Contents

Published by Kensington Publishing Corporation

Almost Home

WITHDRAWN

DEBBIE MACOMBER

CATHY LAMB
JUDY DUARTE
MARY CARTER

ZEBRA BOOKS
Kensington Publishing Corp.
http://www.kensingtonbooks.com

ZEBRA BOOKS are published by

Kensington Publishing Corp.
119 West 40th Street
New York, NY 10018

All Kensington titles, imprints, and distributed lines are available
at special quantity discounts for bulk purchases for sales promotion,
premiums, fund-raising, educational, or institutional use.

Special book excerpts or customized printings can also be created
to fit specific needs. For details, write or phone the office of the Kensington Special Sales Manager: Attn. Special Sales Department.
Kensington Publishing Corp., 119 West 40th Street, New York, NY
10018. Phone: 1-800-221-2647.

Zebra and the Z logo Reg. U.S. Pat. & TM Off.

ISBN-13: 978-1-4201-3104-8
ISBN-10: 1-4201-3104-4

First Printing: August 2009

20 19 18 17 16 15 14 13 12

Printed in the United States of America

Whale Island

Cathy Lamb

To my way-cool sister,
Dr. Karen Straight,
and her special friend,
Matt Farwell,
of the Kindness Ranch,
a home for former laboratory animals.

Hartville, Wyoming

Chapter One

I could not believe I was going to climb up on Stephen's roof in a black burglar-type outfit so I could spy on him through his skylight.

"I have gone over the edge," I muttered, adjusting my black leather knee-high boots. "I'm completely whacked. Brain-fried. Crazed."

"Our mission," Brenda whispered to me before we scurried onto the roof, the stars our only witnesses to this sheer stupidity, "begins right now. One for all, all for one, and don't leave a wily woman behind!" She shimmied her hips, then stuck both thumbs up, her black gloves cutting through the cool night.

My sister Christie and I smothered our laughter.

"Never give up, ladies!" Christie ordered as she pulled a black-knit hat over her blond hair and down her face, her green eyes twinkling through the eyeholes. "Never surrender! Never accept defeat!"

"Women unite!" I said as we high-fived each other.

Brenda fiddled with her night-vision goggles then grabbed the gutter and shimmied her way up the roof. Her agility was impressive, as she'd had a number of strawberry daiquiris.

I yanked my black-knit hat over my face, pulled the eye and mouth holes into the appropriate places, tucked in my black curls, and followed her, trying hard not to laugh. If I laughed while I was climbing I might wet my pants.

"I'm a spy!" Brenda whispered as she climbed. She hummed the James Bond theme song. She has a full head of curling reddish hair, now hidden by her full-face black-knit hat, a huge mouth, huge eyes, and a biggish nose. Men went wild for her. "A sexy spy!"

My laughter broke free, and I had to cross my legs. *Don't wet your pants!* Brenda was wearing black leather pants and a black motorcycle jacket, like me. My sister was wearing a black cowboy hat over the face-hiding knit hat, which was *so hilarious,* and a black coat that wouldn't close over her stomach because she is gigantically pregnant with twins. Normally she is the size of Tinkerbell. Now she is the size of a small bull.

"Chalese is not a sexy spy," I said about my sorry self as I grabbed the gutter to hoist myself up. "Chalese has been dumped. Damn that snaky Stephen." I hadn't even *liked* Stephen. But I didn't appreciate being dumped. Nothing is worse than being dumped by someone you dated because he was *there,* a breathing male, and you desperately hoped he was more than he was but you had to quit lying to yourself in the face of overwhelming evidence of his jerkhood.

A voice inside my blurry head said, *Since you believe him to be a jerk, why are you on his roof in the middle of the night dressed like a burglar?*

Why? Because the three of us, me, Brenda, and Christie, together, are lethal. Daring. Truly ridiculous. And a little drunk. Although Christie is stone-cold sober. She never drinks when she's pregnant.

But, *really,* there was no harm in seeing whom Stephen was dating, even if I had to do it via a skylight. *I didn't care,* not at all, but knowledge is power. "Knowledge is a daiquiri," I intoned as I scrambled up, my black gloves offering a little traction. "Strawberry daiquiri, lemon daiquiri, peach daiquiri . . ."

Stephen's roof was flattish, so our climb to the skylight was not too perilous, even in my fuzzy state. I hummed the *Rocky* fight song, stopping to pump the cool night with my fists, like Rocky did in the movies.

"What's going on, Chalese?" my sister hissed from the ground below, her voice coming in from the walkie-talkie on my hip.

I giggled and held my walkie-talkie to my mouth. "I'm not Chalese! I'm a spy! A secret agent! I am on a serious mission!"

Why are you talking about a mission? Why aren't you home reading a romance novel?

Brenda burped. She says it's her best quality. That is patently not true. Her best quality is writing screenplays for major motion pictures that make women alternately laugh and cry like banshees. She's living with me until she smashes through her writing block.

Christie said, "Copy that, Ms. Bond. All right, 007, carry on."

I carefully—as carefully as I could with two strawberry daiquiris under my belt, well, three, actually, but who's counting—scuttled over to Brenda, who was peering through Stephen's giant skylight, quiet as a tiny drunken mouse dressed all in black with night-vision goggles.

I could see the butcher-block island in the middle of the kitchen. "Mission fuzzy," I whispered.

Brenda put her black-gloved hands over the skylight to angle a better view. "Command center, I report zero activity."

I leaned on the skylight a smidgen, balancing most of my weight on the roof. I could smell Brenda's perfume, sultry and earthy.

I gasped.

Brenda said, "Holy Tomoly."

It was Alanna. *Alanna Post.*

I had known Alanna the Man-eater for years. I avoided her at all costs. She was perfect. Blondish hair, highlighted just so, curling under right at her shoulders. Heavy, but annoyingly perfect, makeup. Thin. Oh, I hated how thin she was! Probably a size six. Designer clothes. And always, always, a condescending sneer or raised eyebrow to make it clear that she thought I was a chubby spider beneath her feet. An awkward orangutan with a poofy butt.

And there she was in Snaky Stephen's house, the doctor that I was going to dump anyhow! I leaned over the skylight, scooching toward the center, then hissed, "It's the female praying mantis."

Why are you spying on Stephen on his roof? What about that romance novel? How about getting down?

I gurgled as Alanna the Man-eater slipped off her dress. Underneath, she was wearing a red negligee, black fishnet tights, and black heels.

This I could not have! Stephen had dumped me a month ago. I hadn't even slept with him, and already he was getting in the flesh with Alanna the Man-eater?

"She has deplorable taste!" Brenda whispered. "If I had an outfit like that on, I would have added a halo and tail."

"That patronizing witch," I muttered. "Did I ever tell you Stephen has a flabby bottom?"

We leaned over for better viewing angles.

"Those boobs!" Brenda said, dismayed. "They have to be fake. No one has boobs that upright, do they?"

"No one should have boobs that bouncy-ball perfect, even if they're fake. It isn't fair. It's against the sisterhood of women, the Society of Decent Females."

Brenda and I scooched a bit more onto the skylight. Alanna had stretched out in front of the fire on the fake thick white fur. If I was wearing that red getup my stomach would be slouching over like a bag of red flour, with the wrinkles etched through my thighs doing little for my sex appeal.

"I wanna be up there, I wanna be up there," my sister whined from the ground. "Why don't I ever get to do any of the fun stuff with you two?"

"That's easy," I snapped. "It's because you're always

THE CAREER OF CARL MICHAEL YASTRZEMSKI

Born August 22, 1939, at Southampton, N.Y.
Height, 5-11. Weight, 185.
Throws right- and bats left-handed.
Attended University of Notre Dame, Notre Dame, Ind., and received bachelor of science degree
in business administration from Merrimack College, North Andover, Mass.

Signed as free agent by Boston Red Sox organization, November 29, 1958.
Named Carolina League Most Valuable Player, 1959.
Established major league record for most years leading league in assists by outfielders (7), 1977.
Tied major league records for most seasons, one club (23), most consecutive seasons, one club (23); most home runs, two consecutive games (5), May 19 and 20, 1976; highest fielding percentage by outfielder, season, 100 or more games (1.000), 1977.

Became first American League player to total 400 home runs and 3,000 hits, lifetime.

Established American League records for most games, lifetime (3,308); most seasons, 100 or more games (22); most at-bats, lifetime (11,988); most plate appearances, lifetime (13,990); most intentional bases on balls, lifetime (190); most consecutive seasons, 100 or more games (20).

Won American League Triple Crown, 1967.
Hit three home runs in a game, May 19, 1976.
Hit for the cycle, May 14, 1965.
Led American League in sacrifice flies with 9 in 1972.
Led American League in total bases with 360 in 1967 and 335 in 1970.
Led American League in slugging percentage with .536 in 1965, .622 in 1967, and .592 in 1970.
Led American League in bases on balls received with 95 in 1963 and 119 in 1968.
Led American League outfielders in assists in 1962, 1963, 1966, 1969, 1971, and 1977, and tied for lead in 1964.

Tied for American League lead in sacrifice flies with 11 in 1977.
Tied for American League lead in double plays by outfielders with 4 in 1971.
Named Major League Player of the Year by The Sporting News, 1967.
Named American League Player of the Year by The Sporting News, 1967.
Named American League Most Valuable Player by Baseball Writers' Association of America, 1967.
Named outfielder on The Sporting News American League All-Star Team, 1963, 1965, and 1967.
Named outfielder on The Sporting News American League All-Star fielding team, 1963, 1965, 1967 through 1969, 1971, and 1977. Winner of Gold Glove Award in each of those years.
Named to Hall of Fame, 1989, with 94.6 percent of ballots cast. (First former Little Leaguer to enter Hall of Fame.)

Year Club	League	Pos.	G.	AB.	R.	H.	2B.	3B.	HR.	RBI.	B.A.	PO.	A.	E.	F.A.
1959—Raleigh	Carol.	*2B-SS	120	451	87	*170	*34	6	15	100	*.377	*255	284	*45	*.923
1960—Minneapolis	A.A.	OF	148	570	84	*193	36	8	7	69	.339	243	18	5	.981
1961—Boston.	Amer.	OF	148	583	71	155	31	6	11	80	.266	248	12	10	.963
1962—Boston.	Amer.	OF	160	646	99	191	43	6	19	94	.296	329	*15	*11	.969
1963—Boston.	Amer.	OF	151	570	91	*183	*40	3	14	68	*.321	283	*18	6	.980
1964—Boston.	Amer.	OF-3B	151	567	77	164	29	9	15	67	.289	372	•24	11	.973
1965—Boston.	Amer.	OF	133	494	78	154	•45	3	20	72	.312	222	11	3	.987
1966—Boston.	Amer.	OF	160	594	81	165	•39	2	16	80	.278	310	•15	5	.985
1967—Boston.	Amer.	OF	161	579	*112	*189	31	4	•44	*121	*.326	297	13	7	.978
1968—Boston.	Amer.	OF-1B	157	539	90	162	32	2	23	74	*.301	315	13	3	.984
1969—Boston.	Amer.	OF-1B	•162	603	96	154	28	2	40	111	.255	427	*38	6	.987
1970—Boston.	Amer.	1B-OF	161	566	*125	186	29	0	40	102	.329	816	64	14	.984
1971—Boston.	Amer.	OF	148	508	75	129	21	2	15	70	.254	281	*16	2	.993
1972—Boston†.	Amer.	OF-1B	125	455	70	120	18	2	12	68	.264	498	43	8	.985
1973—Boston.	Amer.	1B-3B-OF	152	540	82	160	25	4	19	95	.296	979	119	18	.984
1974—Boston.	Amer.	1B-OF-DH	148	515	*93	155	25	2	15	79	.301	806	46	6	.993
1975—Boston.	Amer.	1B-OF-DH	149	543	91	146	30	1	14	60	.269	1217	88	5	.996
1976—Boston.	Amer.	1B-OF-DH	155	546	71	146	23	2	21	102	.267	922	55	4	.996
1977—Boston.	Amer.	*OF-1B-DH	150	558	99	165	27	3	28	102	.296	344	*22	0	•1.000
1978—Boston.	Amer.	DH-OF-1B	144	523	70	145	21	2	17	81	.277	523	49	5	.991
1979—Boston.	Amer.	DH-OF-1B	147	518	69	140	28	1	21	87	.270	529	56	4	.993
1980—Boston.	Amer.	DH-OF-1B	105	364	49	100	21	1	15	50	.275	225	13	4	.983
1981—Boston.	Amer.	DH-1B	91	338	36	83	14	1	7	53	.246	353	34	3	.992
1982—Boston.	Amer.	DH-1B-OF	131	459	53	126	22	1	16	72	.275	119	10	0	1.000
1983—Boston‡.	Amer.	DH-1B-OF	119	380	38	101	24	0	10	56	.266	22	1	0	1.000
Major League Totals—23 Years			3308	11988	1816	3419	646	59	452	1844	.285	10437	775	135	988

* Led league.
● Tied for league lead.
†On supplemental disabled list, May 10 to June 9, 1972.
‡On voluntary retired list, October 25, 1983.

CHAMPIONSHIP SERIES RECORD

Year	Club	League	Pos.	G.	AB.	R.	H.	2B.	3B.	HR.	RBI.	B.A.	PO.	A.	E.	F.A.
1975—Boston.		.Amer.	OF	3	11	4	5	1	0	1	2	.455	7	2	0	1.000

WORLD SERIES RECORD

Year	Club	League	Pos.	G.	AB.	R.	H.	2B.	3B.	HR.	RBI.	B.A.	PO.	A.	E.	F.A.
1967—Boston.		.Amer.	OF	7	25	4	10	2	0	3	5	.400	16	2	0	1.000
1975—Boston. ..		.Amer.	OF-1B	7	29	7	9	0	0	0	4	.310	35	1	0	1.000
World Series Totals—2 Years		.....		14	54	11	19	2	0	3	9	.352	51	3	0	1.000

ALL STAR GAME RECORD

Tied All-Star Game records for most hits, game (4), July 14, 1970; most one-base hits, game (3), July 14, 1970; most home runs by pinch-hitter, game (1), July 15, 1975.

Year	League	Pos.	AB.	R.	H.	2B.	3B.	HR.	RBI.	B.A.	PO.	A.	E.	F.A.
1963—American .	....	OF	2	0	0	0	0	0	0	.000	1	0	0	1.000
1967—American .	....	OF	4	0	3	1	0	0	0	.750	2	0	0	1.000
1968—American .	. ...	OF	4	0	0	0	0	0	0	.000	0	0	0	.000
1969—American .		.OF	1	0	0	0	0	0	0	.000	1	0	0	1.000
1970—American .	. ...	OF-1B	6	1	4	1	0	0	1	.667	8	0	0	1.000
1971—American...	.	OF	3	0	0	0	0	0	0	.000	0	0	0	.000
1972—American .	. .	OF	3	0	0	0	0	0	0	.000	3	0	0	1.000
1974—American .	. .. .	1B	1	0	0	0	0	0	0	.000	5	0	0	1.000
1975—American .	.	PH	1	1	1	0	0	1	3	1.000	0	0	0	.000
1976—American .	....	OF	2	0	0	0	0	0	0	.000	0	0	0	.000
1977—American .	....	OF	2	0	0	0	0	0	0	.000	0	0	0	.000
1979—American .		1B	3	0	2	0	0	0	1	.667	5	1	0	1.000
1982—American .		PH	1	0	0	0	0	0	0	.000	0	0	0	.000
1983—American .	....	PH	1	0	0	0	0	0	0	.000	0	0	0	.000
All-Star Game Totals—14 years .	...		34	2	10	2	0	1	5	.294	25	1	0	1.000

Member of American League All-Star Team in 1966; did not play.

Named to American League All-Star Teams for 1965, 1973, and 1978 games; replaced due to injury.

pregnant, Fertile Myrtle!" Christie had three kids at home with her husband, Cary, the nicest man on the planet.

"Well . . . well . . . well!" she sputtered. "Poop!"

I sucked in my breath as Stephen with the flabby bottom stepped into view. He paused when he saw Alanna the Man-eater. I could see his shock. I pushed my feet hard into the roof so I wouldn't fall off of it.

I'm thirty-five, and I'm climbing on roofs to spy on my ex-boyfriend. What's wrong with this picture?

"I have got to use this in my next movie. Do you mind, Chalese?" Brenda asked, pushing her night-vision goggles on top of her head.

"If I said I did, would you not use it?"

"Silly lady. I'd use it anyhow." She winked at me.

"Brenda," I snapped, "how do you think I feel seeing myself in your movies? All the dumb things we've done? Everything stupid I've said in my life since we were kids streaming out of some actress's mouth?"

"Think of it as being famous without the fame. You're never mobbed by paparazzi, are you? There's something to be said for that, sweetie. And you don't need to hire bodyguards."

I grunted and tugged at the eyeholes in my hat. Brenda and I wrote wild, crazy, thrilling, romantic stories, sometimes with talking animals, when we were kids. She went on to write screenplays, and I went on to be a children's book writer and illustrator. Who knew we'd end up clinging to a roof?

We moved onto the skylight a smidgen more when the Man-eater stood up.

"Can't he see the piranha beneath the makeup?" I asked.

"Nope. He's a man. All he can see is the negligee and bra cup."

"Men are beasts." I growled for effect, slashing the air with my claws. Brenda growled back at me, gnashed her teeth.

It was at that beastly second that I heard a crack beneath my hands, then another one.

My face froze in terror.

"Oh no. Move slowly," Brenda panted. "Slowly."

I felt the crack beneath my knees. I couldn't breathe. Couldn't move. This couldn't be happening. *The skylight was not breaking, was it? What was I doing on top of a skylight anyhow?*

I watched the alarm in Brenda's eyes grow to free-flowing fright as another crack ripped through the night. My mouth went dry as stone, and my body started to shake.

"Back up, Chalese!"

I tried, I did, but panic turned my bones to liquid.

Another crack. As Brenda and I locked mortified gazes, the skylight shattered completely, the noise deafening, and we went smashing through it, our fall broken by Snaky Stephen's butcher-block counter below.

Brenda swore. I screamed. Then she screamed. I swore.

We landed hard, on our knees, but I did not hear any bones crack, any heads splitting open, any limbs disengaging. A piece of glass conked me on the head and splintered.

I groaned. Brenda moaned.

I heard the Man-eater screeching and Stephen yelling "What the hell? *What the hell?*"

Perhaps he wouldn't recognize us with our black-knit hats on? Our black leather biker jackets? Our leather pants?

The Man-eater was still at it with her high-pitched, ear-splitting howls.

I turned to Brenda and whispered, "Let's get out of here."

"Ya think, Sherlock?" she whispered back.

We scrambled off the counter, averting our covered faces, hoping we could slink right out of that house. I'd pay Mervin Tunnel to come in and clean up the mess tomorrow. He'd keep his mouth shut; he owed me a favor anyhow.

We had almost limped our way to the kitchen door, glass trailing in our wake, when I heard Stephen say, incredulously, "Chalese, is that *you?*"

* * *

Crashing through a skylight like a drunken angel was not the worst part of my week.

Stepping on the scale and noting that, yes, all by myself, I had bravely packed on an extra fifteen pounds was not the worst, either. Nor were the two zits on my cheek, as the zits will undoubtedly complement my hot flashes.

Resisting pressure from Gina Martinez, my friend the pet communicator, who was pestering me to stage a "pet rescue" of a horse she was convinced was "depressed and anxious," was not on my list for Most Terrible Part of the Week.

Knowing that my next children's book was already late and I was nowhere close to being done with it had my nerves hyperventilating, but it had not made the list.

Also not on the list was Brenda's dance on top of a bar in town singing the *Pretty Woman* theme song. That I went up there with her does not need to be mentioned, except it was one more humiliating thing in my life that I have done, especially since I cannot sing.

The worst part of my week was when the reporter arrived.

It was the morning after the skylight incident. I limped out of my car after collapsing on the sofa at Christie's for the night, and Aiden Bridger was there, at my yellow house, on my white front porch, one of my slobbery dogs, Mrs. Zebra, in his lap. I was dressed all in black, with a truly pounding hangover and scrapes on my face that made it appear I'd been attacked by a temperamental rat. My long, black, curling hair resembled a dead pelt on my head.

He had that gorgeous, roughed-up, been-around-the-block appearance. He was super tall, a human skyscraper with a lanky build and longish thick brown curls, and I knew that he was gonna be a problem, and not simply because my body about lost all its breath as I took him in. He was . . . *all man*. A manly man. A manly muscled man.

"Hello. You must be Chalese." He stood up, and Mrs. Zebra rolled off his lap and whined. She has no loyalty. If I was ever robbed, she would slobber on the robber. "I'm Aiden Bridger from the *Washington Review.*"

I knew who he was. Oh boy, did I know who he was.

With one look at him, I knew I was toast, too.

Why? Not because he was cursedly, dangerously *hot,* but because that he-man reporter could blow my quiet, private life to Kingdom Come. Everyone would know who I was now, and who I was in my other life, and the scandal would be revived again, the shame, the humiliation, and I'd have to deal with all the other bubbling, sordid, sad memories and secrets.

That, definitely, was the worst part of my week.

And, somehow, the best.

Chapter Two

"I've told you I don't want to talk to you."

I grimaced as I limped up the porch steps and tried to glare at him without salivating. Why did he have to be so yummy-rugged and full of such glorious testosterone? That wasn't fair.

"Yes, I know." For a few long seconds Aiden stared right at me. His eyes were greenish, and he had long lusty eyelashes. The corners of his mouth tilted up, then back down again.

"What happened? Were you in an accident?"

"No."

"Did you fall?"

Pause. "Not really." I glanced away from those bright eyes and reminded myself that men are cagey, deceptive beasts and hairy vermin.

"Did someone hurt you?"

I did not miss the outrage in his tone, the beginning of incredulous fury. My heart didn't miss it, either, but I told my heart to shut up.

"No, no man would ever hit me, because they know I'd flatten them into a kidney-smeared mass of flesh. I don't want to talk about it."

He exhaled, his hands on the waistband of his jeans. "Can I help you? Are you hurt in other places, too?"

Can he help me? Geez. That one little question stopped me right up. How often had a man said "Can I help you?" to me and really meant it? Not often.

"I don't need help Mr. Bridger. I'm perfect. One hundred percent. Fine. Dandy. Do I seem weak? Some damsel in distress who needs an effeminate white guy with skinny thighs charging up on a white horse for a pathetic rescue?"

"No, ma'am, you don't." He grinned. "And I did not bring my white horse anyhow or my skinny thighs."

I immediately stole a peek at his legs. Long, muscled, not skinny, powerful. *Big mistake.*

My breath caught and I glanced longingly at my front door, wanting to escape from He-Man here. I had saved every penny and had this house built in a farmhouse style seven years ago. It was small, fifteen hundred square feet, but there were no walls in the downstairs, so it felt bigger. Upstairs there were two bedrooms and my studio, flooded with light from floor-to-ceiling windows and two skylights. I did not want to think about skylights.

"You have a very nice home," he said, quite serious.

And you have very nice hips. And your shoulders aren't so bad, either, under that beige, outdoorsy jacket you're wearing. And sheesh. That jaw. Even the scar above your eyebrow turns me on. Oh, do shut up, Chalese. To distract myself from the prince's thighs, I said, "Thank you.

"Your view is incredible."

"It calms my nerves." *You, however, have set my nerves on fire.*

"I'll bet." He laughed, low and rumbly. "I think it would calm anyone's nerves."

My yellow home sat on five bucolic acres on Whale Island off the coast of Washington, with a view of the ocean and two neighboring islands through towering pine trees. The pine trees acted as a natural frame for the moving, changing postcard. I watched sailboats and rowboats glide in and out of a small harbor as I worked.

"I'm detecting a longing note in your voice," I said. "Do your nerves need calming?"

"Uh, yes. More than I can tell you at this time."

I nodded. We smiled at each other. Couldn't help myself. My smile hurt my aching face.

"The deer think they own the place," I rattled out to fill the silence. "The raccoons have almost formed a union, there's so many of them. The squirrels have raucous, argumentative family reunions on my back deck, and the birds are bossy and rule the sky."

He shrugged. "Deer are possessive, raccoons should be unionized, squirrels never get along, and birds always have to see what's going on in everyone's lives because they're nosy. Didn't you know that?"

Oh no. A he-man with a sense of humor.

He gazed around, his eyes stopping at my seriously dilapidated barn and then the building with the heated kennels for various abused/stray dogs I had taken in over the years until I could adopt them out to happy homes.

My home, and this island, had been the perfect hiding place for me, my mother, and my sister.

And now, after one award, Mr. Bridger here was going to ruin it. "Mr. Bridger . . ."

"Aiden."

"Mr. Bridger," I started again, trying to sound firm through my throbbing headache. "I have already told you I am not interested in doing an interview with you or your newspaper. Any questions from the media always go through my agent. I believe I forwarded you Terry Rudolph's number already?"

"Got that," he said softly, still staring at me.

"And?" I raised my eyebrows at him and pushed a stray curl off my face. At least I wasn't wearing my black burglar cap that covered all my face except my eyes and mouth. I brushed my leather pants with my hands. Gall.

"And what?" He smiled at me then, his intense gaze never leaving my face. I was doomed, doomed. He was even more yummy smiling.

"Shurx . . ." I tried to speak, could not find words. "Anr . . . Bix . . ." I cleared my throat, studied my red Adirondack chairs, the hanging flowers, the wind chimes tinkling over my porch. "And you should leave. Good-bye, Mr. Gorgeous." I turned away, my kneecaps feeling like they were cracking, then froze.

Oh, please, I begged myself. *Please tell yourself you did not say 'Good-bye, Mr. Gorgeous.'* I hadn't, had I? My body prickled with pure mortification.

It was his laughter that confirmed it.

"Damn," I muttered. "By damn, damn. I *did* say it."

I did not turn around. "Mr. Bridger, please go. I don't want an article written about me, not now, not ever. I'm a private person, have a private life, and I want to keep it that way."

"I understand that. Privacy is one cool thing."

I did not turn around to look at him, because my acute embarrassment was causing a hot flash. Hot flashes at thirty-five years old. Gimme a break. My mother had had them early, too. And her mother. My mother called them her "skin boilers." Her mother called them "the devil's heat spells."

I called them my "sweatfests."

"Ms. Hamilton, it's going to be announced very shortly here that you've won the Carmichael Children's Book Award. Our paper had a contact on the committee, and we want to get the story written on you first. You're already famous under your pen name. Your books are famous. They've sold hundreds of thousands of copies, and yet no one knows anything about you."

"I would bet, Mr. Bridger, that you know a thing or two about me, isn't that correct?" I could feel my spine tingling, that old fear of discovery flaming around me. "After all, you found me, you know my name."

"I know your pen name is Annabelle Purples but very little else. Certainly not enough to write my article."

"There will be no article." I shook my head. Glass tinkled to the porch. "Nada. None."

I saw the alarm on Aiden's face. "You had glass in your hair. Are you all right?"

"Absolutely splendid." I was exhausted. My body ached, I had dried blood on my legs and hands, my hangover was merciless, and I'd hardly slept. First thing this morning I'd paid Mervin to repair Stephen's skylight. Brenda and I had done our best to clean up the kitchen after making a serendipitous call to Christie to tell her to stay out of the house.

The Man-eater in her red negligee had been furious, scathing, degrading. Stephen hadn't been much better. I believe the words "pathetic . . . jealous . . . criminal" had left his mouth. I had promised him a better skylight, immediately installed, and a cleaning woman to fix the rest of the mess in exchange for his not calling the police.

The Man-eater had smirked at me when we'd left. "Get over it, Chalese. Be a mature woman and leave us alone. Stephen doesn't need a jelly maker who is always doing stupid stuff and is obsessed with animals for a wife. *He doesn't want you.*"

I'd scuttled out like a humiliated cockroach after Brenda told the Man-eater her negligee was "uninventive, boring staid" and that Stephen had the face of an "uptight, constipated prune."

"No, thank you very much, Mr. Bridger." I put my key in the lock. "Good-bye."

"Okay. Got it. But you're hurt, aren't you?"

"I'm Zip-a-Dee-Doo-Dah fine. All is well. Calm and collected."

I saw the corner of his mouth twitch. He was trying not to laugh. "It has occurred to me that you've had quite a night. Were you at some biker event? A women's wrestling contest? A costume party where everyone had to wear leather?"

"Take your pick. I get a high out of riding motorcycles,

wrestling has its appeal, and I do have wacky friends who might be inclined to have a leather party. Adios, Mr. Bridger."

"I'm good at putting bandages on."

"I'm sure you're good at a lot of things," I drawled, then snapped that traitorous mouth shut. "I mean I'm sure you have many talents." Darn. I yanked at the door. *Must escape from Mr. Gorgeous!*

"And I'd really like to help you get that glass out of your hair. Please?" His voice was soft and manly and would taste so good hearing it close to my ear. "It's against my chivalrous, princely nature to let a damsel in distress, or a damsel with glass in her hair, fend for herself."

"This damsel is one tough woman and does not need a man in her life to cope or live or be happy or get glass out of her hair. And this is what I know about princes—the prince is probably gay, I'd have to deal with his supercilious mother, the queen, I don't admire men in tights, and if I want a horse I can buy myself a whole damn stable."

"You didn't buy into the whole fairy-tale thing as a kid, did you?"

"No. Why should I? The most interesting things in those stories were the talking mirror that told the truth, the dress-sewing mice, and an apple that could put someone to sleep with one bite. I was also fascinated by the vengeful witches, whom I admired."

"Already you're fascinating to me, definitely not a damsel in any distress at all. Perhaps *you* should ride up on the charging horse."

"I'm boring. I'm dull. Trust me. I write and illustrate children's books. I take care of stray and abused animals found on the islands and try to find them homes. I hang out with my sister, who has been almost constantly pregnant for six years, and my childhood friend, Brenda, who is a menace. I take walks. That's it. That's all."

I opened the door to my home.

"Ms. Hamilton, I'm sorry."

I turned around. The motion killed me again. My back felt like it was splitting. "Why are you sorry?"

"I'm sorry, but I have to write this article. I'm going to stick around Whale Island for a while, talk to people, get a feel for the mysterious children's writer who is going to be even more famous next month when the award is announced. You've been assigned to me, and with you or without you, I have to write it."

My air got stuck in my lungs. I figured it was my past drowning me. I felt a tightening in my shoulders. I figured it was my instincts pushing me to run. My secret would be blown to smithereens. A flood of memories came pouring on in, cameras and furious people, newspapers and reporters, crushing us, shouting, demanding answers.

"People want to know the authors they love. You write kids' stories with these fully developed animal characters, and you're always addressing the problems we have—environmental, social, animal rights, racial issues, politics. You have books that address loneliness, sadness, not having friends, but you use animals to get your point across in a way kids can relate to. It's brilliant."

I leaned my forehead against the door, then banged it lightly a few times. I took the he-man heartthrob reporter in one more time. He meant what he said. He was going to write the story with or without me. Maybe if I talked to him I could throw him off the scent, the article would be brief, six people would read it, and that would be that.

"Mr. Bridger, you are a pain in the butt."

He nodded amicably. "Been called worse."

I left the door open. I had to. I didn't have a choice.

The prince with the powerful thighs followed me in.

* * *

"Let me get this straight. No one on this island knows that you are Annabelle Purples, is that right?"

I let my eyes wander around my home before answering that truly problematic question. The décor was blue and white, with lots of glassworks, pottery, and paintings made by artist friends on the island. Plus stacks of old books, quilts, and three framed pictures of Greece, a country I had promised myself I would visit in this lifetime.

I bit my lip, then nodded at Mr. Gorgeous. "That's right. No one knows except my mother, my sister and her husband, and my friends Brenda and Gina, who has hair all the way down to her rear. Sometimes she sticks real flowers in it. She's a hippie." I wrung my hands, my nervousness unnerving me. "You didn't need to know that."

He blinked. "I respect hippies. But so I'm clear here, the other islanders think you sell jams and jellies and take care of stray and abused animals?"

"That's right again. My, aren't you sharp." I had shown him a storage room that held the jams and jellies I slaved over in between writing books. Each label read "Wild Girl's Jams and Jellies."

"And you want who you are to stay secret?" Aiden leaned toward me across my rattan coffee table, the sunlight streaming through the room.

I rolled my shoulders inside my black leather motorcycle jacket. Even my elbows hurt. "Now you've been right three whole times. You're a freakin' genius."

"Because you're a private person?"

"Yes." And I have something from my past to hide, but no need to split hairs, right? "Privacy is good. Like air. Like cheesy pizza. Like having working intestines."

He paused to consider that bit of wisdom.

"Why?"

"Why what?" My golden, one-eyed cat, Racy, curled around my legs, and I stroked her back.

"Why the secrecy? Aren't you proud of who are, what you've accomplished?"

Proud of who I am? For years I had wanted to crawl in a hole with the worms and wiggle my way farther into the dirt, I was so ashamed. "I'm glad that kids like my books." That was true. If one kid, one place on Earth, learned something from my books, learned to read better . . . Well, that was more than good enough for me.

"They *love* your books, but you didn't answer the question. Aren't you proud of yourself?"

Proud of myself. No. I didn't even really understand what "proud of myself" would entail. "Want some more coffee?" I stood up. Aiden didn't stand. He leaned back in my plush blue-striped chair and linked his hands behind his head.

Why did he have to ooze such masculinity in my pretty messy family room?

"Nice try, Chalese. Why are you dodging the question? And for the third time, can I help you get the glass out of your hair? It's making me nervous. I'm afraid you're going to get hurt again. You could step on it later and cut your foot. . . ."

"I'm not dodging it, and stay out of my hair. Why would I let a stranger paw through the glass in my hair anyhow?" I felt the vague zip of a caffeine headache. "I want coffee. I am going to perish without it. In fact, I want to take these clothes off and get in the shower and wash my hair because it's a wreck." Oh, hell. Had I said that? Had I said "take these clothes off"? I stalked to the kitchen, my black leather boots thumping on the wood floor.

Aiden said something. I was tempted to keep marching, but I couldn't stop myself. "What?"

"I said your hair is fine to me."

My face grew hot, so did my neck, and my forehead broke out in beads of sweat. *Hot flash.* Oh, why? Why now? I grabbed the coffee pot and shoved it under the faucet, then fumbled for a bag of coffee beans. I attempted to pour the beans into the grinder, but the beans spilled all over the floor. I grabbed a broom. Aiden grabbed the dustpan. "You don't have to help."

"I want to help. I'm drinking the coffee, right?"

When that was cleaned up, I tried to pour the beans into the grinder with my trembling hands again. Same experience. Beans everywhere. My internal thermometer shot up eight hundred degrees, and I sweated.

I wanted to cry. I stopped, gripped the counter, and turned away.

"Hey," Aiden said, his voice quiet, reassuring. "It's all right, Chalese. It's nothing."

"It's not nothing." I squished my eyes shut and wiped my forehead. It wasn't *nothing*.

"Chalese, I'm not trying to wreck your privacy. To be honest with you, if I don't write the story, someone else will at this point."

I put my cool, wet hands to my flaming face. That was true. That award was gonna rip me out into the open like a hunting target.

I turned away from him and wiped the tears off my cheeks. "Can you write the article without using my real name?"

"Use your pen name, Annabelle Purples, instead?"

"Yes."

"No. I can't."

"Why not?"

"Because it's not your real name, Chalese."

Chalese Hamilton isn't my real name, either. The need to cry ballooned up again. So unusual for me. I've been burying my tears forever.

I felt the inside of me crumbling. I made a muffled sound against my hand.

"Chalese, please," Aiden said, his voice soft and warm. "I'm sorry. I am. Let me take you out to breakfast—"

Whatever else he was going to say was interrupted by the doorbell.

Sniffling, I hurried over to the door, glad for the reprieve. Perhaps it was a Martian and I could go to Saturn with him and be used for alien experiments.

The second I opened the door to a human, not an alien, I wished I hadn't.

I wished I'd skipped out the back door, toward the fields, or to the ocean. Or to my boat at the dock, always waiting to take me on a little jaunt with the whales that circle our islands on their migration journeys.

"Chief O'Connaghey," I squeaked, dread filling my stomach. "What a pleasant surprise."

"Hello, Chalese!" He grinned at me, almost proudly. "It seems we have a problem again. Yep. Another problem." He whistled. "This one is a doozer, sugar. Where's your co-conspirator? She here?"

Chapter Three

Chief O'Connaghey was about sixty years old. He and his wife, Indira, who was from India, were friends of my mother's. He was ultrasmart. Had been a trader in New York City for decades before completely changing his line of work. His wife had threatened to divorce him because she was sick of him working all the time, and that was that.

Two weeks later they were out on Whale Island, where her family lived, and he was training to be a police officer on the mainland. Two years later, he was police chief on the island. He was kind and compassionate, the president of the Whale Island Garden Society, and ran his department with a steel hand. "No crime permitted on the island"—that was his first motto. His second motto was "No crime and we'll all have a good time."

"Chalese, do you want to tell me something?" He wiggled his eyebrows at me.

I hung my head. I felt sick. Utterly ill. We hadn't meant to crack the skylight. Anyway, it was being fixed. . . . I had had too many daiquiris. . . . Brenda always got me into trouble. . . . Sheesh. I could explain. Couldn't I? No, probably not. Guilty as charged. I exhaled. Dear me, my breath should be incinerated. I heard Aiden walking up behind my smelly self.

"Chalese?" the chief prodded.

"Aiden, how about if you go out on my back deck for a sec? Count birds. Make a daisy crown for your head. Nap."

Aiden returned my pointed stare, smiled, then stuck a hand out to the chief. "Aiden Bridger."

"Pleased to meet you, Mr. Bridger. I'm Chief O'Connaghey. Who are you to Chalese here? I know I haven't met you before."

I tilted my head up toward Aiden, beseeched him with my eyes. Pleaded with him. *Not yet, don't tell anybody yet about me, about the article.* I saw something flash in those green sex pits.

"I'm a friend of Chalese's," he declared.

"Ah. A friend of Chalese's." The chief rocked back on his heels. "Where do you live?"

"I live in Seattle."

"Hmmm. Well, pleased to meet you. Now, Chalese, why don't we have a little chat, shall we?"

"Good idea." I scooted out the front door and turned to shut it behind me as quick as I could. Aiden was having none of it. He put his hand on the door and ambled on out. In the distance I heard a low, purring growl.

That would be Brenda in her zippy sports convertible, the top down.

"Well, now!" the chief declared in triumph. "The co-conspirator is coming to turn herself in."

"I . . . uh . . . hmmm . . ." Darn that snaky stiff, Stephen with the flabby bottom. I thought we'd had an agreement.

Aiden was clearly amused.

"Aiden, please go to my back deck and try to catch butterflies or something."

"I think I'll stay."

"This isn't your business."

"I think it is." He grinned. My heart leaped. "Maybe this will explain the leather outfit and those kick-butt boots."

The car door slammed, and Brenda, who had changed into a skimpy, cherry-red sundress, her fluffy hair lush and clean, big glasses covering half her face, and wearing four-inch-high red heels, skipped onto the porch, hips swinging. "I'm guilty, Chief! I'm guilty! Arrest me! It was my idea, and I forced Chalese to do it! Forced her!"

Mrs. Zebra bounded out to say hello. Brenda paused, bent to cup the dog's face and kiss her, then was up again announcing her guilt. She dumped her designer purse and bag on the front step of my porch and held out her wrists to be cuffed, but not before she smiled brightly at Aiden and drawled, "Wellll, aren't you a sight for sore eyes? Chalese! Who! Is! This! My, oh my, you are scrumptious!"

She shook Aiden's hand, then flipped her hair back over her shoulders and her glasses to the top of her head. As usual Brenda was wearing bright red lipstick and elegant, flower-shaped jewelry I knew well. "Scrumptious!" she declared again.

"Yes, indeedy, he is. Let's wrap him up in a strawberry pancake and eat him," I snapped. "A little powdered sugar, and he'll go down fine."

Brenda humphed at me, but then a quizzical expression crossed her face and her brows knit together. "I know who he is! He's that terrible bulldog who wants to—"

I clamped my hand over Brenda's lipsticked mouth. "Not now, my friend, not now."

The chief crossed his arms. He does that when he's analyzing confounding situations.

I released Brenda. "Personal information," I told the chief.

Brenda glared at Aiden, hands on hips, beaded bracelets jingling, "So you're the enemy?"

"Brenda, shush."

"I'm not here for personal, I'm here for the crime committed," the chief drawled. "Can you tell me what you girls were up to again last night?"

"Again?" I protested.

"Yes, ma'am, again."

"But . . ." I shut my mouth. Okay, perhaps a few of Brenda's pranks had gotten out of hand in the past, but really, did he need to say "again," drawing it out real slow, like stretching taffy, right in front of Aiden?

"Again?" Aiden chuckled. "This is gonna be good. My lucky day."

"My fault, Chief." Brenda shook her head sorrowfully. "You can handcuff me first. I'm guilty, but please be careful of my nails, I carefully polished them all by myself! What do you think? Red to match the lipstick, get it?"

The chief stood up straighter, chest out. "This isn't going in one of your movies, is it, Brenda?"

"It could, it could!"

The chief rubbed his hands together. "Good. Something for our family's Christmas card. I'm gonna be famous again. Okeydokey, ladies, let's have some fun here. You want to list the charges against you and Chalese this time around?"

I slapped both hands to my face, then regretted that move. A weak scream emerged as my glass wounds smarted.

"Are you all right?" Aiden asked, worried. "Can I help you with your face?"

Can I help you with your face? I rolled my eyes at him.

"Lemme think! I love police games! What would the official words be here?" Brenda tapped her forehead with both index fingers as if she were trying to jostle her brain. "Eureka, I've got it! It's not stealing, because we didn't take anything this time and put it where it shouldn't be. Remember that time with the truck?"

I cleared my throat to get Brenda's attention about the truck. Didn't work.

"It's not graffiti, because we didn't paint anything this time like we did on that brick wall. It's not attempted assault with a tractor this time, because we didn't—"

"Oh, stop it, Brenda," I interrupted, flushing red. I could not stand to hear her say "this time" again! "For heaven's sake. It's breaking and entering, trespassing, harassment, and destruction of property."

The chief pointed both index fingers at me. "Bingo! You're the winner in today's criminal charges! And for that, you've won a trip down to the police station! Congratulations!"

I did not miss Aiden's befuddled expression.

"Chalese is so smart, isn't she, Chief?" Brenda said, examining her nails by stretching her hands two feet from her face, then slanting another glare toward the Enemy.

"Sharp as a tack, gets it from her momma. Okay, ladies, into the car, I gotta take you two downtown again."

"Do you have to keep using that word 'again,' Chief?" I sputtered. "I'm friends with your wife, and I'm going to tell her that you—"

"Can we take my car and meet you there? That's gotta be a 'Yes,' Chief," Brenda begged. "Last time we were in your car, I got gum on my gold heels! Gum! Pink gum!"

The chief thought about it. "All right, Brenda, we'll make a parade of it. You lead."

"Yahoo. I'm the person out front with the banner, right?"

"That's it. Mr. Bridger here, a friend of Chalese's from Seattle, he'll bring up the rear."

"He's the trash sweeper," Brenda drawled to the Enemy. "They always come at the end of a parade."

"You don't need to come, Aiden," I said, trying not to be profoundly pathetic. "This isn't going to be fun. Go to town until I get back. Shop for . . . something. Corduroy pants? A whale key chain? Buy beer. Ogle women. Scratch. Hang. But don't come."

"But it will be fun," the chief said. "My motto is 'No crime and we'll all have a good time.' We hardly ever get to book anyone. Come on down, Mr. Bridger."

"No, don't—"

"I wouldn't miss it," Aiden told the chief. He slung an arm

around my shoulders, pretending we were the best of buds. "Lead the way."

He patted Mrs. Zebra on the head when we left. She licked his fingers.

I called Gina Martinez, my friend the pet communicator, as Brenda drove her humming, female midlife-crisis sports car to the police station with the chief behind her and Aiden behind him in his truck, like the trash sweeper. I had a feeling I'd be gone awhile, and I wanted Gina to check on my dogs in a few hours if she hadn't heard from me.

Gina loves that her first and last names kind of rhyme. She said all through school kids called her "Poet Girl" because of it. She actually writes poetry, and it's not bad. It is, however, all about animals who are abused and how she thinks abusers should be stuffed with cabbage, oiled, boiled, then hung over a steep cliff attached to a short, skinny tree branch, their hands tied behind their backs.

"I don't know how long I'll be gone, Gina, probably a few hours . . ." I gripped the handle on the car door and whacked Brenda as we careened down roads bordered by pine trees or rolling meadows. "Let's arrive alive, Brenda, okay?"

"I'm already on my way over to your house, Chalese. Reuby is coming with me. He wants to pet the dogs."

Reuby was Gina's nose-and-eyebrow-pierced teenage son. Instead of calling his mother Mom, he called her the Authority Figure. He had blond hair to his shoulders and came over all the time, although he was not allowed in my studio. He loved two things: technology and animals. "How could you already be on your way over? Brenda and I are driving to the police station at this very embarrassing second."

"Joey Bradonovich called me. Her daughter, Toni, works as a hairdresser, and she heard it from Kobi Chao, who was in the police station to pay a parking ticket. By now the whole island knows you girls got yourselves in trouble again."

"Why does everyone have to keep using the word 'again'? It's not 'again,' Gina."

"Yes, it is."

"There may have been a few crazy incidents in the past, regrettable, forgettable—"

"Not forgettable! Not regrettable! That was sooo hilarious when you and Brenda and Christie dressed up the statues of the pioneers in town square with pink underwear and bras."

"I don't want to hear about the bras—"

"Is Gina talking about Pioneer Day?" Brenda asked as she drove, laughing. "You were a daredevil, Chalese. Remember how you hid—"

"Brenda!" I screamed as she took the corner by the glass-art gallery waaaay too fast. "Slow down, it's not a racetrack! You're gonna get a ticket."

Too late. Chief O'Connaghey's blue and red lights started to swirl. I turned around. The chief wiggled his fingers at me in greeting.

"Gina, I have to call you back."

Brenda pulled over, refreshed her lipstick, then rolled down her window. "Good morning, Chief. It's a pleasure to see you again."

I muffled my despair, my head still crammed with tiny knives taking stabs at my cranium.

Chief O'Connaghey grinned. "License and registration, Brenda. Say, I've been thinking these last few minutes, and your last movie, *Pranks and Love on the Island,* was my favorite. We didn't think that Old Man Stuckey needed to die, though. But the movie touched my heart." He touched his heart. "Made me cry. Same with Mrs. Chief O'Connaghey."

I rolled my shoulders. They hurt like holy heck.

"'Course, Mrs. Chief O'Connaghey also laughed so hard she had to leave the theater and run to the bathroom," he added.

Oh, please.

* * *

As we drove into the two-lane town, the ocean sparkling in the distance, Brenda assured me she would keep it quiet about Aiden's occupation and why he was here and not act hostilely toward the Enemy. "I'll tell everyone he's your lover."

"I beg you, no." We both waved at friends on foot and on bikes.

"I'll tell everyone he's your secret lust, your childhood love."

"Let's skip that one, too."

"Hoo boy. I have it. He's a previous husband. . . . No? He's your vacation plaything, and he wants to be serious now. . . . No? Then he's your pen pal, your e-mail pal, and he's come uninvited . . . Or how about he's a previous boyfriend released from his duty in the CIA? Hoo boy."

"Now, don't you go all stalkerish on me, Chalese," the chief reprimanded me in front of Aiden when he was getting the paperwork together at the station. "Stephen can date whoever he wants. Let him go. He was never good enough for you."

"You're a stalker?" Aiden asked. "Now that's cool."

"No one understood why you were dating him in the first place. He's . . . dweeby," Angie Aluko, the secretary, said. She was wearing one of her bright African outfits. She and her husband, a businessman, had six kids. She and Christie were very close. Christie had not been charged, because she'd hid out in the car. The mere thought of giving birth to twins in a cell made her numb with panic.

"I don't care about Stephen at all. I was up on the roof," I said, then lost my words. I tried again. "I was up on the roof because . . . because . . ."

"Hoo boy!" Brenda interrupted with great fanfare. "We had chugged down a few daiquiris and were insanely curious about what Snaky Stephen was up to. So we snuck up on the roof to take a peekie." She smiled at everyone as if we were at some cocktail party. Everyone smiled back. That's how Brenda is. Everybody loves her. "Plus, I needed a real-life experience for my next movie, and you all have been perfect!"

The chief, two officers I played pool with regularly at Old Harold's Bar and Grill, and Angie preened and giggled.

"Could you handcuff me, please?" Brenda asked one of the officers.

"So is this your new special friend, Chalese?" Angie asked. "That's what the chief says."

I froze. Froze like a constipated snowwoman.

Aiden stared at me, green eyes almost twinkling out of his head with humor, and waited for the answer. I couldn't say the truth. Did not *want* to lie, but felt I had to lie to save myself.

"And the answer is . . ." Brenda paused for an imaginary drum roll. "This *is* Chalese's new special friend. Isn't he devilishly handsome? A raw, masculine specimen!" She waved her hand from his head to his feet, then made a growling sound.

Aiden jokingly lifted his arms and flexed his muscles: to the right, the left, then back to the right. Angie hooted. Brenda cackled.

"What exactly is a special friend?" Officer Doytoech drawled. "How is a special friend different from a regular friend, precisely?"

"Yes, what does that entail?" Officer Lopez asked. "Sometimes department stores have special sales—red sales, blue sales. Is this the same thing?"

"I know," the chief said proudly. "This means you're dating."

I fumbled, I blushed, I stuttered. I sounded like this: "Sdfkjlksad . . ."

Aiden grinned. "Well, she's hard to resist. Especially in her leathers. And those boots! Dangerous!"

"She's beautiful," Angie declared. "Not looking so fresh this morning, but other days she's a beauty!"

"A true beauty," Aiden said quite seriously. "Naturally beautiful. That hair, those eyes. She's irritated now, but still."

"Chalese is a superpolite criminal." Officer Doytoech thunked me on the back. "She never argues with us when she's brought in—" I kicked him with my heel. "Ow!"

"Yep, our Chalese is a lady, through and through," Officer Lopez added. "Why, that time we had to go and rescue her and Brenda from the water tower, she was real cooperative. Took a couple of fire engines and a special unit from another island, but we got 'em down. Why were you all up there anyhow? Can't remember . . ."

"It was because Brenda thought she was a terrible writer," Angie jumped in helpfully, "and needed a new perspective. So they climbed up the water tower, and then the ladder broke. I remember that scene in *The Water Tower Diaries*, Brenda! And I loved that Courtnay Hayes played me in the movie!"

They then discussed the movie, at length, with Aiden enthusiastically adding his comments about character development, while Brenda was handcuffed at her request.

"Chalese has said no four times to eager-to-be fiancés," Angie said to Aiden, holding up four fingers.

"Yep, four," Officer Lopez confirmed. "Four men asked her to marry them, she gave 'em a big nope. Nope nope nope nope."

"Why a nope nope?" Aiden asked the group, not me.

Everyone spoke at once. I heard "Too pompous . . . too showy . . . not manly enough . . . too hairy . . . not smart enough for our Chalese, mind like a steel trapdoor . . . no one liked him . . . hot temper, Chalese has a hot temper . . . he was dull/flighty/bum . . . Chalese indulges in crazy stuff . . . wouldn't have worked . . ." And the finale: "She wasn't in love with any of them, we could tell."

"Yoo-hoo! I'm still here!"

No one stopped talking.

"Yoo-hoo!"

* * *

Before we criminals were released on an unsuspecting public, the officers reminded us that Tuesday night was the annual Whale Island Poker Tournament and invited Aiden, who said, "I wouldn't miss it."

But not before Aiden heard again:

That Stephen wasn't good enough for me, to which he said chivalrously, "I can't imagine any man would be good enough for her."

That I was a "treasure, a gift to any man" (Angie), to which Aiden said, "I treasure every moment with her."

That I was "an upright citizen (Officer Lopez said this while laughing like a drunk hyena), to which Aiden said, "I understand she was upright while scaling Stephen's home. Perhaps she should stay off skylights?"

I was also the woman who made the best jams and jellies this side of the Mississippi (the chief), to which Aiden said, "She has so many talents. I could drink her jams all day."

"When's you ladies' next prank?" Officer Lopez asked. "Can I film it? I could probably send it to one of those funny-videos shows and get me enough for a new truck!"

"We'll keep you updated!" Brenda swung her handcuffs around one finger.

I hot flashed.

Before he headed for the fifty-year-old blue bed and break-fast by the bay, Aiden leaned in and whispered in my ear, "I think this is going to be one of my best stories."

I closed my eyes. Heavens. He was even handsomer close up. "Why?" I asked, strangled.

"Because of you." *Would it be inappropriate to tell him he smelled like mountain vistas and sunny days on a clear lake?*

"What do you mean?"

"You are not at all what I expected."

"Gee, is that because you didn't expect to see the creator of Cassy Cat get arrested?"

He laughed, I could almost feel the laughter in me. *Would it be inappropriate for me to deeply inhale his smell and make a moaning sound?*

"Partly. But I think"—he stared into my eyes from inches away—"I think it's *you*, Chalese. Just you."

"That doesn't sound good." *Would it be inappropriate to daydream about this man every day for the rest of my life?*

"It is good." He winked at me. "You're good."

He stepped away, which was *very* good because I was getting dizzy.

I could never say I believed in love at first sight . . . but I did believe in lust.

Too bad the object of my lust could destroy my life.

I inhaled like a drowning rat before I passed out.

"Hi, Mom, yes, I'm doing well," I said into the phone. "How's Provo? You're in Houston? Yes, I'm resting enough. Yes, I have my new vitamins. I didn't need eight bottles of seaweed and echinacea, but thank you for sending them. Yes, I am still taking fiber. I agree that being regular is important. Yes, I will help with more designs when you get home. Love you, too . . ."

Chapter Four

"He's going to find out everything," I choked out to Brenda the next afternoon in my studio.

I picked up a paintbrush, put it down, picked it up, put it down. Hard to paint or use colored pencils when your hand is shaking. "I know it. He's been all over the world writing articles. Researching a publicity-shy writer is nothing for him. He'll dig. He'll find out." I wanted to cry. I wanted to hide. I wanted to move to Alaska. I had had three hours of sleep the previous night. "Last night, I dreamed of a giant hand grabbing me in the middle of the night and squeezing my neck. Everyone was staring at me, pointing."

I gave up trying to work and stalked to the deck outside my second-floor studio with a box of orange truffles. I did not need any more orange truffles. I could feel my butt expanding as I ate. It did not slow me down.

I petted Mr. Earl, a lab-beagle mix who was returned by his ex-new owner last week. He jumped into my arms when he saw me, not feeling the slightest bit guilty that his new owner had found him in, *in,* her tropical aquarium and only three green flashy fish left.

"He may not find out, chillins," Brenda said, linking an arm around my shoulder. She was wearing a red robe with fluffy trim and red heels because she was hoping dressing romantically would lift her writer's block. "Tell him what you've been telling everyone for years." She grabbed a truffle. Brenda never gained weight. She was thin and rangy. I would hate her, but I love her too much.

"He's a man, after all. They want to know what they believe they need to know, which is minimal because they are raw, uncivilized, unrefined animals. They talk endlessly about themselves and puff up their chests. Give him the basics, off he goes." Brenda ate another truffle. "I wonder if I should get Botox done on my lips."

I turned toward her. "Botox? If your lips were any puffier they'd need to wear a bra."

"Hmm. Maybe you're right. Plus, I can't get my head around shooting a dead botulism virus into my body. Seems if God wanted me to have Botox in my lips, I would have been born with a syringe in my hand, right?"

I rolled my eyes. "Right. And if he had wanted us to have laser peels done on our faces, we would have been born with a mini-sandblaster. Can we get back on topic?"

"Yes, sweets." She patted me. "You know I get sidelined when I'm thinking."

I shoveled in another truffle.

"Listen up, dear friend." She turned my trembling body around so I was facing her. "You, Christie, and your mother have managed to keep your whole family's past a secret for more than twenty years."

"Quite an accomplishment since you could always use it for your movies."

"Pshaw, pshaw! I wouldn't do that. But sweetems, we're going to keep this a secret, too. Tell him about the animals, your jams and jellies business, and your always-pregnant sister. Tell him what you think of modern birth control, rabid butterflies, French politics, tulips, the tsar of Russia, spin the bottle, and cannibalism. It'll throw him off the track. He has a deadline, right? He'll be outta here in a couple of days."

I pressed my hands to my forehead. "No. Aiden Bridger will not be gone in a couple of days. He's a reporter. A successful, award-winning, blood-sucking, dirt-digging, story-sniffing, lie-detecting reporter. His job is to find out all about me. And then everyone on the island will know."

A sudden stab of anxiety hit my stomach, and I bent over double. Family secrets die hard. Once you're told, as a child, to keep your mouth shut, you take that into adulthood with you. Revealing the secret is only slightly less difficult than lifting the state of Oregon out of the ground and shifting it to Hawaii.

"A beer. A beer will help," Brenda said. "Two beers? Or, how about if we throw off our shirts and drive naked through the night? That'll get the ole hormones pumping again! Or skinny-dipping! Let's get your sister! The water will hold that mammoth stomach up for her. . . . How that woman walks is a mystery to me. . . ."

"'Morning."

Bent halfway over to pet my new dog, a black poodle named Nutmeg Man, I froze right where I was in the kennel when I heard that gravelly voice.

The man who had kept me up most of the night for two nights worrying about what he would do to my sorry life was right behind me. Staring at my ample buttocks.

"It's you, isn't it?" What a special moment this was.

"Yep, it is. A pleasure to see you."

A pleasure to see your butt. I sagged, then straightened up.

I had no makeup on. I hadn't showered. I smelled like garlic. Brenda had made chicken garlic pasta while she guzzled white wine and whimpered that she would never write a word again, she was lost, done, a failure. That writer's block was *killing* her. She slept on the kitchen floor so she could get a different "perspective."

"How are you today, Chalese?" he asked.

"I'm dandy." *Go away, please. Go away.* "So dandy I feel I will whistle a merry tune and dance a jig."

The dogs barked, and I let them out of their kennels one by one. They kissed me, jumped up to my shoulders, ran around my ankles, then went to sniff Aiden. He got down on his haunches and petted each one of them.

I ran fingers through my hair. I knew I was the spitting image of Mrs. Godzilla.

"I didn't hear you drive up," I said.

"I'm not surprised." He eyed the barking, jumping dogs.

"Right. I call it my Canine Chorus Line. I have to walk them, or I'll never hear the end of it. They'll complain." I winced. I sounded like Gina, my pet-communicator friend who translates for humans what their pets are thinking.

"The dogs complain?" He raised an eyebrow.

"Uh, well, not in English. Not in any other language, either— for example, French or German." *Stop talking, mouth,* I told myself. "They don't have conversations, they don't communicate to me, but they . . . uh . . . they whine and yip and screech."

"I didn't think dogs had conversations, but thank you." He straightened up. The man towered over me. "That clarifies things."

"No, they don't talk. Animals don't talk." Why must I babble? "That's silly. But Gina thinks they do."

"Gina the hippie?"

I paused. Shoot. I could see the headlines now: "Reclusive Writer Friends With Pet Communicator. 'I know what horses think!' Gina Martinez proclaims. 'I can tell you if your hamster is depressed or if your cat struggles with multiple personalities from past lives!'"

I put a leash around Shortcake. "I have to walk the dogs."

"I'll come with you."

"That's not necessary. I won't get lost."

"No." He smiled at me. "I know you won't get lost. You are one of the most 'found' people I think I've met. But I thought I'd help out."

Why did Aiden have to be charming? "Fine. But you have to know that I haven't showered, I was up late last night working, I have paint in my hair, Brenda made me smell like garlic, and I'm tired and cranky."

"I've already seen tired and cranky, and I'm okay with it."

I glared at him.

"I see you have blue and purple paint in your hair, and I love garlic, so all is well there, too, and I've seen what diving through a skylight does to your face. Now, that was precious."

I opened another kennel, and Rocky jumped up and down, a giant dog-rabbit with a long tail. I stole a peek at Aiden's face. He was trying not to laugh.

I scowled at him. "It wasn't funny."

"But I think it was."

I handed him four leashes with poorly behaved dogs on the ends of them. I took another three. Though my property is fenced, I am trying to teach this mangy gang to walk on leashes so they'll be somewhat respectable members of society. The "respectable members of society" part isn't working very well, as they are uncontrollable beasts.

"I've also seen you in the police station. Even in the poor lighting, you still somehow glowed, as if you were pure and innocent."

"Thanks. Gee. I've always been tremendously worried how my complexion would hold up under the station's lighting." We headed out of the kennel, into the sun and down a path lined with ferns and pine trees.

"How long did you date Stephen?"

"I don't know. . . ." I glanced at him. The change of subject threw me. "Three months. I didn't sleep with him." I crammed my eyes shut. "I have no idea why I said that. It's none of your business who I sleep with or don't sleep with at all, and it's not my business who you sleep with or don't sleep with, and I'm not going to ask you anyhow." Message to mouth: Please. Shut. Up. My hot flash began.

"You're not going to ask me what? To sleep with you?"

I flushed harder, redder, sweatier. Darn these sweatfests. "No! Forget it." A vision of me and a naked Aiden on a red blanket in a field filled with daisies appeared in my brain in 3-D. I could almost smell the honey the bees were making.

"I'll try to forget it," he mused. He smiled that friendly smile again. Why is it that some people are born with smiles that demand you smile back? "Yes, I'll try to forget it, but it might be hard."

The dogs decided they wanted to yank my shoulder socket out. I stumbled as they lunged. They yanked again. I stumbled and yelled at them. Nutmeg Man glanced back and smirked at me. No kidding—this dog knows how to smirk.

This lunge-and-stumble routine went on for quite some time as we headed for my blue picnic table in a clearing in the forest. I gave up, unleashed them, and let all the furry monsters run free.

We settled at the table on the same bench, and Aiden studied me for long seconds while I studied the ocean through the trees. Now, if I were skinnier, prettier, I would think the man was interested in me, but my guess is that he was staring at me because I was a strange sight to behold. A she-devil-insanely private, persnickety, overly well-rounded criminal female.

"Can I interview you now?"

That got me back to reality. "Aiden, one more time, please no story. Let it go."

"I can't force you to talk to me, so it is your choice. But I have talked to some interesting people in town about you. Don't worry, I was subtle. I didn't tell them your pen name and I didn't tell them I'm a reporter. It has gotten around that I'm your special friend."

I sagged in relief. He had nice hands. Long fingers, tough, strong. How would they look on my thighs? I shook my head. "What have other people said about me?" I cringed. Did I really want to know? We all have a vague idea of what people think of us, but are we right? Do they actually dislike us? Love us more than we thought possible? Admire us? Are we irritating and don't know it?

For long, treacherous seconds Aiden smiled at me, and I fell into that smile and felt my heart thumping around like it was in a disco.

"Let me start this way," he said. "I have interviewed thousands of people. In all of my interviews, I can find someone who can't stand the interviewee. Always. Sometimes many people."

Man. I wanted to get under that table and hide. He was buttering me up for being Most Unpopular Islander. I knew I was irritating; *I knew it!* I knew I said stupid stuff, but I wasn't realizing how stupid it was! I knew I didn't belong. I had *felt* I belonged here, but now I would become a recluse, a hermit, so as not to offend anyone else. I put my face down on the rough picnic table.

"I can't find anyone who dislikes you."

"What?" Head snapped up.

"I can't find anyone who dislikes you."

"You're kidding."

He shook his head. "No."

"You have to be. I'm a moody freak."

"No. In fact, you may be the most popular person I know. I'm about ready to put a tiara on your head, a scepter in your hand, and drop a banner on you that says "Most Well-Loved."

I sniffled.

I coughed.

I wiped my nose, then my eyes.

Sniffled again.

And then I lost it and started crying. I don't know why.

"Chalese, this is good news. . . ."

"I know, I know! I know!" I put my head back on the table and let the tears out, not the sweet tears fair damsels in distress cry, but shoulder-shaking, nose-running, face-red-and-sweaty kinds of tears. "I . . . I . . . I . . ." I cried again. *They liked me.* I felt like Sally Field when she got the Oscar. That made me cry harder.

He slung an arm around my shoulders. I whimpered, wiped my face, and he pulled me in close.

"That's twice now."

"Twice what?"

"Twice that you've cried on me."

I tried to pull away. He pulled me closer. I leaned into his warmth. I promised myself I would get off the reporter as soon as possible, because I stank.

"There is nothing fake about you, is there? Whatever you feel, you show. You don't hide your emotions. You don't hide what you're thinking. You cry, you're sarcastic, you care, you're daring, you're funny. And you and Brenda . . ." He laughed.

I cried again—more tears! Why was I so emotional? Why such a wreck? But I loved Brenda! She was from my other life, and underneath the froufrou she was one of the most courageous people I knew. Without her laughter and friendship, my home life would have been even more unbearable. "She's the best," I wept out.

And then I was facing him, tears swimming in my eyes, and he was brushing the tears off my face, his warmth seeping into my side, and I wanted to kiss him. I did. One time. One kiss. I leaned toward him. I closed my eyes and prepared for this dizzying passionate kiss with Prince Aiden. I waited a second, then two and whoosh. Cold air.

When I opened my peepers, he was standing up by the picnic table, facing the ocean, running a hand through his hair.

No no no no no, that voice in my head shrieked. *Oh heck, no, say it isn't so. Say you didn't just do that!*

But I did! I had! Hell and tarnation, *I had tried to kiss Aiden Bridger.*

I could not have been more humiliated if I'd stripped off my clothes in front of him and performed a Scottish High-lands dance followed by a double cartwheel.

I wanted *to die.*

I got up and jogged toward those monstrous dogs of mine, my mind drowning in embarrassment.

I heard him call my name, but I kept on truckin'.

I don't know why I let Brenda talk me into it. I don't know why Christie agreed so eagerly to do it, either. I may have mentioned: the three of us together are lethal.

At ten o'clock that night, there we were, in one of the island's lakes, naked, swimming around.

"I want to live in this water," Christie said. "For once I don't feel as if I'm carrying around a Mack Truck in my gut."

"The freedom, the breathless freedom, the ultimate in lib-eration, right here, right now," Brenda said.

"Fat floats," I said as I floated naked on my back and counted the stars, Aiden's face next to every one of them. "I am such an idiot."

We did not drive with our shirts off through town after that, as previously suggested.

"We'll save that exciting event for later, Brenda," I said.

"Agreed," she said. "We'll bring Mrs. Zebra. She's my fa-vorite dog."

My sister moaned. "I'll probably be nursing by then, so I'm gonna miss out! Why do I always miss out on all the fun?"

"We have to stage a rescue."

I put my paintbrush down. I was drawing/painting Cassy Cat. Hard to do when all I could think about was my bumbling kiss-attack on the unsuspecting Aiden. I hot-flashed at the thought of it.

Cassy Cat had white in her golden stripes and wore glasses and simple clothes. Even though she is running for president of her farm, she did not try to get all dressed up as the prissy goose did.

"Gina, I cannot even think of rescuing a horse right now." My cat Troublesome, old and creaky and missing a leg, settled on my feet.

"It'll take one night." She pulled a purple flower from her hair and stuck it back in over her ear. "One night out of your life!"

"I don't even have a night." I would be up all night, again. I hadn't even been to bed yet, and it was eight in the morning.

I rinsed out my brush, stood up, examined Cassy Cat. She had to be presidential, but not snobby. Smart but not superior. Fox was sticking his pointy nose in the picture, as if spying on her, his black tuxedo coat buttoned up tight.

Had I really leaned in to kiss Aiden?

"This is about reaching out to our fellow species! Grasping their humanity, their dignity! Haven't you seen the horse?"

"No, I haven't." I thought of my own Herbert Hoove the Horse. Herbert was humble and sweet and wore bow ties. I get letters from kids addressed to Herbert Hoove the Horse all the time.

"Come and see him."

"No." *I would hide in my studio the rest of my life.*

"Yes. One peek. A tiny gander. You won't be able to sleep at night once you're introduced to Gordon. He's depressed, he's having anxiety issues, and he can't sleep because he's starving."

"Then Gordon and I have something in common, because I'm not sleeping much now, either." I picked up Troublesome and dropped her on my lap. *At least Troublesome hadn't witnessed the kiss-attack.*

"Take a mental break. A break for Gordon. For a hairy old

friend who whispered to me yesterday that he's afraid he's going to die and he has so much more he wants to do with his life!"

Gina is very passionate about animals. Not only is she a pet communicator, she runs an animal sanctuary on the island. Her grandfather bought tons of land here decades ago, and she inherited it. In addition, she inherited money from her father, a megamillionaire software guy, so her full-time job was taking care of animals that had been used in medical experiments. The labs were actually giving her their animals when they were through with them, and a donation, on condition that she never reveal the status of their health when they arrived.

"I have great fondness for hairy old friends, Gina, but right now I'm painting a cat who bears a sad resemblance to a sick porcupine, and I can't stop."

She marched around my studio for a few minutes, her long hair swaying like a horse's tail as she stared at my paintings. "Okay, Chalese. I'll make you a deal."

"No deal."

"Listen up. If you go with me to take a gander, a peek at this starving, troubled, emotional horse, I'll make you one of my frozen chocolate, flourless pies."

My paintbrush stopped in midair. "Really?"

"Yes, really."

I'm a sucker for those pies. "How about two?"

"Agreed. Two for the horse!"

"Done. We're on."

Who knew that a few days later I was going to end up with a horse in my dining room?

Chapter Five

"I'm so sorry, Aiden, so sorry. I should never have tried to kiss you." I could hardly meet the man's eyes as he stood on my front porch, my wind chimes tinkling in the afternoon wind.

How do you explain to someone that your lust carried you away, and you could not resist them? "I am a clumsy elephant, a ridiculous, pathetic, cloistered writer. I don't get out enough, I hot-flash, I talk to my dogs and half the time I expect them to answer back, I hang out with Brenda, who is so wild and—"

He held a hand up. "Chalese"—his voice was a bit strangled—"please don't apologize. Please don't. I mean it. I was flattered, I was. But . . . this is my job. You're my job."

"Absolutely. I know it. The ox in me will never charge at you again." I slapped my hands to my face. Why must I speak about animals so much?

He took three steps closer to me. "You're very . . . engaging. You've got this curious, electric aura about you, this mystery, but at the same time you're so open about who you are and sincere. And you're so smart. I can almost hear your brain ticking away a million miles an hour." He rubbed his neck. "But this is not the time or the place for me to . . ." He coughed. "To return your . . . kiss."

Clearly, it wasn't, that voice in my head assailed me.

He-man Aiden would not ever want to return your . . . kiss. He was trying to alleviate my total humiliation because he was a nice guy, then smooth things over so he could write the article without me making any more awkward kissy-lunges toward him.

"Hey, Aiden," I snapped, feeling my face get red, therefore resembling a fire engine. Perhaps I should make the sound of a fire engine? "You don't have to make me feel better here, okay? I don't need your pity. Ask me the damn questions you need to ask, and let's get this over with. I'll keep my kisses to myself."

His eyes went bleak all of a sudden, his voice gruff. "That wasn't what I meant, Chalese, not at all."

"Sure it is. The frumpy children's book author made a fool of herself, and you're trying to let her down easy by saying it's 'not the time or the place for me to return your kiss.' Shove it, okay?"

"The last word I would use to describe you is frumpy, even if you are still in your pajamas."

"I'm working. This is my work uniform. Got a problem with it, close your eyes."

"I have no problems with your work uniform, even if you do have pink giraffes on your pajamas. And I don't pity you, so don't start with that. We're going to talk about what happened down there another time."

"Sure we are. As soon as I grow a third head out my spine. Let me grab the dogs, and we'll walk down to the ocean." I shut the door, dove into the shower, yanked my jeans on without the usual force, which was strange, and threw a red sweatshirt over my head.

We got all the leaping dogs on leashes and headed for the ocean, the sun golden and warm, shining through the trees in sparkling rays.

The dogs were poorly behaved and rambunctious, as usual, and soon I let them off-leash. They grinned victoriously, their tongues lolling about, and headed off into their high adventure.

Aiden got out a notepad as we strolled along the shoreline and I tried to avoid looking at him. "All right, I need you to trust me a little bit here with a few simple questions."

I quivered inside but tried not to show it. *Trust him. My childhood had about beat my ability to trust any man right out of my body.*

"When did you start drawing?"

"I can't remember *not* drawing." That was the truth.

"So you started as a child?"

I nodded. I didn't want to say that drawing and writing were an escape for me then. That drawing gave me a way to block out my father and the rampant fear he caused, the crushing hurt, the anger, the way I felt when I saw him clock my mother or lock her in their bedroom suite for days in our New York apartment.

Kangaroos in pink aprons I could control. A fox in a tuxedo I could laugh at. A parakeet who braided her head feathers I could handle. Pretty soon, my animals were talking. At first it was simple stuff, from a child's viewpoint. But that child, *moi,* grew up pretty quick in that house, and my kangaroos in pink aprons were soon giving little speeches in Australia about the land belonging to everyone. The raccoons in the forests of Oregon were working with the beavers to fight off pollution that was killing the fish. The polar bears were discussing how they could all get along.

"I loved to draw because it was creative. It was fun. I loved animals. Still do."

I smiled at him with as much confidence as I could muster over my deadly boring answer.

Aiden stared at me. "I know there's more to it than that behind your beaming, fake smile."

My stomach clenched as if two vises were being screwed into it. I tried to seem perplexed. "No, I don't think so. I'm pretty simple. Very normal childhood. Normal life here, too. Normal childhood. Normal. Very."

I heard the dogs bark in the distance. They loved to run. I wanted to run.

"Why writing and illustrating? Why that career choice?"

Because then I could hide like a hot-flashing turtle and live quietly. "I wanted to write books for kids. I wanted them to love my books, love reading. I wanted to teach them what a truthful, kind society should strive for and how we have to take care of each other and the planet."

"And?"

"I wanted to make them think." That was a raw truth. "We often tell kids what they should think. We dump information on them. We tell them what to do, tell them what to learn, tell them how to be. I wanted them to think about their relationships, their lives, their futures, animals, this country, the world, people that look the same as them, and people that are different, people who have different opinions. My animals in my books struggle with the same emotions people do, but reading it from a fluffy bunny appeals to kids more than if I stuck an exhausted mother of three in there."

I stopped.

"Does that make sense, or do I sound like an inebriated rattlesnake?" I hit my forehead and reminded myself once again to lose the animals out of my conversation.

He nodded at me. "Completely. It's admirable."

"Thank you." *Must you be so sexy?*

"How did your *normal, very normal*"—I did not miss his emphasis on those words—"childhood affect your decision to write books with such depth?"

My childhood had affected every part of my life. It's only been in the last years that I've been able to separate "it" from "me," and I'm still working on it. I hugged my arms around myself. "My childhood allowed me the time to draw and write." Lots of time. Times of sheer terror move quicker when one can draw white storks in bikinis while hiding under a bed.

"Were your parents supportive of your work?"

"Yes." My mother was. She snuck me crayons and pencils and pads of paper. My father gave her enough to feed us— barely. He would not allow her to work. It was outrageous, really. We had a fancy apartment on Fifth Avenue in New York, a car and driver for my father, but often no money to buy milk.

The way my mother got my father to spend money for clothes on us once a year was by implying she was worried about what other people would think of our sorry state. We would live through another rage, he'd leave without us for a charity dinner or fancy ball where his face would appear in the society pages the next day—but by morning my mother would have an envelope on her side of the bed. No telling what my mother had to do to get that envelope.

"How?"

I shuddered. "How what?" How come my father seemed to hate me and was much more interested in Christie? How come he often sent me to my room—"Go to your igloo," he'd order—as if he didn't want to see my face? How come he was such an angry man and asked me with a sneer if I wanted whale meat to eat? *I don't know.*

His eyes narrowed. "How were they supportive?"

"My mother bought me pencils and crayons and paper."

"And your father?"

I grimaced, then pulled my arms closer to my body. "He paid for them."

"Was he an artist?"

"No." He was a nightmare. A black-haired nightmare.

"Was your mother an artist?"

"No." She was a survivor.

"What did your parents do for a living? Where did you grow up?"

I was feeling more and more ill. "My father was a business-man." For a while. Until he made his world collapse. "My mother was a full-time mother. I grew up in . . . I grew up in . . . in . . ." What to say? If I said New York, that would give him another door to open. "I grew up in Connecticut."

So that one was a lie. My father had one of his homes there. We visited once. He hadn't wanted us to go there, ever again, without him. Sometimes he'd be gone for a week, and later he'd tell us he was at the Connecticut house. He'd stare right at my mother when he said this and smirk.

"Any siblings besides Christie?"

"No." Maybe. Probably. None that I know of. Mrs. Zebra licked me. Lightning circled, making sure I was okay, then bounded off into the waves again.

"What do you most love about being a children's book writer?"

That was easy. It didn't make me feel nauseous with stress. I smelled the sea instead. "I love talking to kids through the stories. I love the creativity, the color, the smell of paint . . ." I finally unwrapped my arms from the death grip around my worried body.

"You have lots of dogs and cats here."

"I love animals. They were all strays or abused, and I take care of them, then find them new owners who will be kind and loving and appreciate them." I did not mention my gigantic veterinarian and grooming bills.

Mrs. Zebra, almost on cue, put her paws on my shoulders and licked my face.

"Why were you rocking yourself?" Aiden asked quietly.

"I'm sorry?"

"When I was asking you questions about your childhood, you had your arms wrapped around your body and you were rocking yourself back and forth."

"I was not." But I was. I knew he was right.

He waited. "Difficult childhood?"

"All childhoods have their difficult points." I tucked my hair behind my ears when the wind blew it across my face.

"But yours had more than a few."

"That's it, Aiden," I said, suddenly angry. I was used to my own anger about my childhood, but I smothered it. Now it was being triggered by Mr. Gorgeous Skyscraper getting way too personal. "That's enough, okay? I don't want to talk about my childhood anymore."

"Hey, it's okay. I understand."

"You do? I don't think so. I can't imagine that you could. And would you mind not putting it in your article? Please, one favor. You've boxed me into a corner, you've forced me to talk to you because you're going to write it with or without my help, you're going to blow my private life to hell, and I'm asking you for a favor." My voice pitched, then cracked. "Please don't mention anything about my childhood—what I said or didn't say—in your stupid article."

"I didn't mean to upset you, Chalese. I'm not writing an exposé. I'm not going to publicly lampoon you. . . ."

I closed my eyes when they started feeling hot and wet. An image of my father, yelling, disdainful, sprang to my mind. He would rarely come to my room and tell me good-night, but when he did it was with a litany of things I wasn't doing right. He never hugged me. Not once. I remembered the cowering little girl I had been. I felt sorry for that little girl.

"I'm done with this interview, Aiden," I said as I jogged after my troublesome dogs. When they saw me coming, they grinned and ran fast, checking to make sure I was following. "Come back," I demanded, leaping over a couple of logs. They turned and grinned again, barking joyfully. "Right this minute, come back, you monsters."

When I returned to where we had been sitting in the sand, about twenty-five minutes later, he was gone.

Later a huge basket was delivered to my house. It was filled with flowers and gourmet food. The card read, "I'm sorry."

I sunk into my Adirondack chairs as the sun went down and the night came up, the haunting memories of my father pushed back into their box in my mind.

As I said, the second I set eyes on Aiden I knew it wasn't gonna be good.

At four o'clock in the morning I gave up on sleep, wrapped my periwinkle blue comforter around my shoulders, and settled into my rocking chair on the porch. Shortcake climbed on my lap as I listened to the lapping waves, the sky bluish black and scattered with stars.

My mother snuck two stray cats she found next to a dumpster in New York City into our home, and I have been a sucker for animals ever since. She was in a poorer part of the city that day; I have no idea why. Anyhow, she heard mewing, headed down an alley, and there were Star and Moon, as we came to call them, starving and helpless.

She snuck them into her bag and brought them home. Luckily, our father was on another business trip and then was planning on "checking on" our Connecticut home. For one week, Christie and I and our mother played with those cats, loved them, held them.

And right before my father came home, raging, dangerous, asking me where my harpoon was, we had to give them away to another family.

We were lost. Lost in a huge apartment with a mother scared down to her toes, a sister who was favored by our father and, to this day, still has nightmares about their "father-daughter" times, and a father who often told me that I belonged in an igloo with a polar bear for a pet.

My love of animals began right then.

To find new homes for my dogs and cats, I created a simple website. It does the trick. I get a surprising amount of hits and adopt out quite a few dogs and cats every year. I have a few dogs, however, who will always stay with me because of their poor behavior.

Shortcake is one of them. I kissed her head.

She slobbered on me.

* * *

"Help me."

Those two pathetic words wept over the phone sent panic streaking through my heart. I almost swallowed the nub of purple pencil I was clenching with my teeth.

"What is it? What's happened?" I spit out the pencil and dropped the paintbrush in my other hand to the floor. It hit my cat Butterball on the head. She meowed, miffed.

I heard sobbing on the other end of the phone.

"Tell me, right now, tell me." I abruptly stood up, and my cat Freaky went sailing off my lap. She glared, then stalked off to cuddle up to Rocky, who had horrendous gas problems that morning.

More wretched sobbing.

"I'm coming—I'll be there in a few minutes." I felt as if I'd jumped into an arctic lake. "Please tell me what's wrong!" A spray of rain hit my windows, and I took it as a terrible omen, fear scraping its ragged claws across my stomach. I thudded down the stairs, shoved my feet into pink rain boots, and stumbled for the door.

"Christie! Honey, hang on!" I thought of Christie, who always smelled like roses and baby powder, and I could barely contain my panic. "Should I call the chief? An ambulance?"

"No," Christie moaned. "But I . . ."

I sprinted to my truck in my green cat pajamas, sloshing through the puddles, the rain drenching me. Shortcake and Mrs. Zebra leaped off the covered porch and followed me out. I didn't have time to wrestle them into the house, so I yanked open the door to the truck. They clambered in, their tails wagging with joy at a car ride.

"You what? Is it the babies? Are you hurting? Are you bleeding?"

Christie sobbed again, raw, hopeless.

"Oh no." Not the twins! Tears sprang to my eyes. "Oh no!"

"Chalese," she moaned. "Chalese . . . I am . . . I am . . . *I am so fat.*"

My sweating hand froze on the key to the car, my heart trip-trapping.

"I'm fat!" Christie moaned again. "Fat, fat, *fat*. My legs are huge and I've got stretch marks on my stomach and my boobs are the size of cannonballs and my ankles are the size my thighs used to be and even my ears are fat!"

I leaned against the back of the seat, my heart pattering. Shortcake leaned over and licked me.

"And . . . and . . . my skin feels like it's ripping! These babies are so big and the other three won't take their naps and the house is a wreck and I used to be fun and smart and sexy and had a sexy car and now I'm fat and all I have time to think about is poopy diapers and where's the pacifier and I wear frumpy clothes because I'm fat, my hair is greasy because I haven't had time for a shower for two days, and I don't have a career and probably never will because I'm fat!"

I breathed heavily, deeply, sagging like I was a drunken rag doll against the back of the seat.

"Are you there, Chalese? Are you there?"

"I'm here, Christie." Every neuron in my brain had been zapped by stress, but I was still here.

"Can you come over? Please?"

I had so much work to do. I was overwhelmed, exhausted. This book had to get out, or my editor would call and harangue me. He had actually been threatening me with his own heart attack if I didn't get my book in. "It'll be your fault, Chalese, your fault!"

"Please, Chalese?"

The life of a mother of three, pregnant with twins, is almost beyond rational comprehension. This I knew. Shortcake licked me again. "Give me five minutes."

Chapter Six

"I'm still sensing you're hiding something from me, Chalese," Aiden said, his voice soft and low and sexy. "What else do you want to tell me?"

I leaned back in the booth of Marci's Whale-Jumping Café and tried to breathe.

I shouldn't have been surprised by his astuteness. Aiden was a prize-winning reporter, but I still felt struck, as if an elk had charged at me and the antlers were stuck in my gut.

"No, there's not anything else I want to tell you." That was the truth. I inhaled the scent of buttermilk pancakes, bacon, and orange juice and wiped my hot hands on my jeans.

"It would be better coming from you, sweet Chalese."

I tried not to blush at the "sweet" part.

Our charming village on the island, a mix of very old and medium-old, well-cared for shops, churches, and restaurants, was small, and it hadn't taken Aiden any time to find my truck parked in front of the café, a place with blue leather seats, windows to take in the view of the ocean behind the café, and a giant plastic whale hanging from the ceiling wearing a white captain's hat.

"Hey! Chalese!" Reuby, Gina's son, yelled across the crowded room when I first arrived. "Hear ya got a special friend. If he breaks up with you, are ya gonna climb up on his roof and bust the skylight out?"

Everyone laughed.

"Very funny. Actually, if he broke up with me I would bull-doze his home with a tractor. I like tractors."

"Is the skylight thing going to be in Brenda's next movie?" Jefferson Harris called out. He made art out of recycled materials and did pretty well.

"No, it's not. Brenda and I—"

"And your sister," Lavender Mercato called out. "Man, that gal's gonna have five kids quick as a lick and ain't nothin' slowed her down since high school. She's still gettin' in trouble with you two. Did I hear you three were skinny-dipping again the other night?"

I covered my face as they all cackled. "I'm going to sit here and go to a special place in my own gnarled head, have some breakfast, and pretend I'm alone."

"I don't think you're going to be alone for long," Fred Mitchell called out, nodding his shaved head toward the door; the snake tattoos on his arm no longer alarming me as they once had. "Your man's coming in."

"Lookee who's here!" Shadow Morrison drawled. Shadow is a financial planner. She wears dresses over skinny black leggings, flowered hats, and sparkly scarves. She's twenty-six and does almost everyone's investments. A whiz kid. "I think it's the special friend."

Reuby called out to Aidan, "Your special friend is right here, dude. Right here." Now this was a smallish restaurant, but Reuby still felt compelled to point me out. "She hasn't ordered yet, but she always has eggs Benedict, sauce on the side, blueberry pancakes, and her own Marion Berry jelly. Her jellies are awesome rad."

There was loud, general agreement. One of the island's secret multimillionaires called out, "Jam Lady does it best, man."

I saw Aiden's look of surprise at the attention. Then he

covered it, and that easy smile came out. "Well, I'm hoping to eat breakfast with Jam Lady, if she'll have me."

I groaned. Torture me further: he was wearing cool jeans, a black sweater, and a white T-shirt. Studly. I was sunk. I knew it.

"Her sister always orders breakfast for dinner," Reuby said, playing with the ring in his eyebrow. "Pancakes with strawberry syrup and sliced bananas and white wine. 'Cept when she's pregnant. We all know when Christie's pregnant, 'cause that's when she starts ordering the weird stuff. Whole onions fried with garlic butter. Grape juice with her pasta. Guacamole and pink lemonade and sliced apples. She dips the apples in the guac, dude. It's weird. Plus she sucks down Chalese's marmalade like its water."

"Tell him about Brenda," Shadow called, flipping her blond braids onto her back.

"Yeah, Brenda's the third sister, but they don't share no blood. She orders whiskey sours sometimes for breakfast. That's when she's hungover. For dinner, she orders a salad with extra olives and pickles. One time she ate a whole pizza by herself and three beers. Those three, man, I dunno. Strange."

"Strange is good," Aiden said, his voice low and rumbly. "Who wants a boring woman? I don't."

"Cheers to that," Fred agreed, holding up his coffee cup. "Bring me a high-kicker in red knee high boots."

Dear me, the joys of living on an island with not very many people . . .

It took Aiden twenty minutes to walk to my table because everyone had to say hello, welcome him to the island, and then regale him with stories about me, his special friend.

There was the red and pink streamer incident at City Hall (it was a protest, long ago), and the tractor Brenda and I borrowed and drove behind a group of racist skinheads over from the mainland who insisted on having a parade. We kept the tractor one foot from their heels. When they got worried they'd be run over and started jogging, we revved the tractor and followed close so we wouldn't lose them. They called the police, but we explained we merely were trying to keep up with the skinheads!

Charges dropped. We followed them out of town with the tractor.

"Chalese sells the best jams and jellies ever. She sells to the stores, the restaurants. Probably makes a fortune—that's our Chalese," old Mrs. Chittick said. She carefully cultivated the "old, frail lady" image, but I knew for a fact that the woman could split wood faster than you could say "old, frail lady."

But the Chalese who made the best jams and jellies was all the Chalese I wanted to be. Nothing more.

Not one thing more.

"There is nothing else I want to tell you," I whispered back to Aiden across the table, pushing what was left of my eggs Benedict aside. "Nothing."

We shared another one of those gazes. By gosh, why did I feel as if my soul mate was sitting across from me, right past the salt and pepper shakers?

Aiden was clearly disappointed and worried. I was sure there was a miniature goat stuck in my constricted throat. Did he already know something was up? And if he did, how much did he know?

He had another bite of my raspberry jelly. "Everybody's right. This is incredible." He rolled his huge shoulders then leaned toward me. "I know you're hiding something. I can feel it. I'm already searching for it. This is my job, and I will find out what it is."

I blinked rapidly to clear the tears and the exploding fear. *What would my friends here think of me when they knew?*

"The article is going to come out, and I can help you if I know the truth."

"I know the article will be printed, but I'm hoping it will

have minimal impact for me here on the island. Maybe the day it comes out we'll be hit by millions of falling stars and no one will read it."

"And you can continue to be anonymous? No one will know you and Annabelle are one and the same?"

"Yes," I hissed.

"That isn't going to happen, Chalese."

Good-bye, life.

"I have to go. I'll see you later."

"I'll come with you."

"No, you won't. You make me nervous."

I got up to leave the booth. He got up to follow me, and I did not miss what he said under his breath. "You make me nervous, too."

"I don't know why I make you nervous."

"Spend half a second in front of the mirror, charming Chalese, and you'll figure it out pretty damn quick."

I shot him a glance. "You're flirting."

"Not yet. Simply stating a fact."

I heard Mrs. Chittick and Mrs. Meyerson titter in the corner.

"He's a romantic!'

"He's a sex god!"

"He's got a body identical to Zeus!"

"Yep, a sex-god Zeus."

"Do you think he's asked her yet?"

Mrs. Chittick yelled, "Hey, Add-on! Have you asked her to marry you? You know that girl's never said yes. Not once. Four times men have asked her to the altar. Always a no. Smart, she is. Women live longer if they don't marry, you know. Husbands stress us out, make us so mad our insides curdle, so frustrated we believe we're on blipping fire. Better to stay single, if you ask me, but I'd marry you, sexy Zeus god, if you asked!"

"Fifth time's the charm!" a millionaire announced.

"She's broken hearts here on the island. Ya gotta watch out for that, Add-on," Fred the high-kicker said.

I hurried out as another sweat-fest took its time to burn the heck out of me.

I wiped my brow.

"How about a walk on the trail around the island?" Aiden asked me.

"Sure, Zeus," I said. "Whatever."

Brenda greeted us back at my house wearing a gold pantsuit, a sparkling silver headband, and fairy wings. She had a date with a businessman from Seattle who was at his weekend house for a few days. I have no idea why she periodically puts on outrageous costumes for her dates; I don't ask. She gave me a hug, then flapped her arms as she jumped off the porch and into her sports car. I smelled her sultry, earthy perfume.

I grabbed a bag of grapes. Then we leashed two joyous dogs each before heading for the ocean and a nature path around the island. The day was warm and clear, too pretty to miss.

"Aiden."

He turned his head toward me. Now that was a novelty. Most men listen about as well as they can crack walnuts with their knees. "Tell me about you."

He shrugged his shoulders. "There's not much. I was raised by my father. We're still close. My mother died when I was five in an accident in India. He's still in love with my mother. That's why he never remarried. He was an executive, and we traveled all over the world. He continues to work. He's in Zurich right now. I still have friends from Zimbabwe to Saudi Arabia to London to Toronto. It was a great life. I had much more independence than most kids, but . . ."

"But what?" I felt so unbelievably sad for the little boy who grew up without a mother.

"Once my mother died, I never felt I had a home."

"I'm sorry." I hadn't had a *safe* home until Whale Island.

I unleashed the dogs. They leaped into the water. I could almost hear them yodeling, "We're free! Free!"

He shrugged. "People need a home. They need to know they belong somewhere, that there's family and friends around, that there's a place that's set aside for them to be loved, to laugh, to be themselves."

"You don't feel as if you have a home now?"

He thought for a second. "I have a condominium, Chalese. It's nice. It's on the water in Seattle, fantastic view, it's modern, it's sleek. I have a stove that doesn't catch on fire and a sink that doesn't leak, but I wouldn't call it home. It's where I live, not where I feel I belong."

We stepped over a log on the sand, then headed closer to the ocean, took our shoes off, and waded in.

"I felt the exact same way before I came to Whale Island."

"You feel this is home now?"

"I do." I turned to face him. "I know how it feels to desperately want a home. I don't leave the island much, because I feel so right here, so safe. Yes, it's a problem now and then that we all know each other so well, but mostly it makes me . . ." I searched for the right word. "It makes me feel as if I went on a quest for myself and found myself here. It's a gift. It's mostly a good thing, except for when Brenda, the menace, gets me in trouble."

"Not that that would ever be your fault?"

I laughed with him. "Never." I tilted my head. "You've never married?" I applauded my own daring in asking that question so nonchalantly.

"No. I have worked and travelled constantly, and I have never met anyone I wanted to marry. Fifty years is a long time to be together, and I need to be sure. I'm getting married once, and then the gal's stuck with me forever. You?"

I grimaced. "Let's skip that topic."

He paused. "Let's not. I want to hear about those marriage proposals you said no to."

I hung my head, letting my black hair cover the sides of my face. "Let's talk about biochemical engineering, international economics, or the stock market and skip this part."

"Too dull. So . . . have you been married? What about those four proposals?"

"Aiden, I don't want to talk about that, and I sure as heck don't want it in your story." Small, cool waves lapped at our legs until Nutmeg Man galloped on in and splashed us.

He nodded, wiped water off his face with his hand. "This is off the record. A conversation between you and me. It's personal."

"I don't know . . ."

"Trust me on this, will you?"

"Trust you?" Out in the distance I saw a spray of water from a whale. I was a bit of a head case, that was true, and I had serious, free-ranging trust issues, but for this one conversation . . .

"Yes. Trust me." Charlotte, a white mutt missing half an ear, circled our legs, barking.

I took a leap of faith into those green eyes. "I said no because even though all those men seemed right initially— smart, ambitious, interesting, blah blah blah—when I got to know them, their flaws shone like a six-story spotlight. I knew I'd be infinitely happier single than married to any of them." Plus, I kept seeing a bit of my father in each of them. That was enough to liquify my insides with fear.

"Smart woman." He tucked a curl behind my ear, then drew his hand back real quick, as if that motion had surprised him.

"None of them listened well," I said, clearing my throat when desire flamed up and out of control in my nether regions. "Sometimes they didn't even bother to look at me when I spoke, or they'd say 'Yep' or 'Uh-huh,' which really means 'I'm not listening. You're not worth the effort, and the conversation is not about me, Mr. Man, so I'm not interested.'"

Identical to my father's attitude.

"One man was passive-aggressive and controlling. He sneakily put me down when he could, threw out barbs. The second man was a closet drinker with the accompanying problems of denial, blame of others, anger, and depression."

I watched a sailboat leave the dock.

"The third man was a goofball who did not want to take responsibility for anyone, including himself. He was eternally lazy but tried to hide it under the artist/musician mantle. He played the sax."

"And the fourth man who asked you to marry him?"

"He was a liar. I found that out about two days before he asked me to marry him. He hid massive credit-card bills, and his betting and gambling. When I found out, that was it."

"Good decision."

"Yes, it was. In none of them had I sensed a real and true kindness. Compassion. Selflessness. For those men, it was all about *them*. I knew they would never help me, support me, encourage me in my career or anything else. It sure wouldn't come naturally to them, and they wouldn't do it if they had to inconvenience themselves in any way."

And I hadn't trusted any of them.

"So when they asked you to marry them?"

"I felt as if I were suffocating."

"Suffocating." He nodded.

"I couldn't breathe. I can only compare it to having a wedding bouquet smashed over my nose. Had I slept with any of them, which I didn't, I'm sure the feelings of suffocation would've been exponentially worse."

"What about marrying someone else? Some great, kind, smart, handsome bloke who made you laugh? Would you still feel suffocated?"

"Yep. I'd still feel as if my windpipe was being somewhat smashed. I don't think I would be happy married." *Unless it was to Zeus here. I might be able to breathe long-term around Zeus, the sex god.*

"Because . . . ," he prodded.

"I am happy with my life the way it is." I had to hide away, keep things private, and I preferred to do that without a husband strapped to my back. *Unless, perhaps, it was Zeus. He would not be too heavy on my back.*

"You don't want kids?"

"No." *Well, no more than four with Zeus.* "Do you?" I tried not to feel insanely, flamingly jealous of the wife he did not yet have and the kids she would bear him.

"Yes, I want kids."

"But you travel all the time for your work."

"I did travel all the time for my work. I came to the Seattle paper a year ago because I wanted a change in my life. With this job, I knew I could have a life, flexibility. I've travelled almost constantly for twenty years, not counting my childhood. My suitcase is worn out. I have enough frequent-flier miles to go to Saturn. I can't even think about pretzels anymore without feeling sick. I don't have a real home, and I want that. And I want a family—wife, kids, the whole nine yards. I've wanted that for years now."

I tried to make light of it so I didn't bang my head against the ground like a jealous, rabid rat gone wild envisioning his wife-to-be and kids. "I've rarely heard a bachelor admit that. Strike that. I've *never* heard a bachelor admit that."

"I admit it. It's what I want."

"I'm sure your kids will be born ready to be ace reporters, lie detectors in their tiny fists, flak jackets on, pens at the ready . . ."

"And your kids, Chalese? They'll be born clutching paintbrushes and drawing pencils." He paused. "And then they'd be off to spy on someone through a skylight. . . ."

I tossed a grape at him.

He tossed one at me.

I tossed another.

And somehow, some way, our faces ended up so close I could

see the darker green flecks in those eyes, the lines crinkling from the corners, and the wave of those brown curls.

And there we froze.

I should have moved away, at the very least to avoid the abject, eyeball-popping humiliation of the last kiss-attack. This time, I kept my peepers open.

But that electricity, that lust, *that thing* between us, went loose, boinging off both of us. Aiden leaned in to kiss me, his fingers entwining with mine.

His lips could not have been better, a mixture of softness and demand, passion and restraint, rampaging lust and more rampaging lust.

When he pulled me closer, I linked an arm around his neck and gave in to that quivering, sexily sinking, hot sensation until I thought I might self-combust. He pulled me in close, so we had a warm, tingling, full-body press going on. After luscious minutes, he picked me up, *me,* Ms. Plentiful Bottom, and gently placed me on my back in the warm sand and followed me down, his kisses strong, our breath mixing, a pant following a moan and a pant, until I had no idea where I stopped and he began.

He pulled his head up. "Damn. Oh damn."

I tried to speak, couldn't. I did make a sound in my throat, though, like someone would who landed unexpectedly in heaven. *He was an excellent kisser!*

He bent to kiss me again, and I kissed him back, his lips trailing my neck, and lower, and I instinctively arched my back, willingly diving into that pool of passion in a way I'd never dived.

And then there was cool, ocean air where a warm, muscled, male body used to be as he arched up on his elbows, knees to the ground between my legs, shaking his head. "Dammit," he breathed.

I dropped my arms and waited, trying not to smile like a Cheshire cat, but I couldn't help myself.

"I'm sorry, Chalese," he started breathlessly. "Dammit."

"Dammit twice?" Charlotte circled us, then ran off, barking, like she was tattling to the other dogs.

"Yes, twice." He crinkled his eyes, appreciating the humor, before he went back to serious.

I wanted to laugh, wriggle, dance. The man who was going to expose me had kissed me, and the kisses were, well, *outstanding!* Even my throbbing body yelled, "Outstanding!"

"I can't believe I'm in this situation," he said, shaking his head. "Well, I can, I can believe it. You have strung me up since the second I saw you. I can hardly think anymore but I have never gotten involved with anyone I was interviewing. This is totally unprofessional and inappropriate."

"It felt totally appropriate, though. Yes, it did." I grinned up at him, then ran a finger over his lips. Warm. Yummy. His eyes shut, he moaned.

He was a truly delicious male specimen. Truly delicious. The kisses had been the commanding sort of kiss, the "I'm going to take charge here" kiss, the "I want you, and I'm about to lose control over you" kiss.

Awesome! I chuckled.

"This is funny to you?" he said.

"Yep. It is." I cupped his face, and he turned his head more fully into my palm.

"It's a mess."

"That, too," I agreed. I bit my lip but couldn't suppress my smile. How I wanted that man. He was huggable and kissable, and I had never had such a base, magnetic attraction to any man in my whole life. My body was thrumming for him. *Thrumming!* "A beautiful mess, though."

I saw something flicker in those eyes, eyes that never wavered from mine. "Beautiful, tragic. Complicated. And I really must kiss you again."

It was an instant, a millisecond, and we were right back in each other's arms, sweet, hot, desperate, on-fire kisses, hands going this way and that, legs curved around legs, a roll here and there, an arch or two, a semistraddle.

Until he pulled away again and panted, "This is out of control."

I noticed he was breathing really hard, even harder than me.

"But it's fun." I smiled at him. "So much fun."

He gave up, that stressed expression leaving his face as he laughed.

The dogs circled us, barking, tails wagging.

"You are a helluva kisser, Zeus," I muttered.

And maybe, one day, I could trust this man. Maybe.

"Hi, Mom," I said into the phone. "You're in Dallas? Yes, I got the shiny green coat for winter. It fit perfectly. . . . I *do* appreciate the ear flaps on the hood and how the coat reaches my ankles. I resemble an overgrown caterpillar. I'll take the extra vitamin C and green tea you sent, and I'll do the earth mud mask. . . . I love you, too. . . ."

Chapter Seven

Gina Martinez is actually quite famous for her pet-communicating skills. She speaks to animal lovers at conventions all over the country. She's even been on talk shows and has written newspaper articles about her abilities. She 100 percent believes that she can talk to animals and is quite persuasive.

She was especially persuasive the next night, when she got me and Brenda in our black burglar outfits once again and drove us down a dark and bumpy road on the south side of the island for the rescue mission. Gina was dressed in purple, head to foot. I have no idea why. Reuby was there, too. He wore black.

"Don't take any pictures with your cell phone, Reuby," Gina warned. "None. We can't have any evidence."

"Got it, Authority Figure. It wouldn't be cool to be the guy in court who has to tell the judge his mother is a horse thief, he's got the evidence, and she should go to jail."

Gina rolled her eyes. "No wonder your hamster says you drive him crazy, Reuby."

I sighed. Now I could add "horse thief" to my resume.

We watched the dilapidated house and rickety barn where the poor horse who was "battling depression and enduring anxiety attacks" lived. I didn't know about the anxiety attacks, but there was no disputing Gordon the horse was underfed, sickly, thin, weak, and uncared for, as I had noted days before on our spy mission.

Red Scanlon, a cantankerous drunk whom everyone on the island hated because he was a cantankerous drunk, would soon leave for the local bar on his bicycle, that was a given. Twice he'd parked his truck sideways in the middle of the main street of the island and passed out after a foray to the bar.

The second time it happened, with Red locked up in the jail, *someone* took the truck and exploded it in the middle of a field. The insurance paid out, Red got drunk again, rammed the drugstore with his new truck, almost rammed a kid, and whaddya know, his truck mysteriously ended up in a lake. (Perhaps we did that).

The chief made sure he lost his license, locked him up again, fined him to the high heavens, and now mean Red was allowed a bicycle.

When the cantankerous drunk bicycled off five minutes later, we horse thieves pulled our black-knitted hats over our entire faces with only our eyes and mouths showing and went for Gordon.

Gina turned on the light in that sagging barn as soon as we walked in, and that pathetic, bony horse met my eyes. I wanted to cry. I went over and hugged him with my black gloves.

"I'll get the trailer," Brenda said. Though the black hat covered most of her face, I did not miss the tears in her eyes.

The next morning the chief was out hunting down the horse.

Everyone knew that Gina had taken it. About ten people called Gina telling her the chief was on his way out to her property. How did they all know this? The chief stopped by Marci's Whale-Jumping Café and announced quite loudly that old Red Scanlon's horse was missing and he knew where he might find it. Apparently Red had roused himself and called in the loss that morning.

The chief took his time eating his eggs and bacon with three cups of black coffee and pretended not to notice when half the place took out their cell phones.

When Gina got notice, she trotted Gordon over with Reuby to my place through the field and forest separating our homes.

Brenda and I met them halfway. I grabbed the reins. Brenda and I were still in pajamas, our hair flattened and sticking out in strange ways. Gina had fed the horse the night before—"I thought he'd never stop eating!"—and had brushed him out. "He says his self-esteem is growing exponentially!"

"Hey! Can I come over to walk the dogs today, Chalese?" Reuby asked, fiddling with his eyebrow ring.

"Anytime," I said. "You can visit the cats, too. I've hardly paid them any attention, and they're getting cranky and spiteful."

"Radical. I'm going to take their pictures with my cell phone and put them on my MySpace page."

"Fine by me. Shoot away."

Brenda and I led the horse with better self-esteem into my dilapidated but *clean* barn, rustled up fresh food and water, then wearily climbed the stairs to the porch and dropped into the Adirondack chairs to watch the sun warm my land.

"The horse stealers prevail," Brenda said, fists shaking victoriously in the air. "We were probably horse rustlers in a previous life, guns hanging all over our hips, big pink cowboy hats, spurs on our silver heels, golden lassos swinging all around."

"I think you're right. I have often felt a real bond with lassos," I mused. "Horses. Cowboys. The Wild West. Stagecoach drivers. More cowboys."

"I think ya got your own cowboy right now, my friend," Brenda said. "He's a winner, sweetie. Smart, nice, tight ass, good teeth. Try not to get that suffocating feeling around him, will you? You can do this, you know. To relax, why don't you dress up as a pirate? That's what I did the other night with Chatham. I even had a gold ring in my nose. Chatham was the wench."

"Man, Brenda. You are one wild woman."

"It's stimulating to let my creative streak out in the bedroom, hon. It's a rush for the libido."

"I think if I dressed up, I'd be a flamingo."

"*A flamingo? What* are you talking about? Geez, Chalese, why don't you dress as a giraffe? Or a snake? That'd be about as much of a turn-on as a flamingo!"

"I admire flamingos. They're flexible, they can wind around each other's necks—"

The ring of my phone interrupted my flamingo thoughts. "Hide the horse, hide the horse, the chief is coming your way," Gina yelled. "Hide him!"

"Hide him!" I screamed back as Brenda leaped off her chair. "Where? You have the trailer!"

"Put him in your kitchen."

"My kitchen! I can't put him in my kitchen! Too small."

"Hurry!" Gina screamed.

Brenda and I were up and running in our pajamas again, our hair flattened and sticking out in strange ways.

Turns out the dining room was a good fit, although the cranky, spiteful cats were not appreciative of this new guest.

Funny enough, after the chief checked my barn and property, he never thought to hunt for a horse in the dining room.

Later, a friend of Gina's came by with a horse trailer. Gordon was on the mainland and in a cozy horse shelter with a sizeable donation from me by eight o'clock that night, working on his self-esteem.

* * *

"That can't happen again, Chalese," Aiden told me the next day, trying to keep the smile off his face. "I'm sorry. My fault. I never should have kissed you."

I pulled my robe closer to my body. It was eleven in the morning, after all, and I had a deadline. I knew of other writers who didn't peel their pajamas from their bodies until their kids got home from school. At least I'd had a shower and brushed my teeth.

"Uh . . ." I said. "Am I supposed to say thanks? Thanks for apologizing? Thanks for not kissing me again? Thanks for coming by and telling me you'll never kiss me again?"

"I don't need the thanks, Chalese, but I want to apologize."

How surprised would Aiden be if I all of a sudden ripped my robe open and wriggled about naked like a flexible flamingo?

Nah. Couldn't do that. Too much stomach, too much hip. Not enough boob. Still, the image made me smile.

And when Aiden saw that smile, he murmured, "Damn," and then stepped into my house, slung an arm around my waist, pulled me close and kissed me like he never should have kissed me.

When he was leaning back against the door, his jaw tight, and I was leaning on him, I said, "Thanks for not kissing me again, Aiden."

He rolled his eyes.

I laughed.

Laughed with sadness in my heart.

We were in a terrible situation. He wanted to write about me; I wanted to hide.

And all I could think about was what the dear man would look like stark naked on my periwinkle blue comforter on my bed eating orange truffles. *Delicious!*

"Can I make you an omelet?" he asked.

* * *

It's amazing what you can learn about a person over a cheesy omelet, especially when they insist on trying all my jams and jellies and their expressions tell me they believe they're tasting fruit heaven.

I did not bother to change out of my robe. It was one that Brenda gave me, silky and blue, and I loved the feel of it. I think Aiden did, too, as he kissed me after he scrambled the eggs, and again after the chopping of the tomatoes and mushrooms, his hands exploring much of that silk robe and the hot body beneath it. . . .

We took the omelets outside to the deck. Aiden helped me get the toast and orange juice and everything else out there.

On the deck we stayed apart by a table and talked while Thunder and Lightning fell asleep by our feet and snored.

We talked about our work, the island, my naughty goats, who had escaped yet again into town, my desire to see Greece one day, our favorite books, favorite movies, politics, and a social issue or two.

By the end of it I felt as if my brain had had sex. Aiden was witty and sharp and could talk and debate until my cranium rang with pleasure.

I caught him staring at me, and I looked away, looked back. He was still staring.

"I have never talked to a woman as I talk to you. It's relaxing, it's stimulating, funny. I can only compare it to talking to a comedian/sociologist/professor all wrapped up in a blue silk robe. You are one smart lady."

"I'm glad. I wouldn't want any competition, Zeus."

"There is none," he said in all seriousness. "You have no competition, Chalese. None."

Later that day, we took my boat out. We watched the water shoot from a whale's blowhole, Aiden's face reflecting his awe. We held hands as the sun set, the colors a liquid, moving painting against the outlines of the green islands.

The next day, I showed Aiden more of the island.

When we got back to my yellow house, he stared at my barn, our fingers entwined.

"It needs work," he said.

"Yes, it does. I'll get to it."

He held my hand. "We'll get to it. I'll help you rebuild the whole thing."

And in the silky darkness of the night, I thought to myself, *That is the most romantic thing any man has ever said to me.*

She screamed, long, guttural, and piercing.

Then she jumped up and down, indulging her temper tantrum. She punched the air, ripped up paper, threw it over her head, and stomped around. She arched her back and screamed again through clenched teeth.

When she lifted up her laptop to throw it across my studio, I made a lunge and grabbed it from her. "Brenda, not the laptop. It's too expensive."

"I can't get rid of my writer's block." She fought me for the laptop. "I hate this. I hate screenwriting. I'm going to become a . . . a . . . fourth-grade teacher and teach kids about the Revolutionary War and adjectives and how to get a date!" She screamed again.

I wrestled the laptop out of her hands. We ended up in a heap on the floor huffing and puffing.

"Want an orange truffle?" I asked.

She screamed through clenched teeth.

* * *

I blame the Annual Whale Island Poker Tournament, a fund-raiser for the local schools, for the extreme kissing that occurred afterward.

Aiden won third place in the tournament. Brenda won second place.

Mrs. Ailene Brooks, age eighty-five years young, won first place. The woman is a genius. She knows how to count cards. When she won, she climbed up on a table and did a break-dance of sorts.

Five tables practically buckled with desserts. At least sixty women had entered the Whale Island Dessert Contest. The prize was a three-day spa package on the mainland. A number of women started mean-spirited dessert gossip when they didn't win, one repeatedly stabbed her fork into the table, and one stomped out and slammed the door, but hey. Tough break.

On Whale Island, Aiden and I were officially a couple. In fact, each time he won another round, it was announced by Sherilee Rotowsky via the microphone, "The gentleman who is the special friend of Chalese Hamilton has won another round. Let's see, what's his name? Ah, yes . . ." And then his name would be verbally mangled: Aide-on. Or Add-on. Or even Eedon.

Finished by "You know, the man who is dating our Chalese . . . Doesn't she make the best jams and jellies you've ever tasted? Y'all know that she and Brenda had to go down to the police station again." Laughter. "This time it was Stephen's skylight. No one hurt, folks. She never should have dated Stephen in the first place." That last bit was said under Sherilee's breath, but everyone heard it. "He wasn't good enough for her."

I snuck a glance at the back of the building. Stephen's face was bright red. The Man-eater crossed her arms and scrunched up her angry face.

"How many times has Chalese said no to marriage

proposals?" Sherilee asked everyone as I slouched in my chair. "I can't remember."

"It's nine," Forrest Lee declared. He's forty, the town comedian, and owns a pottery shop. "Nine."

"Nine? That's not true. Chalese has said no to six men," Rainwater Nelson said. "I know. I keep track."

"Is she engaged to Add-on?" yelled Beatrice Wong, principal of the high school.

"That's a good question," Sherilee said into the microphone. "Are you engaged to Add-on?"

Before I could say a word, Aiden stood up. He took a second to grin at everyone. "I think I can answer that. Chalese is . . ." He paused, and everyone leaned forward. "Chalese is *not at this time* engaged to me."

Hooting and hollering followed. *Not at this time?*

I stood up on legs that held all the strength of those green noodles that are supposed to be healthy for you. "I am not engaged to Aiden. I am not even *'not at this time'* engaged to Aiden. And to keep the official record straight, I've said no four times." I held up my hand, four fingers up. "Four. *Cuatro. Quatre.*"

Rainwater yelled, "So don't ask her, Add-on. Kidnap her, throw her over your shoulder, and haul her into the church. I'll drive the getaway Porsche." He had three.

"I can come to you," Reverend Tinner said helpfully. "We'll sneak up on her, Add-on."

"For someone who wants to live a quiet, anonymous life, you sure aren't anonymous, Chalese," Aiden drawled to me as we stepped into the cool night two hours later.

"Shut up, Add-on," I said.

And that's where some serious kissing took place, right in the field next to the poker tournament. At the end of it, when I could barely breathe, he swung me around under a shimmering moon as if I were some skinny little thing.

* * *

"I have to go back to Seattle."

Aiden's words sunk straight into my heart as we stood at the front of the ferryboat, passing the emerald green islands surrounding Whale Island.

I really didn't have time to do this island tour, but I could no more have refused Aiden's invitation than I could have invited a boa constrictor to give my neck a good squeeze.

In fact, I hadn't said no a single time as we'd laughed, talked, and danced our way through the last four days. Plus, I was beginning to think about using paintbrushes as weaponry, so I knew I needed a break.

"I'm going back to Seattle tomorrow. I've been here much longer than I intended so I could hang out with you and your smile. I'm going to write the story, Chalese, it's going to print, and then I'm coming back. We'll work through the fallout together, and I'll be here to hold your hand. I promise."

I had two raging emotions battling for space in my head. One: dead panic. And two: liquid, swirling, joyous joy. Aiden wanted to come back and see me!

"I don't want to invade your life." He threaded his fingers through mine. "I don't want to pressure you. I haven't asked you to marry me, so there's no need for you to feel suffocated, but you're too good of a fisherwoman for me to let you go." He winked at me. So intimate, so sweet.

The wind whipped our hair back as I giggled. We'd gone fishing two days ago and ended up kissing in a rowboat I borrowed from Gina. The rowboat capsized. It was one of the funniest things that had ever happened to me. The fish we caught had been lost.

"I can't be anything but honest here. The first time I saw you, scratched up from the skylight adventure, dressed in leather, grouchy, I felt this . . . I don't even know how to say it. It was as if I was seeing my future. You are the most unique woman I've ever met. You live your life so fully, with courage and caring. You're independent and talented and a heckuva lot of fun."

"Even when I'm struggling back onto a rowboat?"

"Especially then. You walk your dogs at odd hours, you have a thing for your pajamas, you dance well in the sand, you laugh from your heart, and you're dedicated to four-legged creatures."

He wrapped our linked hands behind my back.

"And you're sexier than hell. Every bit of you."

I thought of my burgeoning bottom and my hot flashes.

Oh, well. If he thought they were sexy, who was I to argue? "So when we went biking through the mud and I crashed into you, that didn't appear to be a warning that I wasn't the right one?"

He laughed. "No, not at all."

"And when we hiked to Constitution Point and it started to pour down rain and I suggested we do a waltz, that also wasn't a bad sign?"

"Not at all. Kissing you in the rain was one of the best things that has happened to me in years."

"They were wet kisses," I commented.

"True. I'm going to come back, and I want to see you again for more wet kisses. Many times. Please, Chalese. Say yes."

For an answer, I leaned in, stood on tiptoe, and kissed his neck. Once, twice, three times. "Whatever you say, Reporter Man." Pain rippled through my body. I hoped that this would not be the last time I would kiss this man.

The ferry captain tooted the horn, a long, low screech. I jumped out of Aiden's arms at the noise. Up in the captain's booth, my friend Jonathan Solberg waved.

I kissed Aiden again, right on the mouth, and he kissed me back, taking control of that kiss, which was sexier than all get-out.

I would remember that kiss, I knew it. When I was old and

gray and leaning on a walker, that windy kiss on the ferryboat would make me smile.

I worked until three o'clock in the morning.

I drew my strutting rooster and my busy-body chickens. I drew the blue ocean in back of them. I drew Gordon, the anxiety-ridden horse. I drew my barn. And I wrote the dialogue between the animals as they figured out who would be president of the farm.

Goose couldn't simply take over because she wanted to, and Fox couldn't be president, because he was threatening to eat the chickens unless they voted for him. Donkey couldn't be president, because he had been bribing the other animals, telling the pigs he would bring them donuts if they voted for him.

Next I wrote the speech that presidential candidate Cassy Cat gave to her fellow animals. Cassy Cat is a smart, calm cat who wants everyone to have a voice in her government, even the old horses, the weird new goat from a farm with a name no one can pronounce, and the duck with the green feathers who is different from all the other ducks.

I drew and wrote until I couldn't see straight.

I turned off the light, but dancing before my eyes was Aiden Bridger, with his full lips, knowing green eyes, fishing pole in hand. Next to him was a giant newspaper article, my real name all over it next to my books, along with all the old photos, the old scandal, and my latest arrest for the skylight-busting incident.

I trusted Aiden. But after this, he would probably never trust me.

I conked my head on my table.

For the next five days, I worked fiendishly. Hardly moved except to go and help Christie, who was crying because she didn't know why she was crying. I made her pancakes with applesauce and crushed potato chips, as she requested, then put her to bed, as she was the size of a house. She smelled like baby powder and roses, as always.

"Mommy has some big, fat babies in her tummy," Wendi Jo, her daughter, whispered.

"Yeah. I felt the babies in there," Jeremiah said. He's four. "One kick my hand. He wearing soccer cleats. I felt 'em."

"How they gonna come out?" Rosie Mae asked, three years old. "She got a zipper in her tummy?"

Chapter Eight

"You lied."

I sank into my Adirondack chair on my front porch as Aiden stalked up the steps after slamming the door of his truck. He was not happy. "You lied, Chalese. You lied by omission."

My lifeless fingers dropped my coffee cup which smashed on the porch. I stood up, my anger rising. I did not exactly *appreciate* being called a liar. "I was not required to tell you the full truth about myself, Aiden, or my past, when you were writing a story about me for a huge newspaper, one I didn't want written in the first place. Why should I make your job easier? Why should I provide information that I didn't want out there? Because you kissed me? Sorry, Aiden, I'm not that easy."

"You had to know that I would find out." He put his palms up in the air, exasperated. "You knew it."

"Yeah, Aiden, I thought there was a pretty good probability that you would find out. But I was hoping, hoping against hope, that you wouldn't dig that deep, and if you did, that you'd let it go."

His glare about seared me in half. "Maybe you thought if I was turned upside down by my feelings about you I wouldn't do my job? I'd let it slide, let details slide, not do the research

I always do?" His green eyes flashed with all his pent-up anger, the betrayal I knew he felt.

"Maybe. I hoped." He stood two feet from me. I could smell him—island air, mint, aftershave, and him. If he wasn't mad at me, I'd want to kiss that man until my lips fell off. He was drop-dead sexy when he was ticked.

"I know you aren't who you say you are. I know your real name is Jennifer Piermont, your father is Richard Piermont III, your mother is Rebecca Piermont, and your sister Christie is actually Holly Piermont."

I swallowed real hard. Hearing his *name* made me feel like I was eating rocks.

"You're from New York City. Your father, a private investor, was arrested when you were fourteen for defrauding his clients of millions and millions of dollars. It was a huge scandal at the time because of who he was—a pillar of New York society, on all the right boards, went to all the right parties, belonged to the right country club. All those people trusted him with their last dime. He took all their dimes, their quarters, everything."

"He would have taken their shirts if he could have, Aiden. Ripped them right off."

"When the scandal broke, there were cameras and reporters stalking you and your family. During the trial, one of the disgruntled clients tried to shoot your father in open court. He missed and was tackled by a guard. Luckily you and your mother and Christie were already gone by then. Your father went to jail for ten years."

He put his hands on his hips, pushing his leather jacket back. "Your mother arranged to have everything sold, your apartment in New York, the house in Connecticut, the house in the Bahamas, the art, the furniture, and signed it all off to a fund set up to reimburse her husband's clients. She made no claim to anything in the divorce, and in fact left home with you girls and nothing else. You later drove West and came to

Whale Island, a place she had vacationed with her own family several times as a teenager."

There went my world.

It had imploded.

Was the article being printed as we spoke? Was it already online?

"You all changed your names."

"Yes, we did. We spent much of our time in the car thinking up new names, and when we arrived my mother legally changed our names. A new identity, a new life." Why hide anything now? "We covered up our old lives. My mother told everyone we were from the East Coast, she was divorced, and she was a housekeeper. She got jobs as a housekeeper and maid. On the side, she started her own small business."

"And you disappeared."

"Yes, from all those furious people, people who had a right to be furious, but not a right to take out their fury on me and my sister."

He groaned. "Want to hear what else I've learned? Something that makes me feel like pummeling your father?"

I knew what was coming, and I braced myself for a nauseous cascade of black, annihilating memories.

"Police were called to your apartment on Fifth Avenue three times for domestic abuse. Your mother went to the hospital on a number of occasions."

"Well, aren't you the sleuth." I felt hot tears swim to my eyes. "Want to know a tad more, Skyscraper? My mother told me later that when she went to the hospital for her injuries, my father told the doctors there she was mentally ill and had done it to herself. I doubt the doctors believed him, I'm sure my mother denied it, but it put my already unstable mother in an emotional tailspin."

"I can't believe this." He was furious, but I could tell it had shifted somewhat from me to my father. "I can't believe you lived through that."

"Me, either." When I remember that time, I don't know how I survived it—except that my dad was gone a lot on business. "Once, when my mother got up enough courage and left with us when we were very young, he called a private investigator, then hired these huge, scary thugs to bring us back. We left again another time, a year later, same thing. Both times he physically took his anger out on my mother. She was beaten to a pulp."

"Oh God," Aiden breathed.

"My father convinced my mother that no judge would ever let her have me and Christie since she was mentally ill. What a threat to hang over an emotionally devastated woman's head! At that time there was nowhere for an abused mother to run, certainly nowhere that she knew of. They hardly talked about that then. She had been an only child, and her parents were in poor health and living in a facility. She was trapped."

"And to you, Chalese?" he said, his voice low, pained. "What did he do to you?"

I tilted my chin up. "You mean besides the neglect, his hatred for me, the constant fear he evoked? My father always told me I was fat. He said my skin was a dirty color, not pretty compared to Christie's super-white skin and blond hair. He said I waddled, identical to a penguin, and he would make these penguin calls at me when I walked by. He always said Christie was the smart one and I had a brain born in a freezer. He'd tell my crying mother to give me whale or seal meat for dinner. 'She'll gobble it right up, you'll see,' he told her.

"He would turn off the heating vent in my bedroom and tell me since I was a penguin I was used to the cold and I'd be fine. So here we were, living on Fifth Avenue, and I had no heat. And that's just the start."

Aiden was pale, his face tightly drawn. "Chalese, come here, honey, come here." He pulled me into his arms, hugging me close, then swung me up, into my home and onto my couch.

One sad story followed another, as if they'd all lined up in my heart and were now pushing each other to get out.

"I am so angry, Chalese. I haven't been this angry in years. I want to pound his face in."

"Aiden, I didn't want to tell you about my past, because I didn't want it printed. I would have told you after the article came out. . . ."

"I am mad about you not sharing your past, for not trusting me, but I understand. I do. But *damn*, I'm furious about what you went through as a kid! When I was reading the reports, I wanted to smash your father. I wanted to find him and tear him apart. I am so sorry about what happened to you."

"I'm sorry, too," I said, trying to make light of it. "But it's over. It's done. I have a new life. I'm chasing down goats, drawing talking beavers, and going to poker contests now."

Aiden rocked me back and forth. "So help me, if I ever meet this man, he will *not* be able to peel himself off the floor again. He was a sick man, Chalese. No sane man would ever treat his wife or a child as he did."

I nodded. In my head, away from him now for decades, I realized that. It was my father's issue, not mine. But I remembered the kid I was, how unbearably hurt, how despairing, I had been.

He stroked my back, his cheek next to mine, and I clung to him. At one point I tilted my head up, and Aiden was wiping his tears. Huge, manly stud man, toughened, roughened Aiden.

"Aiden, it's hurting me to see you cry." His tears made me cry. A man who cried for what we went through! A man who cared enough about me to cry in the first place! Through all that pain, I saw this light, this golden, sparkly light.

My lips found his. Aiden kissed me back, pulled away, kissed me again, pulled away. I knew he was fighting within himself. He was kissing me, the subject of his newspaper article.

I should have pulled away, made it easier for him, but I couldn't. I would have given up my yellow house with all my art and quilts before I would have given up the next hour of my life. We gave in together in a rush of passion, of bottled-up lust, of trusting friendship, of shared intimacies. My arms went around his neck, he picked me up, and we were on my bed, on my periwinkle comforter, chasing down that heaven I knew I'd find in his arms.

I tried not to sniffle or let any more tears escape, but when I did, Aiden pulled back, kissed my cheeks, cupped my face, and told me I was the most beautiful woman he'd ever known.

In my head I heard these words: *I love you, Aiden, I do. I trust you, too. Whatever happens with this, I trust you.*

And, whew! That Aiden Bridger was indeed comparable to the mighty Zeus in the bedroom.

"Don't print the article, please, Aiden." I leaned over him in bed the next morning, sunlight streaking through the French doors, and kissed his neck. Instead of responding, I felt him go rigid beneath me.

"What?" he rapped out. *"What did you say?"*

"I told you everything last night, so now you understand why I don't want the article written."

He whipped back the periwinkle blue comforter, stalked to the windows, and glared at the ocean.

"Is that what this was all about?" he shot at me, turning around, his arms crossed over that muscled chest. I had enjoyed that chest last night.

"What are you talking about?"

"You slept with me, we made love, then you make your request with a couple of kisses thrown in." His face was hard, completely cold. "Did you actually hope to change my mind with sex? Do you think I'm that naïve, that clueless?"

I clutched the sheet to me. I wanted to let him have it face-to-face, but I sure as heck was not getting out of bed naked. It's one thing to feel fat in the darkness of night, overcome with excitement; it's quite another to parade around and about naked, bouncing bottom, thunder thighs and all. Plus, I was pissed.

"Let's get something straight, Aiden, before I get off-the-cliff ticked. I slept with you because I wanted to. I didn't sleep with you because I wanted to manipulate you or your precious career. Not a bit."

"Somehow I'm finding that hard to believe."

"I don't care what you find hard to believe, you . . . you difficult, rigid, journalistic prick. Things got carried away last night, and I"—my voice shook and wobbled—"I made a mistake."

"You made a mistake?"

"Yes, I made a mistake. I slept with a man who woke up in the morning, and instead of saying, 'Good morning, how are you, can I make you some French toast and coffee, want to go for a walk to the ocean?' he accuses me of having sex with him to get something out of it."

"How can you blame me for thinking that? The first thing you asked this morning was for me not to write the article."

"Hey, Aiden, I blame you for thinking that because you know me better than that. I have never stopped asking you *not* to write the article. Not once. Did you think I would have changed my mind this morning because we rolled around naked? That pisses me off even more than I was pissed off to begin with! How dare you think so little of me! How dare you think I would stoop to sleeping with you to manipulate you, to get what I wanted." The more I thought about it, the more I wanted to throw something at his head.

"I hate this situation, I do, Chalese, but this is the way it is. I can't believe—" He stopped, pulled himself together as his voice got deep and scratchy. "This article has been assigned to me to write. I said I would, and I will. I'll write it with respect for you, with kindness, with care and consideration, but I've got to write it."

"You said you would, so you will," I mimicked him. "Well,

I'm going to throw this yellow pillow at your head." I threw it. "I said I would, and I did. Here's another one." I shot another pillow across the room. "Here's a third," I yelled. "I said I'd throw it, and I will!" Another one went flying, and another.

"Stop it, Chalese."

"No, you stop it, Aiden. Did you sleep with me so you could have a fuller picture? Perhaps you want to know my mind, and my boobs and butt, too? What is this—the full-body interview? Maybe you can give your readers a play-by-play."

He paled, white as snow. "I slept with you because . . ."

"Because what?"

"Chalese . . ." He swore, turned away. "You know why I slept with you."

"Yes, I do know why, and clearly we let passion shrink our brain cells. Get out of my house. Right now!" Two dogs named Sherbert and Mr. Green ran in, tongues lolling about. When they saw me yelling and upset, they stood in front of Aiden and growled.

"Get out, Aiden. Go. Go skedaddle back to that newspaper of yours, tap away on your keyboard, and do your thing." I felt a wave of depression, of black, gooey sadness, take hold. It was a sense of inevitability, a sense of dismal doom. I had been hiding for years, but the hide-and-seek game was over. The game was up. I leaned back against my wooden headboard, bracing myself for what was to come. "We're done. We are completely done." In case there was any doubt about what I wanted him to do, I threw a light blue silk pillow at him.

I did not miss the shattered expression on his face. I felt it in my own heart, which was shriveling, shrinking, dying.

"Can you quit throwing pillows and understand for one second how this is for me? I'm sorry about this—"

"Sorry about this, Chalese," I said, mimicking him. "You poured out everything last night, all about your childhood, and, hey, I'm sorry about blowing your privacy and about dragging up that you are Annabelle Purples, children's writer who has a truly famous crook for a father, but thanks for the sex!" I wanted to run. Run as far as the ocean shore, then jump in and swim until I couldn't swim, swim to the whales, swim with the whales. "Get out. Get out now."

I did not miss the hopelessness mixed with anger in his expression. I felt the same way. Like my life had been crushed.

As soon as he left, I pulled the covers over my head and soaked my one remaining pink pillow with my tears.

"Hello, Mom," I said into the phone, muffling my weeping with a tissue. "You're going to Los Angeles next? I received the box of peaches and the box of kale. Yes, the natural spices from Africa arrived, too. I'll be sure to use them liberally, as your instructions dictated. I love you, too, and yes I've been thinking about more designs. . . ."

I braced myself for the article. Each day I checked online. It did not appear.

I kept working on my book at a frantic pace, while shoveling in orange truffles and coffee, but in my off moments, almost breathless with despair, I took a break and drew away my anger.

I drew Cassy Cat, the presidential contender who usually wore glasses and simple clothes, in a low-cut red gown smoking a cigarette in a biker bar. Above her I drew a bubble that read, "Hey, baby, want some of this? Aiden Bridger, a *little* man, if you know what I mean, sure didn't."

I drew Fox with his pointy nose from behind, his tuxedo coat pulled open by his sharp claws, clearly flashing a group of puppies in front of him. I put a sign on the fox's coat that said, "Aiden Bridger: Exposing Everyone!"

I drew the prissy Goose as a streetwalker. A fat dog with a long tongue leaned out of his truck. "How much?" he asked.

The truck was a twin to Aiden's, and the license plate said, "A. Bridger."

And popular humble Herbert Hoove the Horse? I drew him at a poker table, aces sticking out from his sleeve, his hat, his shoes. He had a name tag on. It said, "Aiden Bridger, Gambler." The bubble above his head read, "I get so tired of screwing people."

It was my silent way of revenge. My way of getting back at Aiden while I raced to meet the deadline. A way to rebelliously cope while the tears streaked down my checks as if I had faucets in my eyeballs.

Little did I know that the rest of the nation would be cackling their hearts out—or screaming in outrage—by the middle of the next week.

It was announced that I had won the Carmichael Children's Book Award. My agent and publisher began fielding calls and requests for interviews.

All were denied.

I wished I felt happy about the award.

It was one of those things, though. If you don't have that special someone to dance around with when cool things happen, the cool things don't seem that cool.

"I think if we grabbed your sister, the crying Christie, took off our shirts, and drove through the night half-naked, I could get rid of my writer's block," Brenda told me, crossing her red and white polka-dot heels on the top of my blue picnic table in the clearing of the woods. "My life would be better. I'm tired of Shane, you know. He wants me to dress up in a superhero costume, and I am *so* done with that." She dropped cherries into her mouth. "I mean, how many times can you be Wonder Woman and still keep it fun?" She clicked her heels together.

I went back to my draft of another picture for my book. I was giving one of my characters, a llama, dreadlocks. He was a hippie sort of llama.

My hair was slung up in a ponytail, I had been wearing the same jeans for days, and I was operating on approximately four hours of sleep a night. I smelled; my hair was gross. Besides Brenda, the only person I had seen in days was Reuby, who came in to pet the cats when I walked the dogs one afternoon.

"Wanna see my new cell phone again?" he'd asked. "It takes awesome pictures. It's sick it's so awesome. I can't believe the Authority Figure bought it for me."

I nodded absently and shoved my bangs off my head.

My book was quite late. Editor was threatening not one heart attack, but two. Agent was having a loud, prolonged fit. PR agent called to bite her nails over the phone.

And in my grossness, I could also hardly breathe. I was so unbelievably . . . *sad*. It was the sad you get when your dreams are almost there . . . and then they're obliterated. The sad you get when everything seems to stop and get stuck in bleakness. The sad you get when you feel you will never be in love again, never feel happy again, never overcome this giant emotional boulder in your path that seems to want to squish you.

But I had a deadline, so I kept drawing under that clear blue sky. Must keep employed, I muttered. Must not end up as scraggly, molting woman pushing cart down street. Nutmeg Man put his head on my thigh under the table and whimpered.

"Brenda, sit down, stifle the hysterics, and write. Don't overthink it." I popped a cherry into my mouth. "Write one word. One letter. Write a paragraph. Describe your costume dates, what you know about men, about life. Be funny. And leave me alone so I can finish these dreadlocks."

"When we were kids and sending stories back and forth to each other I never had writer's block." She dumped a handful of cherries into her mouth and clicked her heels together.

"The romances you sent me were flaming funny. One of your funniest characters was Mr. Hip Swinger."

Brenda laughed. "Already used him in one of my movies." She spit out a pit.

"And Loyolita Chantal Montalshawn. She was an evil woman. A man-shredding feminist."

"Used her, too. Won an award for that movie."

We both turned as we heard the truck flying down my driveway, creaking, shrieking, rumbling.

Gina drove off the driveway when she saw me and sped right toward us. "Please, Chalese," she begged when she hopped out of the truck, the flowers flying from her long hair. "Don't sue me."

Chapter Nine

Inside the truck was Gina's son, Reuby.

"Drag your limp butt out of the car right this minute or I'll use my slingshot against it!" Gina yelled at him.

Reuby slouched on out.

Brenda and I stood up. "What's wrong?" Instant fear clutched my gut. I could tell that Reuby had been crying. Gina was angry enough to spring an intestine. "What is it?"

Gina jabbed her pointer finger at Reuby. Stomped her foot. "Speak, you troublesome rebel son!"

An anguished Reuby pushed back his blond curls and whined, "I'm sorry, Chalese, dude! I'm sorry. I took pictures of the drawings with my new cell phone and put them on my MySpace page. I thought they were so funny, so cool. They were the animals, dude, from all those kids' books I read when I was a kid. The Authority Figure never told me you were the author who did the Jasmine Farm Animal books. I didn't know! I didn't know that you're Annabelle Purples! But that's sick! Sick and awesome!"

My blood dive-bombed toward my feet. "What are you talking about? Which animal pictures?" *Oh, please, not the Bridger pictures.* "Where did you put them?"

"I thought I'd show the pictures to a few dudes, that's it! I didn't know all this would happen. I didn't know that you were trying to keep yourself secret! Can I still come over and walk the dogs?"

"What?" I could hardly speak, my brain mass flogged with panic. "*What pictures?*"

Reuby scuffed the ground with his army boots.

Gina glared. "I'm sorry, Chalese. My own son may become a stray animal when I'm done with him." She whacked him on the head. "Chalese, Reuby wandered up to your studio the other day when he was petting the cats."

"I couldn't find Elizabeth I and Clover. I figured they were upstairs. And that's when I saw all the funny pictures. Dude, you're hilarious!"

"Do not call Ms. Hamilton 'dude' one more time or you will be sleeping in the barn with the cows." Gina yanked a flower out of her hair and threw it to the ground in anger.

"Sorry, Authority Figure!" He pulled on his eyebrow ring.

I found my tongue. "Are you telling me . . ." I gasped for air. "Are you telling me my drawings for my book are on the Internet?" Gasped again.

Gina burst into tears, then whacked her son on the head again. Two red flowers fell from her hair. "It's not your regular pictures, sugar, not the ones for the book. They're the ones of . . ."

"Of?"

I heard Brenda beside me gasp and then swear, the swear word long and low and crude.

"Of Goose as a hooker," Reuby said exuberantly. "Man, that was clever! And Herbert with all the aces saying he's tired of screwing everyone, and of the fox flashing the puppies, I couldn't stop laughing at that one, heck yeah, and Cassy Cat smokin' in a bar—she was always my favorite character when I was a kid . . ."

No breath. I had no breath in me. I squeaked out, "Please tell me you did not put *those* pictures on your MySpace page." My mind about set itself on fire imagining all the possible, truly unspeakable ramifications.

"Yes, ma'am," he said, chastened. "Yes, ma'am, but I'm sorry. I didn't know—"

I took in a ragged, rough breath before I passed out. "Take them off! Now! Take them off your MySpace page!"

Reuby squirmed, pulled at his scraggly hair. "It's too late," he whispered.

"What do you mean 'it's too late'?" I shrieked, my arms waving through the air. "It's not too late! I don't want anyone to see them!"

"I mean, ma'am, dude, they're on my MySpace page, but they're also . . ."

"They're what?"

I heard Brenda moaning as she linked an arm around my shoulder. "I'll take you shopping in Zimbabwe, that'll make you feel better. We'll buy you some high heels, those lacy bras and underwear you need so bad, we'll bring two bottles of wine—"

"I have tequila, Brenda, in my car," Gina hissed. "Does she drink tequila?"

I put my face six inches from rebel Reuby's. "They're what?"

I saw his Adam's apple sliding up and down. "Dude, I'm sorry," he rasped. "But my MySpace friends sent them to their friends, and they sent them to their friends, and now those pictures . . ."

"What?"

"They're all over the Internet, man. They're out there. I mean, they're *out there*." He scratched an arm pit. "Who's Aiden Bridger?"

I staggered away, my hands to my forehead, then screamed. And swore. And screamed again.

My editor called, hysterical.

My agent called, hysterical

My public relations gal called, hysterical.

It wasn't good. It would get worse.

My privacy was now toast.

A little digging here and there, and the reporters had my connection to Aiden Bridger nailed down via the Carmichael Children's Book Award.

The reporters called, they sped on over to the island that night, they were nosy, pushy, insistent. What could have been one article by Aiden about me had now morphed into something uncontrollable, huge, and nationwide.

I moved out in the middle of the night and into Christie's house. Brenda said she would bravely forfeit her high heels for my work boots and take care of the animals. "That's how much I'll sacrifice for you, my best friend. I'll even put on those dirty garden gloves of yours and wear a floppy garden hat. Hoo boy."

I couldn't help getting a little teary.

The flurry of Christie's home kept me somewhat centered. She was in bed because of pre-term labor problems, her husband was stuck out of town on business, worried sick about her, and I watched the three kids.

I could hide somewhat from the reporters on Christie's fenced ten acres of property, but I couldn't hide from the townspeople. The front page of our own newspaper soon ran the story in giant headlines: "Chalese Hamilton is Annabelle Purples, Famous Children's Story Book Author. Whale Island Animal Lover Center of Online Controversy."

My sister's answering machine was jammed. A few people were ticked I hadn't shared my work with them, others were amused or tickled at this juicy secret. Some were shocked. Overriding it all: was Aiden still my special friend?

I put my head between my legs.

"You gonna throw up?" Wendi Jo asked me.

I nodded. "Maybe."

She dragged over a pan. "Always throw up in a pan, not on the carpet. That's what Mommy says."

"You're very helpful, Wendi Jo," I said.

"Yes, I am." She gave me a hug. "Mommy said you're in trouble because you drew a bad picture. Did you get a spanking?"

"The parents are having a fit," my editor breathed. "We may have to postpone your next book. I feel breathless. I think it's my heart, Chalese! My heart!"

"You may lose your contract," my agent hyperventilated. "You may be done. Finished."

"I have a nightmare on my hands," my public relations gal whimpered. "Why did you have to draw Cassy Cat with a boob job and a cigarette? Why?"

I bounced Jeremiah on my lap as I took the calls. My life had collapsed, and, overriding the whole dismal, nerve-rattling, sickening fear of my family's past being drudged up again and poured out for American consumption, I was drowning in Aiden-guilt and the unparalleled embarrassment those drawings would have caused him.

I left him a message. "Aiden, I'm so sorry. I'm so very, very sorry. Remember I told you I'm a clumsy elephant, a ridiculous, pathetic, writer. I don't get out enough, I hot-flash, I talk to my dogs and half the time I expect them to answer back, I hang out with Brenda, who is a menace. Aiden, the pictures were never supposed to be on the Internet. They were private, a way to work out my . . . this . . . us . . . our . . . me and you . . . a mess . . ."

I hung up. What was there left to say, anyhow? That the drawings were a way to work out my bitter hurt, this life-sucking loss? That I wanted to erase my entire self like I did when I drew a caterpillar incorrectly?

* * *

"I'm fine, Mom," I said into the phone. "You're still in Los Angeles? I didn't want to worry you, so I didn't tell you. Yes, I'll use an organic face cream tonight and lay with cucumbers on my eyes. Thank you for the box of blueberries and the new book on how to organically care for a stressed face. . . . Love you, too . . . No, I have no plans to make any more designs for your company right now. . . . Please, Mom . . . I'm fine."

But I wasn't fine.

Every morning since Aiden had left I woke up and this raging flood of grief came for every bone in my body.

Every evening the flood was still with me, after hanging around all day, making me cry at unexpected moments, my chest heavy, my mind slogging through sadness.

When I turned off the light at night, the grief was worse in the darkness because I was alone and figured I'd be alone for years. Maybe forever.

A forever without Aiden.

I would curl up with my pillow, flipping it several times when my tears soaked it.

Brenda slept with me a few times. "Want to dress up as bunnies or something?"

His voice was so cold, so detached, I thought a glacier had removed itself from the North Pole and lodged between us.

I felt sick with pain and loss. I gripped my stomach. For the first time in my life, I couldn't eat, which was not helping this calamitous situation, as I felt nauseous.

"Aiden, nice to hear your voice," I said into my cell phone. "One second."

I raced to the bathroom and slung my head over the toilet, then leaned my forehead against the rim.

I could hear Wendi Jo on the phone talking to Aiden when

I stumbled back into the family room, leaning hard against the wall in my dizziness.

"Yeah, Aunt Chalese is in the toilet. She's still in her pink doggie pajamas. It's after *Sesame Street,* too. Mommy says no one should be in pajamas in the afternoon. I think she's sick. No, my mommy's in bed with the babies in her tummy. She's sick, too. She eats lots of salsa. I the boss now . . . Yeah, I the boss. You stink, Aunt Chalese. Like throw-up."

I grabbed the phone. "Aiden?"

"How are you, Chalese?"

"Aiden, I'm fine but—"

"Good. I think we need to come to some sort of agreement here. I know you didn't want the article written, but we're both backed into a corner. I'm besieged by reporters wanting to know why America's leading children's writer and illustrator hates me so much and how I ended up being lampooned by Cassy Cat and other assorted famous characters."

"I understand. Please listen—"

"So I'm finishing the article now."

"What? I thought it was already written."

There was a deep, heavy silence.

"It wasn't written?"

"Most of it was written, Chalese, but when I got back to Seattle after our last"—his voice trailed off, and I heard his exhaustion—"meeting, I couldn't do it. Couldn't do it to you. I know you want your privacy, and we were already involved. It was also inappropriate for me to write it. I'd compromised my integrity, my professionalism. I'm kicking myself for that. I don't think I'll ever stop kicking myself." He stopped, swore, went on. "I told my editor to send someone else because I was emotionally involved with you."

Not good. "How did that go?"

"Actually, I've known my boss for twenty years. He laughed. Then he told Jackie Consuelez the story was hers."

"So you're saying if my characters hadn't hit the Internet, you wouldn't be writing the story at all?"

"That's right. But now other journalists are already digging, Chalese. Your story—your full story, father and all—will come out shortly. Mine will be first. You will have no more secrets. For my article, and I will be quoting you word for word, so think about what you're going to say . . ." He stopped for a second. "Please tell me why you drew the pictures with reference to me?"

"Aiden, first, you know I have a soaring, estrogen-driven temper. You know I'm off half-cocked much of the time. I do bizarre, inexplicable things, and I am so sorry about drawing the pictures."

"I'm giving you the opportunity to explain yourself, in your own words here, so take this seriously, Chalese. Don't make it personal."

I was so blitzed, so wiped out, I could hardly sit up. Why not put my emotions in a blender and hit Pulverize?

"In my own words, Aiden? I drew the pictures because you charged into my life, turned it upside down, gave it a shake, and left me on the floor. Got that?"

"I think I do. But I can't print that."

"You also kissed me until I couldn't see straight, made me laugh until I hurt, indulged my idiosyncrasies, clicked with my quirky brain, showed me kindness I had rarely seen in a man, hugged me close, treated me like I was someone special instead of a head case, never suggested I change, loved my animals, appreciated the people in my life, as weird as they are, and you held my hand as if you meant it. Got that?"

"I think I do. But I can't print that, either."

"Finally, you are the only person I talked to about my father outside of my family, Gina, and Brenda, and you wanted to smash him for what he did to me. You stood up for me, you believed what I said, you were emotionally open to discuss it. We cried together. You love sunsets, too, and you're a sucker for a romance movie. Don't think I didn't see the tears in your eyes that one night. You kissed me as if we had time for a thousand tomorrows. You are so masculine, you're such a *man,* rough on the edges, toughened up, and I am so attracted to that, but I can also talk to you like a friend, a best girl-friend. Got that, too?"

"I think I do." His gravelly voice cracked. "That's not going in the article."

"And now you're ticked off, rightly so, and you're gone. I'm here. You're there. And we have this whole, huge incident to deal with because I am a schmuck. Put that part in. Write 'She is a schmuck.' I think we're done here."

"Chalese—"

I hung up.

I had to.

I needed to go back upstairs and rest my head against the toilet seat before I lost it.

Strangely enough, overnight the pictures on the Internet had increased my sales, even while a few parents railed against my turning their favorite horse into a gambler who talked about screwing.

My editor called. "My heart is better, you'll be relieved to hear, no thanks to you. Your book is late. Get it in."

My agent called, and I did not hear him slurping a martini in the background. "Book almost done?"

My public relations gal called. She did not yell at me or gnaw her nails. "Can't wait to see the next book!"

It's all about the numbers.

Of course, the pictures were still gathering interest, online and in the press, in chat rooms, et cetera.

Cassy Cat and her boob job sure got me into a lot of trouble.

* * *

Aiden's article came out the next day. I got up, ate two chocolate-chip cookies for a healthy breakfast, then sat down on Christie's deck, with a stunning view of the south side of the island, to read it. Out in the distance, past Christie's grassy field, I could swear I saw water spurting from a whale's blowhole.

The truth about my father came out in glorious detail. One of America's best-loved children's book writers and illustrators had an infamous crook for a father.

Not simply a run-of-the-mill, stupid-headed bank robber. No, my father outdid them all. He was an "investor" who tossed zillions of dollars of people's money into things they really needed: his yacht, his many homes, his vacations with his mistresses, his Swiss bank accounts, his extensive gambling jaunts. The article also detailed the domestic-abuse charges, my mother's hospital trips, and that Christie and I had been taken into protective custody.

He also wrote how my mother willingly sold everything we had to reimburse my father's victims, that we changed our names, moved to Whale Island so we could disappear, and how she became a maid who later started a successful company on her dining-room table.

My father had been out of jail for ten years. He was presently "whereabouts unknown."

Aiden's article also discussed my crash through Stephen's skylight, my minor arrest record because of a variety of pranks that he detailed with humor, added the islanders' very charitable opinions of me, the design of my farmhouse-style home, my animals and the adopting-out that I did, and my small business with the jams and jellies called "Wild Girl's Jams and Jellies."

He talked about Christie's pregnancy and the twins, and even listed a few of her food cravings, which made even me laugh.

Aiden quoted Brenda, who was uncommonly circumspect.

"She is my best friend. She will always be my best friend. She went through a hellacious childhood and survived with class and grace."

He quoted me frequently throughout the article, including how I felt as a child, attacked by the press, mocked by friends, living in a dangerous home. He wrote of my love of children's book writing, how drawing and writing had taken me away from my fear, and how I wanted my young readers to think and dream and believe they could make the world better.

In all, despite the raunchy pictures I'd drawn of my characters, and the mockery of Aiden, I came off as a decent, caring person who had simply wanted to hide herself away from a childhood filled with difficulties.

He explained those raunchy pictures with great humor, stating, "I invaded her privacy, told her I was on Whale Island to write an in-depth article on her that not only would reveal a past she had worked hard to hide but would reveal to her friends on the island that she was the famous Annabelle Purples. I would have been upset, too, although I would not have been able to draw such superb pictures to get revenge. Stick figures are my specialty.

"To be honest, when I returned to Seattle to write the article, I told my editor I couldn't do it. Couldn't invade Jennifer Piermont/Chalese Hamilton/Annabelle Purples's carefully cultivated privacy. Unfortunately, that was about the time a young friend of Hamilton's put her drawings on his MySpace page. That incident forced my hand, and, I believed, as did Hamilton, that since the article was going to be written now anyhow, by other reporters, it would be best if I did it. By then, I knew Chalese and her history.

"As for the drawings? If I thought there was a chance she'd give them to me, instead of flinging them at my head, I'd beg her for them so I could frame them proudly."

I should have been breathless with panic, sitting there on the deck, but I wasn't. This golden peace embraced me as the sun rose in the sky, the rays dancing over the ocean. Yes, it was devastating to have my whole life exposed . . . and yet there was relief, too. I had to admit it.

I would do no more hiding, no more cowering, no more tap dancing around my past, worried that all would come to light. There would be no more evasiveness to others about what I did during the day. There was nothing more to hide. As Brenda and Christie and I had discussed ad nauseum, Christie and I were not responsible for our father or his actions. The family secret that had been written into my blood was out. On the Internet, of all places. I exhaled, breathed in, exhaled.

It was over.

I started to embrace the golden peace.

My editor called and didn't harangue me with his upcoming heart attacks. "Not a bad article, kid," he told me. "Not bad."

My agent called me, chortling. "The publicity! The publicity!"

My public relations gal giggled. "Have any more scandals in your background? It'd be awesome if you did."

And my website, the URL of which Aiden had listed? Bombarded.

Some people wanted to help the animals. Some people wanted to buy my jams and jellies.

I called Aiden and thanked him.

He did not return the call.

Brenda threw her laptop through the French door in my studio. Luckily it was open. It went flying over my deck and crashed onto the lawn.

"Splendid," she said, breathing heavily. "It was a cursed laptop anyhow. Where is my black Zorro mask? I have a date."

Chapter Ten

"There's something wrong," my sister whispered to me over the phone a few days later. "I can feel it. My back hurts. I'm cramping up. It's too soon, Chalese, way too soon. And there's blood. Oh no no no. I'm bleeding, I'm bleeding."

I flew out of my house with Brenda close on my heels. She had returned from a date and was wearing a white Princess Leia *Star Wars* outfit. It did not stop her from coming with me.

On the way I picked up the doctor, a friend of mine and Christie's from high school, and we sped toward her home. The doctor didn't even look twice at Brenda's hair, braided and coiled on the sides of her head.

Christie's husband, Cary, was stunned with fear and grief, the children crying.

Dr. Lana Shoemaker took over in an instant. She worked to stop the bleeding and called for a helicopter.

Within an hour we were at a hospital in Seattle, my sister hemorrhaging, those dear babies' lives in danger.

"She may need blood," the doctor told me, a stricken Cary, and my trembling mother.

"We're sisters. I'll donate," I said.

The doctor nodded. "Good."

"In fact, I'll give her all my blood." The doctor's eyebrows shot up into her blond bangs. Why do I say things like that? But it was the truth. I would give Christie all of my blood in a second. I'd funnel it out myself if I had to.

My mother swayed, and I grabbed her. She had been on her way home from San Francisco, flying into the Seattle airport, and had driven directly to the hospital.

It was hard to reconcile my tailored, gracious mother of today with the woman who had lived with my father. As she told us later, "That woman was young, naïve, and trapped in an emotional torture chamber. She could no longer think for herself."

My mother never remarried. She instead focused her energy on us, her housecleaning, and her own small business at home. From her dining-room table, with a hope and a prayer for a better life, she made jewelry, mostly from sea glass and shells at first. Christie and I helped. When those streamed right out of the local tourist shops, we made more. With more help and more prayer, she expanded her market to Seattle. We added beads and crystals and hammered metals.

When those hopes and prayers morphed into reality, she took another deep breath, told herself she could do it, and found other markets in Portland and San Francisco. We added semiprecious stones.

Pretty soon we couldn't keep up with the orders, and Mom hired women all over the island to make the jewelry. A manager followed, then an assistant manager. I phased myself out of the business after I sold my first book, but still did a few designs here and there.

Christie, however, was the chief designer, the one who kept things humming right along for Island Dreams Jewelry. Everything she designed was a best seller.

"You may not qualify as a blood donor," my mother whispered to me, patting her blond hair, her voice quivering.

"I might," I told her as the doctor hurried off. "I'm her sister!"

Beside me, my mother gripped a chair and fell into it, her face as white as a sheet. "Mom!" I cupped her face in my hands. "What is it?"

"Honey, forgive me." Her big, blue eyes flooded with tears that turned them almost luminescent.

"Forgive you what?"

"I was young." Her voice pitched. "I was scared. My parents said they would disown me. I had nowhere to go. I had no choice. I was seventeen years old!"

"What are you talking about?" I clasped her hands, thinking she'd lost it. Anybody listening to her haranguing me on the phone about natural food and vitamins would think the woman was an obsessed, partially sane, natural-food freak. They could not be more wrong. She was smart and ambitious and focused. Her slight obsession with her daughters' organic health was because she loved us to distraction. Love comes out in crazy ways, and that was hers. "Christie is going to be fine. She'll be okay. She'll get a transfusion from me if she needs one. The babies are small, but they'll be okay, I know it. . . ."

"That's it, honey," my mom wept out.

"What is it?" She was falling apart.

"You, honey, may not be an exact blood match for your sister."

"I'm her sister. I'll be close enough."

She shook her head, caught a sob. "Half." She put her perfectly manicured hands on my shoulders.

"What?"

"You're half, sweetie." Her moon earrings dangled. It was one of Christie's best designs. "Only half." Her face crumpled.

"What do you mean *only half?*"

She wrapped shaking arms around me. "Please forgive me. I felt so trapped. I had to marry your father, had to. Your real father and I . . . It was one summer on Whale Island. He didn't even know I was pregnant, not at all. And my father was livid. Remember Granddad, how he had such a temper? He always scared you girls, almost as much as your father did. Granddad forced me to marry your father. Your real father had to report for military duty. He'd promised to write, but I found out later that Granddad tossed all his letters. It's an old story, so clichéd, so heartbreaking when it really happens, but it's the truth. . . ."

"I am lost, Mom, totally lost. Or you are. One of us has lost our brain, because I have no idea what you're talking about." I felt my lungs tightening, as if there was not enough air for the two of us.

She grasped my hands, her body rocking back and forth with stress. "Chalese, Christie is your half sister. You have different fathers. The man you've known as your father your whole life, he's not related to you at all. I was two weeks pregnant when I married Richard. He knew it. He never let me forget it. Honey, that's why he was so disparaging of you, so unkind. You were a constant reminder that I'd been with someone else."

Once the giant, numbing fog of shock started to clear, I was suddenly able to aim binoculars at my childhood . . . and things began to click into place. My father's patent dislike of me, his interest in Christie, how I didn't share the coloring of Christie or my parents. *That scary monster was of no relation to me.*

"He was from Alaska, wasn't he, Mom?" I whispered.

Her face froze into shock. "Yes, your real father was from Alaska. Richard was so cruel to you with his comments."

"I know. I don't think I'll ever forget being called penguin butt or wolf daughter," I snapped. "Tell me about . . . about . . ."

"Your real father?" My mother's face became even more pained, and yet somehow, as she reminisced, I got a glimpse of the girl she used to be. "His family had lived in Alaska for many generations. We met when my family came to Whale Island on vacation for an entire summer. He was here, too, working on one of the fishing boats. He was such a kind boy, so handsome, so polite. I fell in love with him all at once, with a rush, as teenagers do. It was true love for me, and for him, too. My father hated him on sight. His daughter and a Native American were never going to work out. When I was pregnant, he threatened to kick me out unless I married your dad, who was the son of friends of his."

"But Dad was never nice to you, Mom. He watched you all the time, he beat you, he criticized you—"

"Richard was obsessed with me. He wanted to own me. Control me. I was a pretty possession. I never stopped loving your real father, though, and Richard knew it."

There were more details, more information, and I sank into a chair by my mother as she held my hand, begging my forgiveness for not telling me sooner. "I thought it would complicate things for you, honey. I didn't know if your biological father would want to see you, and you would get hurt again. I thought you would hate me for keeping that secret from you all these years, that you would think less of me, that you wouldn't see me anymore, and then more and more years passed, the lie got deeper. Oh, honey . . ."

Devastation hit me hard, heavy. I knew we would have a few rolling fights in the future, but there was one thing I wanted to know now, immediately. "Who is he, Mom? Who is my father?"

The babies, a girl and a boy, were taken by C-section, and Christie did not, in the end, need a blood transfusion.

Cary fainted during delivery, fell straight back into a doctor and had to be taken out. After the babies were in their little cribs, he wobbled back in to see them, kissed Christie, kissed the babies, took one more weak glance at his exhausted wife, and fainted again. Straight back. This time he cracked his head and bled like a sieve.

"Men are of no help whatsoever, are they?" Christie said,

exhausted. "I've had two babies lifted from my open stomach, and all the doctors and nurses are helping my bleeding husband. Who ever thought that men should be present at the birth of babies? There are many things women do better on their own. This is one of them."

Christie could leave the hospital in two days, but the babies would be hospitalized for weeks. The babies were healthy and beautiful, but too early, and Brenda and I cried over both of their tiny bodies, their tiny fingers, tiny lips, tiny hearts.

"What are their names?" I weeped.

My sister, already shrinking back to her Tinkerbell size and smelling like baby powder and roses, said, "I've named them after two people I love on Whale Island."

"You named them Gina Martinez and Marci Chang?" Brenda asked.

"No, Princess Leia, I didn't," Christie said, cuddling the babies close.

"Shadow Morrison?"

Christie laughed. "No. This one, our boy baby, is named Bren, for you, Brenda. And this one, our girl baby, is named"— she glanced up at me, her eyes filling with that special love we sisters have—"her name is Chalese. Chalese Rae, for my sister. My very, very best friend."

"Ohhh!" Brenda sobbed, clutching her heart. "Ohhh! Ohhh!"

I put my cheek next to Christie's. I could not even speak. But I could cry, and that I did.

Brenda brought the older three kids across on the ferry, her eyes still puffy from all the crying she'd done over the babies.

When she saw the twins, Wendi Jo said, "They look like their faces were squished by somebody mean."

Jeremiah said, "Why are they so purple? Did they eat too many grapes?"

And Rosie Mae said, "Tiny fingers. How they going to eat

peanut butter and jelly sandwiches?" She had brought a gift
for the babies. It was my strawberry jelly.

When all was well, I took a ferry home and worked on my
book, chugging coffee, walking my poorly behaved dogs in
the middle of the night to wake myself up, and eating orange
truffles.

The grief I felt over Aiden continued to follow me around.
I would think of Aiden, skyscraper Aiden, Aiden of the deep
voice and gentle, passionate hands, the smart and funny and
protective Aiden, and the grief would zip and zap up and
down my body.

I couldn't eat; sleep was spotty, I was exhausted, the sadness pulling me down into a swamp of pain. I fought being
pulled into the swamp, but I didn't win very often.

At night, when I turned off my light, the grief still hung
around, all about the room, on my periwinkle blue comforter,
next to me in bed.

"Want to dress up as princesses locked in a tower, sweet
thing?" Brenda asked before she climbed into bed with me.

I went to the hospital often, bringing Christie some of my
marmalade jelly, which she did indeed suck down like water
as Reuby said, and I kept working because I didn't want to
become a scraggly bag lady.

When I needed a break from the book, I worked on another
project. A gift. Just in case.

Amidst the massive amount of work I did, and the soul-
sucking grief, this doo-dad of a refrain kept repeating itself
in my head. *That scary monster was not your father. That
scary monster was not your father.*

At one point, when I was painting tiny ballet slippers on a jumping green frog, I dropped my paintbrushes, headed to the edge of my property, my feet in the sand as the ocean rolled over them, smiled for the first time in days, and yelled, "He was not my father. That creepy, mean, horrid jerk was not my father."

That horrible man had torched my ability to trust men, trust relationships, even to trust myself. He had ruined years of my life and introduced me to raw fear, desolation, rejection, and mind-numbing sadness.

But he was not my father.

Way out in the distance I saw water burst from a whale's blowhole.

I took it as a happy sign.

Many long days later, when my book was finally off (late, as usual), Brenda and I took the poorly behaved dogs for a late-afternoon stroll, then lay down in the sand by the ocean, staring up at the puffy clouds in the sky. One of the clouds resembled a goofy dragon. Another resembled a worm with oversized eyes. A third resembled two dogs on the run, neck and neck.

The backlash I might have expected from people on the island because of my father's insane criminal behavior never materialized, of course. I had grossly exaggerated in my head everyone's reactions because my own emotions were so charged, so wrapped around my father's abuse and that bone-cracking fear, that I couldn't think straight about that particular "family secret" anymore.

They had reached out their arms and covered me in hugs. In fact, I became closer to many of them who told me, in confidence, of their own wily, criminal, bizarre, dangerous, quirky, and otherwise off-beat family members.

"Sit down with me one day," Shadow told me, flipping

back a sparkly purple scarf. "You want to hear about a scary family? That would be mine. Your dad's got nothin' on my relatives. Half of them are in jail. Hey, they may have been cellmates of your dad's. . . ."

Another puffy cloud drifted by.

It resembled Aiden on a ferryboat. I tried not to cry.

"Go get him, girlfriend," Brenda told me for the umpteenth time, her sultry, earthy perfume wafting around me.

"Gee. Maybe I should bring a lasso, ring him around the neck, and haul him on in as I would a runaway bull. I think he'd find that stimulating." I dragged my hands through my hair. I was surprised at how long it had gotten. When was my last cut?

"Whooee! I'd like to see that. In fact, I think playing Lasso Cowgirl and Bull would be . . ." She clicked her teeth together. "Exciting!"

"You are so inventive, Brenda." I watched the sun slipping down the horizon. The clouds were rolling on in. It would rain soon, thunder and lightning, the works.

"Who is that?" Brenda asked, pointing out at the dock.

A woman was hunched over, clutching her knees, obviously positively miserable. "I think it's Gina!" I got up and started running.

"Gina?" I said gently when we reached the end of the dock. She whipped around, her eyes red and swollen.

"What is it?" I asked. Brenda and I settled next to her.

"Flaubert died."

Ah. Got it. Flaubert was Gina's floppy-eared rabbit.

"I'm sorry, Gina."

"He was a loveable guy. I always hugged him, talked to him. Flaubert was trustworthy, honest. At the end, he was having trouble with his kidneys, based on what he told me. He also had some arthritis in his left hip, and he felt . . . old. He missed Genevieve."

Brenda raised her brows at me questioningly.

"His wife," I told her.

Gina nodded. "You have someone one day, you laugh and talk with them, and then they're gone. And you have this huge, empty hole. Part of you is with them, but the other part of you is still here, still dealing with the loneliness and grief and aloneness."

I was already dealing with that loneliness and grief and aloneness.

"Everyone goes on with their lives, and you're in a bubble of pain."

I knew that bubble. It was here, surrounding me.

"Gosh, I'll miss Flaubert. He really understood love."

I patted her back. I understood love. *I understood I loved Aiden.*

"Don't let go of the rabbits you love, that's what I know," Gina sniffed. "Dogs, either. Horses are the best of friends. Cats, cuddly. Keep 'em in your heart."

I kept Aiden in my heart.

"The problem with animals is that they die," Gina said.

But Aiden wasn't dead. Aiden was quite alive and in Seattle. And maybe I could pop the bubble. Surely it was worth a try. For someone who danced on bars, got stuck on water towers, skinny-dipped in lakes, and had lived through my childhood, what would be another rejection? At least I'd know I tried hard enough to get rejected.

"Flaubert was a smart rabbit, and I'll miss him," I said as a raindrop plopped on my cheek. "I'm taking my boat to the mainland."

Oceans are tricky. They seem placid, and then it's as if a giant hand comes out of the sky and whips up the waves. I took my small cabin cruiser out onto the water, intending to sail to the mainland and then rent a car to drive to Seattle.

Although the waves were choppy when I started off, I

dropped my bag and the gift for Aiden in the cabin and didn't worry. I had made this trip for years.

Midway through my journey, I became rather alarmed. The clouds gathered together like the insides of a bubbling cauldron, the waves grew into these angry, gray rushes of water, and the wind came straight at my face, hard, long gusts that seemed to want to rip my boat in half.

In addition to some truly thrashing rain, there was the requisite thunder and lightning, which added to the thrill ride.

I can only compare it to being in an edge-of-your-seat movie about surviving a storm at sea, although I didn't have my growing butt in a chair with popcorn and pop clutched in my hands.

My boat was tossed around like a toy in a bathtub. Each trough seemed to get deeper, the waves above me higher, stronger, more dangerous. I had my life jacket on but scurried out of the cabin to grab two more life preservers from the seats.

That was bad, bad timing. The next wave was a doozer. It did not flip my boat, but it did flip me. I flew through the air, landing on my back. This terrible, shooting pain split right through my head, and then all those rollicking troughs of water, those towering waves, that racing rain and whooshing wind, they all went black, deep black, and quiet.

I woke up in a hazy fuzz of total and complete confusion. For long minutes, I could not figure out where I was or why I was there. All I knew was that my head pounded as if it had an oar stuck in it, the rain was coming down in sheets, and the wind was making that terrible howling sound you never want to hear when you're outside in a boat on an ocean. I was cramped, freezing cold, wet, and dizzy.

I knelt down in the boat, my head throbbing, my dizziness swirling me into a wet mental funnel, my exhaustion pulling me down a dark tube.

* * *

The next time I woke up, my boat was scraping against the rocks of the mainland. I was way off my usual course, but I knew where I was. I also knew I was starving, freezing, soaked, and my head was pounding, but I was alive. The sun was cresting over the horizon, so I knew I had lived to see another day. I kneeled in the boat, my body a teeming mass of on-fire nerve cells, threw my arms up in the air, and laughed.

How I laughed.

It was, really, *so good* to still be a human, on a planet, able to enjoy a truly spectacular sunrise.

And soon I might have the chance to see a truly spectacular Aiden.

Chapter Eleven

I did not realize how seriously terrible I looked until I noticed people staring at me as I walked down the dock with Aiden's gift under my arm and my bag swung over my shoulder.

It was the rental-car guy who finally drew my attention to my scary face and hair.

"Ma'am, we cannot rent you a car."

"Why?"

"Because, ma'am, we cannot rent to people who have been drinking or who appear as though they may have been indulging in legal or illegal pharmaceuticals."

I pushed my hair into a ponytail before I entered the Seattle salon.

Several jaws dropped at the counter when I walked in.

I was friendly. "Put your lips back together. Are you trying to catch flies?"

"Are you all right, ma'am?"

"Yes, why?"

"*Your face.*"

"What about my face?"

They held up a mirror.

Not pretty. Not good. Frightening. Colorful bruise on forehead. Hair like a wicked witch. Clothes like a bag lady. Note to self: this is exactly what you wanted to avoid.

"You'll need a long appointment—yes, indeedy, you will," a man in a pink shirt said, his hands waving. "Perhaps all day? You have all day? You need all day. Let me see what we have."

I changed into the other outfit I'd brought with me. Then those magician stylists fixed my hair with a cut and highlight, something of which I had neglected for, lemme see, months. They did my nails, something I had neglected for, lemme see, years. They gave me a facial, something I had neglected for, gee, decades. Next stop: a store for new clothes, something of which . . . you get it.

I bought cool jeans in my size (bigger than before, but who cares), a reddish, stylish top that clung to my curvy curves, heels, and butterfly earrings and a necklace designed by Christie which I found in a local boutique. I was a new Chalese.

Almost. I darted into a lingerie shop and filled an entire bag with my lacy, satiny, silky, purple and pink and black purchases.

Now I was a new Chalese.

With the gift slung under my arm, I was ready to see Aiden, my very own Flaubert.

"Aren't you even going to talk to me about us?"

I ducked as a fish seller threw a salmon in Aiden's direction. He caught the flying fish, paid for it, and moved back into the crowded aisles of Seattle's Pike Street Market.

Besides the flying fish, we were surrounded by rows of the most lush fruit your mouth could ever want, piles of spices, international food, French desserts, olive oils from around the world, and tapestries, ethnic art, and fabrics so rich and soft I wanted to wrap them around me.

A street performer enthusiastically played the harmonica nearby, and down a ways a band had the blues going.

"I appreciate that you were stalking me outside of the newspaper," Aiden said, "and how much time you must have stood there waiting for me. You're an excellent stalker, Chalese, truly skilled, but I think we should talk when we're back at my condominium and I'm not concentrating on catching fish."

He had been shocked when he'd seen me lurking outside his building, but I caught the expression right after the shock—he'd been happy. Happy to see me. He did one of those blinking things with his eyes that meant *I can't believe it's you.* I smiled, and he stopped in his tracks and smiled back. Then his face shuttered down, his green eyes went flat, and he looked . . . stressed, worn out, tired.

"You are amazingly beautiful, Chalese," he'd said. Although that bruise . . ." He automatically raised a hand to touch the bruise on my forehead, then pulled back. "My God, what happened? Are you okay? Where else are you hurt? How come you're not more careful?"

"Long story. Let's say that I have been prone to impulsive behaviors in my life, and the bruise was the result of one of them." I rubbed the bump on the back of my head, too.

"You're all right?"

How I loved that concern in his eyes, the caring, the stark worry. It gave me hope, and I so needed hope. I assured him several times that I was well and dandy fine. There was a sizzling silence in which we stared at each other, and I drank that man in as if I hadn't had a drink for twenty years.

He reached for me, I reached for him on tiptoe, and in the middle of that Seattle sidewalk, I squinched my eyes shut real tight while we hugged so I wouldn't cry.

When we pulled away, his voice was gruff and he ran a

hand over his own eyes. Aiden and I are such babies. "I was going to the market. Do you want to come along?"

I threw my hands up. "Aiden, if you invited me to Antarctica to study snow, I would follow you even if you insisted I wear a bathing suit and a gorilla mask at all times. So, yes."

"Hang on a sec." He stared up into space, pondering, pondering more, then grinned. "I got that vision in my head now. You. In a bathing suit in Antarctica with a gorilla mask. Kinky, but sexy. Cold, but hot."

I exhaled a wobbly sigh, wiped a tear away when he took my hand, and smiled like an inebriated greyhound when we headed together for the market and the fish thrower.

Aiden's condominium in Seattle overlooked the water. It was clearly a guy's place, with lots of leather furniture and the technology one would expect from a human with excessive testosterone, but it was classy, the view was incredible, and I was in it *with* Aiden, who made the whole place tasty and perfect.

We danced around any serious conversation while he barbequed the fish and I tossed the Caesar salad. We both sliced the colorful fruit from the market. Then Aiden lit the candles on the table on his deck, and we settled down as if we were an old married couple still flaming for each other. Sailboats drifted across the water in the distance as a cool breeze ambled through.

And this is what I thought as those long-lashed green eyes met mine: I wanted to ride our bikes through mud and dirt and watch romance movies with him where we could both sniffle over the sappy, happy ending.

I wanted to have spaghetti picnics on the beach and take my boat out to visit the whales together. Our four kids could come with us.

When I was old and needed a walker to get out of bed, I

wanted to wake up every morning with him to read the paper and eat chocolate croissants before going to dinner at the grandkids' house.

"Chalese," he started.

"Aiden, please let me talk first." I grabbed his hand across the table even though my fear of rejection was scorching my heart. "I am so sorry for what happened. It's entirely my fault. I've humiliated you personally and professionally . . ."

My mouth went on and on until Aiden insisted, "Stop, please, it's not you, it's me. I owe you an apology—"

"One more thing," I pleaded. "One more." I pulled out my gift to him, a framed drawing. "I made you something."

He unwrapped the gift, slowly, with a smile, and when he saw what I'd drawn him, he had to clear his throat, and he got a wee bit flushed and emotional.

I had drawn many of my characters, and my real life animals, surrounding Aiden, who I had spent hours drawing in his leather jacket and cool jeans.

Cassy Cat's eyes were huge and endearing behind her glasses. Goose was prissy and waving a wing. Herbert Hoove the Horse wore a blue bow tie. The frog with the ballet slippers was sitting on Aiden's shoulder, the fat cat was waltzing with Fox, my goats were perched on bicycles, and flowered hats decorated the heads of two of my dogs, Mrs. Zebra and Rocky. Troublesome, my three-legged cat, sat on his boot.

They were framed by the pine trees and ocean view on my property, blue picnic table in the background.

"Much better, isn't it?" I asked. "No streetwalkers, no gamblers, no bar scenes."

His eyes crinkled at the corners as he studied each animal, then he focused those laughing green eyes on me. "Honey, I think our grandkids are going to find this whole story hilarious."

I opened my mouth to speak. This is what came out: "Xwlkjewfr." And then: "Ckgqedlw."

"Thank you. I love it."

"You do?" I felt a snatch of sheer joy sneaking into the hollow bleakness that had surrounded my life since Aiden left Whale Island.

"Yes, I do. It's the most thoughtful gift I've ever received. And, I'm sorry, too, Chalese. I'm sorry that immediately after I met you I didn't back off the story. I should have. We became friends so quickly followed by my wanting to throw you into bed and not let you leave that bed for years. I didn't even know what hit me. I should have been loyal to you, to my feelings, to us. It was wrong on so many fronts to even think of writing the article, but I knew that I would write it honestly, and that you would end up coming off as the smart, vulnerable, talented, quirky, daring, funny person that you are."

"You flatter me. I'll bet you're just saying that so I don't stalk you anymore or climb on your roof."

"You can stalk me anytime you want. Stay off the roof—you could get hurt, and I mean that." He stared at me pointedly. "When I saw the pictures you drew on the Internet, all I could think of was, 'You deserved this, Aiden, all of it.' And, I did. I was out of line, and I am willing to beg you on bended knee for forgiveness. I'll even gallop up in tights on a charging white horse if it'll make things better between us."

He put the picture down on the table and held both of my hands in the warmth of his. "Chalese, knowing you has been an adventure. You're an adventure. With you, I can actually see a real life in front of me, the beautiful, crazy mess that life is. I've finally found love in you. I've found the love I've been hoping for my whole life, and almost stopped believing I'd ever have."

Did he say he'd found love?

"You know how I see us?"

"Please tell me," I snuffled.

"I see us having a great life adventure together. I see us watching sunsets and working here in Seattle and on Whale Island. I see us playing poker in the annual tournament and taking care of the animals. I see us laughing by bonfires and waltzing in the rain and reading the same book so we can discuss it. I see us holding hands as we get older and sitting on rocking chairs in Greece and Italy and New Zealand and wherever else you want to see in the world. I see us making love a lot." He grinned. "I see a lot of that."

"Yes, by golly, I see that, too. I see that on the beach, on the picnic table, my truck, your truck, in the studio." We laughed and kissed again. "Hey! How 'bout here? Your kitchen counter is probably sturdy enough."

"I'll bet it is. So is this table and the couch. We might even be able to swing things on my motorcycle."

"Now that would take a lot of flexibility. . . ." I could see he had the same graphic picture in his mind that I did, and our laughter floated around that deck like music.

"I don't see us as having a totally perfect life," Aiden said, serious again. "Life has not been perfect for you or me, but, Chalese, I can predict that when hard things come down the pike, it's always going to be you I want to be with."

"Aiden," I said, trying not to get too mushy, "if what comes down the pike is good, or hair-raisingly bad, it's you I want to be with, too. I've known it since I met you. When you bent to pet my monster dogs that first day, I felt my heart melt, because a man who loves animals has gentleness. When I saw you chatting so easily with everyone at the police station, my head said you were a respectable man who treated people with respect. When you didn't run from a woman who has been a part of a few funny schemes, I knew you were a man of humor. When you opened yourself up to actually talking about how you *felt,* I knew you were a thoughtful, insightful man."

I leaned over and kissed him, and that kiss felt like life, like love, like a future. "And when you won third place in the poker tournament, well, I figured if we were both ever unemployed, we could send you to Vegas to pay the light bill."

We laughed, and we kissed once again, and our hands went

dancing, our arms went hugging, and our bodies went thrumming against each other in perfect rhythm, perfect time. Perfect music for in-love people.

"I have missed you so much, babe," he whispered. "So much. I was coming to the island this weekend. I thought you needed space from me, needed time. But I never would have given you up. I love you. I loved you when you were a scratched-up skylight diving wreck, I loved you when you dove into the ocean to rescue Rocky when he got tired of swimming, I loved you when you laughed so hard you spat out your wine, I loved you when I saw you chasing your goats down the street in town, and I loved you when I kissed you the very first time. I will always love you, that I know for sure."

"And I love you, Aiden," I wept out. "I wish I could say it more creatively, but I'm better at drawing pictures of talking alligators." *Why do I say such things?*

"Who wants a talking alligator when I can have you?" He kissed a trailing tear, then whispered in my ear, "How about we try out the kitchen counter?"

Chapter Twelve

He hugged me tight, rocking me back and forth. Then his wife embraced us, too, tears rolling down her cheeks.

His six children crowded around, all with black hair and dark eyes, and in the faces of his grandchildren I saw myself when I was younger. Only they were much happier than I ever was as a kid.

I couldn't call him "Dad" yet, as my half brothers and sisters did, and I certainly couldn't call his sweet wife "Mom," but when my eyes met his, eyes that were so like mine, I felt the door in my heart swing open to family.

Takoda Whitefish had never known my mother was pregnant. Even though his letters were unanswered, he still went back to Whale Island when he was on leave, searching for information on her. He was told by an elderly gentleman who owned the bed and breakfast my mother's family stayed in that my mother had gone back to New York and married.

Heartbroken, he had returned to the service and then moved to Alaska and worked for an oil company.

My mother had tearfully given me his name at the hospital, begging forgiveness and understanding. Although I believed I would repair my relationship with her over time, I was struggling. My life would have been so different, so much richer and fuller, filled with not only my father's love, but the love and friendship of his wife and their children, had I known about him.

I had been unexpectedly hit with a tsunami of rage, regret, and grief, to name a few of two hundred galloping emotions charging through my body, and I didn't have much of a life jacket.

Except for Aiden. Aiden had proved to be a darn good life jacket.

I found Takoda's phone number, and Aiden called him at work in Anchorage. I wanted Takoda to be able to answer honestly about whether or not he wanted to meet me, if he wanted his family to know about me, or if he would prefer that I never attempt to speak with him at all. And I thought it would be easier if he didn't have to speak directly to me about it.

Takoda, which means "friend to everyone," was stunned speechless that I even existed, and later, after the enormity sank in of our situation, devastated about the years we had lost. He never wavered in his desire to see me, however, or for me to be a part of his family's life in the future.

Although I do not believe in any fairy-tale endings, and I still do not believe in castles or princes, I could not deny the warmly exuberant greeting from my father's family.

"Welcome home, my daughter, welcome home."

Epilogue

Six months later

"I think we have a pretty sweet arrangement here," I mused as Aiden and I sat on our beach, four dogs leaping around us as the sun scooted behind the horizon, leaving blurry pinks and oranges in its wake. "Living in Seattle part-time and here part-time."

"I love living on Whale Island," he said.

"Yeah, Zeus? List thy ways."

"One, because you're here, Chalese. Two, you're here. Three, you're here." He wrapped both arms around me and pulled me toward his chest. "But we could be living in a cave in a desert mixing our gruel in clay pots and shooting lizards for breakfast, and I'd be happy."

I linked an arm around The Skyscraper's neck and planted a big one on his lips. "Well, it's me and my gang of poorly behaved dogs and a posse of slinky cats. Not to mention the goats, who escaped again the other day when you were in Seattle."

He kissed me back, long and delicious. "As long as you can resist inviting another horse into the dining room, I think I can manage the animals. In fact, I enjoy my new part-time jobs as animal caretaker and jelly maker."

I laughed and relaxed into him. "You're a talented jelly maker. No one handles fruit better than you, and there are a few female dogs who think you're the head honcho. Love is definitely in the air." I planted a big one on his lips. "I love you, Mr. Gorgeous."

"I love you, too, Annabelle Purples."

Aiden had once asked me if I was proud of myself. I hadn't really "got" the question. I did now, and I had an answer. I was truly proud that I had survived my childhood. I was proud that I wasn't going to let it define my whole life and that I hadn't let anger and bitterness swamp me. I was proud of the happy relationships I had with many cool people, and I was proud of how I drew Cassy Cat.

I was proud of myself for not feeling suffocated one whit around Aiden. As I rolled on top of him, I caught the light in my diamond engagement ring. Man, was it a honker.

Aiden had asked me to marry him as we sat on top of my barn, the barn that we had, together, completely remodeled. And yes, remodeled was the right word. It was one classy barn now. He'd handed me a hammer, and attached to the hammer by a string was my ring.

It had been my fifth proposal, and this time I said yes. Yes, yes, yes.

I love you, yes.

We're going to Greece for our honeymoon.

When Christie's husband offered to babysit one night, Brenda and I took it as our chance for one last adventure before Brenda left for Los Angeles with her finished screenplay in hand.

"It's the seminaked drive," Christie drawled as we pulled over to the side of a darkened road, the stars our only witnesses to this sheer stupidity.

"Yep. Let's go, girls," Brenda hooted, yanking off her shirt. "Yowza!"

I yodeled. "We ladies gotta rebel now and then. Shake things up. Be daring." I yodeled again. Mrs. Zebra beside me stuck her tongue out, then licked me.

We sped into the night in Brenda's zippy sports convertible, the top down.

The only thing we were wearing on our top halves was the wind.

It was the beginning scene of her next movie.

She won an award for that one, too. It was titled *The Rebel Ladies and Mrs. Zebra.*

Queen of Hearts

Judy Duarte

Chapter One

Jennifer Kramer studied the computer screen, reading an e-mail addressed to Diana, the advice columnist for the *Fairbrook Times*.

Dear Diana,

I'm dating a man who's forty-three and still living at home with his parents. My friends think I'm making a big mistake by getting involved with a guy who doesn't have a place of his own. But I'm in my forties, too, and can't afford to be picky. He treats me well, but I must admit his closeness to his family, especially his mother, is a bit worrisome.

He said that he's living with his folks to help them out, but his mom still does his laundry, cooks his favorite meals, and packs his lunch. Do you see a problem with that?

Tired of Being Lonely

Every now and then, Jenn—or rather, Diana—received a letter that touched a little too close to home, one that niggled at her own fears and insecurities. And she was reading one now.

Not that she was in her forties or dating a guy whose mom

still took care of him, but last summer she'd been forced to move in with her parents, which had been humbling, to say the least. She wasn't proud of her living situation, nor did she see any big changes in her immediate future if she didn't pick up full-time work.

She returned her focus to the e-mail, intending to offer some words of wisdom, as well as to suggest that Tired's friends might be right. But Jenn didn't want to imply that adult children living at home had issues. She certainly didn't.

Or did she?

That was the trouble with issues and hang-ups. Those who had them didn't always recognize them.

She rolled back her desk chair, got to her feet, and made her way to the window of the apartment in which she lived, a small two-bedroom unit that had been built over her parents' garage. She looked down into the backyard, where her five-year-old daughter played on the lawn with Sadie, the neighbor's golden retriever.

Caitlyn, with her wheat-colored hair, big green eyes, and an impish grin, resembled her father, a man Jenn once cared about but never should have married.

Jason Phillips, the all-league running back at Fairbrook High, had asked Jenn out when they'd been seniors. Everyone in school thought the head cheerleader and the star football player made the perfect couple. And at that time in their lives, they had.

Buying into the myth, Jenn and Jason had a fairy-tale wedding right after graduation, when most kids their age were getting ready to leave for college. But marriage and adulthood hadn't been all they were cracked up to be, and over time, financial stress gave way to disillusionment, causing the stars in their eyes to dim.

Jenn's parents hadn't always been a happy couple, but they'd stuck together through thick and thin. So divorce hadn't been an option. That is, until she found out that Jason had a gambling problem and wasn't willing to seek professional help.

Last summer, when she realized that his obsession had not only drained their bank account but had run up their credit-card debt to the point they had to consider bankruptcy, she finally moved out and filed for divorce.

Jason hadn't even put up a fight, which had hurt the most.

But Jenn had come out okay. She'd gotten a precious little girl out of the union. She'd also landed a job with the newspaper. Of course, right now it was just a part-time position, but she was working in the field of journalism, which would have been a perfect major for her if she'd opted for a college degree instead of a bridal gown.

Okay, so being an advice columnist for the *Fairbrook Times* wasn't the same as being a reporter, but she wouldn't complain. She'd taken the only position available that allowed her to utilize her writing skills and to show the editor what she could do if he'd just give her a chance. Besides, offering advice was right down her alley. At one time, she was the one all of her friends came to when they had a problem, and her suggestions had usually been spot-on.

In the yard below, Caitlyn, who was cuddling the neighbor's dog, glanced up. When she spotted her mommy standing at the window, she smiled and waved.

Jenn mouthed an "I love you" and blew her a kiss. Then she returned to her desk and got back to work.

So what should she tell Tired of Being Lonely?

Dear Tired,

There are many reasons people move back home or remain living with their parents in the adult years. Some of those reasons might even be admirable and no cause for worry. But that's not always the case, so your friends have a valid concern. As you should do in any relationship, keep your eyes open and don't rush into anything.

However, something else struck me while reading your letter. I hope you're not settling just because you're lonely. Ten years from now you might find yourself in an even lonelier place if you hook up with the wrong man because it seems like the right thing to do at the time.

Jenn leaned back in her chair and read over the opening of her response, knowing it would need to be rounded out after she gave it some more thought. She answered each letter as though it would be one of the few that she used in the column, and so far, her efforts had met with success.

A knock sounded, drawing her from her work.

"Honey?" Her mom opened the door and peered into the small living area that doubled as a home office. "I hate to bother you, but I need to run to the market and thought I'd take Caitlyn with me."

"That's all right." Jenn spun her desk chair toward the doorway. "While you're gone, I'll head over to the newspaper and pick up my mail." Most of the letters addressed to Dear Diana came as e-mails these days, but some still arrived via snail mail in care of the *Times*.

Her mom, who'd lost about fifteen pounds in the last few months, wore an oversize pink T-shirt that hid the extra weight and the tummy paunch that still remained. "Is there anything special you want me to pick up for dinner? Spaghetti might be nice. We haven't had it in a while, and I know it's always been one of your favorite meals."

After reading Tired's e-mail, Jenn felt a bit uneasy about the way her mom prepared most of the meals and went out of her way to make something Jenn liked. But two months after Jenn had moved back home, her parents had revealed their own plans for divorce, announcing that they'd been pondering a step like that for years. And since her mom had spent her entire life as a homemaker, it seemed to help her adjust by having someone at home to fuss over.

"Spaghetti sounds great," Jenn said.

"Oh, by the way, Jessica Rawlings called earlier. She wanted to remind you that the reunion committee has another meeting tonight. She hopes you can make it to that one."

"I'll talk to her when I get back." And Jenn would tell her the same thing she'd been telling her for months: she was too busy to get involved in anything right now.

"I'm really surprised that you're not helping with that reunion," her mom said. "You used to be such a social butterfly in high school, writing skits for the pep assemblies and planning dances and proms."

Time had a way of changing things, she supposed. "Actually, Mom, I don't really want to attend the reunion."

"I'm sorry to hear that. Are you saying that because you're afraid you'll run into Jason?"

"He doesn't bother me. Besides, I'm not sure if he's even planning to go. I just don't want the subject of my failed marriage to come up." And since Jenn and Jason had been the homecoming king and queen in their senior year, it was bound to—one way or another. Bottom line? She didn't want to deal with any of it—past, present, or future.

Of course, if she had a full-time job and if she weren't still living at home, it might be different.

Her mom leaned against the doorjamb and crossed her arms. "I can't blame you for that. Maybe you, Caitlyn, and I can go to a movie that night."

"That's an idea."

As her mom closed the door, leaving her alone, Jenn glanced at the bright yellow flier that rested on her desk, the one sent by Jessica and the gang as a reminder to hurry up and RSVP for the reunion. If she decided to go, she'd have to get her money in right away, but she just couldn't seem to generate the enthusiasm and the energy it would take to write a check and address an envelope.

She picked up the flier, reading it again and hoping to

spark some kind of enthusiasm for the event most of her classmates were looking forward to.

FAIRBROOK HIGH SCHOOL CLASS REUNION
The Starlight Room
Mar Vista Country Club

Saturday, June 15th
Cocktails—6:00 PM
Dinner—7:00 PM
Dancing until Midnight

*We're still looking for Marcos "The Brain" Taylor. If you know where to find him, contact Jessica Rawlings as soon as possible.

Apparently, the committee had located all of the other classmates who'd been listed on the last flier they'd sent out. Why had the valedictorian been more difficult to find?

Surely some of his friends had stayed in contact with him. Or maybe some of those he'd tutored during their senior year knew where he was. The short, gangly teen had not only been bright, but he'd also had a way of explaining things to other students in a way that made sense. And Jenn had been one of the kids who'd benefited from his help.

She remembered the day they'd been at the library when all of a sudden something he'd said had clicked. She'd finally understood the algebraic formula she'd been struggling with all semester and had given him an appreciative hug.

Apparently, he'd misunderstood her intention, because he'd asked her to go to a movie with him. She'd been stunned and had turned him down.

Marcos had been sweet and kind of funny. He'd also had the prettiest brown eyes she'd ever seen, although you really had to look beyond his glasses to notice them. But she wouldn't have dated him; he hadn't been her type.

After that, she hadn't run into him much. It was almost as if he'd disappeared from the face of the earth—or at least from the ground she'd walked on.

Still, it was too bad the class as a whole had lost contact with him. She hoped nothing had happened to him.

If she remembered correctly, he'd gone off to college somewhere—one of the biggies like Harvard, Stanford, or Yale. As bright as he'd been, he'd probably been very successful.

If she were on the committee, she'd do a Google search. And if that didn't work, she'd contact the high school and see if she could get a clue as to which college he attended. Surely someone in the office knew something.

But she wasn't on the committee, and while she could have found time to attend their meeting tonight, she wasn't going to.

She dropped the flier into the trash, shut off her computer, and strode into the cramped bathroom she shared with her daughter. While running a brush through her hair, she peered at her washed-out image in the mirror and blew out a wobbly sigh.

Deciding a little color would help, she applied some lipstick, then grabbed her purse, locked the door, and headed downstairs to begin the ten-block walk to the newspaper office.

She could have asked her mom for a ride, but she could use the exercise. Besides, the skies were a pretty shade of blue today, and the temperature was more like summer than spring. A light sea breeze gently ruffled her hair, and the morning sun warmed her face. Still, her mood wasn't much brighter than it had been for the past couple of years. She doubted that it would improve until her life turned around, which could take time.

Speaking of time, she glanced at her watch and kicked up her pace a notch.

As she approached Mulberry Park, children's laughter filled the air. A couple of boys flew a kite, and two girls on

Rollerblades zipped along the sidewalk that wove through the lawn to the cinderblock structure that housed the restrooms.

The playground was abuzz with children climbing up the slides and setting the swings in motion, reminding Jenn how much Caitlyn loved her visits to the park. They'd have to schedule another picnic soon.

She continued along the sidewalk in front of the community church. When she spotted Pastor George carrying a box to the modular building behind the sanctuary, she waved and called out a hello.

He acknowledged her with a nod and a friendly smile. "How've you been, Jennifer? I haven't seen you or your mom in a while."

"We're doing fine. Thanks."

"Hope to see you in services on Sunday," he added.

She didn't respond. No need to make a commitment when she'd made a point of playing each day by ear.

At the corner, she turned left onto Canyon and walked the last few blocks to the newspaper office, a three-story, smoky-glass structure.

In the parking lot, the driver of a silver, late-model BMW climbed from his car and reached for a briefcase. He was about her age—late twenties—and was dressed in a dark blue sports jacket and dark wash jeans that suggested he was laid-back under an expensive exterior.

He wasn't especially tall, but he carried himself with assurance. But why wouldn't he? His vehicle, his clothing, his demeanor all shouted success.

She couldn't help but study the handsome man whose dark hair and olive complexion suggested Latino roots. As their eyes met, he flashed a crooked grin that caused her heart to flip-flop. For a moment, a sense of déjà vu settled over her, but she quickly shook it off.

There was no way—no way at all—Jenn would have ever forgotten meeting a man like him before.

She forced a casual smile to indicate she was a friendly soul and not gawking at him for any reason in particular.

As he reached the entrance of the building, he opened the door that led to the lobby, then waited for her to step inside.

"Thank you."

"You're welcome." A deep baritone voice strummed over her the way a classical guitarist's fingers moved across taut, well-tuned strings.

She couldn't remember the last time a man had turned her head like that. But then again, she'd gotten married just days after her eighteenth birthday and had been wearing marital blinders for as long as she could remember.

And quite frankly, she wasn't looking forward to the whole dating scene. The rules had changed now that she was an adult, and she wasn't sure she was ready to jump into the midst of it.

As the handsome stranger turned toward the reception desk, Jenn headed down the hall to the elevator. Still, she couldn't help taking one last peek over her shoulder, only to have his gaze meet hers.

Suddenly she was sixteen all over again and awed by a rock star who wouldn't know her from one of a thousand other dreamy-eyed teenage girls. Crimson heat warmed her cheeks, and she averted her eyes as gracefully as she could.

She jabbed at the elevator button, signaling it to open for a quick escape. No way did she want to run into that guy again, not when her interest had been so obvious.

And not when she doubted that even Marcos "The Brain" Taylor would find her attractive these days.

Chapter Two

Marcos knew that by moving back to Fairbrook he was going to run into Jennifer Kramer sooner or later, but he hadn't expected it to happen his first week in town. Nor had he expected his heart rate to spike the moment he laid eyes on her, just as it had ten years ago when he'd passed her in the hall.

With long blond hair, big blue eyes, and a surfer-girl shape, Jenn had been the ultimate teenage crush back then, and Marcos had noticed everything about her. Like how she used to pluck a daisy from the bush near gym class every day after P.E. And how she would scrunch her face when she struggled with an algebra problem in the library, and nibble on the top of her pencil. How her eyes lit up when she finally got the answer.

He also knew that she favored a pair of butterfly earrings and that she usually chose them when she had on that light blue sweater or the yellow blouse. And he always knew whether she was wearing anyone's class ring at any given time.

Apparently, old habits never died, because just moments after spotting her in the parking lot, he'd zoomed in on her left hand, which bore no jewelry at all.

She'd gotten married right after graduation, so why wasn't she sporting a wedding band?

When he opened the lobby door for her, he assumed that

she'd recognized him. But once inside, it was clear that she still didn't know him from Adam, which really shouldn't have surprised him. He'd changed a lot since high school, including his last name.

"Can I help you?" a matronly receptionist asked as she returned the telephone to its cradle and scratched out a memo.

"I'm Marc Alvarado. I have a meeting with Frank Bagley."

"Give me just a second," she said as she continued to write, "and I'll let Mr. Bagley know you're here."

Marc took the requested second to steal one last glance at Jenn, only to find her looking at him. His first thought was that she'd finally placed him, but a flush on her cheeks and an immediate break in eye contact suggested that her interest had nothing to do with spotting an old classmate and everything to do with physical attraction.

Now there was a twist. Ten years ago, he'd been the one sneaking peeks at her, the one who'd flushed at being caught gawking.

But a lot had happened since high-school graduation.

When Marc had left Fairbrook, headed for college, he'd been a scrawny little geek, but over the summer, his lagging growth hormones had finally kicked into gear. Over time, he'd earned a couple of college degrees, and a dream position in a prestigious software firm had opened up. Before long, an idea for a brilliant new business venture had blossomed.

Now he was back in Fairbrook, sporting new contact lenses and sitting on an impressive investment portfolio and more cash in the bank than he'd ever imagined.

"Mr. Bagley?" the receptionist said into the telephone receiver. "Marc Alvarado is here." She waited a beat, then added, "I'll send him right up."

After Marc had been given directions to Frank Bagley's office, he took the elevator to the third floor.

Minutes later, he entered the editor's office, a glass-enclosed room that provided a view of busy reporters, some at their desks and others coming and going.

Frank Bagley, a stout man in his late forties, reached out his hand in greeting. "I'm glad you were able to make it this morning. The *Times* has always been supportive of the businessmen and women in our community, and we're glad to welcome Alvarado Technologies to Fairbrook."

Marc returned a firm handshake. "Thanks."

Bagley indicated a chair in front of his cluttered desk, then took his own seat. "I hear you've leased out the top floor of the professional building across from Mulberry Park."

"That's right. We moved in this past weekend and opened for business on Monday." Marc settled into his seat. "But what I'd like to promote is the scholarship foundation I've created for disadvantaged high-school students who can't afford to attend college without assistance."

"That's a good cause."

Marc thought so. He had no idea where he'd be if he hadn't received financial aid in college. "With June approaching, I'd like to get the word out as soon as possible."

Bagley placed his elbows on his desk and leaned forward. "Well, the *Fairbrook Times* can certainly help you with that."

Marc glanced out the glass-enclosed office and into the newsroom, where Jenn stood at a reporter's desk. She held several envelopes. When she looked toward the editor's office, Bagley lifted his meaty hand, motioning for her to come in.

"Will you excuse me for a minute?" he asked Marc. "My new advice columnist is here to pick up the mail, and I need to talk to her before she leaves."

Marc watched as Jenn approached the office. She appeared to hesitate at the door before letting herself in.

"You wanted to see me, Frank?" She glanced at her boss, then at Marc, and back to the editor.

Frank pushed back his chair and got to his feet. "I'm going to let you have an opportunity to prove yourself, Jennifer.

There's a ten-year high-school reunion coming up. Sabrina Goodman was going to cover it for us, but she went into premature labor last night. The doctors managed to stave off contractions, but she's on bed rest indefinitely. So I'm going to give the story to you. There's a committee meeting this evening, and Sabrina made arrangements to be there. She thought it would put a different spin on the story if she covered the planning of the event, and I agreed. So you're up."

Jenn tucked a strand of hair behind her ear. "Sure, Frank. I'll go to the meeting and write the article."

Bagley crossed his arms and shifted his weight to one hip. "For a woman who's been chomping at the bit to get a real story, you don't seem all that excited."

A class reunion didn't seem like a *real* story to Marc, and he wondered if that's why he didn't see the ol' Go-Wildcats spark in her eyes.

"I *am* happy, Frank." She managed a smile that appeared to be genuine. "It's actually my class reunion that's coming up. And to be honest, I hadn't planned on attending."

Marc knew it had been ten years since graduation, but he hadn't heard anything about a reunion. Yet an even bigger surprise was that Jenn hadn't planned to attend. There hadn't been many social events in high school that she hadn't been involved in, and a reunion should have been the kind of event that was right up her alley.

"Well, it looks like your plans have changed. That is, if you agree to cover the story. If you'd like, I can ask someone else." Frank looked out into the newsroom as though ready to select another reporter.

"No, don't give it to anyone else. I'll take it. And I'll do a great job."

A slow smile stretched across Bagley's face. "Good. And we'll take it from there. Show me you can do more than write a report of the event, and you just might land a job reporting for the *Times*."

Was she embarrassed to have her job prospects talked about in front of a stranger? Marc would have been. He wondered what kind of boss Frank Bagley was and suspected he could benefit from some supervisory training.

Jenn's gaze drifted to Marc, connecting for a moment—long enough for him to see her lift her chin in pride and, at the same time, to sense another flash of attraction or interest in him.

"Forgive me for being rude," Bagley said. "Jenn, I'd like you to meet Marc Alvarado, one of Fairbrook's newest businessmen. And Marc, this is Jennifer Kramer, or rather Dear Diana, our advice columnist."

Marc stood and reached out his hand, felt her fingers wrap around his in a warm grip that lasted a beat longer than usual.

He could have clued her in right then, telling her they'd met before—and he probably should have—but the geek inside held him back, reminding him that he'd always been a little speechless around her.

"It's nice to meet you," he said instead.

"Thanks. You, too." She drew back her hand almost reluctantly and tore her gaze from his to address her boss. "I'll get right on it."

"Good," Bagley said. "I'll look forward to reading that story." She nodded, then excused herself.

It took all Marc had not to watch her walk away. Strange, he thought, how some old flames never quite burned out.

He took his seat. "So, Jennifer is the advice columnist?"

"Yes, and doing a great job of it. I probably shouldn't introduce her as Dear Diana. I wouldn't want people thinking her life is anything but picture-book perfect."

"It isn't?" Marc asked, his mounting curiosity about Jenn trumping his distaste for Bagley's indiscreet revelation about his employee's personal life.

"Oh, you know, just the typical California drama. She's a single mom who was divorced last year and is living at home. But I suspect that the readers who've been writing to her would like to have the illusion of perfection. Know what I mean?"

Marc nodded. He figured those with problems would want to think their advice came from someone who'd made all the right choices in life, and in that sense, he supposed Jenn hadn't. She'd been a lot smarter than she'd ever given herself credit for, and he'd always thought she'd sold herself short when she'd gotten married right out of high school.

"At the first of the year, our advice columnist went on her honeymoon, and I was scrambling to find a replacement. Jenn had just applied for a job, and I was about to drop her application into the circular file. But then I wondered if she'd be able to temporarily fill the position. She jumped on the chance and quickly impressed me with her witty advice and her tendency to put a personal spin on her responses. Letters from readers— some with problems and others with comments on the column, her advice, or her candor—began to pour in. Before long, I had no choice but to give her the job permanently." Bagley leaned forward and lowered his voice. "In fact, I haven't told her yet, but there've been some whispers of syndication."

"I'll bet she'll be happy to hear that."

"Yes, I'm sure she will be, although she'd rather be a reporter. But she doesn't have much experience."

She'd worked on the high-school newspaper, but Marc supposed that wasn't enough to propel her into a full-time journalist position.

"Hey," Bagley said. "Let's get back to your scholarship foundation. Why don't we run an article in Sunday's paper? That ought to get the ball rolling."

"Sounds good to me." Marc glanced out into the newsroom, watching as Jenn headed for the elevator with the letters in hand. "Why don't you assign the scholarship article to Ms. Kramer?"

"To Jenn?" Bagley sat back in his seat, the springs creaking in protest. "Like I said, she really doesn't have any experience. And I'd rather see what she does with that reunion article first."

"I understand, but I've always been one to root for the underdog. I like to give people a chance to succeed. In fact, that's the whole philosophy around the Elena Alvarado Scholarship Foundation. So in that sense, Ms. Kramer would be a perfect choice."

"All right. If you have a business card, I'll have her give you a call and schedule that interview."

"Good. I'll look forward to hearing from her." Marc stood, shook hands with Bagley, handed him a card, then headed for the elevator. He wasn't sure why he'd insisted that Jenn write the article for the paper. Or why he even wanted to see her again.

When they'd been at Fairbrook High, and he'd learned she was struggling in algebra, he'd offered to tutor her, and she'd taken him up on it.

"I can't believe this," she'd said one day. "You explain things so much better than Mr. Ragsdale."

And when things finally clicked for her and she caught on, she'd given him a hug that had nearly steamed up his glasses.

She'd been so pretty . . . so breathtaking, that he'd had no choice but to swallow his pride and ask her out.

But boy, had that been a bubble-bursting mistake. She'd stiffened and told him that he wasn't her type.

But who hadn't known that? She'd been a teen goddess, a fairy-tale princess, and he'd been a toad with no sign of a magic wand in sight.

From that day on, she'd acted as though she didn't know him, as if he'd never helped her turn that D- into an honor roll–saving C+.

At one time Marc hadn't been good enough for Jennifer Kramer, but now it appeared the tables had turned.

And maybe the skinny, four-eyed geek who still lived deep inside of him just wanted to gloat for a moment or two over the fact that he had the upper hand now.

Chapter Three

Jenn had no sooner arrived home than Frank called, asking her to set up an appointment with Marc Alvarado. She'd been pleased to get a second assignment, yet was a little uneasy about seeing the handsome businessman again.

In truth, she found him far more attractive than she was comfortable admitting, and if he sensed she had the least bit of romantic interest in him, she could jeopardize the opportunity she'd been given to prove herself as a professional reporter.

Since her only income was a moderate child-support check and what she earned working part-time for the paper as Dear Diana, she didn't want to remain strapped for cash indefinitely. So she'd called Mr. Alvarado's office and spoke to a woman who'd identified herself as Elena.

"Mr. Alvarado is expecting your call," Elena had said, "but he's not available right now. He asked me to make the appointment for him. Would four o'clock this afternoon be okay?"

Jenn would have shuffled her schedule to make it work, but as it was, she didn't have to. "Four o'clock is perfect." The timing would give her a chance to pick up a bite to eat afterward and arrive early enough at Jessica's house to play catch-up with the reunion plans.

How was that for luck? Jenn had gone from having no assignments to two in one day.

She spent the rest of the afternoon responding to letters and planning tomorrow's column. So far, she'd written to a seventy-four-year-old widower who'd grown tired of warding off the advances of several unattached ladies in his bowling league and a bride whose future mother-in-law was refusing to attend the wedding ceremony unless it was performed at the church she attended, a church the bride considered a cult.

Jenn glanced at the clock above her desk. She still had time to read one more letter.

Dear Diana,

I'm a high-school senior and have received a scholarship to attend a college out of state. My parents don't think I'm ready to leave home and want me to attend the local junior college and stay in town. How do I convince them that I need to spread my wings?

Homebound Senior

Jenn slumped in her seat. At this point in her life, she was kicking herself for not spreading her own wings when she'd had the chance.

Ten years ago, she'd been the homecoming queen of Fairbrook High and had the teenage world at her feet. And now she was facing her class reunion, and her only claim to fame was that of being an advice columnist for the local paper.

So far, other than giving birth to her precious daughter, her adult life had been one big waste. She'd spent nearly a decade with a man who refused to put his wife and child above his gambling addiction, and now she was approaching her thirties with no real job, no real home . . . no real future.

Jenn certainly had a knack for advising the troubled people who wrote to Diana. Too bad she couldn't rewind the past and take some of the advice she dished out to others these days.

But she'd taken to heart an eye-opening realization she'd had a few months back, and from here on out, she was determined to make something of herself rather than rely on a man to make her happy.

She'd grown disillusioned when it came to love and marriage, and the letters and e-mails from the lovelorn she received daily didn't nurture the white picket-fence dream.

Maybe if her parents hadn't split up, if she had some kind of living example of a romance in full bloom, she would have been more inclined to believe in happy ever after.

Jenn returned her full attention to the letter on the screen, reading it one last time. Maybe it would be best if she responded to this one tomorrow, after her interviews, when her own future would seem a whole lot brighter.

After shutting off the computer, she dressed in a black suit and a pale blue blouse. Then she brushed her hair and used the curling iron on the ends.

While she leaned forward and applied lipstick, a pint-size knock tapped at the bathroom door, followed by Caitlyn's voice. "Mommy? What are you doing?"

"I'm getting ready for an appointment." Jenn opened the door, letting the five-year-old inside. "Grammy is going to watch you while I'm gone. Why don't you find your new markers and pick out a coloring book to take with you?"

"Okay." Instead of dashing off, as Jenn had expected her to do, Caitlyn remained in the doorway, a slow, bright-eyed smile stretching across her lips. "You look really pretty, Mommy."

"Thanks, honey."

Admittedly, Jenn had put a little extra effort into her appearance, but not for Jessica and the reunion gang.

"How come you're not wearing the necklace I gave you for Mother's Day?" Caitlyn asked.

Last month, in Sunday school, the kids had made gifts for their mothers out of red yarn, dry macaroni, and colored beads. Caitlyn had been so proud of her creation that she'd insisted

Jenn open it up the minute they got in the car. But as sweet as the gift had been, it wasn't at all a professional accent to business attire.

"You said you loved it," Caitlyn added.

"Oh, I do." Jenn turned and stooped to give her daughter a hug. "Thanks for reminding me. I'll put it on now."

"Want me to get it for you?" Caitlyn asked.

"It's too high for you to reach, honey. I put it in my jewelry box with my other valuables."

Jenn strode to the chest of drawers, where the jewelry box her grandparents had given her for her fifteenth birthday sat next to a picture of Caitlyn. She opened the lid, removed the necklace, and slipped it over her neck. A tag made out of masking tape and bearing Caitlyn's name scratched at her neck. She adjusted it, then turned to her daughter and grinned. "How do I look now?"

"Even prettier than before."

"Good. This meeting is really important, so I want to look my best." She would, of course, remove the handcrafted pasta necklace once she got in the car. She'd just have to remember to put it back on before she returned home tonight.

"Now give me a hug and a kiss good-bye."

"I love you a whole-lot-a-bunch, Mommy."

"I love you, too, honey."

After taking her daughter to the big house so her grandmother could watch her, Jenn climbed into her twelve-year-old Honda Civic and drove to the professional building across from Mulberry Park.

She didn't immediately spot Marc Alvarado's silver BMW, which was a bit disappointing. He hadn't been available when she'd called his office earlier, and she suspected that was still the case.

Either way, she did her best to put some confidence in her steps as she made her way to the red-brick building. Armed with a notepad, as well as the virtual press kit she'd downloaded from the company website, she entered the lobby and took the elevator all the way to the top floor.

At five minutes to four, she entered Alvarado Technologies, an imposing office that had been professionally decorated in forest green and shades of brown—and not very long ago, she realized. The scent of fresh paint and new furniture lingered in the air.

Floor-to-ceiling windows provided a panoramic view of the city, making both the man and his business even more impressive than ever.

A woman whose gray hair had been swept into a twist sat at a massive mahogany desk adorned with a couple of potted plants and a bouquet of open yellow roses. She glanced up from her work and smiled. "Can I help you?"

"I'm Jennifer Kramer from the *Times*. I have an appointment for an interview with Mr. Alvarado."

"Oh, yes. I talked to you on the telephone. I'm Elena." The woman rolled her chair away from the desk and stood. "Marc's been tied up in meetings all afternoon, but I expect him back any minute. Can I get you a cup of coffee while you wait?"

"No, thanks. I'm fine."

Elena was much older than Jenn had anticipated—late sixties to early seventies, maybe?—and seemed to look Jenn over for a moment. A slow grin softened the wrinkles on her face and lit her dark eyes. "That's a pretty necklace."

Jenn's hand plopped onto her chest, and she fingered the yarn and dry-pasta gift she'd meant to leave in the car. She'd been so busy rehearsing her interview questions that she'd forgotten all about it.

So much for her plan to come across completely professional.

"It . . . uh . . . was a gift from my five-year-old daughter." She thought about taking it off, but decided to let it stay put. If Elena or Marc thought she was somehow lacking because of it, so be it.

"It's really sweet. My little boy gave a similar one to me a long time ago, and it's still one of my most cherished possessions. I wore it until the pasta began to break apart."

Before Jenn could respond, the glass door swung open and Marc Alvarado swept in wearing the same sports jacket, the same dress shirt open at the collar, the same expressive brown eyes and heart-strumming grin that he'd worn earlier today when she'd met him at the newspaper office. Yet he seemed to be even more handsome in his own territory.

"I'm sorry I'm late," he told her.

"Don't be. I just arrived." She reached out her hand in greeting. "I'm Jennifer Kramer," she said, reminding him in case he'd forgotten her name.

As his fingers wrapped around hers again, encompassing her hand in the warmth of his grip, a heated rush zipped through her.

"I know who you are," he said, slowly releasing her.

Well, then, that made two of them. Now that they'd met, she didn't think she'd ever forget him.

His gaze dropped from her face to her chest and back again. He grinned, his hazel eyes glimmering like Gran Marnier in after-dinner candlelight. Sweet, smooth. Intoxicating.

"That's an interesting necklace," he said.

Her hand inadvertently returned to her chest and fingered a large piece of macaroni. "Thank you. I think so, too. The young artisan who designed and created it is someone near and dear to me."

"You don't say." Marc chuckled. "Come on. Let's go where we can talk."

He led her back to a private office boasting two brown leather chairs in front of a mahogany desk that bore neat stacks of paperwork.

This office, too, provided a view of the city. Yet instead of looking at the six or seven buildings that made up the Fairbrook skyline, Jenn's gaze was drawn to the park below, to the playground and the jogging path that wove around the lawn and meandered along the edge of the canyon, and to the people enjoying their leisure.

If this were her office, she'd have a difficult time focusing on work. She turned to Marc and smiled. "You have a great view."

"Thanks." He pointed to the leather chairs in front of his desk, indicating that she should choose one.

He waited for her, then took a seat across from her.

They made small talk at first, and she let him know that she'd done her homework by researching both him and his company on the Internet earlier. He answered her questions truthfully, yet modestly.

Several minutes into the ice-breaking chat, he sat back in his seat. "What I'd really like to talk about is the foundation I created and the scholarships I'm going to give out."

"Of course." She placed her notepad in her lap and clicked her ballpoint pen, releasing the tip.

"It's called the Elena Alvarado Foundation."

Elena? Wasn't that his receptionist? And *Alvarado* was his last name. Was that merely a coincidence . . . ?

"I assume the foundation was named after a relative," she said, suspecting his mother, his sister, or his wife. Her gaze casually drifted to his left hand. No wedding ring, but then again, a lot of married men didn't wear them.

"Elena's my aunt," he said. "She's also my office manager."

Interesting, Jenn thought as she began to sense a human-interest story in the making.

"I wanted to honor her for taking me in as a child, for loving me, believing in me, and encouraging me to be all that I could be. I owe a debt to that lady that I'll never be able to repay."

"How old were you when you went to live with her?" Jenn asked.

"I was a newborn. My mom was a teenager and didn't want to be burdened by a baby, so her *tía*, Elena, took me in. It was supposed to be a temporary solution, but my mother never had a change of heart."

"I'm sorry."

"Don't be. I came out way ahead. Elena provided me with a loving home. And from the first time she picked up a Little Golden Book and read it to me, she encouraged me to get an education."

"That's touching."

"I think so." He leaned back in his seat. "When I was in the third grade, she told me that I was going to college one day. There'd never been any question about it. She'd had some kind of vision."

"Is she psychic?"

"She says no, but I know people who'd disagree with her."

"Are you one of them?"

Marc shrugged. "She definitely has a gift. That's the only explanation I have."

Interesting, Jenn thought for the second time since entering the office. "So you proved her right."

"I really didn't have to prove anything. It all just fell into place. Besides, school was a breeze for me. It was easy to excel."

"Your aunt didn't have to push you?"

"Not at all. Life was good, and love was plentiful. I did it because I wanted to. The only thing she did to encourage me was to make learning a game."

"How so?"

Marc paused a beat, as though he needed to think through his response. "Elena had a limited income while I was growing up, so we never got a chance to visit theme parks like Disneyland or Sea World. Instead, she took me on adventures to the local library. We'd visit foreign countries and take rocket ships to the moon."

"It sounds like fun."

"It was. In fact, she enjoyed learning so much that she decided to take adult-education classes and eventually managed to earn a high-school diploma of her own."

Jenn, who'd gone to theme parks a lot while growing up, couldn't help feeling as though she'd missed out on something special by not having library adventures. And she made a mental note to attempt something similar with Caitlyn in the near future.

"My plan isn't just to provide scholarships to low-income students," Marc added. "I'd really like to offer them to the kids who are struggling to stay in school, kids who've got a few strikes against them but still want to pursue higher education. So in some cases, their grade-point average wouldn't be the determining factor in deciding who would receive a scholarship and who wouldn't."

"That's definitely a unique approach."

"I want to meet with each applicant and find out if he or she is willing to sign a contract to put their education first. Sort of a business venture, you know? I'd offer them work during the summer, too."

"You're planning to mentor them?" Jenn asked.

"Yeah. I guess that's what I'd be doing."

Jenn had no idea what to say. The man and his game plan had thrown her for a loop. He was offering kids a lot more than money. He was handing them a lifeline.

"You know," she finally said, "there's a man in town named Ramon Gonzales. I think you ought to talk to him. He's working with a sports organization that's geared to kids at risk. I'm not suggesting that you work together, but I definitely think you'd have some things to share with each other. Ideas that might help his organization and your foundation at the same time."

"Is he related to Eddie Gonzales?"

"Yes, he's his younger brother. Do you know Eddie?"

"We went to school together."

Jenn had gone to school with Eddie, too. "At Fairbrook High?"

"We were in the same economics class."

Jenn hadn't taken economics, but surely they'd passed each other in the hall once or twice. "I ought to remember you, but I don't."

"I was pretty quiet and unassuming, so I don't think many people did."

She supposed that was a nice way of saying that he wasn't popular, but she couldn't understand how a guy like him could have slipped under her radar. She didn't care how shy he'd been.

Without being too obvious, Jenn studied Marc, trying to remember all the glossy photos of her classmates but coming up with a mental blank.

She'd been busy during her high-school years, and her life had been a social whirl. But what girl would have missed noting a guy like Marc?

Maybe he only attended FHS for a short time and transferred to some other school. If she had any idea where she might have packed her old yearbooks, she'd go home and do a search. But she'd stacked boxes of stuff at the back of the garage, and she had no idea where to look.

Marc glanced at his watch, then looked at her with soulful eyes she could have sworn she'd seen somewhere before—in her dreams, maybe?

"Would you mind if we finished this interview at Café Del Sol?"

His question and the intensity of his gaze threw her an unexpected curve. Was he asking her to have dinner with him?

She cocked her head slightly to the side. "Excuse me?"

"I worked through lunch today, and I'm starving. I'm going to have a hard time focusing if I don't put something in my stomach."

Oh, okay. The question had been practical, and his mind was definitely still on the business at hand.

"Sure." She made one last note on her pad and put her pen away. She'd planned to get something to eat before heading for Jessica's house anyway.

Marc opened the door and waited for her to walk out of his office first, which was merely a polite gesture and nothing for her to read into. They were just two hungry people grabbing a bite to eat while they continued to work.

Yet as they walked down the hall and toward the exit, she couldn't seem to quell a feminine flutter of excitement that suggested it was a whole lot more.

Surely the rush was due in part to the unexpected chance to learn more about the real Marc Alvarado and the opportunity to create a story that would dazzle Frank Bagley into hiring her as a full-time reporter.

But something deep inside wasn't buying it.

Not when she got that same buzz whenever she caught a glimpse of the successful businessman's heart-strumming smile and gorgeous brown eyes.

Chapter Four

As Marc led Jenn out of his private office, he glanced toward Elena's desk. Her files had been put away, her chair had been pushed into place, and her computer screen was dark.

He was glad to see she'd left for the day. She always took more interest in his comings and goings than a typical office manager would, which was understandable. And he'd always been okay with that. But since she knew about the unrequited crush he used to have on Jenn, he didn't want to encourage any speculation or romantic notions. All he needed was for her to think she could help imaginary things along.

After he locked up the office, he and Jenn took the elevator to the lobby.

"Thanks for being a good sport about this" he said as they left the building.

"You mean about dinner? Actually, this works out great. I have another appointment after our interview, and I was going to have to eat by myself. Now I don't have to ward off any sympathetic stares."

"What do you mean?" Marc had eaten his share of meals alone—a lot of them, especially when he'd moved to California as a freshman in high school—and he'd never picked up on any sympathy. Nor any stares at all, for that matter. He'd gotten used to eating alone back then, which was good. These days, it seemed he was always on the go, so he grabbed a bite whenever and wherever he had a chance.

"I guess it's just me," she said. "I don't like going to a restaurant by myself, so I usually find a drive-through and eat in the car."

"That sounds like it would be more of a pain to me."

They walked across the parking lot and made their way to the storefront shops and eateries that were located along Applewood, the street that bordered the east side of the park. They stopped in front of Café Del Sol, a trendy bistro that provided sidewalk dining.

Marc had spotted the colorful striped awnings and café-style black tables and chairs from his office window. He'd also passed the place on his way to the bank and had been planning to try it out eventually. So now seemed as good a time as any.

"Do you want to sit indoors or out?" he asked. "It looks like they have heaters in case the breeze kicks up and it gets chilly."

"Then let's eat outside."

A young man wearing black slacks and a crisp white shirt stood at a podium and smiled. "Two for dinner?"

"Yes," Marc said. "And outside, if those heaters are working."

"They are." The man snatched two menus and led them to the back of the patio, next to a red bougainvillea that grew in a big clay pot. He pulled out a chair for Jenn, and she sat at a white-linen–draped table adorned by several votive candles and a small vase of daisies.

Marc wondered if she would notice the simple flowers, if she still favored them like she had in school.

He supposed it really didn't matter.

When they took a seat, the waiter passed out the menus, then returned with water, a basket of homemade bread, and butter.

Jenn studied the list of entrees and sides, but Marc found himself studying her instead. She was still just as pretty as ever, although he couldn't help missing those go-team smiles that always reached her eyes.

But who was he to find that the least bit remarkable? Time had a way of changing things, especially him. And to be honest, after years of being considered both a top-notch student and a second-rate classmate, it had taken Marc time to deal with the changes his late growth spurt had put into play.

He'd always been a fast learner, so he'd caught on to the intricacies of attraction and flirtation quickly. But that didn't mean he hadn't struggled some with the whole male/female mating ritual in the beginning. There'd been the typical first-date jitters and awkwardness, and he'd decided that some things were best muddled through when a guy was still a teenager. Of course, now that he'd accumulated a healthy stock portfolio and an impressive bank account, women just naturally flocked to him, and the awkwardness had disappeared.

A lot of guys might have let that go to their heads, but Marc never had been like other guys. And when he settled down with one woman, he wanted her to be able to accept the ninety-pound weakling he'd once been. The guy who sometimes still felt a little backward in a crowd.

He opened the menu, yet his thoughts were on Jenn and the changes that had taken place in her life over the past ten years.

How was she dealing with her divorce? Was she still grieving and hurt? Was she glad to be free?

Those weren't the kinds of questions he could ask over a business-related dinner, which is what this was.

Nor could he write a letter to Dear Diana and ask, although a wry grin tugged at his lips at the crazy thought.

Dear Diana,
   People always tell you their deepest, darkest secrets and fears. So now it's your turn. Why did you get a divorce? How are you feeling about it? Have you been scarred for life? Are you ready to date?

                                        Curious in Fairbrook

Marc's grin morphed into a full-blown smile as he imagined her response in print.

> Dear Curious,
>   I made the mistake of settling for the wrong guy and was never really happy. I can't help feeling as though the last ten years of my life were a complete waste. What I wouldn't give to be able to wind back the clock, return to high school, and start over. Maybe, had I given the right guy a chance, if I'd been willing to wait for him ...

Frank Bagley had mentioned something about Jenn putting a personal spin on her responses, but going the Dear Diana route was too wild to contemplate.

Still, earlier this afternoon, while heading to the accountant's office, Marc had picked up a copy of the *Fairbrook Times* along the way. Instead of reading the front page or checking out the business section of the newspaper, which was his practice, he'd turned to section B and the social pages, looking for the Dear Diana column. But he supposed he didn't know enough about her these days to pick up on the personal spin Frank had mentioned.

Yet her advice had been solid to those who'd written in, and Marc could see why she'd get a nod from the editor.

On a whim, he said, "I read your column today."

The menu, which had been blocking Jenn's face, dropped six or more inches, and she looked at him, lips parted.

He couldn't quite tell whether she was flattered or embarrassed. Either way, she seemed uncomfortable.

"I wish Frank wouldn't have mentioned that," she said. "He knew I wanted to remain anonymous."

"Don't worry. Your secret's safe with me." Marc tossed her a friendly smile, but as their gazes met, something blood-stirring rushed between them. He'd be darned if he knew exactly what that something was, but he'd felt it whenever he'd looked at her in the past. Only this time, she seemed to be as affected by it as he was.

Doing his best to shake it off, he said, "I thought your advice to that secretary was pretty good."

"Thanks." Jenn reached for her glass of water and took a sip.

According to the secretary who'd written to Diana, her boss was having an affair with a cocktail waitress at a bar he frequented, and the secretary was morally opposed to what he was doing. She felt the need to call the boss's wife or to at least be more forthcoming than she'd been in the past. Still, she needed her job and couldn't afford to quit or allow herself to be fired.

"Telling her to confront her boss was the best way to handle it," Marc added.

"I thought so, too. It wasn't her place to tell the man's wife what he was up to, although my heart goes out to that poor woman, too. I think it's terrible when people make a commitment to each other to be best friends and life partners, and then one of them cheats."

Had Jason cheated on Jenn? Had he given her reason not to trust him?

Marc supposed he shouldn't try reading into her comment. And it really wasn't his business, but he couldn't help saying, "It sounds as though you can easily sympathize with the boss's wife."

"Yes, but not because I had to deal with another woman, although the trust issue definitely came into play."

Marc suspected she was about to open up and tell him the rest, to mention her divorce. Instead, she sat up straighter and seemed to stiffen.

"I guess we're not here to interview you," Marc said, making light of the fact that she'd flashed a yellow caution light when they'd veered off topic.

"That's okay," she said, lowering her guard again. "It's probably not a big secret. My ex had a gambling addiction, and he chose the ponies and the casinos over my daughter and me."

"I'm sorry."

"Me, too—for my daughter's sake. But it's over now."

Was it? When people had serious gambling issues, there were usually financial repercussions, some of them long-lasting.

Had Jenn been left to deal with creditors? Or maybe even bankruptcy?

"You know," she said, lowering her menu again and peering at him over the top, "getting back to the interview, I'm really impressed with the goals of your scholarship foundation. And I'm curious about your selection process. How will you choose the recipients?"

"They'll have to fill out applications. And they'll be required to provide letters of recommendation. There's also going to be an interview."

"You'd said you'd want to meet with them personally."

"The applicants will have to meet Elena, too. I'd like for her to have a say in who gets a scholarship and who doesn't."

Jenn lowered her menu, set it on the table, leaned forward, and cast him a warm smile. "I think it's nice that you're including her by letting her sit in on the process."

"Oh, it's not as a courtesy to her. It's just that she . . ." Marc paused, unsure whether he wanted to explain or not.

"Off the record?" he asked.

"Sure."

"It's that . . . gift . . . of hers that I mentioned."

"Her psychic ability?"

"No, it's not that."

Jenn furrowed her brow. "Then what is it?"

"I'm not sure what you'd call it. Some people might consider her a psychic, but she says she's not."

"You believe her?"

"She, more than anyone, ought to know what to call it. I suppose you could say that when she prays, she seems to have some kind of hotline to Heaven, a communication that goes both ways."

At least, it sure seemed that way to Marc.

He wished that he could say he shared her unwavering faith, but he didn't. Yet he still came to respect her divine connection—or whatever it was.

"She's got a way of just knowing things," he added. "Knowing people. It's hard to explain, but let's just say that I've grown to appreciate her foresight, even if I don't always end up taking her advice. So I definitely want her to meet the scholarship applicants."

Jenn graced him with a smile that caused his heart to lurch. "Elena sounds like a special lady."

"She is."

The deeply religious widow was generous, too. Taking in an extra mouth hadn't been easy on a limited income, but she'd never complained. She also gave regularly to the church, even when money was scarce and she'd had no idea how they'd pay the rent. "Don't worry," she would tell Marc time and again. "The Lord will provide." And, inevitably, the money would show up somehow, either with an unexpected side job someone offered her or when a check came out of the blue.

Fortunately, the waiter stopped by at that time to take their orders, and the conversation hit a lull.

Yet that didn't mean the pheromones had stopped swirling overhead. Or that Marc's heart rate had returned to normal.

Nor did it mean that he would make an attempt to pursue anything more than a professional relationship with Jenn. After all, he still had some of the old geek pride, and she'd had her chance.

The problem was, he was still attracted to her. And even if he did want to gloat and let her know what she'd missed out on, he didn't want to get involved with a woman who couldn't appreciate the man he really was—the inner man who had nothing to do with the status he'd achieved and the money he'd earned.

Over the past ten years, Marc had convinced himself there wasn't anything more to Jenn Kramer than met the eye.

But as he watched her reach across the table, pick up a fallen daisy petal and study it almost reverently, he couldn't help wondering if maybe he'd been wrong.

As much as he'd like to let Jenn and the past go, he wasn't quite ready to wrap up their interview, eat dinner, and send her on her way. Yet he couldn't for the life of him decide on a reason to stretch things out—not one that made any sense. Nor could he explain why he found himself suggesting that she get involved in something that would keep them in contact.

"You know," he said, "I haven't been back in town for ages and don't have a lot of contacts right now. But both my attorney and my accountant suggested I get at least the skeleton of a board of directors chosen."

She let the daisy petal drop to the table and looked at him as though wondering where he was going with that.

To be honest, he wasn't entirely sure. But the words slid out before he could reel them back in and give them more consideration. "Would you be interested in serving on the board?"

Her lips parted even more. "*Me?*"

"Why not?"

"I . . . uh . . ." She cleared her throat. "Actually, while I hate to admit this to anyone, I don't even have a college degree. It seems both wild and bogus for me to take on a position with a scholarship foundation."

And it was wild and bogus for him to try and drag her into his life, yet he had. Shaking off his reservations, he leaned back in his seat. "You're actually a good choice. You've got connections with the newspaper. And you'd be helpful in creating brochures and writing letters."

She seemed to actually contemplate his suggestion, and when she finally looked up, her gaze burrowed into his. "I've never been offered a board position before, and it's an honor to be asked. It's also a cause I could easily champion . . ."

"I get the idea there's a big 'but' coming."

Jenn took a deliberate breath, then slowly let it out. "All right. Since I'm only working part-time right now, I don't mind helping out, but I don't want to get caught up in volunteer work when I'm seriously seeking full-time employment."

She hadn't come right out and said it, but she hadn't needed to. Marc could read between the lines. Jason's gambling addiction *had* taken a toll on her finances. It wasn't so much that she wanted a full-time job; she needed one.

Again, a response rolled off his tongue before he had the chance to stop it. "I also have some brochures and news releases that need to be written for Alvarado Technologies. So if you're interested in working for me in that respect, I could hire you to do both jobs."

She waited a beat before responding, and he watched her brow form a V in concentration—much like it had when he'd tutored her in algebra.

"Of course, it's only a temporary position," he added.

"That's fine. Although, to be honest, I've never created brochures before. But I'm willing to give it a try. And I can definitely write press releases. So, yes, I'd like to work for you. I'll have to file my story first, but I should be able to do that in the morning. When do you want me to start?"

He couldn't very well backpedal and take back his offer now. "How about tomorrow at ten? I have a meeting first thing and want to be sure I'm at the office when you arrive."

"Won't Elena be there?"

Yes, she'd be there. But all he needed was for his aunt to get some crazy idea about playing matchmaker.

Jenn might consider Marc Alvarado an eligible bachelor now, but he already knew how she felt about Marcos "The Brain" Taylor.

And Marc didn't want to go down that path again.

Chapter Five

The next morning, Marc stopped by Fairbrook High and talked to both guidance counselors, as well as Mr. Sturgis, the principal.

At the end of their meeting, Bob Sturgis stood and shook Marc's hand. "It's always nice to have our students come back to visit. But we really appreciate seeing those who return and try to pay it forward. You're doing a wonderful thing with that scholarship foundation, Marc. But correct me if I'm wrong. Wasn't your last name Taylor when you were in school?"

"Yes, but neither of my parents played a part in my life. So when I was in college, as a tribute to my aunt, I legally changed my surname to hers."

"I'm sure that pleased her."

Bowled over and touched beyond measure had been more like it. Elena hadn't known what he'd done until they'd called "Marcos Ramon Alvarado" at the commencement ceremonies. And afterward, when she'd looked over his diploma, her tears had started anew.

As Marc and Bob walked together down the corridor that led to the administrative secretary's desk, the older man said, "I remember your aunt. She was a member of our parents' group."

Marc nodded. Even though Elena's work schedule hadn't

allowed for much free time, she'd managed to bake cookies whenever they were needed and to go to a couple of meetings.

"My wife taught adult-education classes," Bob added, "and she told me that your aunt attended school at nights to get her high-school diploma."

"It took her several years, but she finally made it. I'm proud of her."

"Which, I'm sure, is why you named the foundation after her."

Marc nodded, although that had been only one of many reasons.

When they reached the secretary's desk, Bob slowed to a stop. "Eileen? Can you please give me one of those yellow fliers?"

"Of course." The woman took one from the top of the stack and handed it to the principal, who then offered it to Marc.

"Your class is having a ten-year reunion," Bob added. "This has all the details."

Marc only gave the flier a cursory glance, since he had no intention of attending. For the most part, high school had been a real pain for him and the other kids who'd never found a place for themselves. But there was no need to mention that to Bob. "Thanks. I'll have to check my schedule to see if I'm free that night."

Either way, Marc wasn't going.

After leaving the high-school administrative building, he opened the driver's door of his vehicle. As he climbed behind the wheel, he tossed the flier onto the passenger seat, where it would remain until he got a chance to throw it out at home. Then he drove back to the office, hoping to arrive before Jenn did.

In the lobby of the building, he glanced at his wristwatch, realizing he still had a couple of minutes to spare. So he stopped at Mug Shots, a coffee cart located near the elevators, and picked up a cup of decaf for Elena. He usually had to remind her to take a break, to have lunch, or to clock out for the day.

He'd never expected her to be so industrious, so determined to run his office efficiently.

Over the past five years, he'd tried time and again to subsidize her income, but she'd always refused his money. "Don't worry about me," she would say. "I've been blessed and have everything I need."

But while she might believe she'd been blessed, she deserved so much more than what she had. So Marc had done the next best thing. He'd asked her to work for him, telling her he hadn't been able to find an office manager who was discreet or who had a sixth sense about people.

"Stick with me until I can hire a competent staff," he'd told her.

Fortunately for him, Elena had jumped on the offer and was doing an amazing job organizing the new office and setting up interviews. She also took great pride in looking after her boss.

Marc entered the office with an insulated cup of decaffeinated coffee and two packets of sugar. "Ready for a break?"

His aunt looked up from her desk and smiled. With silver-gray hair pulled back into a twist and a sparkle in her dark brown eyes, she looked ten years younger than a woman who'd turned seventy last month.

She saved the work she'd completed on an Excel spreadsheet, then spun her chair to face him. "How did your meeting at the school go?"

"Great." He handed her the coffee and sugar. "They have several kids who fit our parameters. So as soon as I can develop the application forms, I'll forward them to the school administrative assistant. How are things going here?"

"I coordinated and scheduled that meeting with the accountant and the attorney, and unless you've made any appointments I'm not aware of, they'll be here tomorrow at three-thirty."

"That's fine." Marc glanced at the clock. It was almost ten, so Jenn would be arriving soon.

Elena moved a file and repositioned one of several potted plants on her desk that had added warmth and a homey feel to the office. "Do you have time to pull up a chair and join me?"

There was an official break room down the hall, but until Marc hired more staff, there was no one to answer the telephone or greet clients, so Elena rarely strayed far from her desk or ventured into the kitchenette to brew a pot of coffee.

Before he could take a seat, Elena glanced toward the glass door that opened to the elevators. "It looks like your new hire is here."

"*Temporary* hire," he corrected.

"I didn't realize that your new office employee was the same woman who interviewed you yesterday. And I left to meet my bridge group before I got a chance to tell you that *Ms. Kramer* looks a lot like *the* Jennifer Kramer who broke your heart in high school."

Marc took a sip of coffee, not wanting to have this conversation now. Not while Jenn was approaching the glass door to the office.

"Why didn't you tell me what you had in mind?" Elena asked.

"I didn't see any reason to. Besides, she doesn't even recognize me. So what difference does it make? She has no idea there's any kind of connection. And I'd like to keep it that way."

As Jenn swung open the door and entered the office, he could have sworn Elena uttered something under her breath. But his focus was on Jenn, whose breezy smile turned his heart on end. She wasn't wearing anything special today, just slacks and a blouse, yet it took some concentrated effort not to gape at her in awe.

"Good morning," she said, her brow furrowing, her gaze searching his expression. "Is something wrong?"

Oh, for Pete's sake. He must have been gawking at her in

spite of himself. Morphing out of geek mode, which seemed to be his default, he sobered. "Nothing's wrong. Would you like a cup of coffee?" He could go back downstairs and get her one.

"No, thanks. I'm a tea drinker. And I've already had plenty this morning."

"Then let's get started." He made the mistake of glancing at Elena, who was sporting a Cheshire-cat grin. Something told him he'd better steer Jenn away from his aunt.

As Marc led Jenn to the office she would use while she was here, he realized he was going to have to set Elena straight. He might have had a major crush on Jenn as a teenager, but that didn't mean he had feelings for her now. At least not the kind that insisted no other woman would do.

He wasn't in high school anymore and pining over the only girl who'd interested him.

Back then, his aunt had picked up on his infatuation and advised him to be patient. "Love takes time to develop," she'd said. "One day, Jennifer will see you for who you really are, and then love will blossom. I'm sure of it."

That was the only thing Marc could ever remember his aunt saying that didn't eventually come to pass. But so what if it hadn't? Other things far more important than that had happened just the way she'd said they would—like her insistence that he would not only be accepted at Stanford, but that finances wouldn't be an issue.

"That scholarship will come through, *mijo*. Just wait and see." And as if her words had drifted straight up to the Almighty's throne, Marc had received a full-ride academic scholarship and moved to northern California that fall.

But that was then.

Things were much different now.

As Marc opened the door to Jenn's office and waited for her to enter, he caught the alluring scent of her shampoo—something springtime fresh and laced with citrus—which compelled him to take a second whiff.

As she stepped inside, she surveyed the room, which wasn't nearly as large as his.

"This is great," she said, her eyes brightening as though she really meant it.

"I'm glad you like it." He nodded toward the small mahogany desk with the new computer that was already up and running. "The drawers are fully stocked with supplies, but if you need anything else, just let me know."

"What would you like me to do first?"

He approached the desk, where he'd left his notes and files for her to go over. "If you'll read through these papers, you'll get an idea of what I envisioned for the brochures and what I hope to accomplish with them. I left instructions for the artwork and details that need to be included. You'll also find a couple of samples to use as a model. Why don't you work on a rough draft? Then we can go over it together."

"All right." She placed her hands on the top of the chair's backrest, but she didn't sit. She merely looked at him as though waiting for him to leave her alone.

Or was there something else going on?

He tried to read her expression, but the geek in him kept getting in the way.

"Well, then," he said, taking a step back. "I guess I'd better let you get busy."

When her gaze locked on his, he was struck by the sincerity in her eyes.

"Thanks, Marc."

For getting out of her hair? For providing her with a job and an office?

Rather than ask, he tossed her an unaffected smile and accepted her appreciation. "You're welcome."

Then, true to his word, he left her to her work.

But returning to his own office wasn't nearly as easy as he'd thought it would be. Knowing she was just down the hall did a real number on his ability to focus, and it was nearly twelve-thirty by the time he finally threw up his hands and decided to check in on her.

He found her seated at the desk, studying his notes, then glancing at the computer screen, where the mock layout she'd created was displayed. But instead of looking over her shoulder at what she'd done, he felt compelled to watch her, noting the way her hair brushed against her cheek. The way she nibbled on her bottom lip.

Finally, he knocked lightly on the doorjamb.

She looked up from her work and, upon seeing him, broke into a pretty smile. "Oh, hi. Come on in."

He remained rooted in the doorway. "It's lunchtime."

She checked the clock on the wall as though questioning his comment. "I can't believe it. I was so involved in what I was doing that the morning whizzed by."

"Would you like to get a bite to eat? There's a deli not far from here that offers great sandwiches. They have salads, too."

"Thanks, but I'm meeting my mother and my daughter at the park for a picnic." She shrugged. "You know how it is."

Actually, he didn't. And a surge of disappointment rushed through him, reminding him of the rejection he'd suffered the day she'd shut him out. But he shrugged it off.

"Have fun," he told her before heading to Elena's desk.

"Are you up for a sandwich?" he asked his aunt.

"I'm sorry, Marc. I packed a lunch today."

Then he'd just go to Dagwood's Deli by himself. "That's okay. I'll be back in a few minutes."

Yet as he walked to the elevator, intending to dine alone, he couldn't help wishing he'd packed his own lunch.

And that he could eat it in Mulberry Park.

Chapter Six

As Marc sat outside Dagwood's Deli munching on barbecue potato chips and eating a turkey on sourdough, he couldn't help checking out the park, hoping to spot Jenn having lunch with her mother and daughter.

Sure enough, she and her mom were seated at a picnic table, watching several children play on a colorful climbing structure.

He watched her talk to her mom, saw her nod and smile. As she took a bite of her sandwich, a little girl in pigtails, her hair a darker shade of blond, ran up to her and chattered animatedly about something. After listening intently, Jenn wrapped her arms around the child and gave her a hug.

Marc had spent a lot of time in high school studying his teenage crush, but there was something even more appealing about her now that he'd spotted a maternal side to her.

He'd never actually dated any single moms before, although he hadn't avoided them. One of the guys he used to work with once told him that he preferred only to go out with women who had children. "For the most part," the guy had said, "they're more responsible and less self-centered. They also tend to be a lot more nurturing than those who are unattached."

Marc hadn't given it much thought before now, but as he

watched Jenn with her daughter, he wondered if his coworker's observation was true.

If he asked her out . . .

Whoa. Who said anything about *dating* her?

Besides, did he really want to complicate his life in that way?

No, he didn't.

But after he finished his lunch, instead of going to the office, he found himself turning left instead of right, crossing the street and walking to the park.

It was warmer than it had been yesterday, a perfect day for eating outdoors. Birds chirped in the treetops, and the vast array of colorful flowers near the water fountain had turned toward the sun and opened in concert.

As Marc neared the green fiberglass table where Jenn sat, he noted that she was still wearing that macaroni necklace, and his coworker's words came to mind: considerate, more nurturing.

When Jenn looked up and saw him, her breath caught. "Oh. Hi."

"I was heading back to the office and saw you out here," he explained. "So I thought I'd stop by and say hello."

Her lips parted as though she was dumbstruck by his presence.

Great. Super Geek strikes again. On his first day at Fairbrook High, he'd made the mistake of sitting at the wrong table in the cafeteria and had been chased off by a couple of jocks. Had he made a mistake in crashing Jenn's family get-together?

"I . . . uh . . ." She turned to her mom and managed a smile. "This is my boss, Mr. Alvarado."

He reached out his hand in greeting. "Let's not be formal. Call me Marc."

"Susan Kramer." The woman smiled as though she'd met someone noteworthy or famous. "I've heard a lot of nice things about you."

Marc glanced at Jenn, whose cheeks were a telltale shade of pink.

Had she been talking about him?

Jenn turned to her mom. "I didn't realize you even knew who Marc was."

"I did a Google search," Susan said. "And it's no wonder that the community has welcomed you with open arms. The Fairbrook branch of your company will provide jobs for a lot of people."

Jenn's cheeks grew pinker still.

Marc had gotten used to women finding him attractive, but he'd realized many of them were especially enamored with his financial success. Some guys might find that helpful or even appealing, but he didn't. Sure, he hoped the woman he got involved with would be proud of him and his accomplishments, but he didn't want his success to be the deciding factor.

What would happen if he lost his money or was crippled or scarred in some way? He wanted a woman to be interested in him because of the real man inside. And he wanted to know that she would stick by his side no matter what the future might bring.

Before he could conjure a graceful exit, Jenn's daughter, the cute little girl in pigtails, skipped up to the bench. "Can I have a cookie?"

"Did you finish your sandwich?"

"Yes, but not the yucky crust. I threw that part in the trash."

"And the apple slices?"

When the child nodded, Jenn reached into a brown paper sack, withdrew a plastic baggie that held what looked to be homemade chocolate-chip cookies, and gave one to her.

"Thanks, Mommy."

"Jennifer," Marc said so the little girl would hear. "Did I tell you how much I like that pretty necklace?"

The pixie turned to him and grinned, her eyes bright. "I could make one for you, too. Some men wear necklaces, like the man who came to see Daddy and wanted money. He had a big gold chain."

A bookie, Marc suspected, but he smiled at the child, noting that while she looked a bit like her mother, she favored her father in looks, too, getting the best of both of them. "If you have time someday, that would be great."

Caitlyn lifted the cookie to take a bite, then paused. "Mommy, will you come and push me in the swing before you have to go back to work?"

Susan quickly got to her feet. "I'll do it, honey." Then she ushered the child back to the playground, leaving Jenn and Marc alone.

He had the feeling that had been her plan all along, but he figured he'd never know for sure.

For a moment, he considered asking Jenn out to dinner so that he could get to know her as an adult and let her have a chance to meet the real Marcos. But in spite of his self-confidence and accomplishments in the business world, as well as having a couple of successful romantic relationships under his belt, when it came to Jenn, he still harbored a little more adolescent insecurity than he was willing to admit.

"Well," he said, "I'd better get back to work."

"Me, too." Jenn got to her feet. "I'll be right behind you."

As Marc turned and made his way back to the office, he had the strongest compulsion to look over his shoulder. He couldn't be sure, but he had an unshakable feeling that Jenn was watching every step he took. But he didn't dare look.

He would have been disappointed to learn he was wrong.

Jenn watched Marc cross the lawn until he reached the sidewalk. Then she finally tore her gaze away and went in search of her mother.

Susan Kramer was returning from the swings at a pretty

good clip and grinning like a yenta. "I have a really good feeling about you and Marc hitting it off."

Jenn crossed her arms. "I can't believe you did that."

Her mom's smile drooped, and her brow lifted. "Did what?"

"Implied that Marc was a great catch. And to his *face*." She tucked a strand of hair behind her ear. "What's worse, you made it sound as though I'd been talking about him at home."

"I said I did a Google search. And I *did*."

So had Jenn, but that was beside the point.

"He clearly would be perfect for you," her mother added. "He's tall, dark, handsome, successful, rich. . . . What more could you ask for?"

"*Mommm,*" Jenn said, dragging out the word. "Come on. I'm working for him. He's my *boss*. I don't want to jeopardize a paying position right now. Besides, what makes you think he'd be interested in me? After all, I'm . . ." She glanced at the slide, watched her daughter climb up the steps. "Well, let's just say it's going to take a big man to step into a ready-made family and to be the husband and father Jason never was."

"Marc Alvarado would be lucky to have you, Jennifer. Any man would."

Yeah, right. Even with a FICO score that had dropped to the cellar? Jenn blew out a sigh of resignation. Not that she wasn't working on paying off her debt and improving that score, but it was going to take time—a *lot* of time.

"And he'd be even luckier to have Caitlyn to round out his family." Her mom's glowing smile threatened to split her face in two. "Didn't you notice how sweet he was with her?"

"Yes, I saw that." And to be honest, she'd quit thinking of him as her employer right then. Instead, she'd momentarily considered him a potential romantic interest. And that was not only crazy—it was unthinkable.

"You're too young to be alone," her mom added.

"I'm not alone, Mom. I have you and Caitlyn."

"Yes, but you need more than us."

"No, I don't. And even if I did, I'm not going to throw myself at the first eligible bachelor I meet."

"Why not? My mother always used to say that it was just as easy to fall in love with a rich man as a poor man. And from what I've read, that company Marc owns is worth millions."

Jenn smiled. "Then what happened to all Daddy's millions?"

Her mom chuffed. "I didn't listen to *my* mother. But looking back, I wish that I had."

"Then you wouldn't have had me," Jenn said, looking at her own daughter and realizing how much her life would lack had she not married Jason and had his child.

"I hope you're not down on matrimony because neither of our marriages worked out."

"You have to admit," Jenn reminded her, "that we *are* two for two."

"I know. But try not to let it make you bitter. Some people are really happy, no matter how old or how young they are when they tie the knot."

"I'm not down on men and marriage," Jenn said. "It's just that I made a big mistake by jumping into a relationship so young."

"Your father and I married young."

"Case in point."

Her mom's eyes grew misty. "We were happy once."

Jenn couldn't remember when. And try as she might, she just couldn't seem to believe in happy ever after anymore.

"You know," Jenn admitted, "I thought marriage was my only option after high-school graduation, but that wasn't true. I wish I would have gone to college first and then gotten married when I was older and wiser. And I wish that you and Daddy would have encouraged me to do that."

"You weren't a studious child," her mother said. "And you never brought home the kind of grades that would have led us to believe you were college material."

Maybe not, but Jenn could have excelled in school if she'd wanted to. She'd loved working on the yearbook staff and had pulled As in journalism, even if, admittedly, her heart hadn't been in math or science. The trouble was, she'd been one of the popular kids and extremely social, so homework had always taken a backseat to fun and extracurricular activities.

"Besides," her mom said, "you were in love."

Had she been? She really wasn't sure what she'd felt for Jason. Attraction, to be sure. But over the years she'd wondered if she'd been riding on the tail of high-school popularity and all that homecoming king and queen hype, which the entire senior class had bought into when it had voted her and Jason the couple most likely to get married.

Last night, at the reunion meeting, she'd learned that Danny Litman, the guy voted most likely to succeed, had gone on to do just that. However, Marcos "The Brain" Taylor, the valedictorian who'd been in the running for that position and had shown even more promise than Danny, seemed to have disappeared from the face of the earth.

So who knew what the future might bring?

She wondered what would have happened if she and Jason had continued to date and had enrolled in the local junior college. Would they have eventually outgrown each other? Or would their marriage have been better? Stronger? More durable and better able to withstand life's storms?

That was the trouble with hindsight. It usually pointed out the error of one's choices, but there was still no guarantee of actual outcomes.

Either way, she wished her parents had tried to talk her out of marriage and into college. There was a great big world that went beyond Fairbrook city limits. But at eighteen, how had she been able to know that?

Jenn had grown up believing that life was a modest home on a quiet street in Fairbrook, that all fathers went to work at blue collar jobs and most mothers were housewives. That parents were content when their kids had average GPAs and an occasional mention on the honor roll with no effort whatsoever.

That college was only for students like Danny and Marcos. And that a pretty smile and a full calendar of social events was enough to guarantee a bright and happy future.

"Mommy," Caitlyn said, drawing Jenn's attention away from the dark realities of the past and back into the sunlight of the here and now.

Jenn turned to see her daughter carrying a pink Gerber daisy with a short stem.

"This is for you, Mommy. Somebody left it on the teeter-totter, and I found it. Isn't it pretty?"

"It sure is. Thanks, honey."

"You can take it back to work with you," Caitlyn added.

"I'll do that." Jenn looked at her watch. She still had a few minutes left in her lunch hour, but maybe she ought to start back now. No need to be late on her first day.

After giving her daughter a hug good-bye, she brushed a kiss on her mom's cheek, then returned to the office. She was a little uneasy about seeing Marc after her mom's comments, but she figured she might as well get it over with.

However, when she reached the eighth floor, stepped out of the elevator, and looked through the glass door and into the office, Elena was the only one in sight.

"Good afternoon," Jenn said as she entered. "Did you have a nice lunch?"

The older woman smiled warmly. "It was all right. And it was quiet, which gave me a chance to read for a while."

"Good." Jenn peered down the hall, wondering if Marc had gone into his office already.

Apparently, she'd been caught craning her neck, because Elena said, "Marc had to leave. Two of our best customers have gotten into a tiff, and he's going to try and smooth things over."

"Will it hurt business if they don't work things out?"

"No, it won't hurt us at all. But Marc's always been a good mediator."

That was yet another plus, Jenn thought as she twirled the

short stem of the pink daisy in her fingers and considered Marc's many attributes.

"That's a pretty flower. I'll get you something to put it in." The silver-haired woman slipped away, then returned with a paper cup filled with water. "This ought to work."

Jenn took it from her. "Thanks."

"Did you enjoy your picnic in the park?" Elena asked.

"Yes, I did. It's nice that the playground is so close. It'll give me a chance to see my daughter during the middle of the day."

"It's heartwarming to see a young woman put her children first. Not all mothers do that." Elena smiled. "I hope Marc finds someone like you someday. He's going to make a perfect husband and father."

Uh-oh. Was Elena playing matchmaker?

Whatever Jenn did, she'd better not bring her mother to the office. Between the two women, they'd drive Marc and Jenn crazy.

Besides, Marc wouldn't have any trouble finding a woman on his own.

A woman who didn't already have a child or a mountain of debt.

Chapter Seven

The next morning, Marc rolled out of bed before the alarm went off. Ever since starting his own business, he faced most days with a smile. But now that Jenn would be at the office, he was even more eager to get to work.

Originally, he'd wanted to see her reaction when she learned who he was. He wondered if she would be sorry for giving him the cold shoulder in high school. But after seeing her at the park, he was beginning to like the idea of asking her out to dinner, although he couldn't quite bring himself to do it.

He wasn't ready for another let's-just-be-friends response.

After taking a shower and shaving, he put on the coffee, then went outside to get the morning edition of the *Times*. The dew-covered grass chilled his bare feet as he crossed the lawn to get the paper, which had been tossed into the hedge again. As he reached through the branches to grab it, a thornlike twig scratched the top of his hand, and he grumbled under his breath.

The newspaper carrier, whoever he was, had a lousy aim.

On the way back to the house, Marc removed the rubber band and unfolded the paper enough to scan the headlines. When he was convinced there weren't any world, national, or state calamities that needed his attention, he entered the house and returned to the kitchen, where he poured a cup of coffee and sat at the table.

He turned to section B and looked for Jenn's column. After learning that she was Diana, he'd been reading the letters and her responses, which gave him some insight into the woman she'd become.

The first letter in today's edition was from a woman whose friends were concerned that the man she was dating was forty-two and still living at home with his parents. She signed her letter *Tired of Being Lonely.*

Marc figured there were a lot of reasons why a person that age would live with his parents and wondered what Jenn's thoughts were.

Ten years from now, Jenn wrote, you might find yourself in an even lonelier place if you hook up with the wrong man because it seems like the right thing to do at the time.

Marc wondered if she was reflecting on her own situation. Was she implying that she'd hooked up with the wrong guy for the wrong reason? Was she in a lonely place?

She certainly didn't seem unhappy, but she wasn't nearly as effervescent as she'd once been.

As Marc continued to read, he found the next letter interesting, too.

Dear Diana,

Six months ago, I went through a midlife crisis and left my wife of nearly thirty-seven years, thinking that I deserved to find happiness. But being single isn't all that it's cracked up to be. I've come to realize I've made a big mistake.

Trouble is, now my wife is having a midlife crisis of her own, and she doesn't seem to be as miserable as I am. The other day I stopped by the house and told her I wanted to come home. But she said she wasn't so sure she wanted a husband anymore.

What can I do to convince her to give our marriage—
and me—one more chance?

Kicking Myself

Thirty-seven years was a long time to be married. Marc
couldn't understand how a guy could leave on a whim and
wondered what Jenn's advice would be.

Dear Kicking,
  Your wife may still love you. It's also possible that
what she's really saying is that she just doesn't want to
be married to the husband you became over the years.
  Marriages take work, and so do apologies. Start by
asking her out to dinner—and make sure she knows
that it's a date. If she agrees to go, take her someplace
nice and romantic. Treat her the way you did when the
two of you were starry-eyed and in love. Let her know
she's special and that you're sorry for letting her go.
Then, if you truly mean it, tell her you're willing to give
150 percent to make your relationship better than it
ever was before.
  There are no guarantees in life. But maybe, by reading
your letter, other married couples will feel compelled to
climb out of their own ruts and to re-create the romance they once shared with their spouses. Good luck.

Not bad, Marc thought. She didn't give the guy false hope,
nor did she make him feel like a jerk for leaving.
  The last letter was from a woman who hadn't spoken to
anyone in her family for more than ten years because her parents and siblings hadn't approved of the man she'd married.
But she'd just learned that her only sister was diagnosed with
breast cancer.
  The woman wrote: I called my sister two days ago to let her
know how sorry I was, but she didn't answer. I left a message,

of course, but she hasn't called me back. I must admit that I had refused the olive branch she offered me a couple of years ago. So how do I go about mending fences now?

Jenn, or rather Diana, had responded: Unfortunately, it sometimes takes a tragedy for us to count our blessings and to place the proper value on the time we spend with those we love. Send your sister a handwritten note telling her that you love her and are hoping or praying that all goes well for her. Then do it again the next day. And the next. With each note, share one of your memories with her and let her know why she's always been special to you.

Please let me know what happens. I'll pray for you both.

Marc wondered if she really meant what she said about praying or if she'd merely written that for the sake of other readers. She certainly seemed sincere.

He poured the rest of his coffee into the sink, rinsed his cup, then headed back to his bedroom to slip on a pair of socks and shoes. But as he neared the den, his steps slowed. At the open doorway, he peered into the room and looked at his computer. And while he did, an idea sparked.

On a whim, he stepped inside and took a seat at his desk. Then he signed on to the Internet and, using one of his Gmail accounts that didn't have an identifying moniker, addressed an e-mail to *Diana@TheFairbrookTimes.net*.

He didn't have any real problems to write about. At least, nothing he couldn't handle.

Of course, that hadn't been the case ten years ago, when he'd had more than his share of teenage angst. Back then, he could have written for advice nearly every day of the week.

As he pondered his words, a second idea evolved from the first.

Taking on the persona of a teenage geek enamored with the head cheerleader, he typed Dear Diana.

The rest of the words flowed easily, and he wrote from the heart.

What kind of advice would a grown-up Jenn give now? What insight would she have on her feelings back then? Would she have done anything different if she had it all to do over again?

Had she changed?

Was she being honest?

Without giving what he was about to do any more thought, he hit Send, and his letter hurtled into cyberspace.

Then he signed off the computer and prepared to leave for work.

And to see Jenn again.

Balancing the demands of two jobs, as well as those of being a single parent, wasn't an easy task. So Jenn had set the alarm for five in the morning to allow her time to answer the most recent e-mails for Diana and to create her column for tomorrow.

Three hours later, she was ready to sign out when a new e-mail popped up. She really ought to leave it until another time, but she wasn't completely happy with the layout of the column she'd created so far and clicked open the new e-mail.

Dear Diana,

I'm in love with the hottest and most popular girl at my high school, but she doesn't even know I'm alive. I guess you could call us Beauty and the Geek.

For a while, I was tutoring her in math, and it seemed to help her. She was struggling to maintain a low D in the class, and now, with my help, she's pulled it up to a high C. The other day, she gave me a hug. I know it was in appreciation, but when she wrapped her arms around me and I caught a whiff of her perfume and felt the warmth of her embrace, I couldn't help thinking that I stood a chance with her.

But I blew it. I asked her out, and she turned me

down. I can understand that, but now she treats me as though I have leprosy. How do I turn things back to the way they were? At least being ignored was better than getting the cold shoulder.

The Geek

The poor kid's problem sounded familiar. Marcos Taylor had tutored Jenn in algebra, and he'd gone on to ask her out. Of course, that was ten years ago. Apparently, the situation wasn't uncommon.

As Jenn pondered the poor kid's plight, she tried to imagine the pain of being attracted to someone who clearly didn't share the same feelings. As a teenager, she'd been the head cheerleader, as well as homecoming queen, and had never lacked for a date. In fact, there hadn't been enough days in the week to go out with every adolescent male who asked her out. Nor had she wanted to.

She'd tried to turn each of them down nicely, although some of them remained more hopeful than they should have.

When she'd feared a guy might continue to pursue her, she would ignore him until he realized there was no chance of romance. At the time, it had seemed like the most humane way to handle it, but as she pondered the angst in Geek's letter, she realized her method had been a lot more hurtful than she'd realized.

"Mommy?" Caitlyn said as she entered the living room and approached Jenn's desk.

"Yes, honey?" Jenn turned away from the screen and, while still seated in her desk chair, gave her daughter her undivided attention.

Caitlyn placed her hands on Jenn's knees and looked at her with puppy-dog eyes. "Can we go the library for story time today?"

"I'm sorry, sweetie. I have to go to the office."

"*Again?*" Caitlyn had been used to having her home all the

time, but after the divorce, Jenn had been forced to go to work. Fortunately, the child hadn't complained too much and had been fairly understanding about the quiet time Jenn needed to work on her column.

"Yes, I'm afraid so. But we can talk to Grandma about going to the library. And maybe she can bring you to the park at lunchtime again."

Caitlyn brightened. "Promise?"

"I promise to talk to Grandma. We'll have to see what she says." Jenn gave her daughter a hug. "Now go and get your things. It's time for me to leave."

As Caitlyn dashed off, Jenn took one last peek in the bath-room mirror, checking her hair and adding a bit of lipstick.

Then, after dropping Caitlyn off with her mom and sched-uling another lunch date at the park after story time at the library, Jenn headed for work at the nicest professional build-ing in town.

How weird was that? She felt as though she'd made some-thing out of her life after all. She had a real job in an impres-sive office. She also had a handsome boss who turned her heart on end.

It was hard to ignore the irony, though.

At one time, she'd been at the top of the pecking order at Fairbrook High. But now? The tables had turned.

Jenn felt like the Geek compared to Marc's Beauty.

Chapter Eight

The next day, Geek's letter and Diana's response ran in the morning edition of the *Fairbrook Times*.

Jenn was always concerned about the feelings of those who had written in, but she was even more so today. Geek was young, brokenhearted, and undoubtedly vulnerable. So for that reason, she'd hoped to offer him comfort, although she feared her words might not be enough. And if not, maybe he would contact her again.

Some of the readers who'd written with a problem had responded to her advice—usually favorably, and sometimes with further questions or explanations. She rarely answered those second letters in the newspaper again, but she did e-mail or write back privately. And in this case, she hoped Geek would reach out to her again. She would hate to have him continue to suffer in silence.

Of course, since she had his e-mail address, she could always touch base with him later and ask how he was doing. His letter and his plight had touched her and made her hope she'd never inadvertently hurt anyone like that.

But Jenn hadn't been the only one moved by the unpopular teenager's plight.

While at the dry cleaners, she overheard a heavyset woman

talking about the subject with the owner, a small, slender man in his fifties.

"Poor kid," the woman said. "Some of my worst memories were in gym class. You have no idea how awful it felt to be thirty pounds overweight and have a locker next to one belonging to Angela Williamson, who went on to be crowned Miss Fairbrook the very next year. Talk about having a poor self-image."

"Tell me about it." The owner took the woman's dirty clothes and placed them in a blue mesh bag. "It seemed as though I was always the one who was the butt of a practical joke or the target in a cafeteria food fight. In fact, once a couple of football players put me head first in a trash can. I had to finish the rest of the school day smelling like rotten milk and wearing a pair of glasses with a cracked lens."

The woman sighed. "You know, those high-school days remind me of a book we had to read in sophomore English—
A Tale of Two Cities."

"How is that?" the owner asked.

"'It was the best of times, it was the worst of times.'"

As Jenn waited her turn to pick up her clothes, she pondered the comments she'd overheard, yet kept her thoughts to herself. She hadn't realized how many kids had high-school experiences that weren't as fun and upbeat as hers had been.

After leaving her own clothes to be cleaned, she drove to the office, arriving early enough to stop by Mug Shots for some hot green tea. She carried her cup to the counter that provided cream and sugar and other condiments. While reaching for a packet of sweetener and a stir stick, she overheard two women seated at one of the café-style tables.

"Diana's column sure struck a chord with me today," the redhead said. "The teen years were downright miserable for a lot of us."

As Jenn added the sweetener to her tea, she tried to focus on her drink and to ignore the women's conversation. For the past few months, she'd downplayed her role as an advice columnist. Sometimes she'd even been embarrassed by it. She'd meant it to be a stepping stone to bigger and better things, but now she wasn't so sure. For some reason, she felt as though she owed something to someone, that she was a spokeswoman for geeks everywhere.

Odd, she thought. Was there a need for a full column devoted to the struggles of the kids who lacked the happy high-school experience she'd had?

As she carried her tea into the elevator and up to the eighth floor, she decided to call her mom and cancel lunch plans at the park. Instead, she could meet her mom and daughter at Chuck E. Cheese's after work, which would allow her time to check her Dear Diana e-mail while eating a sandwich at her desk. Sometimes, when readers were impressed with her advice—or when they disagreed wholeheartedly—they wrote in. And she suspected this column might be one that would touch the memories of a lot of people.

"Good morning," Jenn said, as she entered the office.

Elena, who held a cup of coffee in one hand, set down the newspaper she'd been reading. "You're here early."

"So are you."

Elena smiled. "I had a doctor's appointment at eight this morning and didn't get a chance to read the paper, so I brought it with me. And I'm glad I did. It was pretty good today."

"The newspaper in general?" Jenn had only taken time to read her own column.

"Yes, but I was actually talking about Dear Diana. Do you ever read it?"

Jenn stiffened. For a moment, she wanted to skirt the truth, but Marc already knew she was Diana, and Elena was his aunt. It was just a matter of time before her secret was out.

"Actually," she admitted, "I write that column."

"*You're* Diana?"

"I have been for the past six months or so."

Elena chuckled. "Well, then I won't offer to let you read it."

Jenn took a sip of her tea and smiled. "Which of the letters interested you the most?"

"The one from . . ." Elena paused as though thinking it through. "The letter from the man having a midlife crisis."

"What did you think about my advice?"

"I thought it was great. And realistic. But to be honest, his wife might not want to take him back, and if she does, I hope she makes him wine and dine her for a while. Marriages take work, and romance needs to be cultivated."

"You're right," Jenn said. "I always hate to suggest divorce as an option. And that probably sounds ironic since I'm a divorcee."

"Was the separation your idea?" Elena asked.

Jenn nodded. "My ex had a gambling addiction and refused help or counseling."

"That's too bad. Divorces aren't easy. And while the split is often for the best, there are always a lot of adjustments that need to be made."

"Are you divorced?" Jenn asked, making the assumption.

"No, I was widowed. My husband was killed in a car accident while we were living in Mexico, so I understand dealing with the loss, with living alone, with coming to grips with all the changes that need to be made. And in my case, the grief. After Fernando died, I thought the pain would never go away."

"Did it?" Jenn asked. "Ever get better, I mean."

"Yes, with time." Elena's hand lifted to her chest, and she fingered the gold cross she wore around her neck. "I'm confident that he's in Heaven and that we'll be together again one day."

"How long has he been gone?"

"It'll be thirty-four years this coming April."

Before she'd taken in Marc, Jenn realized. "I'm sorry to hear that you lost your husband, but it's nice to know that some people have found their soul mates. I'm afraid that after my parents split up a few months ago, I've grown a lot more skeptical of people truly being happily married."

"How long were your parents married?" Elena asked.

"Over thirty years."

"And they have a daughter and a grandchild?"

Jenn nodded.

"They certainly have a good reason to work things out."

But should they? They hadn't been happy in ages.

"I'm afraid I've become jaded," Jenn admitted. "You have no idea how many letters I receive from people who are either divorced or teetering on the edge of one."

"I'm sure you do. But don't forget that the happy couples aren't writing you letters. They don't need help. It's just the ones who are struggling and miserable who ask for advice, so you're getting a skewed sample."

She had a point. "I hadn't thought of that."

Elena smiled and took a sip of her coffee.

"Well," Jenn said, glancing at the clock on the wall. "I'd better get to work."

"Me, too." Elena reached for a pen and a steno pad. "What are your parents' names?"

"Susan and Brad. Why do you ask?"

"Because I'm going to pray for them. I have a feeling things are going to work out."

Jenn arched a brow. "The divorce will be final in a couple of weeks."

"Don't ever limit the power of prayer."

Jenn thought about "the gift" Marc had said that Elena had, but not for long. Her parents' relationship was too far gone to be helped, and besides, her dad hadn't even stopped by the house in months.

Before Jenn could take two steps toward her office, the door swung open and Marc walked into the reception area. His hair was damp and stylishly mussed, and he wore a day-old beard that gave him a dark and dangerous edge, something she hadn't noticed before. Something she hadn't expected now.

He must be wearing clothes—slacks or a dress shirt, she supposed. But she couldn't seem to tear her gaze from his face long enough to look.

Was it possible for a man to grow even more attractive overnight?

Marc was the first to look away, and the disconnection left her a bit unbalanced.

"Can you please call a plumber?" he asked Elena. "See if you can get one out to my place as soon as possible. There's something wrong with the hot-water heater, and I'd like to have it fixed before I get home tonight."

"It's a new house," Elena said. "Shouldn't there be some kind of warranty?"

"I'm sure there is, but I had to take a cold shower this morning, and I don't want to wait any longer than I have to."

"I'll get right on it. But if you don't mind, I'll give the sales agent a call first. Her number should be with the closing docs." As Elena got up from her desk and walked toward the file cabinet, she looked at Jenn. "Marc just moved into a four-bedroom house at The Bluffs."

One of the most exclusive neighborhoods in town, Jenn realized, where almost every home had an ocean view. But that shouldn't surprise her. Marc was obviously a successful man who could afford the best.

She had work to do, and Elena certainly had everything under control, but for some reason her feet remained rooted to the floor, and her eyes sought Marc. He reminded her of someone, although she couldn't put her finger on who it might be. An actor on his way to movie stardom? A model for men's cologne or underwear or something?

Oh, for goodness' sake. She was going to find herself fired if she didn't get her mind back on work.

Shake it off, she told herself.

As her feet began to comply, Marc turned to her, stopping her in midstep with just one look.

"How's the brochure coming?" he asked.

"The draft is ready for you to look over whenever you'd like. I also finished that press release before leaving last night."

"Good. I'm looking forward to seeing it. I've got a conference call scheduled first thing, so if you'll give me a few minutes, I'll come in and take a look at it."

"All right."

As she headed toward her office with sure, steady steps, she overheard Elena speak to Marc.

"Have you read the paper yet?"

"No, I haven't had a chance."

"I think you'll find it especially interesting. Here, take my copy."

Elena had mentioned that she'd enjoyed reading today's issue. So Jenn told herself not to put much thought into that comment. There were a lot of articles in the *Times*. Surely Elena wasn't encouraging Marc to read Dear Diana.

And if she was, why would Marc find that letter about a guy's midlife crisis interesting?

Chapter Nine

Marc sat in his office making a few notes after speaking with his second in command at the home office and a labor advisory group that had been providing supervisory training for several of his top managers. The conference call had gone into overtime, and now it was nearing eleven o'clock.

So much for telling Jenn he'd be right in.

But rather than rush to her office, he glanced at the morning edition of the *Times* that sat on his desk.

While Elena had no idea that Marc had written a letter to Diana—and he wasn't about to confess—she'd been well aware of the crush he'd had on Jenn while growing up: the tutoring session, the hug, the ill-fated question about taking her out, the cold shoulder he'd gotten the rest of the school year. So he suspected she'd picked up on something in the column.

His first guess was that his letter had come out in print. And that even if Jenn hadn't recognized the similarities in the past and in Geek's situation, Elena probably had.

He set down his pen, shoved his notes aside, and opened the newspaper. And sure enough, on the right-hand side of page B-6, his letter was the first of three that had scored ink.

Dear Geek,

Some girls your age have a lot to learn when it comes to dealing with others. And a few of them are just plain mean.

In Beauty's case, she might be ignoring you so that you won't waste your time pursuing her. She may think she's doing you a favor by encouraging you to move on to someone who will truly appreciate you. There's even a good chance that she doesn't realize how badly you feel and how confused you are by her behavior.

In ten years, when Beauty attends your high-school reunion, she'll probably kick herself for letting a great catch like you go without a fight.

I know it hurts now, but believe me, your pain and embarrassment will pass. While you go on to make something out of your life, the right girl will come along, and you'll be glad you didn't hook up with Beauty after all—at least, not when she was too young and too immature to recognize your value.

You're not alone, Geek. I'm here, and I care.

                                                    Diana

Interesting, Marc thought. Apparently, Jenn had sympathized with "the kid" who'd fallen for the popular girl who was way out of his league.

But had she connected the dots? Did she see the similarities between the guy who called himself the Geek and the kid she'd known as Marcos? Did she suspect that Marc and the Geek were one and the same?

While he was at it, Marc continued to read the other letters, as well as her responses. And just like yesterday and the day before, he was seeing a side of Jenn that he hadn't expected. A compassionate side that intrigued him more than ever.

He ran a hand along his chin, felt the bristles he'd refused to shave with cold water this morning, which left him feeling scruffy. Unkempt.

Now what? Did he dare step out on a limb and ask her out again? Did he want to risk the embarrassment of her refusal?

Putting his dilemma on hold, he got up from his desk and went to her office, where she was folding the mock pamphlet. He could have said something, let her know that he'd finished his conference call and was now ready to give her his undivided attention. But he continued to watch her fuss with the brochure she'd created, to watch how her concentration formed a V on her brow, to watch the way her hair hung along her cheek. The way she nibbled on her bottom lip.

She must have sensed his presence, because she turned to him, her lips parting. "Oh. I'm sorry. I didn't realize . . ."

"No problem. I didn't want to startle you." He eased into the office and made his way to her desk.

She took a step back, making room for him. Her hand lifted to her chest, and she fingered her necklace, a single pearl on a silver chain. His eyes were drawn to the soft spot on her throat where her pulse throbbed. If he didn't know better, he'd think that she was actually nervous around him. And maybe not only because he was her boss.

Trying to steer his thoughts back on track, he asked, "What do you have there?"

She pushed the brochure across the table, and he studied it carefully—the colors, the wording, the design. She'd captured everything he'd wanted, and it was apparent that she'd followed his notes to create a pamphlet that was even more eye-catching than he'd imagined. But instead of the paper that detailed the scholarship he was prepared to give out, his interest was on Jenn.

When he thought she wouldn't notice, he stole another glance her way, only to find she'd been studying his reaction. Or had she been studying him?

Marc wasn't sure what—if anything—was going on

between the two of them. Was it just his imagination? An old fantasy resurrected?

Had she figured out who he was? Did she suspect that he was "The Brain"? Did she think she'd made a big mistake by turning him down when they were seniors?

Forcing his focus back on work, he said, "This is great, Jennifer. I like the colors you chose. And it's short and sweet."

"That's what I thought. Do you think we should mention the application deadline?"

"Probably. It's important that we get the word out as soon as possible."

"That's an easy addition." She tucked a strand of hair behind her ear, revealing a simple pearl stud that matched her necklace and releasing the hint of her floral scent. "I'd like you to take a look at the press release I created." She handed him a hard copy.

He nodded slowly as he read it over. Then he gave it back to her. "This is perfect."

"I hope we're not getting a late start," she said. "I did some Internet research and found that most kids have already been accepted by the college they want to attend."

"We're late if we were targeting seniors," Marc said, "and while I'll give them a chance to apply this year, I'd really like to offer the scholarship to juniors. That way, during the mentoring process, they'll have an idea of the funding they'll be receiving, which should guide their college choices. That knowledge should also encourage them to work hard through their last year in high school and to keep their academic future on track. And since the kids I want to help will be dealing with a lot of outside influences that could thwart their efforts, not to mention the regular struggles brought on by adolescence, I think it's really important to reach them early."

"You know," she said, "high school was a wonderful experience for me, but I'm just beginning to realize how tough it is for some kids. So I think offering this opportunity to juniors is great. But then . . ." She smiled. "Something tells me that was on your mind all along."

She was right, but he didn't want to imply that he'd suffered through the social jungle otherwise known as high school—unless, of course, she already knew that.

"I read your column today," he admitted. "And I noticed your response to the Geek."

"What did you think of it?" She turned to face him, those expressive blue eyes hopeful. "Not his letter, but what I said to him. I know how sensitive teenagers can be, so I hope my advice was helpful. And that he'll be okay with what I said."

"I thought your response was good, but is that what you really believe happened? That the girl actually thought she was being helpful by ignoring the guy and treating him like he was pond scum?"

Jenn crossed her arms. "He never said she treated him badly. Just that she ignored him."

"I guess that depends on what side of the cafeteria you sit on."

"What do you mean?"

Marc managed a just-messing-with-you grin. "I figured that's what Geek would have said if he'd been sitting here with us."

"Oh. You mean the invisible lines that were drawn between high-school groups."

Some weren't all that invisible, Marc thought, but he let it go.

"You know," she added, "that letter was a real eye-opener for me."

"In what way?"

"First of all, I never had to deal with some of the heartache that Geek is suffering through. I was popular and never lacked for friends, dates, or things to do on a Friday or Saturday night. So hearing about how the other side lived was sadly illuminating. And so were the responses I've received from that column."

"Responses?"

"I get letters from people all the time, especially when they read something that evokes emotion or they remember something similar that happened in their own lives. And I've received a surprising number of replies to that column, especially Geek's letter."

"You're getting replies already?"

"I'm sorry. I was going to wait until lunch to check my e-mail, but I'd already caught wind of a buzz in the community this morning, and I was curious. I just skimmed the letters so far, but it looks as though readers of all ages and genders are recalling their teenage years and sharing their pain, as well as offering me insights."

"That's interesting—and a little surprising." Marc would have guessed that a lot of people would rather keep those memories locked away someplace, like he did.

"One letter referred to an upcoming high-school reunion, so it probably was from a former classmate of mine, although it was impossible to identify her in any specific way." Jenn gave a little shrug and smiled. "I'm seriously thinking about writing a special article about teen angst and teen cruelty. I'm hoping that with the hindsight I've acquired in the last ten years, I might be able to . . ." She shrugged. "I don't know. Help, I guess."

So she had a heart for geeks.

Possibilities began to swirl in Marc's mind, but before he could comment, Elena stepped into the open doorway of Jenn's office.

"Excuse me, Marc. Am I interrupting anything?"

"No, you're not." In fact, Marc realized, Elena might have come in at the perfect time. He'd been about to extend a dinner invitation to Jenn, and he wasn't sure whether that was the route he really wanted to go. Not today, when he needed a shave.

"Jennifer's mother and daughter are waiting in the reception area," Elena said. "We've been chatting, but they'd like to talk to Jennifer when she's free."

Jenn's eyes grew wide, and her expression sobered. "Is something wrong?"

"No. Your mom had a change of plans today and wanted you to know."

Jenn turned to Marc. "Do you mind? Can you excuse me for a moment?"

"Of course."

He probably ought to return to his office, but curiosity got the better of him, and he followed her and Elena to the reception area.

Susan Kramer, who was holding Caitlyn's hand, stood next to Elena's desk. "I'm really sorry for barging in like this. I hope it's not a problem."

"Not at all." Marc offered the older woman a welcoming smile. He had clients stop by at all times, and if he'd wanted a private conversation, he would have had it in the conference room.

"We won't stay long," Susan said. "But Caitlyn wanted to see where her mommy works, and I wanted to let her know that we won't be able to meet for lunch today. In fact, I might have to get a sitter to come over before she gets off work."

"A sitter?" Jenn asked.

"You're not going to believe this," Susan said. "But your father called me about thirty minutes ago and asked me to have dinner with him tonight. And you'll never guess where."

Jenn's brow furrowed. "Dad called you? Just out of the blue?"

"Yes, but even more surprising than that is where he wants to take me." Susan broke into a smile that shed about five pounds and ten years off her. "To the Starlight Room at the Marina Hotel."

"He wants to take her on a date," Elena said, "just like the guy who wrote to Diana."

Susan's smile intensified, and a flush on her cheeks

deepened. "I noticed the similarities, too. And to be honest, I didn't tell you this, Jenn, but your father came by the house a while back and said he might have made a mistake by leaving. I figured that he really just missed his workshop in the garage. But Brad would never write a letter to an advice columnist, especially since he knows she's our daughter. And even if he didn't, who would write a phony letter?"

Marc stiffened and scanned the group of women, hoping no one was looking his way, but . . . bingo. Elena's gaze had zeroed in on him, seeing right through him. Thank goodness he could trust her to keep her suspicions to herself.

"Maybe you should get your hair done," Jenn said. "And buy a new outfit."

"Do you think I should? This is so not like Brad." Susan bit on her bottom lip, as though giving the whole thing some serious thought. "You know, maybe he just wants to talk about the settlement. Or to ask for something he forgot in the garage."

"I'll bet he's going to tell you that he wants to save your marriage," Elena said, her brown eyes taking on a romantic gleam.

Marc had to admit his aunt had a point. Dinner at the Starlight Room wasn't the kind of setup a guy chose to discuss a divorce settlement.

A smile tugged his lips, and he turned to Jenn. "Why don't you take the afternoon off and go shopping with your mom?"

"I really . . ." She turned to him, clearly surprised by his offer. "Are you sure?"

"Absolutely." Who was he to stand in the way of love?

She slid him a crooked little smile that was downright adorable, and for a moment he thought she was going to hug him, which would have really sent him for a loop, since it would remind him of the embrace he'd misread while they were in school.

But Jenn was no longer the self-centered cheerleader he'd once tried to convince himself that she was.

"Thanks for doing a great job on the brochure," he told her.

"If you copy the file onto a disk, drop it off at the printer, and ask for a thousand copies, you'd be doing me a big favor. Then, tomorrow, we can work on the company project."

"If you're sure it's not going to be a problem." She looked at him with those expressive blue eyes, and even if her leaving would have left him in a major lurch, he wouldn't have admitted it.

"I'm sure," he told her. "Have a good time."

After she went back to her office to prepare a disk and to grab her purse, she took off with her mother and daughter.

Marc continued to watch her through the glass doors until she disappeared into the elevator.

"You've still got it bad for her," Elena said.

Marc was going to deny it, but he'd never been a good liar.

"Why don't you ask her out?" Elena said. "She's clearly attracted to you."

"She might be attracted to the man she thinks I am, but not to the guy I used to be. And the truth is that I'm both of them."

Elena blessed him with a warm, loving smile. "Some things are meant to be, *mijo*. Don't let pride get in your way."

Marc remembered how his aunt had always told him that Jenn would eventually see him for what he was, that things would work out for them with time.

And while he didn't want to fall into the trap of believing that Elena truly had some kind of hotline to Heaven, a part of him desperately wanted to.

The part of him that had never stopped loving Jennifer Kramer.

Chapter Ten

Elena hadn't been able to get anyone to check the hot-water heater at Marc's house until sometime between three and five o'clock, so Marc left the office early to go home and wait for the plumber to arrive.

Normally he would have hired someone else to hang out at his place, but ever since he'd given Jenn the afternoon off, he'd had a difficult time keeping his mind on business and not on her. So he figured he might as well do it himself.

As he'd walked past Elena's desk on his way out of the office, she'd finally broached the fact that Geek's letter sounded a whole lot like Marc's experience with Jenn in high school.

"There are a lot of guys who are attracted to girls who don't give them the time of day," he'd replied, unwilling to confess that he'd actually written the letter, even though she'd already figured it out.

"Yes, I'm sure you're right, *mijo*. But now, more than ever, I think you and Jennifer are meant to be. The timing wasn't right before."

"What makes you think the timing is better now?"

"I've seen the way she looks at you when you're not aware of it. And she definitely has feelings for you."

Feelings for her boss, maybe. But what about feelings for

the guy she'd once known as Marcos? A guy who was still a large part of who Marc really was.

"Things are more complicated now," he said, thinking of Caitlyn. She was a cute kid, but Marc didn't know anything about being a parent.

"You mean because Jennifer has a daughter?"

Marc shrugged. She was also an ex-wife, and if Marc got involved with her, if he became a part of her life, that life would also include an ex-husband, a guy who'd teased Marc incessantly about being a shrimp during gym class.

For the longest time, he remained silent, wondering if his aunt was right and hoping that she was. He had to admit that there was something going on between him and Jenn, although he wasn't exactly sure what.

Okay, so he knew what was happening on his part. He was attracted to her—still. And he'd seen a side of her that was warmhearted and genuine, a side he'd like to get to know a whole lot better. But for a guy who'd gained a world of self-confidence since college, he was certainly skating around a direct approach now.

It had taken him a long time to get over her rejection. So what would happen if she blew him off with the cold shoulder again?

Last time, in his heart, he'd known he hadn't reached his full stride yet. That he'd been a late bloomer and didn't stand a chance physically against guys like Jason Phillips, the all-league running back who'd married her. He'd also known that, at least back then, he hadn't had anything to offer her. But that was no longer the case, and if she shut him out this time, he'd have to deal with the fact that his best wasn't good enough.

Still, if he didn't do anything at all and lost the last opportunity he had, he'd kick himself for the rest of his life.

Should he level with her? Let her know who he was and what he felt for her?

The answer wasn't that easy.

Too bad he couldn't play the write-a-letter-to-Dear-Diana card again.

Or could he? What if he dumped the teen-geek persona and took on a new one?

He pondered his dilemma all the way home. Once inside the house, he glanced at his wristwatch. He still had at least twenty minutes before the plumber might possibly arrive, so he went to the refrigerator, reached for a can of Coke, and snapped open the pop-top. Then he took the soda back to his home office, sat at the desk, and stared at the computer screen until the words finally came.

Dear Diana,
    I read the letter from the Geek and was reminded of a similar time in my life, when I carried a torch for one of the cheerleaders at my high school. Now, as our ten-year reunion looms on the horizon, I've run into her several times and found out that she's single.
    Times have changed, but I can't handle being turned down again.
    Do you have any advice for an insecure geek who's still got a crush on his Beauty?

                                                      An Older Geek

Not bad, he thought as he read over his letter. He'd given her enough information to hint that it was him. Maybe that was all he needed to do. Maybe fate would take over from there.

Tomorrow morning he would go to work and try to pick up on her vibes. If she was friendly, warm, or flirty, he'd ask her out. And if not? He'd pretend he hadn't even read her column, let alone taken time to write.

Pleased with his game plan, he hit Send.

The ball was now in Diana's court.

* * *

Jenn had helped her mother find a simple but classy black dress that was perfect for a romantic dinner at the Starlight Room.

"I know I shouldn't be getting my hopes up," her mom had said, "but your father sounded so . . . so . . . sure of himself, so sure of us, that I had to give him a chance."

Jenn understood, yet her parents had been so unhappy. Not that they'd fought, but for years they'd moved through the house like unfeeling robots, taking great effort to avoid any physical contact or connection.

"I thought the divorce was a joint decision," she'd said.

"In many ways, it was." Her mom had blown out a sigh of resignation. "When your dad mentioned the divorce, I'd been living in an emotional vacuum for so long that I hadn't wanted to expend the effort to talk him out of it. But now . . . ?" Her mom had burst into a radiant grin. "It's like I'm going out with a new man, a stranger. And it's exciting."

They'd stopped by the Clip 'n' Curl on their way home, and her mother had gotten her hair colored and styled in an elegant twist. Now she was taking a bubble bath.

Jenn hadn't seen her mom so vibrant and giddy in ages, and she couldn't help getting caught up in the excitement. She just hoped her dad meant what he'd said, that he wanted to work on their relationship.

At a quarter to four, Jenn entered the house and sent Caitlyn to play in her room. Then she whipped up a meat loaf and put it and a couple of russet potatoes in the oven.

While she waited for dinner to bake, she sat at her desk and sorted through the letters she would use for tomorrow's column. She chose one from a man who'd been having trouble sleeping, thanks to the neighbor's new dog, and another from an elderly woman whose son wanted her to sell her home and move in with him and his family. She also included a couple of letters from people who'd commented about

Geek's situation, but she kept the best ones for use in the article she would write on teen angst.

She was just about ready to send off her column to the editor when a new e-mail arrived. This one was from a self-proclaimed geek who still harbored a crush on a woman who'd been a cheerleader at his school. Since he'd mentioned the upcoming reunion, she suspected it was one of her classmates, although she wasn't sure. It was possible that a senior class from another local school had similar plans.

Without knowing the two people involved, she kept her answer generic.

Dear Older Geek,
    I understand your reluctance to approach your Beauty and ask her out, but you'll find that honesty is always the best policy. I suggest that you bite the bullet and ask her to go someplace with you—maybe to lunch or to a movie. The worst thing that could happen is that she'll tell you no. But if you don't ask, you'll never know.
    Good luck! I'm pulling for you!

                                                    Diana

"Mommy?" Caitlyn asked, drawing Jenn from her thoughts. "How come Grandpa took Grandma out to dinner and we didn't get to go?"

"Because it was very important that they have some special time together."

"But we're special. And I want to wear my party dress and shoes, just like Grandma."

"Maybe you and I can go out together some night."

It had been ages since Jenn had gotten dressed up and looked forward to a night on the town. The senior prom, maybe?

As a married couple, she and Jason had rarely gone anywhere that had required them to dress up. How sad was that?

She returned her focus to the letter she'd just read and considered the guy who'd written it, the upcoming ten-year reunion, the one-time cheerleader who wasn't married.

For a moment, she wondered if the geek in question had harbored a crush on her for ten years. After all, Jenn was now single and had once been a cheerleader.

But so had Devon Carmichael and Alisha Torres, who'd never married at all and would be much better catches.

Still, a sense of anticipation settled over Jenn, a sense that a big change was about to take place. Or maybe that was just wishful thinking on her part.

Of course, that's what it was. The old Jenn was clamoring for a little passion in her simple life, and her mother's excitement was contagious.

Unwilling to latch on to unrealistic expectations, she did her best to chase away any misspent hope. Instead, she finished preparing dinner for her and Caitlyn, oversaw bath and story time, and then called it a night.

The next day, Jenn arrived at the office at ten minutes before nine, only to find that she'd beat Elena there, which was surprising.

She hadn't beat Marc, though.

He stood near Elena's desk, a cup of coffee in hand and a smile stretched across his freshly shaved face.

"How was the shopping trip?" he asked.

"It was fun—and productive. We found the perfect dress. And from what my mom told me this morning, my parents are officially dating now. Dad's coming back tonight to take her to see *Mamma Mia* at the La Jolla Playhouse."

"That's great." His eyes glimmered, causing her pulse to slip into overdrive.

They stood there for an awkward beat, caught up in something warm and vibrant, something she had no business feeling.

"I've been meaning to go to the Playhouse," he said.

"Me, too."

Another beat stretched between them, this one longer than

the last, warmer. More vibrant. And her senses went on high alert.

"How about Friday night?" he asked. "We could have dinner first."

Was he asking her out?

Yes, of course he was. And now he was waiting for her answer. But for some reason, the words refused to form.

She was flattered, of course. Thrilled, actually. But she pondered the wisdom of getting involved with her boss, a man who signed her paycheck. A man who'd find her financial situation a shameful mess. A man who'd probably never failed at anything in his life.

Think, Jenn. Think.

"I . . . uh . . ." She willed herself to collect her thoughts, but it didn't seem to work. "I'd like to, but . . . I'm . . . not sure what I'd do with Caitlyn. Or what my mom's plans are that evening. Can I take a rain check?"

"Sure." The spark in his eyes faded, but he managed a smile and nodded down the hall. "I'm expecting a call from the accountant, and I need to get some numbers together for him. I'll talk to you later."

"Okay. I should have a draft of the company brochure ready for you to look at later this morning."

"All right. I've got a lot on my plate right now. Just e-mail it to me as an attachment." Then he turned and walked away.

What had she done?

The most attractive man she'd seen in ages had just asked her out. She ought to be clamoring to find a sitter. Instead, she'd hesitated and put him off.

She told herself that another opportunity to go out with Marc would present itself again. But would it?

Ever since she realized that she and Jason were headed to divorce court, she'd claimed that she didn't want to ever get married again, but that wasn't true. As the final papers were signed and a lifetime of loneliness stretched before her, she'd known that she didn't want to remain single forever. But the next time she got involved with anyone, she wanted it to be with a man who would work at a relationship as hard as she would, a man who was her equal.

Marc had achieved so much more than she had. Dating him would throw all of her insecurities in her face each time she was with him.

In truth, she was afraid to go out with him, afraid she wasn't ready for someone like him, afraid she never would be.

Would he consider her a loser when he realized how much baggage she had, how much debt?

She hadn't actually told him no. Instead, she'd asked for a rain check, which gave them both some time to think about what was happening between them. But as Marc disappeared into his office, as his door clicked shut, she wondered if he'd misread her apprehension. Or if she'd misread her own mind.

As the morning wore on, Marc seemed to have holed up in his office for good, and while she told herself it didn't matter, it really did.

By noon, he still hadn't come out. On her way to meet her mother and daughter at the park, she stopped by Elena's desk before heading out the glass doors to the elevator. "Have you seen Marc?"

"He left about ten minutes ago, but he didn't say where he was going. Why?"

Jenn nibbled on her bottom lip. "I get the strangest feeling that he's avoiding me."

"Why would he do that?"

"Because . . ." Jenn shrugged. "It's probably just my imagination."

"He was pretty quiet," Elena said. "His mind was clearly somewhere else."

"I'm sure you're right." Jenn labored over her decision to confide in Elena, then gave in. "It's just that . . . he asked me out, and I may have blown it."

Elena's expression sobered. "He asked you to go on a date?"

Jenn nodded slowly. "To dinner and the theater."

"And you told him no?"

"Not exactly. I . . ." Jenn wasn't sure if she should explain to Marc's aunt why she hadn't jumped at the chance to date a handsome, successful man who most women would give their right arm to go out with. But maybe it would help if she did. Maybe it would ease some of the tension in the office. "Marc's a wonderful man, a perfect catch, especially for a woman like me. And that's why I'm dragging my feet about dating him."

"I'm not sure I know what you mean."

"I probably should have gone to college when I got out of school, but I didn't. I got married instead. And now I'm a step behind some of my classmates." Jenn ran a hand through her hair, messing it up, no doubt. "I also have a child and a mountain of debt, thanks to my ex. And Marc deserves so much better than me."

"Is that why you told him you wouldn't go out with him?"

"It's why I needed some time to think it over." Jenn's shoulders slumped, and she leaned her hip against Elena's desk.

"Don't worry about Marc. He's always known what he wants."

"I *am* worried about him. He's a hero in the flesh, and the answer to a woman's prayers."

"Funny that you should mention that," Elena said. "I've been praying for Beauty and the Geek, and I hope that she'll give him the chance he deserves."

What did Beauty and the Geek have to do with anything? Was Elena comparing Marc to the Geek? Impossible. She was reading way too much into her nephew and those letters.

Or was she?

Jenn had caught Marc looking at her. And she'd picked up on some heart-spinning vibes. If she felt just a little bit better about what she was bringing to the table, she might have told him yes.

Maybe Marc had been shy about asking her out.

He'd been following the column. Had he taken Diana's advice to the Geek, mustered his courage and asked Jenn to dinner and the theater? Or was it all just a coincidence?

She had to find out.

"Oh snap," Jenn said. "I forgot to do something."

Then she strode back to her office, took a seat at her desk, and signed into her e-mail account as Diana.

Chapter Eleven

Marc had no idea where he was going, but he hadn't been able to get anything constructive done all morning, not while his disappointment and embarrassment ran amok. So he'd decided there was no point in hanging out at the office when he could be working from home.

But while he sat in the den and stared at his computer, he still hadn't been able to get a single thing done.

Yesterday he'd written to Diana, baring his heart and soul, and she'd suggested he ask his crush out. So when the opportunity arose, he'd jumped on it, only to crash and burn.

Not that Jenn had actually said no. She'd asked for a rain check, which was clearly her grown-up way of rejecting a guy she wasn't interested in dating.

Marc seriously considered writing back and letting Diana know that her idea had bombed. But then, maybe she was aware of that already. Maybe she'd put two and two together and figured out that Marc was the geek in question.

On a whim, he opened his e-mail account to re-read the response she'd sent him yesterday, the one that had encouraged him to step out on a shaky limb and ask her out.

But lo and behold, he had a new e-mail from Diana, one she'd sent just minutes ago.

Dear Geek,

   I've had some time to think about the advice I gave you and realized that I should have come up with a better response.

   In your case, I failed to realize how difficult it might be for you to ask your Beauty out. After all, you've been carrying a torch for a very long time, and I have a feeling you're probably shy.

   Why not start slowly? Consider sending her flowers. Do something romantic. Make her see you with new eyes.

Diana

What was that all about? Marc wondered. He'd already asked Jenn out, and she'd come up with a lame excuse for why she didn't want to go with him.

Didn't she realize that she was the beauty he'd been pining over for years?

He drummed his fingertips over the desktop and studied the letter on the screen. This was crazy. He didn't want to play the game anymore. Yet on a whim, he replied to her e-mail.

Dear Diana,

   It's too late. I asked; she declined.
   End of story.

Geek

There it was, the painful truth. But he couldn't quite bring himself to hit Send.

Was it too late? Was it really the end?

Why had she changed her advice?

As he continued to stare at the screen, he couldn't decide whether to revise the e-mail he'd written or to delete it completely and let Jenn go without another word.

And that was one decision Diana couldn't help him make.

* * *

As soon as Jenn got home, and while Caitlyn was still at the big house, she went immediately into the garage and dug through box after box until she found one that stored memorabilia. She pulled out all four of her yearbooks before putting away the mess and going to get Caitlyn.

After dinner, while Caitlyn kept herself busy playing in the bedroom, Jenn sat on the sofa with her yearbooks and scanned each picture to see if anyone resembled her new boss. His name hadn't sounded familiar, but he'd said he'd attended Fairbrook High.

She hoped she wasn't wasting her time. After all, Geek's letter to Diana followed by Marc's invitation to dinner and the theater was probably just a coincidence, but she couldn't seem to let it go.

As she studied each high-school photograph, she found a girl named Monica Alvarado who'd been a sophomore when Jenn was a senior. Could Monica have been Marc's sister? Or maybe a cousin?

Jenn continued to turn pages, to peruse each student until she reached the senior pictures and found Marcos "The Brain" Taylor, a small, wimpy guy with glasses. His dark hair, short and wavy like Marc's, wasn't unusual, so she couldn't consider that a telltale sign.

She wondered what Marcos would look like if he'd worn contact lenses.

Did Marc wear contacts?

She carried the yearbook closer to the lamp so she could study the photo in better lighting. For the longest time, she looked at the image and wondered if Marcos could have made that big of a change in his appearance. She tried to imagine him filled out and grown up. Marcos definitely had some similarities to Marc—enough that they could be brothers.

And Marcos certainly had been smart enough to graduate from college and be a successful businessman now.

But why the name change?

That part didn't make sense.

She thought back to the day in the library, when "The Brain" had tutored her. He'd been so sweet and helpful. And he'd taken all the time in the world to help her understand a concept that had been foggy. Never once had he made her feel stupid.

Relieved that algebra had begun to make sense, she'd given him an appreciative hug, felt the tender strength of his embrace, caught the whiff of his woodsy aftershave.

For a moment, she'd actually been drawn to his embrace, flattered by it, warmed by it. But when he'd sensed her reaction and asked her out, she'd balked.

Ten years ago, she hadn't been physically attracted to Marcos, even though she'd found him likable as a person. But she was older now, wiser.

And so was he.

The physical attraction that had been missing before soared whenever she looked at him now, whenever he spoke. And that kind and generous nature she'd noticed before had blossomed, making him an awesome man.

That is, if Marcos truly was Marc.

Two hours later, she hadn't been any closer to a decision, and at a quarter to eleven, she'd finally turned in for the night. But sleep had been a long time coming, as she'd tossed and turned and dreamed of her boss, a man who sometimes wore a pair of geeky glasses in her nocturnal imagination and sometimes didn't. A man who alternately asked her out for burgers and fries one minute, then dinner and the theater the next.

At three-thirty, she climbed out of bed and fixed herself a glass of warm milk, which helped a bit, but she still wasn't any closer to having an answer.

What was she supposed to do? Go up to her boss and ask

him if he'd once been a geek named Marcos and if he'd once had a crush on her?

No, she couldn't do that.

The next morning, after fussing with her hair and makeup longer than usual, pulling several different outfits from the closet and trying them on, she selected a pair of brown slacks and an off-white knit top. Then she drove to the office, hoping Marc would own up to being Marcos. That he'd do something romantic to tip his hand.

She had to know for sure who he really was.

Once she stepped through the glass doors and into the office, she spotted Elena at her desk, where a small bouquet of daisies sat next to the telephone.

The older woman looked up from her work and smiled. "Good morning, Jennifer."

"Good morning." Jenn pointed to the vase on her desk. "Those are pretty flowers. I've always been partial to daisies."

"They are, aren't they? Marc brought them in this morning."

"That was nice of him. They really brighten up the room." Jenn scanned the immediate area. "Where is he? In his office?"

"No, he came and went already. The Fairbrook Kiwanis Club is hosting a charity breakfast this morning, and he volunteered to make the pancakes. He should be back in an hour or so. Did you need to talk to him?"

No, she just wanted to see him. If she looked a little more closely, would she spot any similarities to Marcos Taylor?

But for the same reason she hadn't wanted to come right out and ask Marc, she wouldn't discuss her suspicion with Elena. Instead, she said, "I had a question about the brochure I'm working on for Alvarado Technologies, but it can wait until he gets back."

As Jenn strode down the hall, she entered her office, where

another bouquet of daisies sat, this one larger and fuller than
the one on Elena's desk.

Do something romantic, she'd suggested in her last e-mail.
And flowers definitely counted.

But not if Elena got them, too.

Jenn took a seat, but instead of diving into her work, she
pulled a petal from a daisy that dangled over the edge of
the vase. "He loves me," she whispered. Then she plucked
another. "He loves me not."

Did it matter if Geek and Marcos and Marc were one and
the same?

Would it make her any more enthusiastic about dating
her boss?

For some crazy reason, the answer was yes.

Disregarding the work she had to do, she signed into her
Diana e-mail account, which had several new messages in the
in-box. Yet only one set her heart strumming—the one sent
by Geek.

Dear Diana,
    You're right about me being shy. My Beauty turned
me down years ago, and it was a tough blow. And while
I appreciate you reconsidering your advice and suggesting I do something romantic, I'm afraid it's too late.
I asked Beauty to go out with me yesterday, and she
declined.

                                                    Geek

Jenn's heart dropped to the bottom of her chest. Marc had
asked her out yesterday, but other than that, there was no information in the letter that would suggest that Geek was actually Marc. Besides, Jenn hadn't really declined; she'd asked
for a rain check.

Unable to help herself, she typed in a response.

Dear Geek,
   I'm sorry that Beauty refused to go out with you. Does she know who you are?

Diana

She hit Send, then returned to her e-mail. She'd no more than read the first one, when a click sounded, alerting her to a new letter in her in-box. She knew it couldn't possibly be from Geek, yet when she checked, she was both surprised and shocked to see that it was.

How could *Marc* have sent that so soon? He was at breakfast, which meant there was a flaw in her assumption already.

Feeling more than a little disappointed, she read his words.

Dear Diana,
   I don't think she recognizes me, but it's hard to say. I've changed a lot in the past ten years. I'm also going by a different name than the one I used when I was in high school.

Geek

Marcos Taylor? Marc Alvarado?

Again, the assumption didn't seem to be that big of a stretch, although she couldn't understand how Marc could be flipping hotcakes and sending e-mails at the same time.

Did he have an iPhone or a BlackBerry?

She supposed it was possible.

Her senses reeled, and excitement pulsed through her veins.

But if she was wrong, if Geek was another guy, she couldn't encourage him to chase after a woman who clearly wasn't interested in him.

Still, what if he *was* Marc? What if Jenn was the beauty he'd pinned his heart on . . . ?

Would it change things?

Would that cause her insecurities to worsen?

What a mess she'd stumbled into. But she couldn't let it go on any longer.

Dear Geek,

I might be jumping to a faulty conclusion, but someone asked me out yesterday. And I was so touched, so nervous, so scared, that I stumbled over a decision. I asked for a rain check, hoping it would give me time to think it over. Because, believe it or not, a lot of people aren't nearly as self-confident as they seem. Sometimes they find themselves in situations in which they become shy and insecure.

After I suggested that you do something romantic, I received a bouquet of flowers. But I wasn't the only one in the office who did.

So …

Okay. To be honest, my thoughts are scampering here. But if you placed those flowers on my desk, thank you. It was sweet and thoughtful, since I love daisies. But unfortunately, that wasn't a big enough clue for me. You need to declare yourself in person. And you might be surprised at what a heart-to-heart talk might do.

Diana

Jenn read over the letter one last time, then hit Send and waited.

And waited.

And waited.

But Geek never replied.

Chapter Twelve

Geek still hadn't responded to Jenn's last e-mail, and Marc never returned to the office, which left Jenn feeling uneasy.

The longer she went without hearing from either of them, the more she thought it was best if she gave Marc her two-week's notice.

The job at Alvarado Technologies had only been temporary and would be ending soon, so there was no need for her or Marc to feel uncomfortable around each other any longer than necessary.

Now, as she sat with her mom and Caitlyn in the park, munching on a turkey sandwich, she couldn't help thinking that her whole life had fallen apart.

Of course, her mother and father appeared to have gotten their acts together. And as long as they were both happy and seriously considering a reconciliation, then she was okay with it, too.

She turned to her mom, who was eating an apple slice. "Do you and Dad have plans for the weekend?"

"We're going to dinner on Friday night, and we're driving to Julian for breakfast on Saturday morning. Why do you ask?"

"I just wondered. How are things working out for you? I mean, will he be moving home?"

"We still have a few things to talk through, so I'm not in any hurry for him to move back into the house, especially if that means our relationship would revert back to the way it was. But so far, it's going well. And believe it or not, he even suggested we go to church on Sunday."

"*Dad?*" Not that he'd been a hellion or a complete nonbeliever, but her father had always been selfish with his weekends and preferred to watch ball games on television or tinker around in the garage rather than socialize with friends or family. "Now that's a surprise."

"I know. That's what made me realize he's serious about changing the dynamics of our relationship. I think he's even read some books and articles on the subject, too. Weird, huh? The old Brad wouldn't have even considered reading a novel, let alone a self-help book."

"I know. So what's behind the big change?"

"He mentioned something about having an epiphany after talking to some homeless guy who was on his way to the soup kitchen at Parkside Community Church." Her mother chuckled. "I didn't even know your dad could spell 'epiphany,' let alone have one or use it in everyday dialogue. Of course, he's been using a lot of new words lately, like boundaries and communication and even romance."

Jenn had to admit that her dad had been pretty closed-lipped during the past few years, and that her mom hadn't been that talkative, either.

"Well, would you look at that?" Her mother pointed toward the street, where a shiny, black limousine had parked along the curb.

The driver, wearing a dark suit, got out, walked around to the side of the car, and opened the door for the passengers—or rather one passenger, a man carrying a bouquet of red roses, a gold-foil box, and a white teddy bear.

Jenn looked to her right and left, wondering what was

going on at the park, but as far as she could see, it was just the usual lunch and playground crowd.

As the man began walking toward her and her mother, she thought that, in the distance, he bore a striking resemblance to Marc. He wore glasses, though—like . . . Marcos?

A very grown-up Marcos.

He continued his approach, and her heart took off like a runaway freight train. She lifted her hand and pressed it against her chest as though she could keep it from breaking free.

Do something romantic, she'd told Geek yesterday.

Again, she scanned the grounds, trying to determine whether Marc—or Marcos?—had come to visit someone else, but realizing he was clearly headed straight for her.

The daisies weren't a big enough clue, she'd told him earlier this morning.

Declare yourself in person. And you might be surprised at what a heart-to-heart talk might do.

Her pulse rate continued to race, and the blood swooshed through her veins in a heady rush.

"Oh, my goodness," her mother said. "It's Mr. Alvarado. And he's coming to see you."

Jenn didn't know what to say—to her mom or to Marc. She'd made a big mistake earlier by freezing up when he'd asked her out, and while she was still struggling to wrap her mind around the fact that he was the self-proclaimed geek who'd written to Diana and was coming to lay his heart on the line, she didn't want to screw things up again. So she got to her feet and began walking toward him.

"I . . . uh . . ." She took a deep breath and slowly released it. "I can't seem to talk around you."

"I know what that's like. Maybe it's best if you let me do the talking."

"I . . . yes. Okay." She smiled. Their gazes locked, and her peripheral vision shut down, leaving only the two of them standing in the entire park.

He handed her the flowers—blood-red, long-stemmed, and de-thorned. She took them, unable to avoid taking a long, drawn-out whiff. So fragrant. "They're beautiful, Marc."

And so was he.

She'd asked for something bold and romantic, and he'd given it to her.

"I brought something for Caitlyn and your mom, too." He lifted the stuffed animal, a little white bear with a pink ribbon around its neck, and a gold box of Ghirardelli chocolates.

As if on cue, Caitlyn ran up to Jenn and tugged at the sleeve of her sweater. "Is it your birthday, Mommy?"

"No, it isn't." But it was certainly turning into a very special day.

"Then why is he bringing you flowers and a teddy bear and a present?"

Marc stooped to one knee and smiled at the child. "Your mom suggested a romantic move and thought my daisies were too subtle." He handed Caitlyn the teddy bear. "This is for you."

"For me?" Caitlyn looked at Jenn. "Is it okay? He's not a real stranger 'cause you know him, right?"

"Actually . . ." Jenn turned to her boss and studied him carefully for signs of Marcos, finding glimpses of the boy who'd shared himself and his knowledge, glimpses of the generous man who'd created a scholarship foundation so kids at risk could pursue higher education and make something of their lives. The depth of the man he'd become was almost staggering. "This is Marcos, Caitlyn. He's an old friend of mine. We haven't seen each other in years, but we're going to . . . renew our friendship. So, yes, honey. You can keep the teddy bear."

The little girl took the stuffed animal and cuddled it in her arms. "Thank you. I have another teddy at home, a brown one. But now he has a friend."

"Friends are special," Marc said.

That was true, and something told Jenn she'd just found one who was more special than the rest.

"I'm going to show my new bear to Grandma," Caitlyn said as she dashed off to the bench where her grandmother continued to sit, a smile bursting across her face.

"Do you think your mom would mind watching Caitlyn while we talk?"

"I'm sure she'd be happy to."

Marc nodded toward Jenn's mother. "Then let me give her the chocolate."

Jenn followed him to where Susan sat, her eyes glimmering.

"Mrs. Kramer, I brought you some chocolate."

"Thank you, but you didn't have to do that."

Marc grinned. "It's a bit of a bribe. I was hoping you'd keep an eye on Caitlyn while Jenn and I talk."

"Of course. Take all the time you need."

Marc looked at Jenn. "Should we go for a walk or take a drive?"

She glanced at the limo, where the driver stood next to the door like a Buckingham Palace guard. It was all very sweet, very romantic, but she wanted to talk to Marc alone. "Let's walk."

"Okay." She handed the roses to her mother for safekeeping. "We'll be back."

"No rush," her mom said.

As they made their way across the lawn toward the jogging path that ran along the perimeter of the park, she said, "I'd wondered where you were this morning. And yesterday, too. You haven't spent much time at the office, and I thought . . . well, I thought maybe you were avoiding me."

"You were right. I was."

Her steps slowed, and she turned to her right, checking out his expression.

He smiled, and those eyes, beautiful brown eyes she could clearly see through the lenses of his glasses, glistened. "I'm glad we're having this talk, Jenn. I couldn't continue to work from home and make up meetings that didn't exist."

"I ran you out of the office?"

"I'm afraid that was the old Marcos reacting. I've come a long way from those high-school days, but I've always had a thing for you. I thought I'd outgrown it, or rather you. But when I saw you again, those feelings came flooding back, and so did my adolescent insecurities."

They continued to walk, the sun warming them, the birds chirping in the treetops.

New life, new hope.

"I've changed, too," Jenn admitted. "I've got a lot of baggage now. And the insecurities I seemed to have bypassed in school have come home to roost lately."

"You don't have anything to feel insecure about. You're a beautiful woman, a loving mother."

"Thanks, Marc. But I'm not as successful as you are. And I'm not as smart. I don't have a college degree, so I might not fit in with your friends and colleagues."

"You'll fit in just fine. But for what it's worth, if it makes you feel better, you can always take some evening and Saturday courses at the local junior college. That's what a lot of people do. In fact, that's how Elena got her AA degree."

She hated to tell him that she'd already considered doing that, but she couldn't afford the registration fees right now. Instead, she said, "I'll have to check into it."

They continued to walk along the concrete jogging path, winding away from the park.

"That's not all the baggage I'm carrying," she said.

"Are you talking about Caitlyn? I know the two of you are a package deal, and it doesn't scare me. I'm willing to read parenting books and go to theme parks and watch cartoon movies—whatever you suggest."

"Something tells me that having a child around won't be a problem for you."

"Then why do I still detect reluctance?"

"It's not reluctance on my part. I'd love to get to know you better, to date, to . . . whatever."

"Then what's holding you back?"

"The fact that I have a lot of debt."

"That's not a problem. I can—"

She reached for his arm, as if she could hold the offer back. "No. I don't want to be rescued by some guy riding a white horse." She laughed. "Or in this case, a black limo."

They stood like that, gazes locked, her hand resting on his forearm. She'd made her point; she could have let go and stepped away. But she didn't want to lose the physical connection, the warmth of their touch, the surge of attraction, the rush of pheromones swirling around them.

"I understand why you want to pay off your own debts," he said, "but if you need money, either as a gift or as an interest-free loan, all you have to do is say the word."

"I appreciate that."

She could certainly drop her hand now, take a step back, look away, but the intensity in his gaze was spellbinding, and she couldn't imagine being anywhere but here, with anyone but him.

Marc had already made his move when he'd arrived in the limousine, bearing roses and wearing his heart on his sleeve. So now it was her turn.

She lifted her hand, cupped his jaw, brushed her thumb against the faint bristles on his cheek. "I don't know what's happening between us or what I'm feeling, Marc, but I like whatever it is—a lot."

He placed his hand over hers, holding her fingers to his face, strengthening their connection, stirring the heat of their touch. "I like it, too."

When her heart fluttered, she wondered just how deep her feelings had gone. Was this love? This soon? It was possible, she thought. So very possible.

So now what? she wondered. She hadn't wanted a man in her life who wasn't an equal. Nor had she wanted a rescuer. Yet she no longer saw Marc as someone bigger than life or better than she deserved. He had a few flaws and insecurities, just as she did. And he cared for her in spite of them.

Marc was a gift, she realized. And maybe he'd always been, but the timing hadn't been right before.

Now it was right. The past ten years had changed them into people who would truly appreciate each other from this day forward.

Slipping her hand free of his, she urged her fingers along his jaw and around to the back of his neck. Then she drew his face, his mouth, to hers.

The kiss started with the brush of his lips against hers, gently and tentatively, like an innocent kiss between young lovers testing their feelings and desire for the very first time. But as it intensified, as their breaths mingled and he drew her closer, her lips parted.

When his tongue touched hers, the kiss exploded into a heart-pounding, earth-moving kaleidoscope of colors.

She found it hard to breathe or to keep her knees from buckling. All she could do was to hang on tight and relish the taste of him, knowing that just one kiss wouldn't be enough.

Their first embrace had pushed them apart, but this one was binding them together in a way she hadn't expected.

As the kiss came to an end, they continued to hold each other tight, to see the truth in each others' eyes, to validate what had just happened to them.

Falling head over heart in love with Marc suddenly seemed to be a whole lot more possible than it had been even moments ago.

"That kiss is going to be a hard act to follow," she said.

"Something tells me it's only going to get a whole lot better." Then he took her by the hand and headed back to the park, back to her mother and daughter and the waiting limousine.

She glanced at her bangle wristwatch. "It's almost time to go back to work."

"Not today. I've got the limo rented for the rest of the afternoon and evening. And I feel like having an adventure. Let's see where we end up."

Jenn gave his hand a squeeze. "That sounds like a great idea to me."

She'd been given a second chance at love, and she didn't intend to let one single minute of the adventure slip away.

Chapter Thirteen

By the time the evening of the reunion came around, Jenn and Marc had been dating for ten days—each one a unique adventure that proved they were meant not only to be together, but to be a family.

They'd taken Caitlyn to Roy's Burger Roundup, as well as to a matinee at the Fairbrook Movie Palace, where they watched the latest Disney flick. And they'd been to Chuck E. Cheese's twice.

But they'd also found time to be alone.

Last weekend, he'd surprised her by taking her for an awesome ride in a hot-air balloon. And on Tuesday, just before midnight, they'd walked barefoot in the sand—hand in hand and heart to heart. The full moon had shined bright, and as the waves rolled back, they spotted a scattering of grunion, the silvery fish that had come to lay their eggs in the sand. Marc had felt a part of something much bigger than the two of them, and he'd only been further convinced that he was meant to be with Jenn for the rest of their lives.

On Wednesday, they'd had a romantic dinner for two at the Starlight Room and seen *Mamma Mià* at the La Jolla Playhouse. And last night, after getting a babysitter, they'd double-dated with Susan and Brad Kramer and gone bowling.

Marc liked Jenn's dad, and he suspected the man would be moving back home soon.

Now, as he pulled up in front of the Mar Vista Country Club and waited for the valet to open Jenn's door, he adjusted his tie. As magical as the past week and a half had been, he wasn't all that keen on attending the reunion, but Jenn had thought they should at least make a showing.

He felt a little awkward about being with the former homecoming queen, but he shook it off. He wasn't a nobody any longer.

As Jenn climbed out of his car, wearing a black dress and heels, her hair pulled up in a pretty twist, he had to pinch himself to believe that this day had truly come, that he and Jenn were finally a couple.

He reached out his hand, and she took it.

"Thanks for coming with me," she said. "I know you weren't really up for all of this, but we don't need to stay very long. Just long enough for me to interview a few people. Then we can take off."

He gave her hand a gentle squeeze. "I understand. You can't very well wrap up that article about the reunion if you don't attend."

They walked into the lobby of the country club and followed the music to the main dining room, which had been decorated in blue and silver, the Fairbrook High school colors.

A disc jockey had set up his equipment next to the dance floor, where he was playing a hit that had been popular ten or more years ago.

They'd barely made it inside when Jason Phillips approached.

Jason looked at his ex-wife and smiled. "You look good, Jenn."

"Thanks."

Jason's focus shifted to Marc, but his words were aimed at Jenn. "I see you brought a date."

"This is Marc Alvarado," she said. "You probably remember him as Marcos Taylor."

"The Brain?" Jason's assessment deepened. "You've changed."

Yes, quite a bit, Marc thought. And Jason really hadn't. But what good would it do any of them for Marc to make some kind of snide retort? So he refrained from mentioning anything about growth and maturity and gave a half-shrug.

"Where are you guys sitting?" Jason grinned, but not in what Marc would call a snobbish way. "With the brains, huh?"

"I hope so," Jenn said. "I'm writing an article for the *Times*, and I thought it would be a nice twist to find out what's going on in some of our classmates' lives."

"Well," Jason said, "I'll let you get after it, then. I was just heading to the bar to meet up with a couple of buddies of mine. They're watching the Padres game, and I need to check the score."

Marc figured he had a bet riding on the outcome.

Jason's gaze again turned to Marc. "Take care of her."

"I intend to." Again, Marc held back on implying that Jason hadn't done a very good job of looking out for his wife, his marriage, or his family. But then again, maybe the guy already knew it. Maybe he was the one making comparisons and falling short now.

"I'll see you guys later." Then Jason excused himself and went off to join his friends.

When the guy was out of earshot, Marc asked, "Who do you plan to interview?"

"Some of the honor students. And remember Darren Jackson? The guy who used to sit under the tree on the senior lawn and strum his guitar?"

"Yeah, I remember him. He used to keep to himself a lot, and he probably got as much ribbing as I did."

"I heard he just landed a major recording contract, and I'd like to talk to him. Jessica told me he was coming. I think it would be cool to talk to some of the kids who hadn't been popular, but who made something out of their lives."

Like me, Marc thought.

He suspected that she'd show Frank Bagley that she was a talented journalist who knew how to create a story that would appeal to the community at large, and a surge of pride shot through him.

As they entered the dining room, they spotted Jessica Rawlings and another girl Marcos didn't recognize sitting at a table, passing out name tags.

"Hey!" Jessica brightened when she spotted Jenn. "You look great."

"Thanks."

Jessica's eyes swept from Jenn to Marc. "And you brought a date. I didn't have him on the RSVP list, but we can squeeze him in." She glanced at the sheet of paper in front of her that bore the names of those attending and their seating assignment. "I have you at table three now, but if I switch you to table nine, that'll work. Ken Clausen and his wife canceled at the last minute."

"We'd like table nine so we can sit together, but my date is already on the list, Jess. This is Marcos 'The Brain' Taylor, now known as Marc Alvarado."

"No kidding?" Jessica brightened. "You found him."

Jenn turned to Marc and smiled. "You bet I did. And I'm never going to let him go."

Marc slipped an arm around his queen and held her tight. He'd been successful in school, as well as in business, but his true calling was to be a good husband to Jenn, a devoted step-father to Caitlyn, and a daddy to the other kids they would have together.

Tía Elena had said there would be three—two boys and a girl.

Marc hadn't said anything about it to Jenn, thinking she'd like to be surprised. But Marc didn't doubt his aunt's gift anymore.

Love takes time to develop, she'd told him when she'd found him down in the mouth as a teenager. *One day, Jennifer will see you for who you really are, and then love will blossom. I'm sure of it.*

And sure enough, she had—and it did.

"Maybe I can move some other people around," Jessica said. "Most of the old gang will be seated at tables three and four."

"Don't bother," Jenn said. "As long as Marc and I are together, we'll be fine."

Marc couldn't agree more.

"Do you want to know who you'll be sitting with?" Jessica asked.

"It really doesn't matter." Jenn turned to Marc, a smile lighting her pretty face, drawing him into an inner circle that only included the two of them.

"Come on," he said, escorting her into the dining room in search of table nine.

They planned to enjoy meeting the adults their classmates had become. And when the night was through, they would continue the adventure they'd started ten days ago—getting to know each other and becoming the couple they were meant to be.

Love and second chances didn't get much better than this.

The Honeymoon House

Mary Carter

Chapter One

She had no choice—it was a direct order from the Bride-monster. *Get rid of everything romantic. I don't want a single trace of anything lovey-dovey in the house, do you hear me?* Amanda actually said, *"Do you hear me."* Kate Williams stood on the front porch of the adorable Gingerbread cottage, key in hand, gearing up to execute Mission KR: Kill Romance. Not the duties she'd expected when she signed on for the role of Amanda's maid of honor, and rushed to Martha's Vineyard for what, if Amanda was to be believed, was to be the Wedding of the Century.

Kate inserted the key into the lock, but didn't turn it. Instead, she surveyed the front porch, doused in bright greens and blues with icicle-like trim dangling above her head. Then she lifted her gaze to the nearest neighbor, and beyond. Near-replicas of the fairy-tale cottage she stood in front of were rolled out in front of her, dominating the street like a parade of grown-up tents splashed in bright colors and boasting varying arrays of dangling, geometric trim. Kate felt as if she were the lead float in the parade, and imagined herself waving to the unseen crowds. The cottages, a tourist attraction born of the Methodist revival tents that dominated the area in the nineteenth century, were sandwiched so close together, Kate felt like the new guppy dumped in the proverbial fishbowl.

Hopefully, the nearest neighbors were out for the day, strolling the beach or brunching in a local café. She didn't want anyone spying her in her disheveled, yet remarkably still fluffy, plum bridesmaid dress. Although truth be told, her colorful gown blended in with the cottages perfectly; she looked like a fairy-tale princess coming home on her lunch hour, but that was definitely where the similarities ceased. Because one thing was for sure—this princess was, at thirty-one, much older than your average Cinderella–Snow-White combo pack (definitely too old to still be wearing a hideous bridesmaid's dress), and furthermore, this particular vision in plum was extremely hungover.

She and Amanda had pulled an all-nighter, first in a local bar until they were tossed out at two, then on the beach with a bottle of Candy Apple Liquor Amanda had been given as a bridal-shower gift. They passed the bottle back and forth as Amanda purged months' worth of minor complaints about Pete. Then they passed out on the beach, an almost-bride and her maid of honor sunk in the sand like drunken teenagers dumped by their dates on prom night. When Kate awoke several hours later, Amanda was hovering over her with breath Kate could only wish smelled like candied apples, and a self-professed brilliant idea in her head: she and Kate were going to stay in the cottage that was supposed to have been her honeymoon house with Pete.

The fact that the cottage was on loan from a childhood friend of Pete's, not Amanda's, didn't seem worth worrying about. They could stretch "girls' night" out for an entire month. Could Kate get the time off work? Kate didn't mention she'd been laid off and had all the time in the world. Instead, she said yes, she was definitely due some vacation time. It was settled. The girls would move into the cottage. But first, Kate had to go to the cottage and do Amanda a favor.

Thus, Operation Kill Romance was born. Go directly to the cottage, do not pass Go, do not collect your sweatpants and T-shirt.

Kill romance. Who was Amanda kidding? Why was Kate following the directions of an unglued almost-bride? Because she was her best friend, and she needed her. If Amanda wanted the place stripped of love, Kate was going to strip it of love. But did that include the flowerpots resting along side of the porch, bursting with flagrant color? And what about the wooden swing swaying in the slight breeze? A swing could be considered romantic, couldn't it? And while she was at it, would she have to find a way to get rid of the scent of honeysuckle in the air?

Kill romance? What about the beaches, the ocean, the Vineyard's signature pink sunrises and sunsets, the romantic little restaurants, the panoramic views, the cliffs, the lighthouses? Seemingly, they could never leave the house. Kate would have to cover all the windows in a shroud, mark the door with a bloody *X*. At least she would have to move the flowerpots to the tiny backyard or put them on the neighbor's porch. That's when Kate looked down and spotted the welcome mat.

Custom-ordered for the happy couple, portraying a handsome groom carrying a blushing bride over the threshold, it shouted WELCOME MR. AND MRS. Oh. My. God. That was the sweetest thing ever. That was definitely going to have to go. Kate flipped the offending mat upside down. Then she gathered the flowerpots, which wasn't an easy feat since there were six of them, and snuck them over to the neighbor's porch. She came back and was all set to enter when she made the mistake of looking up. Little lights were strung up in between the dangling trim. Upon closer inspection, she could see they were shaped like little hearts. A tear came to her eye as she started yanking them down. It was such a pity she wouldn't get to see them lit up at night.

Your mission, if you choose to accept it . . .

Not that she had a choice. Amanda was on a rampage. She reminded Kate of the movie *Gremlins,* where, when you accidentally doused the cute, fuzzy, little buddies with water, they freaked right out and turned into slimy, snarling monsters.

Kate ripped out all the lights and bunched them up near the steps. She felt awful. Someone had put considerable time and thought into welcoming the nearlyweds, someone who was obviously a romantic at heart, just like Kate. Who did Amanda say owned this cottage? A photographer friend of Pete's, if she remembered correctly. A man did this? He must be gay. Or he hired a woman to decorate it, being that women were much more romantic, Kate thought as she spied another flowerpot and, not feeling like sneaking next door again, smothered it with the upside-down welcome mat instead.

She stopped and surveyed her work. Better, but not completely deromanticized; the swing was definitely going to have to come down.

Or was that going too far? *I don't want to look at anything that smacks of romance, Katie, or I will lose it. I WILL LOSE IT.* Better take down the swing.

Amanda and her prenuptial tantrum. Because let's face it, that's all this was, a tantrum. A stressed-out, sleep-deprived bride throwing a fit, and a clueless groom who walked into her trap just because he didn't know how to keep his own trap shut. Oh, how clearly Kate could see the flaws in others!

She unlatched the chain from the top of the hook, and the right side of the swing fell with a bang. Kate winced at the noise, hoping she hadn't damaged the swing. She could see herself sitting on it at night, enjoying a glass of Chardonnay after a leisurely stroll on the beach. Maybe she'd sneak out here when Amanda was in bed and hang the lights and reattach the swing so at least someone could enjoy the luxuries the cottage had to offer. So far, everything Kate had heard about the island was true. Martha's Vineyard was a little slice of heaven. Maybe a bit too elitist for a common girl like Kate from good Midwestern stock, but that just meant she was in a better position to truly appreciate what the Vineyarders probably took for granted. Should she leave one end of the swing up or collapse the whole baby?

She'd leave half of it up, mess with Amanda's mind a little. Shame on her. Poor Pete. The wedding was so beautiful, too. If you could call it a wedding since it crashed and burned just before the vows. And Kate was finally going to face her fear of singing in public again. She'd even spent the last few months with a vocal coach getting her voice back in shape . . .

It didn't matter. It was Amanda and Pete she was thinking about, not the fact that she had been looking forward to the reception—a little cake, a little champagne, perhaps a dance with a handsome stranger.

It was so typical of Amanda to pull something like this; still, Kate was trying not to judge. It would be easier to do if she could just get out of this ridiculous dress and maybe get a cup of coffee and some aspirin.

Kate couldn't help but wonder how things would have gone if Jeff had been here. He'd always had a way of calming people down, making them see sense. Yes, it definitely would have been Amanda's older brother to the rescue. He would have made an expert negotiator, would have excelled at anything he put his mind to. He just had that way about him; Jeff lifted everyone around him. He was order out of chaos. Kate couldn't believe the silly things she used to get upset about, the inordinate amount of time and attention Jeff would spend trying to make her feel better. Looking back, she realized that was all she was after, Jeff's attention, but she couldn't believe she used to play such games to get it. Regrets played in her mind like a song you couldn't get out of your head, and it wrenched at her heart. Just like the games Amanda was playing with Pete. What a waste. If Kate had it all back—had Jeff back—just for a day . . .

But she couldn't think about Jeff right now, and she

couldn't get mad at Amanda, or at her own younger, immature self, the one who'd thought love would last forever. She was on a mission. She hadn't been a very good friend the past five years; in fact, it was Amanda who'd had to hold Kate up after grief swallowed her like a swarm of locusts. Now Amanda needed her, and for once Kate had the strength to be there for her. If Amanda wanted her to Kill Romance, she was going to make sure it never lived to see another day. That is, until Amanda was ready to see the light.

Amanda Panda, as Kate called her when they were children, was her best friend in the whole world. They'd lived across the street from each other since they were six years old. Kate fell in love with Amanda's brother Jeff the same day she became best friends with Amanda. It would take eight-year-old Jeff, however, another twelve years to return her feelings. They dated for five years, and then Jeff asked her to marry him. But a run-down Ford with faulty brakes and icy roads on a Saturday night wiped out that dream in a matter of unimaginable seconds.

But that was five years ago. Kate needed to move on. She had been so invested in this wedding taking place—looking at it as a chance to heal, a chance for love—even if she wasn't the recipient. She loved Pete, too; he was perfect for Amanda. Why couldn't Amanda see that? How could people be so careless with love? Why did some people throw it away like it was nothing, while others had it ripped out from underneath them?

Amanda still had a chance, and Kate was going to do everything she could to make her see that.

There, the porch was done. Plant covered, swing disabled, lights ripped out, and the last of the flowers smothered by the welcome mat. Not so welcome now, girl. It was time to trash the inside. Ah. Always the bridesmaid.

Kate unlocked the door and stepped into the living room. The cottage was just as adorable on the inside: wood floors, ogee arches, leaded-glass windows. It was small, but bright and cheery. It was a perfect honeymoon house; Kate had her work cut out for her. There was a gorgeous vase of long-stem red roses on the bamboo coffee table. Those would definitely have to go. It was hard to believe such perfection grew in nature. Should she give them to a neighbor? She didn't have much time. Amanda had to check out of the inn by ten, and it was only a ten- or fifteen-minute bike ride to the cottage, which gave Kate exactly twenty-five minutes. If only she hadn't taken her time riding over here, she could have saved the roses. She shouldn't have stopped at the beach to pet the little gray cat, or chat with the lovely elderly couple collecting seashells. How she would love to give the roses to the woman, Margaret was her name, but since that wasn't possible, at least she'd brought a large black garbage bag with her.

Kate grabbed the roses with both hands and, forgiving the thorns that dug into her palms, brought them up to her nose, smelled them, and then softly kissed them good-bye before whispering apologies into their soft petals, snapping their stems, and shoving them into the bag. When Amanda was in a better mood, Kate would replace the roses, she promised, but for now they were casualties of war. Into the garbage bag they went, bulging out obscenely, a few piercing through the bag, making Kate feel immeasurably guilty. But she had to admit, the place looked a lot less romantic with nothing but a couple of leaves floating on top of a vase of water like the last inner tube deserted in a pool. Hurry!

Chocolates in a dish on top of the television, gone. Fresh-baked cookies on a plate in the kitchen, in the bag you go—except for one; Kate had to eat at least one. The minute they were in the bag, Kate regretted it. Surely chocolate was a necessity. Too late now; those were honeymoon cookies, and they were gone. Kate and Amanda would venture out and get a nonromantic pint of Ben and Jerry's. Kate might even pick up a jar of peanut butter and some quality dark chocolate. Just like Jeff used to bring her. No Jeff. No cookies. No roses.

She tore through the rest of the downstairs and was ready to head up to the second level when she rounded a corner leading to the spiral staircase and WHAM. Oh. No. God, no. Wedding gifts. Loads of them. An entire hallway table full. No way was she going to toss those in a bag. They were so beautiful. A mountain of glittering paper topped with good wishes, and white bells, and fat bows. Boxes of all sizes and shapes decked in glitter, hearts, and shine.

Kill romance, kill romance, kill romance. This was an awful day. Of all the things she could be doing, even with a hangover, this was the worst. She was a love sniper. There was no other alternative; she would have to rip the presents open. She started with a box wrapped in silver topped with a crème brûlée bow. She took a deep breath, grabbed a corner of the wrapping paper, and mercilessly ripped. Tearing off the paper revealed a triple-slotted toaster. Much less romantic. She couldn't turn back now; she was committed. She began exposing the gifts one by one. Margarita pitcher, fondu set, candles, silver gravy boat. She was so into the groove that when she tore the paper off the next gift, she almost overlooked it.

She could tell it was a picture frame, and she was expecting to see a generic silver or gold wedding frame, but instead she found herself looking at a close-up photograph of Amanda and Pete framed in driftwood. It was absolutely stunning in its simplicity. The photograph looked as if it had been taken right outside the cottage. Amanda and Pete were looking at each other and laughing. It was as if they hadn't been aware of the camera, as if no one in the world existed but the two of them.

This must have been taken by the photographer friend of Pete's—the very man who had gone to great lengths to welcome the couple to their honeymoon house. The man whose romantic efforts Kate was methodically destroying. She set the framed photograph against the wall and made a mental note to explore the upstairs to see if she could find any more of his work.

Her gift to the happy couple was in here, too—oh, the time she'd spent picking out the wrapping paper alone. She'd gone to three boutiques until she found the perfect shade of glittery plum, an exact match for the bridesmaid dresses. From the looks of it, everyone had gone to great lengths to celebrate the young couple. Amanda and Pete should be opening these gifts, daydreaming about the ones they thought they'd use, stockpiling the ones they'd return for other things they dreamed they'd use, but probably never would, and wouldn't see again until one of them insisted they clean out their garage and have a yard sale. They'd hold a few of them back—let's keep the fondu set; let's really make fondu this year—and price the rest at five bucks each, so they'd at least get three. When she thought of it like that, Kate didn't feel as guilty. Otherwise she was no better than a cannibal, eating through their dreams. Hurry!

She was going to have to knock some sense into Amanda, that was for sure. Really, wrangling Amanda's moods was like taming a wild animal. Maybe that's where Jeff honed his skills, in childhood, with his little spitfire of a sister. Precaution must be taken. There, the presents were all revealed. Kate siphoned the cards off and put them in a neat little pile next to the photograph that so captivated her. It was romantic, there was no doubt about that, but Kate wasn't going to touch it or even turn it to face the wall. She had boundaries, after all. Black plastic bag bulging, Kate stood back and surveyed her destruction. The exposed boxes stared back at her with contempt. Much less lovey-dovey. Onward and upward. It was time to tackle the upstairs.

Chapter Two

What the hell? Andy Beck looked at the sky to see if there was any lingering sign of the tornado that had apparently torn through his front porch, but it was clear and blue. What happened to his porch swing? Why was the welcome mat upside down? Where were the flower pots? Was this the work of vandals? On the Vineyard? It just didn't fit. And although Andy wasn't naïve about the ways of the world, the brutal truth that tragedy could strike anywhere, he'd been coming to Oak Bluffs since he was a kid, and he liked to think it was untouched by time and protected from the harsh realities you'd expect more from big-city living than his island haven. The neighbors may not keep their doors wide open, but they certainly said hello and looked out for each other. And they would never think of vandalizing each other's front porches. This was definitely the work of an outsider.

Although he had to admit, haven or not, the island certainly had seen its share of tragedies over the years, and he wasn't just talking about spotting Bill Clinton in his swimsuit. Weddings in particular seemed cursed on the Vineyard; you didn't have to look any further than the plane crash that took JFK Jr., his wife, and her sister all those years ago.

Andy had certainly had his share of bad luck here, too—

his own disaster of a wedding three years ago was eerily reminiscent of what was happening to Amanda and Pete. Although, as unreasonable as she'd been last night, at least Amanda hadn't been caught making love to another man the night before the nuptials, which was more than he could say for his ex-fiancée, Michelle. That's right, the night before he was to pledge his love to her forever, she was out having sex on the beach, and unfortunately, he didn't mean the drink.

But this was a new day. A clean slate. Just once, Andy wanted to see a wedding on the Vineyard come to fruition! And now he was dealing with a break-in. If bad luck came in threes, this was number two. Amanda freaking out at the wedding and calling it off was, of course, number one. Andy's only consolation, as he surveyed the damage to the porch, was that the newlyweds hadn't come across this mess. It wouldn't have been much fun to carry a bride over this demolished threshold. Whoever did this had better be long gone.

The work he'd put into getting the place ready for Pete and Amanda! Risked his reputation as a guy's guy in the process. Not that he was insecure about his masculinity, but come on, he wouldn't buy a special welcome mat, gussy the place up with flowers, and shower the bedroom in champagne and rose petals for just anyone.

The front door was ajar—whoever did this could still be inside. It wasn't Amanda or Pete; Andy had just left them at the Black Sheep Inn, arguing with each other through a slammed door. He crept to the front door, once again thinking how weddings on the island seemed cursed. Pete and Amanda were supposed to break the curse. What a ridiculous scene. He didn't mean to be judgmental, but Amanda seemed downright crazy yesterday. When, and if, Andy ever got involved in a romantic relationship again, he wanted a nice, normal, woman. No blowups, no erratic behavior, no drama. Poor Pete. Although, to be fair, up until last night Andy had always liked Amanda. What had come over her? Yes, Pete should have kept his mouth shut, even Andy had to concede that one—but her reaction was way out of proportion. He could see Amanda getting a little miffed, but calling off the wedding? Obviously, Andy was a little biased. Pete was his childhood friend, and that's where his loyalties had to lie.

He looked at the door again, and wondered if he should call the police. No, it was better if he checked it out first. But not without a weapon. There was a baseball bat on the corner of his porch. That would have to do. For the first time in three years, Andy felt protective of the cottage. The idea of anyone else treading on it enraged him. It had taken a while, but he could finally gaze upon it without being overtaken by negative emotions. Anyone walking by might stop and stare at the tall man crouching by the front door, wielding a baseball bat, completely oblivious to the fact that he was actually smiling. Not because he was a violent man and looking forward to a fight—quite the opposite; he tended to funnel all his energy, including his anger and disappointments through the lens of a camera. No, Andy was smiling because it dawned on him that he was finally free. The honeymoon house was no longer haunted. The ghost of Michelle was gone.

He had no desire to sit on the front porch with her, and a glass of wine, at the end of the day. Nor did he dream of sharing a cup of coffee and the morning paper at the little breakfast nook, discussing their prospective days, eagerly anticipating their night. And it wasn't just his fantasies of Michelle that were gone; it was all gone. The jealousy, the anger, the longing, the regret. Gone, gone, gone, gone. The cottage was neutral. Of course, it helped that they never spent their honeymoon here, or moved in for that matter—Michelle had never even known about the existence of the cottage; things imploded long before he could tell her about it. He'd been saving the surprise for their wedding night. But as it turned out, he was the one in for a big surprise.

It seemed like such a good idea at the time, not seeing his bride the night before the wedding. Little did Andy know, Michelle's ex-boyfriend had no such plans. He'd actually rented a boat and sailed to the island at the eleventh hour, surprising Michelle at her hotel-room door with two red roses and a single plea for her heart. Maybe Michelle hadn't meant for it to happen. Andy would never know. Did she tell him to go away, or was her answer an immediate yes? Did she agree only to a walk on the beach, a few last words before they said good-bye forever?

And what if Andy hadn't decided to take a walk on the beach that night? He never would have seen the lovers entwined on the sand, lit by the moon. The sick part was, even Andy had to admit it was kind of romantic. He tormented himself with what-ifs. What if roles had been reversed and Michelle had been about to marry another man? Would Andy have ever thought of doing something like her ex did? The guy didn't even know how to sail. Rumor had it he almost got arrested pulling into the dock, because he didn't know how to maneuver the boat and clipped a couple of yachts. That was the kind of love everybody wanted, wasn't it? Deaf, dumb, blind, and sailing-impaired. Willing to risk everything. Had Andy ever felt that for Michelle? It had taken him a few years, but he came to realize unequivocally that the answer was no. He even hoped they were still together. He hoped they were happy.

He couldn't say the same thing for whoever was hiding in the house. In fact, if they were still there, he was about to make their life very, very miserable. Maybe he should call the police after all. What if they'd broken into his makeshift darkroom? The pictures hanging in there had long since processed, so he didn't need to worry about anyone letting in the light. But just the thought of anyone seeing those pictures . . .

He quickly entered the house, careful to avoid the first three floorboards, which had a tendency to squeak. The living room wasn't destroyed per se, but Andy didn't know quite what to make of what he was seeing. The two dozen roses he'd spent a fortune on had vanished. But the vase was still there, mocking him with two little leaves floating on top. And the chocolates on top of the television, the ones from the Sweet Shack, his favorite candy store on the Vineyard, gone.

Andy crept into the kitchen. The cookies were gone, too. Was the thief some kind of a diabetic? He tensed, straining to listen. He was sure he heard noise upstairs.

Baseball bat over his shoulder, he rounded the corner to the stairs. Just as he was about to take the first step, he caught sight of the wedding gifts out of the corner of his eye. He'd loaded all of them into his Jeep and brought them over last night. They had definitely been wrapped. This was outrageous. And weird. A thief taking the time to unwrap his loot? Pile the cards neatly on the table? And the photograph he'd taken of Amanda and Pete was propped up in the middle of the table. At least they hadn't destroyed it. Nevertheless, knowing someone else had violated his gift enraged him. Now he was hoping they were still in the house. Now, right or wrong, he was very much looking forward to a fight.

Andy took the stairs two at a time. When he reached the top, he heard the unmistakable sound of ice rattling in a bucket followed by the pop of a champagne cork. Was he about to burst in on some kind of weird Bonnie and Clyde couple, prematurely celebrating the break-in? He hurried toward the master bedroom, flattening himself against the wall at the last minute. He had to keep the element of surprise; the intruders could be armed. But he didn't hear whispering—or moaning. Just someone . . . guzzling champagne? Unable to help himself, he snuck a look through the doorway and stared in disbelief. There, standing in the middle of his bed in a hideous purple dress, was a woman with a bulging black garbage bag in one hand and his three-hundred-dollar bottle of Dom in the other, guzzling it down like the bridal version of *The Grinch Who Stole Christmas*.

Andy tried not to stare at her cleavage, wet with droplets of champagne, the one bright spot he could see in this bizarre sea he found himself swimming in. He was so flummoxed he forgot all about the baseball bat he was wielding. Unfortunately, it was the first thing the woman saw when she came up for air. Her eyes widened, and she screamed. Before Andy knew what was happening, the champagne bottle was hurtling straight for him. God, the woman had some arm on her! It was only natural to swing the bat in response. In a series of split-second revelations, Andy realized what he'd done, but it was too late—he'd already hit the equivalent of a home run. Only instead of breaking it, he'd boomeranged it, and the champagne bottle was now whizzing straight for the woman's head.

"Duck," Andy screamed. "Duck!" Oh God, it was going to kill her. Luckily, the woman's reflexes kicked in, and she fell facedown on the bed. He'd never seen anyone drop so fast. The bottle, which would have taken her head clean off had she not hit the deck, sailed past and slammed into the back wall, finally shattering, exploding bits of glass and champagne like bomb fragments. Too bad the bed had never seen any action, no maiden voyage, for it had definitely just been christened.

Andy dropped the bat and bent forward, head down, hands on knees, trying to catch his breath. When he looked up again, the woman raised her head off the bed, and they stared at each other for the first time without the fear of imminent danger.

"Hello," she said as if they were meeting over biscuits and tea.

"Hello?" he parroted. "Are you kidding me?" The woman pulled herself into a sitting position, looking completely at ease sitting on her knees, her dress billowing out like ripples of a wine-colored river. She folded her arms across her chest and stared. Andy felt like he had to defend himself, even though she hadn't said another word. "You're trespassing! You've vandalized the house! You stole the plants off the front porch—"

"Transferred."

"You ravaged the—what?"

"What? What?"

"Transferred? What?"

"The plants. I simply transferred them to the neighbor's porch."

Andy shook his head and held out his hands in confusion. He didn't know quite how to handle this. His desire for a fight was conflicting with the energy coming off this woman, drawing him toward her and equally disorienting him. It was as if she'd sideswiped him, and he was stumbling around, trying to figure out exactly where the hell he was. Luckily, focusing on the black garbage bag in her hand helped him revive a little bit of his anger. He marched over to it, pried it open, and made a triumphant noise as he yanked out a rose.

"And where are you 'temporarily transferring' these, m'lady? These prize-winning, top-dollar roses? To the dump?"

"They're beautiful, yes," she admitted. "But 'prize-winning?' You're stretching it."

"And that," Andy yelled, pointing at the enormous champagne stain splashed against the back wall, "was not yours to drink."

"You're referring to the bottle that almost killed me?" she yelled back.

"I told you to duck!"

"I can't thank you enough. Because my natural instinct would have been to stay and pray."

"Screw you." Andy couldn't believe he was having this ridiculous argument with this psychotic woman. Even if she was extremely attractive; even if he did have an urge to rip her dress off and—

His lurid thoughts were interrupted when he glanced at the floor. It was immaculate. So was the bed cover.

"Where are my rose petals?" Andy said. The woman looked guiltily at his Hoover, which was propped near the foot of the bed. Its bag was bulging.

"You sucked up my rose petals?" Then, he made the mistake of looking around the room. He couldn't believe what he was seeing along his side wall. He walked over and just stared.

Every single photograph from his dark room was out and lined up against the wall. Every photo he had taken of Michelle for the book. The photographs no one knew existed; the photographs nobody had ever laid eyes on but him.

"Did you take those?" the woman asked. "They're incredible. They're—"

"Shut up," Andy said. His voice was low and serious. For once, she didn't snap back a reply. He ran his hands through his hair, not sure how to handle this. "Get out," he said.

"But—"

"Get out."

"I can explain. I'm Kate. Amanda sent me over here . . ."

Kate continued to ramble, but Andy stopped listening to her. So that's who she was. Amanda's maid of honor, the best friend. He'd heard quite a bit about her from Pete. In fact, a few things he'd been told had intrigued him. He'd been looking forward to meeting her. None of it mattered now.

"You seriously need to get out of here right now," Andy said. "I don't care who you are. I don't care what you think you're doing." He turned to face her, and even though he couldn't mistake the look of fear on her face, he was too angry to care. "These weren't yours to touch," he said. "These are none of your business."

"I . . . I . . . didn't realize. They're so beautiful—" Andy put his finger up to his lip. The woman stopped talking.

"You need to promise me something," Andy said.

"Anything."

"You won't mention these pictures to anyone."

"Okay."

"Not Amanda, not Pete, not your mother, not the mailman." Kate held up her right arm like she was testifying in court. "I swear."

"Okay then. Now get out."

"Okay, okay. But I have to ask. Why in the world wouldn't you want anyone to see these? They're amazing. They could be in a gallery, or a book—" Andy cut her another look. "I won't say a word," she said.

"Good-bye, Kate."

"Amanda will be here any minute—"

"You can wait on the porch. You know—the one you disman-tled piece by piece."

"I can explain—"

"Oh, you can explain everything, can't you? Well, don't bother. I wouldn't really be listening anyway."

Kate squared her shoulders and lifted her chin. "Again," she said. "I apologize." She walked to the door. "I never should have let Amanda rope me into being a love sniper. But she's my best friend, and she's in pain. And I shouldn't have taken your pictures out of that room. But I couldn't help it. They're so amazing—just like the photograph you took of Amanda and Pete. It was like I was standing right in front of them. You captured them so well. And this woman . . ."

Kate pointed at the photographs lining the wall. They were truly stunning. The subject was a beautiful blonde wearing a billowing white dress in some, a sleek red one in others, and in the last one a little black dress. There were shots from all over the Vineyard, the lighthouses, the Gay Head Cliffs, the marina, the golf course. The colors were so vivid, the images almost haunting.

"You just have to know," Kate began. "These pictures—"

Andy loomed in front of her.

"These pictures," he interrupted, "are none of your business."

Kate turned away, but stopped when she reached the door, and spoke her last piece without turning to look at him.

"You might be very talented You might be very generous," she said as Andy studied the back of her. "Loaning your house to Amanda and Pete for their honeymoon . . . You may even think you're extremely attractive—I couldn't say. But what I do know . . . is that Amanda was right about one thing. You. Are. An egotistical ass."

Chapter Three

Amanda knew it was a waste of time, playing it over and over again in her mind, but she couldn't help it. She sat on a boulder overlooking the marina, sipping a latte and regretting all the lemon-drop shots from the bar last night, not to mention the Apple Pucker on the beach. Her overnight bag was beside her, and she was dressed in a simple white sundress that should have been her honeymoon outfit. Pete should have been at her side, enjoying the sea air, nuzzling her neck, and whispering "Good morning, Mrs. Dean" into her ear. But here she was, alone, unnuzzled, and still Amanda Bailey.

Had she made a mistake? How could she not go over and over it in her mind, replaying every second up until the wedding? Amanda gazed at the line of sailboats docked at the pier, swaying gently in the breeze. In the distance a catamaran skated across the ocean. This was the life. Amanda loved every bit of the island. She loved its cleanliness. She loved the shops on Main Street. She loved the boating culture. She loved the up-to-date summer outfits. She loved the beaches and the celebrity sightings. Unfortunately, she and Pete would never be able to afford to live here, but they'd been lucky enough to know Andy—he'd arranged the whole thing: the exclusive reservation for the ceremony and reception at the Harbor

House, the offer of his cottage for an entire month—an offer that quite frankly surprised Amanda, given what she knew about the man. Pete had sworn her to secrecy, but despite the fact that Andy was a gifted artist, and would clearly do anything for Pete, he was a player, a gambler, and an egotistical ass.

Still, if the wedding had gone the way it was supposed to, she would have been thankful for his generosity. Amanda hugged her knees to her chest and breathed in the scent of the ocean. At least everyone who flew in for the wedding had a beautiful day ahead of them. Amanda made sure they were all still going sightseeing as planned. She'd begged her parents to orchestrate the outings without her. Some were going golfing, others wine tasting and shopping, and the last bit sailing. They would meet up for dinner in the evening. Everyone except for Amanda and her almost-husband. Amanda wasn't going to face any of them, that was for sure.

They'd still gone on with the reception, even after the wedding had been canceled. After Amanda ran off with Kate to the nearest bar, Pete convinced everyone else to stay and party. Although, what choice did he have? It had all been paid for, not to mention their friends and family had traveled near and far, spent money, and taken time out of their busy lives to celebrate with them. Poor Pete. That's what everyone was saying behind her back, she just knew it. Poor Pete. They thought she was to blame. Was she?

She'd gone over it with Kate and the bartender last night, but she couldn't help but feel they'd been coddling her. So she went over it again this morning with her mother, her aunt Jessica, and three of the six bridesmaids. Of course they agreed that Pete had been out of line, everyone agreed that, but the verdict seemed to be they weren't sure it raised to the level of calling off the wedding. And then her mother said the worst thing she could have possibly said: "Amanda you're the one who will have to live with Pete day in and day out, and you're the only one who can make this decision."

What a thing to say! How could she speak the truth at a time like this? Amanda's friends had always loved Amanda's mother, her straightforward style, her laissez-faire parenting. Good for sneaking out and doing wild things as a kid; bad for devastating moments where you just needed a little comfort in the form of good old-fashioned maternal lies.

And the people at the coffee shop where she bought her latte this morning hadn't been that helpful, either. One woman said men were like dogs and needed to be trained, but even that depended on whether you had a purebred or a mutt. Another woman shouted at Amanda not to pay any attention to that nonsense, that men were just like us only some of them could fix things. At this, the woman looked pointedly at the man sitting across from her. He shook his head and shoveled food in his mouth without a word. None of it had been helpful.

Why couldn't someone just tell her what to do? What if it was just a case of cold feet? Isn't that what bridesmaids and the mother of the bride were for? To push her off the matrimonial cliff no matter how much she protested? Amanda had gone tandem skydiving once; Pete had set it up as a surprise, all because, on one of their first dates, Amanda had bragged she was going to go skydiving on her thirtieth birthday. She'd lied, of course; she had no intention of doing any such thing, but she was trying to impress Pete with her sense of adventure. How was she to know that he would take her seriously and surprise her with a tandem instructor and a little plane? All the way up she thought she was going to be sick. When they reached their destination altitude of 12,000 feet, Amanda stood at the mouth of the plane and revolted. No way was she doing this! She didn't care if the pilot said she had no choice now; what kind of person would willingly jump out of a perfectly good plane? She grabbed the top of the door with both hands and braced herself against the instructor, who was trying to push her out. Did the instructor let up? Did he say, "Oh, well, you changed your mind, we won't go."

No. He pried her fingers loose and pushed her out of the plane. And it had been the most exhilarating time of her life. What a rush! At first the air hit her like a brick wall, temporarily clogging her eardrums, so all she could feel was the pounding of her heart in her chest, and then they were falling, falling, falling. She spread her arms out and bent her legs back as she'd been taught, and suddenly she was flying. After several glorious moments of free-falling, the parachute opened, the world fell silent, and they soared.

It was the greatest feeling you could imagine, down, down, down, arms spread out, head held high. The ride was way too short, the ground coming up way too fast. Amanda started to worry once again, convinced she was going to slam face-first into the ground. But after a few tugs on the strings from the instructor, they were calmly gliding feetfirst as the ground came up to meet them. And even though she stumbled a bit on the landing, causing herself and the instructor, who was still strapped to her, to topple over and kiss dirt, it was still an incredible rush. And when they finally managed to pick themselves up, there was Pete on his knees in front of her, with a big grin and a diamond ring. It had been the most romantic moment of her life. And none of it would have happened if the instructor hadn't given her a big shove. Maybe she should have made him her maid of honor instead.

Soon she would go to the cottage and go over it again with Kate. She would make Kate give a definite, thought-out opinion. But first, she had to get it straight in her own mind. It all started with the dress-fitting. True, the fitting had nothing to do with her fight with Pete, but if she was going to go over everything again, she might as well relish how happy she was before it all went to hell. Of all the wedding advice she'd tried to glean from magazines, websites, and friends, you would think someone, anyone, would have warned her to muzzle the groom.

One day before the wedding. The fitting.

"Don't cry." They were standing in the back of the bridal shop, in the dressing area. Amanda was in the middle of the floor in her wedding gown. If Kate started crying, she was going to lose it. "I mean it," she said, pinching Kate on the back of the arm.

"Ow, that hurts."

"It was supposed to. If you start crying, you're going to make me cry, and I'm not going to have red eyes, do you hear me?" Kate nodded and told Amanda how beautiful she looked.

"I know that's what everyone tells brides," Kate said. "You know? All babies and brides are supposed to be beautiful when we all know there are some really ugly ones out there. I'm sorry, that's an awful thing to say. But it's true. You are stunning. Truly stunning."

Amanda looked in the mirror and flushed with pleasure. Her wedding gown was simple, but gorgeous. With its empire waist, V-neckline down to her ample breasts, and tiny diamonds and pearls around the waist, she even took her own breath away.

But what was threatening to make both of them start crying and never stop was the thing they weren't mentioning, the cloud hanging over both of them all morning: Jeff should have been here to see this. He would have loved the Vineyard. He would have loved all the relatives coming together; he had a way with everyone, including Uncle Arthur. An uncle by marriage, Uncle Arthur was a Southerner and a religious conservative whom most people couldn't take for more than five minutes once he started in on whiskey and the war. But Jeff would have happily chatted with him, and it wouldn't have been long before Uncle Arthur was putty in his hands. Jeff would have no doubt even slipped in a point or two of his own, and Uncle Arthur would have wound up agreeing. Jeff just had a way with people, an easy way in the world. And by now he would have explored every nook and cranny of the island, with Kate on his arm. At the wedding they would have danced all night long and toasted Amanda and Pete, declaring them the second luckiest couple in the room. Jeff would have made it clear that he and Kate were still the luckiest, and he would have done it in a way that wouldn't have offended anyone.

And even though her father was still alive, if she could have Jeff back for just one night, Amanda would have asked Jeff to walk her down the aisle. It was impossible to believe he'd been gone for five years. One awful night, one icy intersection, and he was gone forever. Kate had been the lucky one; she was in the car, too, but despite a large scar on her left arm that she'd kept covered ever since the accident, she came out unscathed.

"He's not going to know what hit him," Kate said. "I've never seen such a beautiful bride." Amanda reached out and took Kate's hands in hers.

"You're going to find love again, too," Amanda said. Kate squeezed back and looked away.

"This weekend isn't about me," she said. "And I couldn't be happier for you and Pete."

"I know that. But Jeff would have—"

"I don't want to talk about it." Kate tried to pull away, but Amanda wouldn't let her go.

"It's been five years. He would be so proud of you—"

"Mandy, please." Amanda was proud of Kate, too. After a year of grieving, she went to Guatemala and taught English to local schoolchildren. Then, when she returned to Iowa City, she became involved with a nonprofit foundation that Jeff had supported. And she'd remained single all these years. Amanda knew Kate had loved Jeff since she first laid eyes on eight-year-old him flicking marbles in the driveway. He didn't even give her a second glance when she trampled over to play with Amanda. Amanda loved Kate like a sister. And now that she had Pete, she understood how utterly love could transform your life. She was going to make it her mission to help Kate find love again. She had no doubt that's what Jeff would have wanted her to do.

And here they were on Martha's Vineyard, one of the most romantic places on earth, and they'd only been on the island a day. Maybe Kate would like one of Pete's friends. A couple of them were cute, all right. She could have any of them except Andrew Beck. She was thrilled when he told Pete he'd photograph the wedding, and over the moon when he loaned them the cottage for their honeymoon, but there was no way Amanda was going to let him put the moves on Kate. She knew all about Andy Beck and his sick little games with women. Pete had told her all his dirty little secrets. Still, she had a sneaking suspicion Kate was going to like him. And she couldn't blame her. He was talented, handsome, and filthy rich. And Kate didn't know what she knew—so why wouldn't she like him?

Nevertheless, she wouldn't say anything to Kate unless she absolutely had to. She wasn't a gossiper by nature, and again, Andrew had been extremely generous. She was a little surprised Pete had accepted Andy's offer, but as Pete pointed out, just because Andy had a bad reputation when it came to women didn't mean he wasn't a good friend. Besides, Pete and Andrew went back almost as far as she did with Kate. She wouldn't judge Andy as long as he didn't try to get his paws on Kate. No way. Not after all she'd been through.

"A couple of Pete's friends are single," Amanda said. Kate smiled, but Amanda noticed it didn't reach her eyes. "Would you like to try your dress on again?" Amanda asked.

"No need," Kate said. "It fits." Her voice was tight and high.

"Kate."

"It's beautiful."

"You're not mad?"

"Not at all."

Amanda let her breath out. The bridesmaid dresses were all

sleeveless; she'd thought for a minute Kate might refuse to wear it.

"I'll just have to find a shawl or a wrap," Kate said as she unzipped Amanda.

"But none of the other bridesmaids will have a shawl or a wrap," Amanda said, stepping out of the dress. "Don't you think you'll kind of stand out?"

"I don't mind standing out," Kate said. "Unless you want someone else to do the honors." Amanda didn't reply right away. She didn't want to upset Kate when she was handling her dress.

"Of course not," she said at last.

"Good," Kate said. "It's settled, then." Kate put the dress away while Amanda reluctantly put her regular-people clothes back on. It was such a waste that you could only wear your wedding dress once. Even the bridesmaids would be able to wear their dresses again; Amanda had picked them out with that in mind. There should be some kind of tradition where brides wore their dresses all week. Or at least all day. Just like French women wore crowns or some kind of fancy hat on their thirtieth birthday.

"What's next?" Amanda asked.

"French toast and mimosas?" Kate suggested.

"I have to fit into my gown tomorrow," Amanda said. "I'll skip the French toast."

"Mimosas it is," Kate sang, hooking her arm into Amanda's. "I'll eat your French toast."

"You're the best," Amanda said as they headed out of the shop. The dressmaker would keep her gown until tomorrow. The rooms at the inn were small and crowded, and Amanda didn't want to take the chance of anything happening to it. Amanda didn't broach the subject of Kate's dress again, although she was thinking as they headed down the street and around the corner for breakfast that there wouldn't be much Kate could do about it if the shawl or wrap were to disappear minutes before the ceremony. Sometimes friends needed space to work out their issues, and sometimes they needed a little shove.

Wedding day. Early evening just before the ceremony.

"It's wrinkled, isn't it? It looks wrinkled."

Kate took a deep breath and then treated Amanda to a fake smile. "Honestly Amanda. It's perfect."

Amanda whirled around. "What about the back? Is the back wrinkled?"

"No. Nada. Perfecto."

"Don't do the Spanish thing. I'm not in the mood." Amanda didn't mean to sound so curt, but it just seemed like every little thing that could have gone wrong today had. Relatives had missed plane connections, caterers called and said the credit card on file had been rejected, a couple of brides-maids had gained too much weight to fit into their dresses and Amanda's aunt was busy trying to tailor them . . .

Not to mention she and Pete had been so busy this week they'd barely slept. And her wedding dress was wrinkled. Why didn't Kate just admit that?

"What can I do?" Kate asked. Everyone was waiting. Amanda was late to her own wedding.

"Are you sure everyone else is ready?" Amanda asked, stalling for time.

"Yes," Kate said. "They're all waiting."

"Don't put it like that."

"Anticipating, then. Everyone is patiently anticipating your arrival." The wedding ceremony was outside, on the great lawn of the Harbor House, overlooking the ocean. The sun was shooting dark pink rays across the sky. And even though it was summer, it grew cool at night. Everyone was probably anxious to get under the heated tents and start the party.

"What about Pete? Are you sure Pete's out there?"

Kate pulled her wrap around her, which she hadn't let out of her sight for a second. "He's out there," she said. Her voice was strained, trying way too hard to sound chipper.

"Did he remember the rings?"

"I'm sure he did."

"You're sure or you know?"

"Amanda. What is going on? This is it. The part where you need to forget about everything, go out there, and marry the man you love."

"You're right," Amanda said. "I'm sorry. I'm so sorry." Kate stepped up to give her a hug but stopped when she saw the look of horror on Amanda's face. After all, a hug could generate another couple hundred wrinkles. So at the last minute, Kate simply air-patted her on the shoulder instead.

"You look absolutely gorgeous," she said.

"Thank you." A rap on the door interrupted them. Amanda turned her stricken face to the sound.

"Who is it?" Kate asked.

"It's Pete."

"Oh my God," Amanda said in a loud stage whisper. "What is he doing?"

"Hi, honey," Pete said. "Are you ready?"

"Don't come in!" Amanda yelled.

"I'm not coming in," Pete said. "But are you ever coming out?"

"Yes. I'm coming, I'm coming." You could almost hear Pete's sigh of relief through the door.

"Good, good," he said. "Everyone's getting worried that you changed your mind." Pete laughed, the kind of laugh he always gave when he was nervous. It sounded like the bark of a wolf, or a really sick coyote.

"Couldn't you have sent someone else?" Amanda asked. "It's bad luck to talk to each other before the ceremony."

"I'm going—but you are coming, right?"

"Of course I'm coming." Amanda shot Kate a look that

gave Kate a good glimpse of who was going to win all their future fights.

"We'll be right there, Pete," Kate said.

"Good," Pete said. "Because any longer and I'm going to just close my eyes, grab the nearest bridesmaid, and marry her!" Amanda's jaw literally dropped. She looked at Kate, whose face mirrored her own horrified expression. Kate tried to cover it up with a little smile and a shrug, à la "boys will be boys."

"Amanda," Kate said. Amanda marched back to the door and threw it open. Pete had just turned away, but he was still within striking distance.

"What did you say?" Amanda demanded. She hated the fact that this was how Pete was going to first see her—glaring at him from the dressing room instead of sailing up the aisle with everyone smiling. Pete must have had the same thought, for he slapped his hand over his eyes and turned around.

"Hey," he said. "You said it was bad luck. Honey, shut the door." Amanda did no such thing. She put her hands on her hips.

"Look at me," she said. "And say that again. To my face."

"Say what?" Pete said. Amanda narrowed her eyes. "Honey," Pete pleaded. "It was a joke."

"Which bridesmaid would you 'grab'?" she asked. "Will any of them do, or is there one in particular you had in mind?"

"Kate?" Pete called.

"You want Kate?" Amanda said.

"No! I want you! I was just calling for Kate—asking her to help me handle you."

"Handle me? Handle me?"

"Honey, please. You're stressing me out." Amanda turned to Kate, who seemed to be cowering in the background. Amanda's eyes filled with tears.

"Don't cry," Kate said. At this Pete's head snapped up, and he went to Amanda, tried to put his arms around her. She pushed him away.

"Honey, I'm sorry. I'm sorry. It was a joke. A really bad joke. I love you. We're getting married. I can't wait to make you my wife."

"Really?"

"How could you even ask? Compared to you, all your bridesmaids are dogs. No offense, Kate."

"None taken," Kate said, giving a little "woof." Nobody laughed.

"That was a horrible thing to say," Amanda said.

"Again?" Pete said. "I can't say anything right, can I? I'm sorry, okay? Let's just assume from now on, no matter what stupid thing comes out of my mouth for the rest of my life, that I'm sorry. Okay? Do you want to add that to the vows? It's not too late."

"I can't believe you're talking to me like this right before our wedding," Amanda said in a quiet but deadly tone of voice.

"I'm sorry," Pete said again. "I'm just hot. And tired. Andy kept me out a little too late last night—"

"You were out last night? The night before our wedding?"

"Just a little."

"Are you hungover? Did you go to a strip club?"

"Yeah. When it comes to strip clubs, Martha's Vineyard is second only to Amsterdam's Red Light District!"

"Where's your dad?" Kate interrupted. "Is he ready to walk his little girl down the aisle?"

"Is that the only reason you didn't go to a strip club— because there aren't any on the island?"

"What am I supposed to say here?" Pete asked. "That I never want to see another woman naked as long as I live?" Amanda watched Pete catch the look of warning on Kate's face. "Oh," he said. "I am supposed to say that, aren't I?"

"Not just say it," Amanda said. "You're supposed to mean it."

"You're being ridiculous. I love you. I want to marry you. But if you're seriously asking me to say I never want to see another woman naked for the rest of my life—I won't do it.

Because that would be a lie, and I don't want to lie to you, honey. Ever." Pete smiled. Amanda just stared. Kate shook her head. "Oh," Pete said. "I don't mean I will see naked women. I would never cheat on you, honey. Not ever. You know that. I mean like on the Internet—accidentally, of course. I might accidentally see women naked on the Internet. I won't linger or anything. I'm not a pervert. I'm just saying from time to time I'll probably *want* to see other women. Not emotionally. Just—you know. Naked."

Present day. Marina.

What a complete ass. Amanda was convinced she'd done the right thing. The only question left was—what the hell was she supposed to do now?

Chapter Four

"Amanda, we really shouldn't be doing this," Kate said. It had only been twenty-four hours since the girls commandeered the Honeymoon House, and Amanda had already come up with a diabolical mission for the two of them to carry out. They were standing in front of the Black Sheep Inn holding photocopied pictures of Pete's "mugshot," a picture of Pete that Amanda had blown slightly out of proportion, adding a tinge of red to the eyes to make him look like the featured escapee on *America's Most Wanted*.

"He's left me no choice," Amanda said. "How am I supposed to grieve and move on with him hovering around?"

"Amanda, it's only been a day since the wedding—"

"There was no wedding."

"The almost-wedding, then. And where else is Pete supposed to go? You two rented out your apartment for the entire month." Amanda and Pete lived in Brooklyn in the trendy neighborhood of Park Slope and took advantage of craigslist for furniture, tickets, rants and raves, and renting out their apartment whenever they were out of town for more than a day.

"He could stay with his parents," Amanda grumbled. "And thanks for reminding me that one of us is going to have to start looking for another place to live."

Kate sighed. She'd been listening to Amanda gripe nonstop for the past twenty-four hours. She kept thinking any minute Amanda was going to come to her senses and admit she'd overreacted and never should have walked out on Pete. Instead, she'd grown crazier by the minute, in large part Kate suspected because Pete hadn't called or texted since they argued at the inn. Amanda pretended not to care, but she was checking her cell phone so often, Kate feared she was going to get carpal tunnel from flipping it open. Now here they were again, about to "out" Pete as some kind of criminal.

Kate didn't want to do it, and even though it seemed to be a losing battle, she continued to gently try and talk sense into her friend. "It's defamation of character," Kate pointed out. "We're pushing the limits here. He could sue."

"Pete doesn't have enough money to take me to court."

"His friend Andy does, though, doesn't he?" Kate had been trying to slip Andy into the conversation whenever she could. Either Amanda hadn't noticed or she simply didn't care to talk about Andy, because so far she'd ignored all references to him. Kate couldn't stop thinking about their meeting and how angry he'd been with her for taking out his pictures. She was dying to talk to Amanda about it, to see if she could relieve some of her guilt—what was wrong with looking at an artist's work? You think most people would have been flattered. He was completely livid. She promised him she wouldn't mention the pictures to anyone, and when she and Amanda moved into the Honeymoon House, the pictures were gone, not a trace of them anywhere. Kate decided if Andy could be magnanimous enough to let them kidnap his cottage, the least she could do was keep his secret. Although what choice did the poor man have, he probably didn't want to incur Amanda's wrath anymore than the rest of them. "Don't poke the bear," Jeff used to say whenever Amanda was in a mood. Kate shuddered to think what Amanda would've done if Andy hadn't let them stay at the house.

"This island isn't big enough for the two of us," Amanda said as they stepped up to the inn. Kate wanted to point out that they'd managed not to run into Pete the past twenty-four hours despite trouncing around to every beach, restaurant, golf course, and marina, wearing as little as possible and flirting outrageously with every bellboy and bartender in town in hopes that a certain someone might be lurking nearby and overcome with jealousy. Kate was exhausted; pretending to have fun all day long was a drag.

"He wants to see naked women," Amanda said as she dragged Kate around the island. "Well, I want to see naked men." In truth they'd seen ones in swimsuits, boxers, and a couple of ill-fitting Speedos, but to Kate's relief, none of them had been in the nude.

A little bell above the door tinkled as Amanda and Kate entered the inn and approached a slight woman behind the counter.

"Have you seen this man?" Amanda asked, heaving against the counter and slamming the picture of Pete's face on top. Amanda knew very well Pete was staying here, down to the exact room. The woman peered over her reading glasses, her lips already quivering. Kate couldn't believe how quickly Amanda had morphed into a cynical detective, on the force twenty years too long, with the disposition of one who'd quit smoking, drinking, and eating carbs all on one go. The lady licked her dry lips and shifted her gaze to the stairwell on her left.

Amanda leaned in as if she knew a confession was forthcoming. "He wanted a room for a full month," the woman whispered. "It was just his luck Mr. and Mrs. Griffith had to fly back to Miami. They booked their room for the entire summer, I couldn't just let it remain empty." She looked around before leaning into Amanda and Kate. "They had to bring their eldest boy to rehab. It's his fifth stint." She shook her head and then reached for a sanitary wipe in a container by the phone. She pulled one out and began wiping the mouthpiece of the phone. Then she used the same wipe on the counter. Finally, she glanced upstairs. "He paid in cash," she said.

"What kind of rehab makes you pay in cash?" Kate asked. "Isn't that like a debtors support group making you pay by credit card?"

"What?" the woman said.

"She meant Pete paid in cash," Amanda said.

"Oh," Kate said. "That makes much more sense." Amanda banged the counter with her fist. Both Kate and the woman jumped.

"I knew it," she said. "I knew it!" Then, as if remembering she was supposed to stay in character, she shook her head with a "tsk-tsk" and threw a loaded glance to Kate. When Kate didn't mimic the "tsk-tsk," Amanda kicked her in the shins. Kate weakly delivered at least one "tsk" and slightly shook her head at the woman.

"I'm sure the cash is good," Amanda said in a tone that conveyed the opposite. "You checked it out, though, right?" Amanda mimicked holding a bill up to the light to see if it was real or counterfeit. The woman, who was starting to look sick, shook her head no.

"No problem," Amanda said. "I wouldn't worry too much about it. Although if I were you, I'd try to pass those bills off as fast as I could."

"Is he dangerous?" the woman asked, picking up the picture Amanda had been edging closer and closer to her. Amanda unconvincingly shook her head again. Kate wished she were anywhere but here and wondered if she should put a stop to the madwoman she barely recognized as her best friend.

"Look," Amanda said. "As long as you kick him out, we're authorized to refund the money he paid." She turned to Kate and held out her hand.

"What?" Kate asked.

"You have the authorized credit card, don't you?"

"Me?"

Amanda nodded vigorously and then leaned in and whispered.

"I'll pay you back."

Kate hesitated. She shouldn't be using her credit card when she was out of a job. But Amanda didn't know that. Amanda was also slightly forgetful when it came to things like paying a person back.

"I'm not sure they authorized it," Kate said.

"Let's just try it," Amanda said. Kate sighed and dug out her card. Amanda snatched it out of her hand and handed it to the woman. The woman hesitated, and then took it.

"I'm not sure what to do," the woman said, turning the credit card over in her hand.

"Maybe you've suddenly had a convention come to town," Amanda said. "Or relatives. Yes, relatives came in to surprise you for your birthday!" Amanda leaned so far over the counter her feet were lifted off the floor. She picked up the credit card and swiped it into the machine. "I'm not saying he's a pervert," Amanda said as they waited for the card to process. "But this witness herself heard him say he's on the prowl for naked women." Amanda landed back on the floor and shoved Kate forward. The woman put both hands over her mouth.

"He seemed so nice," the woman said, ripping the receipt out of the machine. Kate didn't even want to look at the amount. "So heartbroken. He was left at the altar you know."

"Liar!" Amanda shouted.

"Panda," Kate said. "Calm down." Amanda leaned over the counter again until she was only an inch from the woman's face.

"Seconds before the bride was about to say 'I do,'" Amanda said in a voice that would have scared the most seasoned exorcist, "the groom was contemplating molesting one of the bridesmaids." The woman gasped, flipped Pete's picture upside down, and picked up the phone.

"Mr. Dean," she said after a moment. "I'm afraid I have some bad news. My sister is coming to town, quite unexpectedly, and she's bringing. . . all of my cousins."

Kate waited until they were on their way home, and Amanda announced she wanted to take it easy the rest of the day, to break the news that she was going out for the evening. A nice old man from Grapevine Books, an adorable book-shop she managed to sneak into without Amanda on her back, had invited her to go on a group sail that evening. He'd caught her looking at books on Martha's Vineyard, stood right over her shoulder while she was looking at a picture of a sailboat, and asked her if she'd ever been. She soon warmed up to him. His name was Tony, and he was the owner of the little inde-pendent bookstore. Her plan all along was to see if she could find out anything about Andy Beck, and she hit pay dirt. One casual mention of his name and she learned Andy had been working on a photo book of Martha's Vineyard, but the proj-ect fell through. It was apparent Tony had been counting on showcasing the book in his store; when he spoke about the project he sounded like a jilted lover complaining about their ex. Kate was about to push for more information when Tony said he had to go—there was a ladies' book club coming in. That's when she agreed to the group sail; hopefully they could pick the conversation back up.

Besides, she desperately needed a break from Amanda. Breaking it to her, however, was proving difficult. "I can't wait to get into our pj's, drink wine, and talk," Amanda said. Kate smiled. She couldn't think of anything worse. Besides turning the island into her own personal edition of *America's Most Wanted,* and searching for naked men, all they'd been doing was sitting in their pj's and swilling alcohol. Kate was going sailing no matter what. Did Amanda really think she was going to spend her impromptu vacation getting drunk and man-bashing? It was a small enough island, and if they weren't careful they were going to become known as the Man-haters of Martha's Vineyard. Who was Martha anyway, and how did she get a vineyard? Kate would have to google it next time she was on the Internet. She'd also have to google "scorned almost-brides" and see if there were any tips.

Because so far, Amanda showed no signs of turning into the insecure ball of mush Kate was sure she could mold into sanity and roll back to Pete so she could get on with the business of getting on with her life. A life that didn't include Andy Beck. So why was she thinking about him nonstop? It was being in his house, Kate decided, surrounded by his things. And she was dying to see his photographs again. Maybe Tony from the bookstore had copies. She had to go sailing. She had to find out more about Andy.

"I think I'll just stay dressed," Kate said as they walked up to the porch.

"Nonsense," Amanda said. "We'll change into pajamas."

"I can't very well go sailing in pajamas," Kate blurted out. Amanda stopped, blocking Kate from the door.

"Sailing?"

"Yes. I'm sort of going tonight."

"Sailing."

"Sailing." *There, this isn't so bad. Except for the whole time I say sailing, she says sailing, I say sailing bit.*

"With who?"

Kate wondered if Amanda realized she was bellowing. It was probably not the best time to tell her.

"Tony from the bookstore," Kate said.

"Tony from the bookstore?" Amanda parroted. Kate noticed she said "bookstore" like a Sunday-school teacher would say "porn." "You'd rather go sailing with Tony from the bookstore than drink wine in your pajamas with me?" If Kate wasn't careful, she was going to walk right into one of Amanda's verbal traps.

"Of course not," Kate said.

"Good." Amanda marched up to the front door. Kate meandered over to the swing. She picked up the fallen chain from the disabled right side, and before she could chicken out, she reattached the hook. She could feel Amanda's glare on her, but she couldn't turn back now. Kate sat on the swing like a prisoner cutting the first slice of a barbed-wire barrier.

"I'm kinda surprised you don't want me to go sailing," Kate dared to say. "You're the one who told me I needed to move on with my life."

"That was before I learned my fiancé was a total perv," Amanda said. "I've changed my mind. We're done with men."

"We?"

"You're never going to find another Jeff, Kate. You know that, don't you?"

Kate used her feet to push off, swinging the little porch swing harder than she should.

"I know that, Amanda," Kate said. "But I'm not going to just shrivel up and die!"

"But I'm on my honeymoon, Kate. You can't go on a date and leave me alone on my honeymoon!"

"It's not a date," Kate said. "It's a group sail."

"Katie!" It was Amanda's alarmed tone of voice that finally got to Kate. She was truly upset, like a psychotic patient on the verge of a meltdown, and only Kate had the medicine.

"Okay, okay," Kate said. "You know me and things that float. I'd probably get seasick anyway." It was all a lie. Kate had never once had a problem with things that float, but Amanda seemed to buy it hook, line, and sinker.

"Thank you, thank you, thank you," Amanda said, joining her on the swing. "I promise, we'll go sailing another night."

We?

"Great," Kate said, wracking her brain for a way out of this. Unfortunately, if she wanted to escape the cottage tonight, she was going to have to go all soap opera on Amanda's ass and drug her nightcap.

Chapter Five

"Someone is in the backyard," Amanda said, dragging Kate to a window in the kitchen. "Look."

Sure enough, there was a man in the yard, setting up a large, green tent. Kate's first thought was that the army had given up on the inner city and was recruiting in Martha's Vineyard. The man turned around, and she recognized Pete. Kate felt a strange stab of disappointment as she realized she'd been hoping it was Andy. This couldn't be happening to her, could it? Could she have a crush on some guy she didn't even know? One who hated her guts, no less?

"What is he doing?" Amanda demanded as if Kate had sold him the tent.

"You took his mug shot to the inn," Kate said, wondering if there was any room in the tent for her. "What do you think he's doing here?" At that, Pete discovered Amanda and Kate in the window and waved. Amanda hit the floor. "He's not armed," Kate said, nudging Amanda with her toe.

"Get down," Amanda said in a low whisper.

"He can't hear you through a closed window," Kate said, staring at Pete while Amanda fussed with her hair.

"I look like shit," she said. "He had to see me when I look like shit." Just then, a second head emerged from the tent. It was Andy. A little bird took flight in Kate's chest. She wasn't even aware of drawing in her breath until she felt a sharp pinch on her shin. Then Amanda's head popped up next to hers.

"What? What did you see?" Andy had disappeared back into the tent. Pete was still securing one of the lines.

"Andy Beck is with him," Kate said, now whispering herself. "He just went into the tent."

"Let's go." Amanda pulled Kate so hard she almost yanked her arm out of the socket. Soon they were flying up the stairs. Amanda immediately threw open her suitcase and scoured it for the dress she'd been wearing all week, the one designed to catch Pete's attention.

"Nice pajamas," Kate couldn't help but say.

"I have a master's degree in business," Amanda said, pulling off her sweatshirt, "and sometimes I still feel like I'm in the seventh grade, waiting to be asked to the dance."

"I know," Kate said. "I should be thinking about my career. Instead I'm like a little girl with a crush. It must be the island. Takes me back to summer vacations when I was a kid."

Amanda pulled off her sweats and pulled the sundress over her head. It was a tight fit; in other words, perfect.

"Hold on," Amanda said. "Crush? What crush?"

Kate was still staring at her suitcase. She was fine, she realized, in her jeans and top. As usual, she had a lightweight blouse over her tank top that came to just below her elbows. It would look too out of place with a sundress.

"Kate?" Amanda said. "I said, what crush?"

Kate went to the bedroom window and peered into the backyard. Andy and Pete were throwing a football. Their shirts were off. Kate was thrilled to see Andy had nice arms, but he wasn't completely buff. He was slightly pale, which suggested he wasn't one to lounge on the beach. He wasn't hairy (a big plus for Kate), and he had a tiny little paunch. Not a gut by any means, but he wasn't a gym rat. And although Kate was slim, she by no means considered herself on par with models, and she was very aware of the fact that she was in her thirties now, no longer even young by most standards. And with her scar . . .

In other words, she was imperfect, and as sexy as Andy Beck was with his shirt off, she was thrilled to see he wasn't picture-perfect, either. Unfortunately, it made him even sexier in her eyes. She wanted to put her hand on his tiny paunch— and although she probably wouldn't have had such thoughts in the seventh grade, she was definitely feeling more schoolgirl than grown-up. Amanda followed Kate's gaze out the window.

"Since when do you know Andrew?" she asked. "You met at the wedding?"

"No," Kate said. "We met here."

"Here? What do you mean here?"

"You sound pissed."

"You didn't tell me you and Andy met here."

"He came in on me when I was . . . getting the house ready for you."

"And?"

"And I thought he was cute, and he thought I was a total lunatic for hiding the roses, and tossing the chocolates, and unwrapping the—"

"Woah, woah. What roses? What chocolates?"

"Oh, they were gorgeous, about a dozen of them—"

"From Pete?"

"I guess, I don't know. And the sweetest box of local chocolates—the Sweet Shop, I think . . ."

"The Sweet Shop?" Amanda cried. "I love the Sweet Shop. Where are they? What did you do?"

"You sent me here to destroy them, remember?"

"No. I definitely do not remember that."

"You said kill romance. You said to get rid of anything that would remind you of Pete and the wedding."

"So you threw away completely good roses and chocolates?"

"I only had fifteen minutes. Look, can we get back to me and Andy?"

"Oh, so it's you and Andy now, is it?"

"I just think he's incredibly sexy. That's all."

"Stay away from him, Katie," Amanda said, pulling her back from the window and closing the blind. "He's trouble, believe me."

"What do you mean?"

"Look. Haven't I already told you he's an egotistical ass?" Amanda said.

"Yes," Kate said. "But that's all you've ever said."

"Isn't that enough?"

"No. I want details." Amanda slumped on the edge of the bed.

"I met Andy the same summer I met Pete. I was waitressing for the summer. In fact, I had a little crush on Andy at first."

A ball dropped in Kate's stomach. "Did you sleep with him?" Kate asked. If she had, it was game over. There was a limit to what she was willing to share with her best friend.

"No. Thank God. Pete told me what he was like before that happened."

"What do you mean, what he was like?"

"Andy's a con artist. He's a player."

"Come on." Kate turned back to the window and peeked through the blinds. Andy was laughing at something Pete said. And then, even though he couldn't possibly see her, Andy looked up. It was like one of those moments where Kate was convinced the news anchor on television was making eye contact and talking directly to her.

"It's true. He lies to women all the time," Amanda said. "I think he only goes for rich ones, though. Where do you think he got the money for this house? It's not from snapping pictures, believe me." Kate wanted to tell Amanda how good of a photographer she thought Andy was, but she felt as if she'd be betraying Andy by doing so. Plus, she realized, she wanted to keep his photographs all to herself. Could it be true? Was he a con artist?

Kate's thoughts were interrupted by music blaring. It was "My Girl." Amanda tried to snap open the blind, but it stuck halfway up. It took three tries of raising and lowering it before she got it to stay up again. Next to the tent, a large boom box was hooked up to enormous speakers.

"It's his song for me," Amanda said.

"Aw," Kate said. "That's so sweet."

"Yes, well," Amanda said. "I guess he couldn't find one called 'I Love You but I'm Going to Want to See Other Women Naked for the Rest of My Life.'" Then she headed into the bathroom to do her makeup. She had completely forgotten about Andy Beck, and, Kate realized, whatever bad things she was about to say about Andy Beck, she didn't want to hear them. A few minutes later, Amanda emerged from the bathroom armed with cleavage, shiny hair, and wet lips. They headed for the stairs. Just before going down, Amanda grabbed Kate by the arm. "No matter what happens," she said, "do not leave me alone with Pete. Capice?"

"Got it."

"I mean it. No matter what I say, or what I do, do not let me."

"Okay."

"And do not go off with Andy. I already told you—he's trouble."

Yes, Kate thought. But why did she have the feeling that it wasn't that Andy was trouble that was bothering Amanda, it was simply the fact that Kate liked Andy. Was Amanda jealous? Was that why she was being so critical of him? After all, he was the one who fixed up the cottage and gave it to them for their honeymoon. Of all the things to do with your summer, Kate thought, crashing someone else's honeymoon had to be at the bottom of the barrel.

* * *

"Andy," Amanda said the minute they hit the backyard. "Can I talk to you for a minute?" Andy caught the football and held it for a moment. Kate couldn't help but notice he was looking at her. He pulled his hand back and made like he was going to throw to Pete, and then, at the last minute, heaved the football to Kate. She caught it with ease. He grinned. All of his previous anger at her seemed to be gone. It had been a couple of days since they'd met; maybe he was starting to trust that she wouldn't tell anyone about his photographs. Kate could feel Amanda's glare.

"What do you say we leave these lovebirds alone?" Andy said, ignoring Amanda and walking toward Kate. Amanda's head swiveled around like a demonic bobblehead doll.

"Kate can't go anywhere with you," Amanda shouted. "She's going sailing."

"I didn't know you sailed," Andy said to Kate.

"She's fabulous," Amanda said. "And she's late."

"Who are you sailing with?" Andy asked, apparently unfazed by Amanda's demeanor.

"Uh—owner of the bookstore—Tony?" Kate said. Andy's smile evaporated, and before her eyes Andy turned back into the brooding man she'd met in his bedroom. Kate wondered if it had anything to do with the photography book Andy had been working on. Once again, she got the feeling that something had gone sour with the deal. Kate was dying to know what.

"Oh," Andy said. "Well, good for you."

"It's not a date," Kate said quickly. "It's—uh—a group thing." Kate said. That didn't sound good either, Kate thought, wishing she could take back her words.

"And you're late," Amanda piped in.

"I'm going to the marina myself," Andy said. "I can give you a ride."

"Great," Kate said before Amanda could protest. "Let's go."

* * *

"Do you think they'll kiss and make up by the time we get back?" Andy asked as he walked Kate to his Jeep.

"I hope so," Kate said. "Although I'll have to find another place to stay."

"There's room in the tent."

"Lovely."

Andy laughed at Kate's reply. It was a deep laugh with a hint of badness in it, and coupled with the cramped quarters of his Jeep, Kate was very aware of the proximity of his body to hers. He smelled good, too, but she stopped short of asking him the name of his cologne. And now she couldn't stop picturing herself in the tent with him. Kate complained about Amanda while Andy drove. She knew she was talking fast and loose about nothing, but besides trying to get her mind off her palpable attraction to the man, she was still extremely nervous whenever she was in a car, and she was trying not to grab the side of her door, or "air" brake. People tended not to like it when you did things like that.

Kate made sure to get back in a car shortly after the accident—otherwise she probably would have stayed away from them forever. But then "it" would have won, whatever "it" was. A nameless, faceless enemy called Fate. Still, she couldn't say she enjoyed riding in a car, and she was relieved when Andy pulled into the marina.

They took their time walking to the boats, neither in any hurry to leave the other. While Kate tried to shove lurid thoughts of the brooding artist out of her mind, Andy removed a deck of cards from his pocket and flipped them up in the air one-handed. They spurted up and folded under like a pop-up book of the Gateway Arch. What was he, some kind of shark? Kate wondered if that was how he made his money. Maybe Amanda was right. Maybe he was a player, a con artist.

"You play poker?" Andy asked. His tone was casual. Was this how he roped in his victims? Invited them to a friendly game and then sucked them dry? When she caught Andy's friendly gaze, she felt guilty. She was becoming as cynical as Amanda. Why was she being so hard on him? She knew the answer: it was because she'd been so attracted to him, she couldn't help but size him up as a possible mate. But he wasn't. He was just some guy on a summer vacation. She'd had true love once in her life; that was all she was ever going to get. That was the sad but obvious truth.

"I know how to play," Kate said. "But I'm not a shark or anything." Now why did she say that? Was she testing him? Andy laughed again. He had a sense of humor, she'd give him that.

"Me neither," he said, sending the cards into the air again. "I've just got a little game going a few evenings a week on the *She-Devil.*"

"*She-Devil?*"

"Oh, it's just a boat."

"Ah."

"That's why I offered to walk you—I was going the same way anyway."

"I see." Did he have to go out of his way to let her know he didn't really want to be with her? She was back to being suspicious and cynical; she couldn't help it. He had a cottage and a boat? It was probably just a little sailboat, but still. The thought rolled around her head and then, to Kate's surprise, rolled right out of her mouth as well.

"You have a cottage and a boat?" she heard herself say.

"I'm lucky," Andy answered. "I've made some good investments over the years."

"Oh," Kate said, thinking of his photographs. Were those part of his "investments"? If so, why was he hiding them away? She didn't ask him to clarify, and he didn't do it voluntarily. "If I had that place, I'd be here all the time," Kate said of the cottage.

They had reached the docks. Sailboats and yachts bobbed at anchor, and they could hear voices filtering through the dusk. People were out on their decks with food and drinks, waiting to toast the sunset. Several dogs romped about, all shapes and sizes, groomed to the hilt as if they'd just come from a dog show. Their bejeweled collars glittered in the dregs of the sun. The sky was a jaw-dropping shade of pink with a streak of dark red filtering through, topped off by a faint purple line. The tangy smell of barbeque mixed with the scent of the ocean, and waves lapped rhythmically against the side of boats large and small. It was the large yacht front and center that made Kate stop dead. It loomed over the other yachts like a lifeguard on the beach. "She-Devil" was painted on the side. Just a boat her ass.

"Darling!" a woman on the dock yelled. "Come back to Mommy." Andy laughed at the look on Kate's face.

"I think she's talking to him," he said, pointing at the Standard white poodle running by.

"Oh," Kate said, wondering if Andy was going to make any apologies or explanations for his monster of a boat.

"You're going to the sailboat over there," Andy said, pointing down the dock. "The *Bookworm*," he added, his breath brushing against her ear. Kate felt a stab of disappointment. He wasn't going to be her summer fling after all. He would think she was after him for his money, which, apparently, he had loads of. She'd never been a gold digger, not remotely, and she wasn't going to be thought of as one, either. It was ironic, probably the first time Andy Beck had ever been turned down because of his money. Too bad she couldn't share this little tidbit with him.

"Thanks," she said, heading off in the direction of the *Bookworm*.

"Hey," he said. "Why don't you come to the *She-Devil* when you're done? I'll give you the tour, and maybe even let you in on the game."

"No, thanks," Kate said without even turning back to look at him. "I don't play your type of games."

"Hey," he said. She stopped but barely turned around, and

when she did, she was looking everywhere but directly at him. "Seriously. Come by when you're done. I don't think it's safe to walk home alone."

"I'm a big girl."

"I meant me."

"You drove here."

"Yeah, but I'll be all liquored up and probably losing my shirt in there. And I don't drive drunk, so I'll have to walk home. I'll need your protection and company for the sojourn back to my little tent." Kate turned and walked away again, but she'd at least broken into a little smile. She couldn't help it. She was definitely hoping he would lose his shirt.

Chapter Six

Andy knocked on the table, and the dealer dealt the flop. He normally loved these nights playing Texas hold 'em with the guys. But tonight he was definitely off his game. *I don't play your type of games.* What did she mean by that? Obviously it was a dig, so what type of "games" was she referring to? She'd turned cold since she'd spotted the *She-Devil.* Although she'd given him a smile in the end. Would she stop by when she was done with the sail? He really didn't want her walking home alone. He had binoculars somewhere; he was going to have to see if he could sneak out on deck with them and keep an eye on her. What was her sudden problem with him anyway?

Yes, he was angry with her when they'd first met, but as far as he could tell, she'd kept her word and hadn't said a thing about his photographs to anyone. Andy was sure Pete would have mentioned it if he'd heard about them. So, giving her the benefit of the doubt, she'd kept quiet. Which meant she had integrity. Some men were breast men, others leg men, but Andy's aphrodisiac was a girl who could keep her word. Now, that was sexy. Not that she didn't have the other aforementioned attributes as well—along with gorgeous eyes—but she wouldn't have looked at her twice if she were a gossip. But of course now that he was willing to give her a chance, she was the one who seemed to be cooling off.

Was she against yachts? If she'd allowed him to give her the tour, she would see the *She-Devil* was made out of recycled materials and used energy-saving lightbulbs. Not to mention she wasn't really his boat, just like the cottage wasn't really his, but that was another story. One he was never going to get into with Kate Williams. Not that he was ashamed of being a starving artist. His happiest moments had been behind the lens of a camera. The things he captured were the things money couldn't buy. Sunsets. The ocean. The silhouette of a beautiful woman. That was another thing. Why was Kate always wearing long sleeves? For some reason, it made him want to see her arms even more. He chuckled to himself; he'd never imagined a scenario where, if he had a choice, he'd rather see a girl pull up her sleeves than anything else. What was this woman doing to him?

"Earth to Andy," one of the guys said. "Are you in or what?" Andy glanced at the cards on the table and increased his bet. What games was she talking about? And if she didn't like him now, what were the chances she was ever going to look at him again after spending time with Tony and his son, Mark? Tony was a good guy, but Mark was a complete jerk. He would probably be all over Kate, too. Hell, he was probably the one who invited her "sailing." In the old days he would have grilled Pete about Kate. He couldn't get the image of her sprawled out on his bed out of his mind. But he hadn't said a word to Pete about Kate; he didn't want anyone to know he was even thinking about her that way. His last romance had been way too public, way too dramatic.

What was he thinking? He couldn't get involved again. But there was one thing he knew for sure as he threw his cards down and watched the fallen faces of his friends as they took in his straight; he was definitely going to see what she was hiding behind those long sleeves. It was that obsessive thought and too many drinks that made him start talking about Kate out loud, which led to him doing something really stupid, something he regretted the minute he accepted it. People should not only hedge their bets, they should know when to turn them down as well.

Chapter Seven

"Kate. Great to see you again. Look at you! You look great." Tony grabbed her in a bear hug. "This is my son, Mark," he said when he finally let her go.

"Hello," Kate said, extending her hand to Mark. Mark smiled, revealing teeth that were large and slightly protruding but a perfect fit for his moon-shaped face. He had spiky blond hair of the sort typically found on a teenage boy, but the beer belly of an old-timer. Based on the lines on his face, Kate pegged him to be in his early forties, but it could just be that his Coke-bottle glasses were throwing her off, making him appear older than he actually was. The way he was staring at her without speaking made her feel like a very small bug in a very large jar.

"Who was that you were with?" Tony boomed. They were standing on the deck of a tiny sailboat. It couldn't have been more than a fourteen footer; even the twenty-four footer next to it dwarfed the vessel. Kate ignored the question and looked around to see who else had been invited, fearing just one more person would sink them. But nobody else was in sight.

"Am I too early?" Kate asked. Mark looked at his watch and appeared to be taking the question very seriously.

"Not at all," Tony said. "Punctuality is an admirable quality in a woman. Right, Mark?" Mark stared at Kate again.

"I think it is," he said. "I think it is." From their tone, it was as if the two men were discussing a much more sinister topic.

Do you think she could be a danger to herself and others? I think she could. I think she could.

Where were the others?

"How many people are coming?" Kate asked, once again wondering how much weight the little sailboat could hold. She was happy she'd eaten a light lunch.

"We're all here," Tony said with a wink. Kate did her best to manufacture a smile, all the while feeling as if she'd been ordered to walk the plank.

"Oh?" she said. "Just the three of us." *You said party! This is not a party. This is a setup. I'm being set up. Am I going to take this? Run. Run now. Tell them you're sick. Amanda's sick. She just texted you. You thought you saw a shark.*

"Yep," Tony said. "Just us sea chickens!"

"Why?" Mark asked. "Did you want to invite your boyfriend? Andy Beck?" He punctured Andy's name like a fencer lunging forward for a final thrust of his sword. He looked at his dad and winked.

"Mark," Tony said.

"Andy's not my boyfriend," Kate said. *Now why did I say that? That was my chance!*

"Did you hear that, Mark?" Tony said. "He's not her boyfriend." They were reciting lines like soap-opera actors dumbing down the plot for a long-lost audience.

"Man friend?" Mark asked. "At our age, we should probably say 'man' friend. Don't you think, Kate?"

Sometimes I don't think at all. Like right now my mind is a horrified blank.

Mark stuck his hands in his pockets and tucked his chin to his chest. His glasses slid down his nose. "Let's get her out on the water before it gets too dark," Tony said.

"You should stay away from Andy Beck," Mark said. Kate didn't respond. "He's a shyster," Mark continued. "We'd like to kill him." It was the first time Mark had raised his voice above a whisper; he was practically yelling.

"Mark," Tony admonished, looking down the dock. "People's dogs are sleeping."

"But we do hate him," Mark said.

Tony held up his index finger and thumb in the form of a pinch. "Just a smidge," he admitted.

Kate tried to stare through the line of boats and catch a glimpse of the *She-Devil*. She thought she could even hear Andy laughing. She knew absolutely nothing about him. Rich man? Troubled photographer? Playboy? Now "shyster." The thought of meeting up with him tonight was consuming her. Would she? She tried to push the question away as the little boat pushed out from the dock, gently rocking from side to side.

The boat may have been small, but she could really sail. Father and son handled her effortlessly, and despite Mark hovering around like an alien craft, Kate was enjoying herself. There was a gentle wind, but strong enough to pick up the sails of the little boat and glide them across the water. Kate realized as she took in the magnitude of the ocean, and the beauty of the sleepy little community now disappearing into the distance, how lucky she was to be spending a month on the island. And she wouldn't let anyone take that away from her. She was in control of her happiness. She would do her best-friend duty when it came to Amanda, but the rest of the time here she would spend going for long walks on the beach, reading good books, and drinking wine on the dock.

Thoughts of spending time on the island brought Andy's photographs to mind. The woman had been stunningly beautiful, and the way they were shot made her look almost spectral, with her white dress billowing in the wind, her hair blowing around her face. She was so sexy. Was he madly in love with her? What a stupid question. Of course he was.

"What are you thinking about?" Mark asked as Tony disappeared into what Kate could only assume was a tiny hole for a cabin. Kate laughed, embarrassed Mark had caught her thinking such silly thoughts. So what if Andy had been in love with her? That was probably what made the pictures so outstanding. Why had he never published the book? Romance be damned; if Kate did nothing else with her month on the island, she was going to get to the bottom of that question. Maybe she should broach the subject of Andy with Mark. She decided to warm up to it by chatting with him about his work first.

"So what do you do, Mark?"

"You're kidding, right?" Kate looked out the side of the boat, half expecting a giant camera crew to pop up through the waves and end her misery by announcing she was on *Candid Camera*. "I'm sorry," Mark said. "Everyone on the island knows what I do."

"Well, I'm not a native, you see," Kate said. Mark removed an object from his pocket and threw it at her. Kate automatically reached for it, but the flashlight hit her in the stomach as she grabbed it.

"Shine it on me," Mark said. Kate accidentally aimed it directly at Mark's eyes. "Ow, ow," he said, shielding them with his hand.

"Whoops," Kate said, bringing the flashlight down a tad and smiling in the safety of the dark. Mark unzipped his coat and held the flaps open. It took Kate a few minutes of finagling with the flashlight to see his T-shirt. On it a giant cockroach was being strangled by a mouse who was in turn being choked by a human hand. The word CROAK! was splashed across the top in large red letters.

"I'm the island exterminator," Mark announced proudly. "My motto? 'We can't kill just one.'"

"Oh," Kate said.

"You know. Like potato chips—you can't eat just one."

"Uh-huh."

"And you know for every cockroach you see, there are at least a thousand more in hiding."

"I did not know that." Whatever Tony was doing in the tiny cabin, he wasn't coming out any time soon. He was biding time, leaving her to bob out here with Mr. Buggy. Nighttime sail. It sounded so romantic. She could throw herself overboard and swim to the *She-Devil*. She wondered what was going on inside Andy's yacht and suddenly she wished she were—no pun intended—a fly on the wall.

"Did you ever consider getting into the bookstore business?" Kate asked, wondering when she was going to be offered a glass of wine. A bottle and two glasses were sitting prominently on the little built-in bench on the side of the boat. When staring at it didn't clue Mark in, Kate walked over and picked up the bottle, pretending to be interested in the label. She didn't care if it tasted like two-buck chuck, she was going to get a glass.

"You know three of the islands on the Vineyard are dry?" Mark asked, eyeing her as she searched for a wine opener.

"Yes," Kate said. "Those are the islands I avoid." It was a joke, but Mark's humor didn't seem to reach that far. "Technically," he said, slicing the air around him with windmill hands, "we're probably in dry waters right now."

"Mark," Tony suddenly yelled up from the cabin. "We talked about this. A little wine is good on a date. It doesn't always mean she's a loose woman." Mark nodded, took a wine opener out of his jacket, and tossed it to Kate.

"Tony," Kate yelled as she struggled to pierce the cork while the boat was moving. "Why don't you join us?" *Steer this boat back to shore!*

"What other bad habits do you have?" Mark asked as she stuck the wine bottle between her legs and started to yank on the cork.

"Besides alcohol," he said. "Do you smoke? Gamble? Are you promiscuous?"

"Mark," Tony yelled. "I told you not to ask that!"

"You said 'Don't say slut,'" Mark yelled back. "I changed it to promiscuous!"

"I'd like to go home now," Kate yelled. She put the bottle of wine up to her mouth and drank.

"You do have nice childbearing hips," Mark said. "I'll give you that."

"Tony," Kate yelled. "Let's get this baby back to shore!" Shit. She should have said "puppy." Let's get this puppy back to shore. She didn't want Mark to think she was acknowledging his "childbearing hips" comment.

"We planned on a couple hours of drifting," Mark said. Kate stared at the doughy exterminator. She looked at his shirt and then imagined her hands wrapped around his neck, squeezing for all she was worth. She knew she would swim for it before she drifted anywhere with this bozo. If he was sizing her up for a potential wife, he was about to get a picture of the not-so-pretty variety. Two could be obnoxious. Kate chugged from the bottle again and flopped herself on the tiny bench. She spread her legs in a very manly, non childbearing way. She would have let out a belch, but she just couldn't do that one on command.

"What can you tell me about Andy Beck?" she asked. Mark shifted several times and glanced at her spread legs.

"Why?" Mark asked.

Kate let out a dog whistle. "Because he's totally hot," she said. She leaned forward and whispered, "I'd totally do him."

"Dad," Mark yelled. "The North Star is in the sky."

"Seriously—tell me everything you know about him."

"The North Star, Dad!"

Kate chugged from the bottle again. "I heard he was going to publish a book of photography."

"He didn't follow through with it," Tony said. Kate jumped

out of her seat. She hadn't even heard Tony come up, but he was sitting next to her on the bench. She closed her legs and put down the wine bottle.

"What happened?"

"He found his fiancée procreating with another man on the beach the night before their wedding," Mark said.

"His fiancée?"

"Duh. The star of his book?" Mark said.

So that was who the woman was, Kate thought. Shyster or not, Kate could relate to the pain Andy must have gone through, and she felt for him. Suddenly the woman didn't seem so beautiful. "That's terrible," she said, meaning Andy's plight.

"It's criminal!" Mark said. "He cost Dad thousands of dollars!"

"Mark," Tony said. All the volume and excitement had gone out of Tony's voice. He suddenly sounded like a little old man.

"What do you mean?" Kate asked, turning to Tony.

"We just told you," Mark said in a tone of voice that clearly conveyed he'd crossed her off his future potential wife list.

"You mean because he dropped the book, he cost you potential sales?" Kate asked.

"No," Mark said. His tone of voice was patronizing. Kate was really starting to dislike this guy.

"Dad spent thousands of dollars on a surprise book party for that prick—"

"Mark . . ."

"Not to mention we were counting on the sales. He'd just been reviewed by the *New York Times*—an article raving about his talent."

"He is talented," Kate said.

"The book would've been a huge hit—and Andy promised it would only be sold through Dad's store."

"Which was very generous," Tony said. "It was supposed to come out at the beginning of summer, the height of the tourist season."

"Prick!" Mark said.

"It must have been too painful for him," Kate mused, "after what she'd done to him."

"Bullshit!" Mark said. "It's because he's a phony. They were probably all crap. I'll bet he saw how lousy the pictures were, so he made up some story—"

"They aren't crap," Kate said. "They're gorgeous. I've seen them myself—"

"Somebody broke in—the camera was stolen—the photos were destroyed—"

Mark and Kate yelled over each other like squabbling siblings. It took Kate a moment to process what Mark was saying, and only then did she fully understand what she had just done. Looking back, Kate wasn't sure which came first, the simultaneous gasp from father or son, or their faces, only inches from her, staring her down. She could smell their breath, which, cheap wine and all, definitely blew hers out of the water.

"You saw what?" Mark asked.

"The photos exist?" Tony asked.

"Um," Kate said, wondering how to take it all back. "I probably saw the wrong pictures—"

"Gorgeous woman posing in a white dress at various locations on the island?" Mark asked. Kate took another sip of wine and sunk into immediate regret that she didn't have a poker face. *There was a red dress, too,* she thought but didn't say.

"Well, I'll be damned," Tony said. "I'll be damned." Father and son got to their feet. Without speaking, Tony reached for the wheel of the sailboat, and Mark lowered the sails, then came back to rev the engine. The little boat jerked and then leapt out of the water before slamming back down and skidding forward.

You think they would have warned me to watch my wine, Kate thought as she was lifted off the bench and thrown back down with a thud. She didn't have to ask where they were going. I was obvious. They were headed straight for the *She-Devil.*

Chapter Eight

Andy sat in the small library next to the game room, gazing out the porthole. Voices and laughter trickled in through the thin-paneled wall separating him from the poker game, but Andy couldn't concentrate on anything other than Kate. Especially after the bet he'd just made. Had Tony and Mark already turned Kate against him? Andy had to admit, he knew Tony got the raw end of the book deal gone bad, and for that he was sorry. "We'll stick it to the man," Tony said, pumping his fist into the sky when Andy told him he could have exclusive retail rights to the book. "We'll stick it to the man!" His excitement tripled when Andy told Tony he and Michelle would be happy to do book signings the first week of its release. With the buzz from the *Times* article, and the amount of traffic the island did in the summertime, it was bound to be a best seller.

Then the look on Tony's face when Andy told him there wasn't going to be a book—there would never be a book. How could he tell him the truth? That he'd never be able to look at those pictures of Michelle without seeing her locked in another man's embrace? That he'd die before those pictures saw the light of day? Before he knew it, he was making up a story about a break-in. Everything was gone—the camera, the originals, the film.

"How long will it take you to reshoot?" Tony had asked. Andy couldn't believe it. By now everyone had heard the gossip about Michelle and the wedding, yet here Tony was acting like Andy should go back to business as usual with the woman who betrayed him. As if she deserved to profit from Andy's dream. She'd actually called to ask when the book would be coming out, and then she told him she was still planning to be there for the book signing—she didn't want to disappoint her fans (her fans?), and would he mind very much if she brought what's his name? Then she had the nerve to ask about royalties. That's when Andy lost it. He set her straight on all accounts. His place had been broken into, ransacked— there wasn't going to be a book. He felt guilty, yes, but not guilty enough to publish those pictures. Not now, not ever.

It had been Andy's only act of revenge, pulling the plug on the book. His agent tried to persuade him to reshoot the book using a different model, but Andy wouldn't hear of it. At the time he was too immersed in his own pain, and couldn't imagine doing the book with anyone else. And he'd certainly paid the spiritual piper for that decision—his muse had evaporated as fast as his love. He'd experienced absolutely no creative joy since. He hadn't even the slightest stir of interest in photography. Until Kate. The interruption. Sprawled out on his bed chugging champagne from the bottle and sucking up rose petals with his Hoover. He couldn't get that image out of his mind. He wanted to stage it again and photograph her from every angle.

A sudden thud against the side of the yacht startled Andy out of his daydream. He ran to the porthole just as the second thud hit. When Andy looked out, he couldn't believe what he was seeing. Someone was deliberately ramming their joke of a sailboat into the side of the yacht. It wasn't going to do much other than scratch it, but it enraged Andy nonetheless. He quickly mounted the stairs to the deck with the guys in tow.

"What the hell are you doing?" Andy yelled. It took him a

minute to recognize the sailboat; it wasn't until he spotted Kate cowering in the back that he realized it was Tony and Mark.

"You liar!" Mark yelled, preparing to ram the yacht again.

"Cut it out," Andy said. "You're going to hurt yourself."

"Let us up," Tony said. Andy tried to ignore the guys behind him, jeering and laughing, and as he lowered the emergency rope ladder down to the little sailboat, he implored them to go back to the game. Apparently, they decided the show they were about to see upstairs was way more exciting than the money they stood to lose downstairs, and none of them budged.

Kate climbed up first, and as Andy helped her over, he thought whatever was about to go down was worth it for the chance just to touch her hand. But he also noticed she wouldn't make eye contact with him, and as she slipped past he could have sworn she muttered "Sorry." He was the one who should be sorry, especially after making that ridiculous bet. He would have to tell the guys it was off. He'd probably lose his place in the games—men didn't like it when you retracted your bets—but it was the right thing to do.

Mark climbed up next, refusing Andy's hand, followed by Tony, who was about to accept some help up when Mark elbowed in and hauled his father the rest of the way over himself. Andy tried to ignore the sound of laughter and bottles clinking behind him.

"Are you having boat problems?" Andy asked, hoping there was a reasonable explanation for the ruckus.

"We're having 'you' problems," Mark said. Andy glanced at Kate, who was looking overboard as if considering jumping.

"Did you lie to us?" Tony asked.

"About what?" Andy answered.

"The photo book. You told us the pictures were stolen. You told us the film and camera were stolen. You told us Michelle wasn't willing to do the shoot over. Was any of it true?"

"Why are you asking me this? Why now?"

"Because you're a liar," Mark said. "You still have the pictures. She saw them!" Mark pointed at Kate. Stunned, Andy
stared at her. Some of the guys murmured "whoa" and tried to
clink glasses again, but the ones who knew Andy well enough
to stay clear of any talk of Michelle came to their senses and
guided the rest of the drunken gamblers back down to the
game. To her credit, Kate looked up and met Andy's eyes.

"I didn't know," Kate said. "I—"

"You gave me your word," Andy said. He didn't go any further. There was nothing more to say. He couldn't believe he'd
been falling for her. Once again, he was betrayed by a woman.
At least he found out now before he really fell in love with her.

"Andy," Tony said. "Just tell us the truth."

"Obviously you know the truth," Andy said. "Is there anything else?"

"What do you mean is there anything else?" Mark said.
"Give us the book. You owe my father the book!"

"I don't owe your father anything," Andy said.

"Well, that's that," Tony said. "Let's go."

"No," Mark said. "He cost you thousands of dollars, Dad!"

"Mark," Tony said.

"What do you mean?" Andy asked. "He didn't have to pay
anything for the book—"

"He had a whole surprise party planned for you."

"Mark."

"It cost him a couple thousand dollars. Plus he was taking
advance orders and had to pay that money back—plus he
took out loans because he was counting on the sales of the
book to pay them back."

"I had no idea," Andy said. "I had no idea, Tony."

"It's okay," Tony said. "Now let's go."

"Why don't you just give us the pictures?" Mark asked.
"Why don't you just publish the book?"

"Why don't you just write a check," Kate mumbled. She

was also looking around the yacht like it was disgusting he had so much money. Well, let her think that; he didn't care anymore. He stared at her long sleeves. She'd obviously gotten wet from the sailboat charging the yacht. Her sleeves were translucent and sticking to her skin. Andy could see a deep scar on her right arm; it was long and jagged, shaped like a lightning bolt. He had to force himself to look away.

"What if I shoot the pictures again with a new model?" Andy asked. At this, Mark and Tony perked up.

"Do it," Mark said.

"Would your publisher still honor the contract?" Tony asked.

"Are you kidding?" Andy asked. "He'd be over the moon."

"Who were you thinking of using?" Tony asked.

Andy paused, relishing the moment.

"Her," he said putting his arm around Kate. The look on her face! Why didn't he have his camera handy? He'd never wanted to snap a picture more in his entire life.

Chapter Nine

"You're sure you don't hate me?" Amanda asked. Kate finished zipping her suitcase and smiled even though she felt more like choking her for asking the same question over and over again.

"Of course I don't hate you," Kate said again. "I'm happy for you." In the few hours Kate had been gone, Amanda and Pete had made up. Although talk of another wedding had been shelved, the lovers planned on going through with their honeymoon. Which meant Kate no longer had a cottage to stay in for the month.

"I can drive you to the airport," Amanda said.

"I'm not going to the airport," Kate said. "I'm checking into the Black Sheep Inn." Amanda was right on her heels as Kate headed to the door. Just as she opened it and was about to step out onto the porch, Amanda reached around her and shut it.

"You're staying on the island?" Kate had been anticipating—and not looking forward to—giving Amanda the news. She wanted to lie to her, but the thought of Amanda catching her in a lie was enough to terrify her into telling the truth.

"I am," Kate said. "In fact, I kind of . . . got a job."

"What do you mean, 'got a job'?"

"Um—you know Andy?"

"You know I do."

"He wants to . . . take some pictures of me . . . for his new book."

"You're kidding." Amanda and Kate turned to the voice. Pete was just out of the shower, one towel wrapped around his waist, the other his neck. "Andy's doing a new book? That's unbelievable!"

"You can't do it," Amanda said.

"You have to do it," Pete said. Amanda seared Pete with such a look that Kate expected his towel to fall off.

"I don't know what he's up to," Amanda said, turning back to Kate. "But stay away from him. He's a user."

"No, he's not," Pete said. "Andy's a great guy."

"That's not what you told me," Amanda said. "You said he was a con artist, remember?"

Pete laughed and started toweling his head. "That's just because I was afraid you were going to get a little crush on him, and I wanted you for myself."

"So you lied?"

Pete shrugged and grinned.

"He's not a con artist?" Amanda asked.

"Nope," Pete said.

"He really is wealthy?"

"Why?" Pete asked. "Is that important to you?"

"I just want to know the truth," Amanda said. "How many lies did you tell me?"

"Panda," Pete said. "I'm just messing with you. All I'm saying is—Andy isn't your typical rich jerk. He's always made his own way."

"Oh, it must have been so rough on him with his little house and his big yacht . . ."

Pete walked over to Amanda and rubbed his wet head on her neck.

"Eww," she said, pushing him away. But at least she was laughing.

"You know what your reputation was when we first met?" Pete asked.

"That I was gorgeous and young and wonderful?" Amanda answered without hesitating.

"No," Pete said. "That you were a gold digger."

"Who said that?" Amanda demanded. "Andy?"

"Would you give Andy a rest?" Pete said. "I told you he's a great guy. One of the best." Amanda reached out and yanked on Pete's towel. Kate turned her eyes as it fell to the floor.

"He asked me out!" Amanda said as Pete scrambled to cover himself with the towel. "You're the one who told me not to go out with him. You said he was a player—a liar—a con artist!"

"I told you that so you'd go out with me instead."

"That's a cheap thing to do!"

"Are you saying you wish you'd chosen him?" Pete asked. Kate threw Amanda a look of warning, but as usual Amanda ignored her.

"Well, why wouldn't I?" Amanda said. "He's gorgeous, talented, and rich."

"There it is," Pete said. "Money, money, money. Is that all that matters to you?" Pete threw out his arms in frustration, and the towel fell off again. This time he didn't seem to care. Kate averted her eyes until Pete finally grabbed the towel.

"You know I'm not like that!" Amanda said. "If it was money I was after, I never would have married you!"

"Guys," Kate said. "Stop fighting. You already kissed and made up."

"Well, why don't you go for Andy now?" Pete yelled. "You're single, he's single—be my guest."

"I don't need your permission to seduce someone."

"Amanda, let's just drop this," Pete said.

Kate crossed her fingers behind her back.

"Tell me you know Andy would fall in love with me if I wanted him to, and I will," Amanda demanded.

Kate couldn't believe what she was hearing. Amanda was

being immature, pure and simple. Kate was embarrassed listening to their fight. If Amanda was going to continue to act like this, she was never going to have a successful marriage. Not that Kate knew anything about marriage. Or Andy. Maybe he would fall in love with Amanda. Why did the thought bother her so much? Why wouldn't Pete just put on some pants?

"I will catch up with you guys later," Kate said.

"No," Amanda said. "You're staying here. Pete's leaving."

"Like hell I am."

"Then what do you have to say to me?"

"What do I have to say to you? You're acting like a child! This is my friend's cottage. The 'man of your dreams.' You want him? Go for it. But I'm staying right here. If you don't like it, your tent awaits, sweet cheeks."

"Seriously," Kate said. "Andy paid for a room at the inn for me." Amanda and Kate were lying on their backs in the tent, staring up at the pitched ceiling. With their suitcases, makeup, and every sweet and salty thing they could find in the kitchen, there wasn't much room left in the tent for them.

"I'll bet he did," Amanda said, tearing open a bag of Nutter Butters. "Mr. Moneybags." She crunched on the cookie.

Kate sighed and rolled away from Amanda. She had never been one for camping unless it included blow-up mattresses and down comforters. She was getting claustrophobic and the smell of peanut butter was suffocating. Kate started to unzip the front flap. Amanda grabbed her wrist.

"Where are you going?" she asked.

"Outside," Kate said, pulling her wrist out of Amanda's grasp. "Going to check the yard for bears."

"We have to stay in here until we figure out a plan."

"I've got a plan. Let's stay at the inn!"

"No! I've got to keep an eye on Pete." Amanda started to paw the ground around her. "Where are the binoculars?" she asked with the same alarm an asthmatic would if they lost their inhaler.

"Is that what I'm lying on?" Kate asked, reaching under her. Sure enough, there was a pair of binoculars sticking into her back. She maneuvered them out and handed them to Amanda. Then she forced herself to take a deep breath. "Amanda," she said. "I think you're being ridiculous." There, she'd said it. That wasn't so bad. Except for the look on Amanda's face. Kate had never seen so many shades of purple and red in one go. She had better do a little damage control. "Pete loves you," Kate continued. "And you love him. So he's not rich. So he told a couple of white lies. So he wants to see other women naked. At least he's honest about it."

"Honest about that," Amanda said. "But lying about other things."

"About Andy Beck, you mean?" Kate prodded. Amanda didn't respond. "Come on, Panda. Would you really rather be with Andy? From what I hear, he's pretty moody." Kate held her breath, praying Amanda would assure her she had no interest in Andy.

"Andy really asked you to be part of his photo shoot?" Amanda said, playing with the binoculars.

"Yes." Kate knew the tone of voice Amanda was using, and although she didn't come out and say it, Amanda was jealous. Kate hated to acknowledge that, but it was true. Amanda was a gorgeous thin blonde, used to men falling all over her. But instead, Andy asked Kate to do the modeling gig. Amanda was thinking what Kate herself had been wondering—why her? Kate wanted to think it was because there was something between them—there had to be. It was impossible for only one to feel chemistry that strong, wasn't it?

"He must be up to something," Amanda said.

"What do you mean?" Kate sat up and hit her head on the top of the tent. Either it was a tent for midgets or it was starting to cave in.

"You saw his ex!" Amanda said, oblivious to the fact that their house was falling down around them. "She's a model. I mean, you're supercute—don't get me wrong. But come on, Kate—you're not a model." So there it was. Not so subtle now. Kate knew Amanda wasn't trying to be intentionally mean, but it hurt nonetheless.

"I guess *he* thinks I'm beautiful," Kate said quietly. Amanda quickly put her hand on Kate's shoulder.

"Oh, you are! You are. Just—"

"Not a model. I know. I heard you the first hundred times." Kate grabbed her suitcase and started crawling for the flap.

"Where are you going?" Amanda grabbed the other end of the suitcase and pulled.

"To the inn," Kate said as they wrestled with her bag.

"Kate. You know I love you. You know I think you're gorgeous."

Kate stopped. "Then why can't you understand why Andy Beck would want me? As if that would be impossible—"

"I didn't—"

"There's something between us, Mandy." They stopped playing tug-of-war with the suitcase. "I really, really like this guy," Kate said. "And you know I haven't felt this way in a long, long time."

"Oh, Katie."

"Be happy for me," Kate said.

"I am. I think."

"You think?"

"I just don't want you to get hurt. You have to understand. Thanks to Pete, I've had a bad impression of Andy Beck for years. I just don't want you to get hurt."

"Believe me," Kate said. "I'm strong enough to handle it if I do. I learned that the hard way." Amanda lunged forward and hugged Kate. Kate wanted to tell her she was squeezing her too hard, but she let it go. Thankfully, Amanda let her go as well.

"What about work? Don't you have to get back to work?" Amanda asked, handing Kate a Nutter Butter.

"I was laid off," Kate said.

"When?"

"A couple of months ago."

"A couple of months? Why didn't you tell me?"

"I didn't want to ruin your wedding," Kate admitted. Amanda laughed and flopped on her back. Kate put the suitcase down and did the same. The ceiling was definitely a foot closer than it used to be.

"Turns out you didn't have to," Amanda said. "I did that all by myself."

"Go in there and tell him you love him," Kate said.

"You really think that's what I should do?"

"Absolutely."

"Because you think we're meant to be together?"

"That," Kate said. "And this." She reached up and poked the ceiling of the tent. It wobbled for a minute and then collapsed on top of them.

"I really do love him," Amanda tried to say from underneath the tent.

"I have to tell her," Amanda said. She and Pete were lying by the fireplace, legs and arms entwined. It was too warm to actually have a fire going, so Amanda planned on filling the fireplace with lit candles, but thanks to Kate the only ones she could find in the house had their wicks ripped out.

"Don't you dare," Pete said. "I told you that in confidence."

"She's my best friend."

"Let Andy handle this." The lovers eased up on the conversation for a moment and just held each other.

"I knew there had to be a reason he wanted to photograph her," Amanda said. "I just didn't think it would be so mean."

Pete pulled Amanda in tighter and spoke softly. "It's not mean. He's an artist. He likes the unusual."

"She's not going to do it."

"We'll see. I think it's about time, don't you?"

"Does he know what happened?"

"A little."

Amanda pulled back so she could look at Pete. "Does he know Jeff was my brother?"

"Yes," Pete said.

"What did you tell him?" Amanda asked. "Word for word."

"I told him Kate and your brother dated, and five years ago they were in a horrible car accident and Jeff didn't survive. Since then, she's worn long sleeves."

"Jeff and Kate weren't just dating. They were more in love than any two people I've ever known."

"They were young," Pete said. Amanda supposed Pete was right, but when it came to Jeff she had a bottomless need to defend him. In her eyes, he was perfect.

"So it doesn't count?" Amanda demanded. Pete sighed.

"I didn't mean it like that," he said. "I'm just saying their love had never really been tested."

"We've never really been tested," Amanda said. "And look at us." Pete laughed loud and long. Amanda's first instinct was to defend herself, but at the last minute she relaxed and laughed with him.

"What?" she said after a minute, which made Pete laugh even louder.

"I'd say you freaking out and canceling our wedding was a test, wouldn't you?" Pete said. Amanda stopped laughing as a wave of guilt rolled over her.

"Will you ever forgive me?" Amanda asked. Pete made a noise in the back of his throat and kissed her neck.

"I already did," he said.

"What do we do now?" Amanda asked. Pete moved his hand lower.

"Not that, silly," Amanda said, stopping his hand with her own. "About our wedding."

"The guests have all gone home. I say same place, same time, next year."

"Next year?" Amanda sat up. "Next year?"

"Or we elope," Pete said, pulling her back down. "Panda. You can't just ask people to turn around and come back. Think about all the money they spent flying here." Pete stopped when he saw the look on her face. He kissed her. "I'm sorry."

"No. You're right. It's all my fault."

"We could have a civil service so that you and I would really be married, then next year—or six months from now—we could have a wedding for friends and family. How does that sound?" Amanda squeezed Pete's hand in consent.

"What about all the presents?" she said, lifting her head and gazing in the direction of the table where they were all stacked up and waiting.

"Etiquette says we have to give them back," Pete said, covering her eyes with his hand.

"All of them?" Amanda said, swatting his hand away.

"You want waffles, don't you?"

"I want waffles," Amanda said. "And fondu."

"No margaritas?"

"And a margarita. But we can return the toaster."

"It's triple-slotted."

"Oh, right. That baby isn't going anywhere, either."

"We're terrible people."

"No," Amanda said. "I'm a terrible person. You're just in love with a terrible person."

"You're not a terrible person, sweetie," Pete said. "You're just a little piggy." He oinked and pinched her on the bottom. Amanda swatted him away again.

"Did anyone give us a frying pan?" she asked.

"Because you want to hit me over the head with it?"

"It's amazing how well you read my mind."

Chapter Ten

It wasn't going to be anything like the first book. That was the beauty of it. The first book had been a picturesque guide, a people pleaser, color photos of tourist attractions and designer dresses for Michelle. It was the scar on Kate's arm that gave him the idea. From the inception of the book, Andy had wanted to do something more artistic, something that communicated what he wanted to say to the world. "Golf on Martha's Vineyard" was not it.

Unfortunately he'd made the mistake of discussing his ideas with Michelle first, and then before he knew it she'd invited herself to lunch with his agent, and he definitely shouldn't have had two drinks during lunch because suddenly Michelle was selling the book idea—not the artistic visions he had in mind, but the tourist photo book of the Vineyard. And Andy didn't stop her. He let love trump art, which in his eyes made him no artist at all. He'd given up his vision to please her. But this time would be different. He already knew he wanted to shoot the next book in black and white, but when he saw the scar on Kate's arm, he had a flash. Almost literally. The scar looked like a lightning bolt. He would photograph her on various spots of the island, all in black and white, but he would illuminate the scar with a golden glow, make the lightning bolt really stand out, and then he'd pick an object outside her, the keyhole of the lighthouse door, a shell on the beach, the handle of a golf club, whatever, and he'd highlight it in the same glow. He couldn't even explain to anyone exactly why he wanted to do the photos this way, but it excited him, and that was the whole point—the love of it.

Of course, there were a couple of problems. Getting his agent to agree to the new concept was one. Getting Kate to agree to it was the other. He wasn't sure which he was looking forward to least.

He approached Pete first, luring him out with an invitation to golf. As Andy and Pete started the course, Andy listened as Pete talked about Amanda.

"It's the best thing that could have ever happened," Pete said, taking a swing. "She's been all over me ever since. I'm telling you—you want a woman to go crazy for you, almost marry her, then say something stupid."

"I'll keep that in mind," Andy said. "So what else can you tell me about Kate?" He'd planned on waiting until they were finished golfing and settled in the pub with a few pints, but he couldn't help it—he had to know more about her. Besides, he'd heard enough about Amanda and Pete's renewed sex life to last him a lifetime. He wanted to ask if they were going to plan another wedding, but he was afraid of the answer. When Pete groaned, Andy hoped it was because he just overtopped the hole.

"Amanda was right," Pete said. "You're after her. Is that why you want her for the shoot?"

Andy didn't answer until he hit his ball. It fell perfectly on the green, only a few feet away from the hole.

"You get to play more than me," Pete grumbled as they walked. "So are you like into her, into her—or what?"

"As an artist, yes. She's ignited my interest artistically."

"Yeah, right. Well, you've got Amanda all wound up about it."

"Why?" They reached Pete's ball. He swung, and they both watched as the ball bounced pathetically before rolling to a stop near the base of a tree. A squirrel scrambled over and sniffed it.

"I like fishing better," Pete said, struggling to hit his ball away from the massive tree. "We should go fishing."

"What's Amanda's problem with me?" Andy asked. Pete's ball finally made it onto the green and rolled a hair past Andy's. Pete jumped in the air and roared. His gloating was cut short when Andy's third shot disappeared into the hole.

"Bastard," Pete said.

"She called me a bastard?"

"No. I'm calling you a bastard," Pete said. "Isn't that your third birdie?"

Andy laughed. "I've had a lot of free time on my hands," he said. "But maybe you should let the squirrel take this shot," he added as Pete prepared to swing. Pete gave a fake laugh as he swiped at the ball. "Seriously," Andy said. "What's Amanda's problem?"

"I told you Kate dated her brother right?"

"I think you mentioned that."

"Well, they were attached at the hip. Madly in love. The works. Kate's been through a lot. Amanda doesn't want her to get hurt."

Andy thought about the project. Would it really hurt her? It certainly wasn't his intention. He had to think like an artist. The scar made her interesting, period. And it was shaped like a lightning bolt. He couldn't let emotions destroy his vision.

"And," Pete said as he chopped the grass with his golf club, "Amanda kinda thinks you're a player." This got Andy's attention.

"Why the hell would she think I was a player?"

"Might have been something I said."

"What did you say?"

"I told her you were a player." Andy shook his head as Pete laughed.

"Well, she needn't worry," Andy said. "I've no romantic interest in Kate. She's work to me. That's all."

"Does she know that?"

"Why wouldn't she?"

"Look. I'm not as paranoid as Amanda, and Kate's a grown woman—but she has been through a lot. And truth be told, I've seen a bit of a spark in her lately. I wouldn't want to see her get hurt, either. She used to be a singer, did you know that?" Andy shook his head. "Well, she was going to sing at our wedding. She hasn't sung in public in five years. Just like she hasn't taken off her long sleeves. Just go easy on her, man."

Andy didn't answer. He was way too conflicted. He was full of shit; he had feelings for her, and that was that. But this time he wasn't going to play the fool for a woman. This was about work. She was work. Kate's pain tore at his conscience, but he pushed it away. All great artists faced this. Not that he was comparing himself to the great artists, but whether you were a writer, musician, painter, or a photographer, every artist had a duty to his vision—was compelled to tell the truth as he or she saw it, even if it hurt someone's feelings. He didn't want to hurt Kate. He thought her scar was beautiful. And maybe, truth be told, he was attracted to how vulnerable and self-conscious she was about it. To the outside eye, it wasn't as hideous as she seemed to think it was. But the fact that she felt that way about it made her very human. *We all have private pain,* Andy thought. He wasn't trying to exploit hers. But he couldn't pass up this opportunity.

"Tell Amanda not to worry," Andy said. "I won't mislead Kate. I'll be up front, and nothing but professional."

* * *

"Why can't you be happy for me? Do you know how long it's been since I've had a crush on someone?"

"So you admit it," Amanda said. "You have a crush on him."

"Yes," Kate said. "And believe me, it's mutual."

"You don't know that for sure."

"Why are you acting like this? Why can't you be happy for me?"

"He's going to hurt you, that's why. He's not like Jeff, Kate. Very few men are like Jeff." Kate pedaled faster, because what she really wanted to do was ram her bike into Amanda's and knock her over. Did Amanda think she was a child? Did she not realize that Kate knew there was no one else like Jeff, never would be anyone else like Jeff? Tears stung her eyes as she sped up. What was she to do? She was young and hopefully had a long life ahead of her. She couldn't just lie down and die because Jeff did. She used to feel that way. She spent many nights angry she was still alive. Endless nights where she wished she were dead, where life didn't seem worth living without the love of her life. It had taken an enormous effort to get this far. And Jeff would want her to be happy again. So why didn't Amanda?

"Hey," Amanda said in between heavy breathing. "Why are you going so fast?" Amanda caught up with Kate, and when she saw her face, she almost steered her bike into a bench.

"Are you crying?" she said. "Kate, I'm sorry. I didn't mean it." Kate put on the brakes. The bike screeched, and Amanda almost plowed into her.

"Yes, you did," Kate said. "You don't want me to be with anyone else." The women stared at each other as Kate's words sunk in. Kate was in full-blown tears now. "You think I'm betraying Jeff, don't you?"

"Kate."

"There isn't a single day that goes by that I don't think of him," Kate said, barely able to speak through the lump in her throat. "Not a single day."

"Oh, Kate, I know. I'm sorry."

"I know a man like him only comes around once in a lifetime. Lightning doesn't strike twice. Don't you see? That's why Andy's the perfect rebound."

"I don't think it's a rebound if it's been five years," Amanda said.

"It feels like yesterday to me," Kate said.

"I know. Me, too."

"But I still have needs."

"I know."

"And Andy's perfect. A player like you said. A perfect summer fling."

"And the fact that he's gorgeous and rich has absolutely nothing to do with it, does it?" Amanda said. Kate smiled. Amanda reached over and wiped the tears off Kate's cheeks.

"I just miss him," Amanda said.

"I do, too," Kate answered. "But he would want me to live."

Amanda tugged on Kate's long-sleeved shirt. "He'd hate this," she said.

Kate didn't reply, but the look on her face was enough to stop Amanda from pursuing it any further.

"So are we done with the exercise shit?" Amanda said instead. "Can we have some wine now, please?"

"Race you to it," Kate said.

Kate could barely contain her excitement as she got ready for the evening. It was nice to know she could still feel this giddy, still get butterflies in her stomach. They were much better than the knots that had taken up residence the past five years. Andy was taking her to the Break House, a five-star restaurant overlooking the ocean. It was a celebration for the shoot, which was to start the next day.

"You have to tell me everything," Amanda said. "Or—Pete and I could just happen to show up and sit near—"

"No," Pete yelled from the other room. Kate laughed and turned back to the mirror. She was ready. She'd chosen a pink dress with a matching wrap. Her hair was up in a bun, and she was wearing dangling earrings with little diamonds. It was the outfit she'd planned on wearing after the wedding ceremony, as soon as she could sneak away and get out of the hideous plum dress.

"I can't believe you just happened to have a dress like that with you," Amanda said, eyeing her suspiciously.

"Lucky, huh?" Kate said. No bride ever wanted to hear they'd picked a hideous dress. Many a bride went to great lengths to convince the poor maids she'd picked one they'd be sure to wear again and again. Hell was probably full of them.

"Well," Amanda said, "it's 'game over' after he sees you in that dress."

Kate tried to diminish the compliment, but the grin taking over her face gave away her pleasure.

Andy had offered to pick her up, but Kate wanted to meet him at the restaurant. It was a short walk along the beach and up the street. She was nervous and hoped the walk would help calm her down. Just a few weeks ago she was regretting this trip. It was such bad timing, what with being fired, broke, and having no idea what she was going to do with the rest of her life. But look at her now. Andy was going to pay her to do a modeling shoot, and she was going on the first date she'd had in five years. Oh, men had asked, all right, but Kate had first thrown herself into her grief, and then into her work. Traveling outside the country left little time to date, and saying "No" to every offer didn't help, either. She would have thought she would have missed sex, but even that didn't bother her after a while. Until Andy. Meeting him the way she did, in his bedroom, on his bed—was that why she was suddenly sex-crazed?

It didn't hurt, of course, that he was incredibly sexy. She

could tell by his demeanor that he would be good in bed—they would be good together. And what was more romantic than a man taking pictures of you? If the photo shoot turned out anything like the photos she'd seen of Michelle, she would have beautiful dresses to wear, flowing hair, flawless makeup. Would he have professionals to help her with that? It was fine if he didn't; she was pretty good at doing it herself.

As Kate climbed the steps to the entrance of the Break House, she turned to take in the panoramic views of the ocean before going in. She took a deep breath and laughed at the tripping of her heart. She couldn't wait to sit across a candlelit table from Andy. She couldn't wait to get to know him better. She couldn't wait to see what he looked like, what he was wearing, and the look on his face when he saw her in the dress. It was going to be a great night.

The restaurant was a stately old mansion divided into exquisitely decorated dining rooms. They boasted cherrywood floors, original crown molding, crystal chandeliers, deep-set stone fireplaces, and floor-to-ceiling windows whose sole purpose was to draw in the Break House's oceanfront views. Kate's eyes feasted on every gorgeous detail, and when she looked outside she noticed the shade of pink threading through the sunset matched her dress perfectly. That, she decided, was a very good omen.

Chapter Eleven

Kate was having difficulty making sense of the table in front of her, given that it was filled with people. Mark's mushroom-face was the first one she saw. Then Tony. Andy was seated in the middle of the table, but he didn't look up at her. He actually had a portfolio on the dining-room table and was studying it as if trying to save the world from imminent disaster. To his left sat a nice-looking black man in a suit and trendy glasses. He smiled at her and motioned to an empty seat next to him, across from Andy.

"So this is your new model," the man said. He held his hand out to Kate. "Harris George," he said. "I'm Andy's agent."

"Nice to meet you," Kate said quickly, trying to cover her shock. Amanda had been right; this was no date.

"You're late," Andy said, still not looking up. Kate smiled at the faces around the table as she tried to swallow the irritation and humiliation she could feel building up inside her.

"I'm sorry," she said. "I didn't realize this was a business meeting." Andy finally looked up. If he noticed how beautiful she looked in her pink dress, it didn't show.

"What else would it be?" he asked so smugly she wanted to swipe the silver candlesticks off the table and whack him over the head.

"Andy's going to show us his concept for the new book," Tony said.

"It's all here," Andy said, closing the portfolio. "But let's eat first. Then we can get down to business."

There was no doubt about it, the food was probably delicious. They started with fat cocktail shrimps sitting in parfait cups with cocktail sauce, mussels, and crab-stuffed mushrooms. Then there was a mesclun salad and a lobster bisque that normally would've sent Kate straight to heaven. Each course was paired with a glass of wine. For her main course, Kate ordered a steak, but only because it was the most expensive thing on the menu and she was praying Andy was picking up the bill. It was a waste, though; she could barely eat with the hole in her stomach. Apparently, he wasn't over the fact that she'd "outed" his lies about the photos. He was obviously pissed about doing this book again, and she was going to be his scapegoat. So much for sex and romance. Moody artist was right.

The men talked freely about island gossip, politics, the food, the view, and the upcoming project while Kate concentrated on chewing, swallowing, and not crying. The wine had loosened her up, and she was afraid, given her severe disappointment and embarrassment at actually thinking Andy had asked her on a date, that she was going to dissolve into tears. Luckily, she knew how to turn into steel when she had to; she'd learned that the hard way.

"I hope we can cover this quickly," Kate said. "I have plans this evening." Andy looked at her, only the second time that evening that she could tell, and continued staring until she looked away.

"I think Andy just wants to discuss the concept and the shooting schedule. Then there is a contract for you to sign, and we'll be all done," Harris George said. Kate nodded, and despite her anger, she was looking forward to hearing the concept. She thought again of the pretty dresses worn by Michelle. Would she get to keep any of the clothing? Andy reached under the table, pulled out copies of his portfolio, and silently passed them around the table. At least this time, Kate wasn't the only one stunned as those present thumbed through Andy's proposal.

The locations were the same ones Andy had chosen for the first book. It was easy to recognize all five lighthouses on the island, Andy's favorite golf course, the winery, and several of the local beaches. That wasn't the reason everyone's jaw was hanging open. It was his markup of the model that was captivating everyone's attention. There were no pretty, flowing dresses. Instead, the model was wearing ripped jeans and tank tops. Her hair wasn't soft and billowing around her face; in fact, it was downright messy. And even more outrageous, he'd drawn her scar—everything was in black and white except for it, which was painted to look like a lightning bolt. In addition, each sketch showed a strike of lightning coming from somewhere above her, as if she were about to be struck by lightning in every single picture!

Kate frantically searched her memory. When had Andy seen her scar? She thought back to the last time she'd seen him. They had all been on the yacht—she thought she'd caught him looking at her arm. Her sleeves had been wet. He'd seen through them. Heat invaded Kate's face as the realization sank in.

Harris George was the first to speak. Kate kept her face glued to the book. She felt like a slab of stone, paralyzed, with no idea how she was going to react. Options ranged from storming out of the restaurant (just after setting it ablaze) to appearing absolutely unfazed (because somebody who would do something this cruel to her didn't deserve to see her pain). Or she could simply walk out without a word to any of them.

"I don't understand," she heard Harris say. "This is nothing like the first book."

"Is this a joke?" Mark asked.

Kate had never been so aware of breathing in all her life. She should definitely look up. Otherwise she was going to play her hand without a conscious decision. She forced her chin upward. Her only victory was the slight jerk Andy gave when he met her eyes. She wasn't going to have to follow through with any of her storming-out-and-setting-the-place-on-fire plans; her look had hit its target. Andy had definitely flinched.

"I know it's not what you were expecting," Andy said, turning to his agent. "It's less touristy and more artistic. . . ."

"Artistic," the agent repeated, rolling the word around his tongue.

"Is it all going to be like this?" Tony said. "In black and white?"

"What's the deal with the lightning bolt?" Mark asked. "Is she supposed to be like a superhero?"

"Take it or leave it, gentlemen," Andy said. "An artist has to follow his visions. I simply can't repeat the same book I did previously. That would make me nothing more than a wedding photographer. If you want me to do the book again, this is what it's going to have to be. If not, we'll all just agree the project should be shelved and move on."

So that's what was going on, Kate thought, her anger growing by the minute. Andy had no intention of doing this book. He never did. He was just working it so that he was no longer the bad guy. At least she wasn't going to have to do it anymore. She wouldn't ever have to see Andy Beck again.

"There is something intriguing about this idea," Tony said. Kate couldn't believe what she was hearing. Apparently, neither could Andy.

"What?" Andy said.

"Everybody likes superheroes," Mark agreed. "Especially hot, grungy female ones." Hot, grungy females? What did the chubby bug killer know about hot, grungy females? Then Kate realized the extent of his relationship with women probably came from comic books. No wonder. She turned to the agent, waiting for him to shoot down the project.

"The New York art circle might really get into this," Harris said instead. "And all those high falutin' people who come to the Vineyard love to be exposed to local 'art.' I would suggest adding some other colors—I mean the sunsets here are outstanding."

"Nope," Andy said. "Everything in black and white, except the lightning and . . . Kate's scar." The heat in Kate's body really soared as everyone looked at her. She was very aware of the wrap covering her arms.

"She really has a scar like that?" Mark asked.

"Even though all of you gentlemen are on board," Andy said, ignoring Mark's comment and looking at Kate, "we still haven't heard from the lady. I'm sure it wasn't what she was expecting. I'm afraid she has the right to back out, and if she does we all need to respect that. And that's the last word I ever want to hear about this book."

Again, all faces were on Kate. She suddenly felt like a superhero, for she was hyperaware of every single sound in the room. Silver spoons clanking against china. People toasting in the next room. Laughter. Low voices. Her heart beating. She thought of her scar. Up until this point, it had been a reminder. A reminder that she lived and Jeff didn't. It wasn't vanity that made her cover it up; it was regret. Regret that she had to keep on living when the rest of her world had died. And now she knew Amanda had been right about something else. She would never find love again. There was only one Jeff. But he would always be with her. The scar was part of him. He was her lightning bolt. If Andy Beck wanted a fight, he was going to get it.

She slipped the wrap off her shoulders and let it fall. "Are you kidding?" she said, keeping her voice as steady as possible. "I love it." She turned to Harris and smiled. "Where do I sign?"

* * *

Andy moved to the bar long after everyone else had left the table. He couldn't think to do anything but drink. He had so many thoughts swarming him, he didn't know how to organize them. His first thought was that he'd never acted like such a complete jerk in all his life. He truly hadn't planned on his concept coming across as cruel. But there was no confusing the look on Kate's face when she saw the markups. He'd only seen that kind of pain in people's eyes on the news, when horrible tragedies were being covered.

He was scum. Art be damned, he was total scum. And even after all that, they were all still on board for him to do the book. It was impossible. And how dare he be thinking about how stunning Kate looked tonight. What a sick man he was. He'd actually been relishing her discovery that they weren't on a date. When had he become this man? When did his pain over Michelle's betrayal turn him into someone capable of such cruelty? Kate wasn't Michelle. She hadn't done a thing other than stumble into his darkroom. She'd invaded his privacy, yes, but her intent hadn't been to hurt him like he'd just hurt her. Maybe it wasn't too late to change the book. He could be a wedding photographer if he had to. He could give Kate pretty dresses to wear and shoot traditional poses.

His only saving grace, at least in his own mind, was that his ideas for the shoot were intriguing. It wasn't all about revenge or getting the others to drop the project; he really did like the idea of pulling out the stark, natural beauty of the island and throwing it against a stormy background. The island was already gorgeous. People already knew everything about Martha's famous sunsets, and beaches, and bike paths, and golf courses. That's why the rich and famous came here in droves. Why not explore the starkness of the cliffs, the black and white to its color, the storm to its calm?

The pictures were cool. They really were. And Kate could

have said no. He was sorry she was embarrassed about her scar, but it made her stand out in a crowd. And she would definitely stand out in the photos. After his third whiskey and no small amount of self-talk, Andy felt a tiny bit better about himself, and extremely excited about the shoot. But he hadn't come close to figuring out how he was going to accomplish his other goal. Because tonight, no pun intended, it had hit him like a bolt of lightning. Kate Williams wasn't just your average woman. Any fool could see that. She was the type that, if you were lucky enough to have her walk into your life, you never let go. She was the type you fell head over heels in love with. She was the type would sail all night in a rickety sailboat for. He might never be able to repair the damage he'd done to her tonight, but he was sure as hell going to try.

Chapter Twelve

Looking over the expanse of the Gay Head Cliffs, Kate could almost imagine what the area once looked like without houses, restaurants, boutiques, and the Clintons. The terrain was gorgeous, rugged, and fresh. Standing on top of the cliffs and looking out at the ocean reminded Kate how petty her problems were, and just how miraculous planet Earth was. Mankind just couldn't compete with Mother Nature. She had purposefully arrived half an hour early, and had also declined Andy's ridiculous offer to pick her up. As if she would ever spend a single minute she didn't have to with the man.

But to her dismay, he was already there when she arrived, standing down by the water's edge adjusting his camera. There was no crew, no makeup girl, no trailer, no table full of bagels and fresh fruit. It would just be the two of them. She'd come dressed in the outfit sketched by Andy: ripped jeans and a tank top. Andy offered to buy her the outfits he wanted her to wear, but Kate didn't see the point since she had already raided the local thrift shop, there was no sense in wasting money even if she did want Andy to "pay." Kate sat on the cliff, stoic, and silent. She was going to speak to him as little as possible, if at all.

"I brought you coffee," Andy suddenly yelled without

turning around. "It's sitting on top of my equipment behind you."

What the hell? Kate had been watching him since she arrived, and he hadn't once turned around. He must have seen her through the camera somehow, some kind of digital rearview mirror thingy. She opened her mouth to refuse, but realized she really wanted coffee. At this early hour, all the stores had been closed, and thanks to three of them now staying at the house, they were out of coffee at the cottage. Kate plodded over to Andy's equipment, wishing she'd brought packets of Splenda and hoping it wasn't black or with just a tiny drop of skim milk—as if all women did nothing but watch their weight. Since she saved calories on the Splenda, Kate liked her coffee with plenty of half and half.

There were two cups of coffee sitting on a black equipment box. One had a sticky note on it.

Kate: One Splenda and half and half. Extra Splenda in the bag. I was a jerk. I'm sorry. But I truly believe in the artistic merits of this project and appreciate your participation. Lunch will be provided at noon, and there will be a fifteen-minute break every two hours. Let me know if you need anything else. Sincerely, Andy.

Sincerely, Andy? The nerve. Amanda must have ratted out how she liked her coffee. If he thought that was going to make everything all right . . .

Hoping Andy was watching, Kate stuck the note in her mouth, chewed, and spit. Then she took her coffee back to the cliff. It felt strange, going sleeveless, and she was surprised at how alive the memories still were. She could still feel herself lying underneath the car, still smell the sharp scent of gasoline and blood, still hear the screams of approaching sirens, which were nothing compared to the screams coming from her. Jeff was lying just a few feet from her, but she couldn't move, couldn't touch him. She didn't know it at the time, but he was already gone.

"Kate?" Startled, Kate looked up to find Andy directly in front of her. She'd been so lost in her memories, she hadn't been paying attention to him.

"We'll get started in ten minutes, is that okay? I want to catch the sunrise." Kate glanced at the horizon, where the tiniest touches of light were flirting with the horizon.

"We can start now if you'd like," Kate said. "And I don't even need breaks or a long lunch. The sooner we finish this project, the better." Andy's face didn't change expression, but even in the bare light of the sunrise, Kate could see that she'd hurt him. Well, so what. He was a player, after all, and acting the wounded man was probably his easiest role. She wasn't going to let him get to her.

"Fine," Andy said. "I'd like you lying down for the first shot, on your right side, with your elbow propped up, supporting your head in your hand. If it's comfortable, cross your left knee and bring it up to your stomach. We're going for rebellious and sultry, so no worries, that fuck-off expression you're wearing right now is perfect."

With that, he took the coffee cup out of her hand and walked away.

Kate lay on her side, propping her head with her hand as requested. When she brought her knee up, her tank top rose slightly, exposing her belly button. She didn't make a move to pull her shirt down, and Andy didn't ask her to. She had to admit, it was a nice feeling, having a camera aimed just at her. Andy moved around snapping shots from various angles as she kept her body as still as possible, letting only her mind wander.

What was she going to do for work? She'd known the minute she was laid off that she no longer wanted to stay in

Iowa. It was time to move on. Maybe she'd move to a big city. Maybe she'd travel first. Maybe—

"I don't mind you showing your stomach," Andy said. "But stop sucking it in."

"I'm not sucking it in!"

"Yes, you are. Just be natural. Exhale for God's sake."

The nerve! Kate wanted to scream. Here she was thinking she was all sexy. Kate let her breath out and pulled down her shirt. When she heard Andy chuckle, she seriously considered picking up a big, fat rock and throwing it at his big, fat head.

"That's good for this shot. Ready to move?" They were going to the golf course next, before the bulk of the retirees were out on the greens walking in their ugly pants. Kate quickly got up and didn't bother to thank Andy as he handed her coffee cup back. Instead, she slipped silently into his Jeep and waited as he loaded in the equipment.

A short while later Kate lay on the golf course with her arms stretched out, the fourth hole just above her head. A golf club lay to the left of her body as if she'd tossed it there in a fit of rage and thrown herself on the ground in an act of submission. In her mind's eye, Kate thought she could see where Andy was going with the shot, lightning striking the club, bouncing off her arm. It would probably look really cool, not that she was going to tell him that. Andy was standing directly over her, going for a close-up. Kate prayed he wasn't shooting up her nostrils but didn't dare say anything for fear of appearing vain. Andy suddenly stopped shooting and simply stared at her.

"What?" she said after a minute. Andy kneeled down with a knee on either side of her body and bent in toward her. For a split second she thought he was going to kiss her.

"Don't move," he said.

"What?" Kate asked. "Is there something on me? What is it? A bee?" Andy laughed, and Kate was furious with herself. His voice was deep, and his lips were so close to hers, she definitely wanted to kiss them. She hated him for that, but she hated herself even more.

"I just want to do something with your hair, but don't move—okay?"

"Okay," Kate whispered, dreading his touch simply because she couldn't wait for it. Still kneeling over her, he took both hands and spread her hair out so it almost seemed to be flying from her scalp, finger-in-a-light-socket look. All the effort she'd gone to with her makeup and hair to look pretty, and he was ruining it. She wondered about the other woman, Michelle—a real model. How different her shoot had been. Michelle wouldn't have been caught dead letting Andy arrange her like a science experiment.

And even though he was looking at her very intensely, almost passionately, Kate knew she was nothing more than an artist's subject—it was his work he was intense and passionate about. She was simply the by-product of that. Certainly nothing to be flattered about.

"There," he said softly in her ear when he was done arranging her hair. "You're perfect." *He didn't mean I'm perfect*, she reminded herself as he started shooting again.

"Close your eyes," he said. Kate was only happy to. Andy's words had set off a memory.

"You're perfect," Jeff said. They'd just made love, and Kate had tried to cover her body with the sheet. Jeff pulled it away. Kate reached for it again, and Jeff gently caught her wrist and held it above her head. He took her other hand, holding both her wrists now above her head with his hands. She could have pulled away, of course, and he would've let her go, but she didn't.

"What are you doing, mister?" she asked.

"Who do you think you're hiding from?"

"I'm not hiding. I'm just cold."

"It's ninety degrees in here."

"I just like the feel of a sheet on me."

"Liar."

"I'm modest."

Jeff growled into her neck.

"Coulda fooled me just a few seconds ago," Jeff said. Kate laughed. Jeff leaned in and kissed her.

"If you want to hide from yourself, hide from yourself," Jeff said. "But don't ever hide from me. Because in my eyes—you're perfect."

"Kate?"

She'd done it again, lost all sense of where she really was.

"Sorry," Kate said, sitting up. "Are we moving?"

"We're moving." In the distance she could see golfers taking the course, standing in plaid and tweed clumps, pulling shiny golf clubs out of bulging bags. Andy packed up and they walked silently toward the Jeep. Kate's prayer that Andy hadn't noticed the tears in her eyes was blown out of the water when he silently handed her a tissue.

Chapter Thirteen

"I saw a *Dateline* special once about men addicted to porn," Amanda said. Pete groaned and rolled over. He and Amanda were cuddled in the tent. They'd just had what he thought was the best sex ever, but that was quickly changing given their pillow talk was reverting back to what Amanda insisted was his "perverted desire to undress every woman you see." The biggest difference between men and women, Pete thought, was that a man could forgive and forget, but a woman could beat anything to death. Even the Headless Horseman wouldn't have been safe; she would still have been trying to beat him over the head despite the fact that he didn't have one. Pete thought that was pretty funny, but he kept it to himself. Laughing when she was like this was apt to piss her off even more.

"Panda," Pete said. "I am not addicted to porn."

"But how do I know that?" Amanda said. "How do I really know that? You didn't see *Dateline*. Did the wife of that judge know that? Did the little seventy-five-year-old woman know that—"

"Oh my God."

"—did the soccer mom know that?"

"The soccer mom knew," Pete said. "The soccer mom definitely knew." Amanda punched Pete on the shoulder. He tick-

led her side and then wrapped his arm around her waist and
kissed her.

"No porn, honey," he said. "I promise."

"You swear?"

"I swear."

"Because I consider that cheating."

"Yes."

"And demoralizing."

"Uh-huh."

"It objectifies women—"

"Amanda, I get it, okay!"

"Okay." They hugged in the silence of the tent.

"What about paintings?" Pete asked after a few moments
of bliss. "Can I look at naked women in paintings?"

"Are you ready for a lunch break?" Andy asked. Kate
thought about it. She was hungry. After the golf course they'd
shot a few pictures of Kate riding a bike, standing underneath
a twisted oak tree, and running on the beach. Who knew modeling could be so strenuous? But she wasn't going anywhere
to eat with Andy. The only problem was, she was so tired
when she'd left the house, she'd forgotten her purse. She had
no money and hadn't thought to bring lunch. Andy didn't
need to know that. She could spend lunch napping on the
beach or walking along the water.

"Fine," Kate said. "What time should we meet back up and
where?"

"I thought I'd take you to lunch. I know this great little—"

"No," Kate said. There was no way she was going to lunch
with him. He was being so nice. She'd felt like the center of
attention all day; she'd felt like the most beautiful woman in
the world. The closeness of his body when he'd come in for
special shots had driven her crazy. She wanted to touch him;
she definitely wanted to kiss him.

He'd be good in bed. There was no question in Kate's mind. If his intensity in the sack was one tenth of what he gave to his work . . .

She felt so vulnerable. She couldn't let him anywhere near her, or she was definitely going to do something she would live to regret.

"Are you sure?" Andy said. "Because lunch is part of the contract."

"I brought my own," Kate said. "And I just need some time to be alone."

"Okay," Andy said. "We'll meet here in an hour—"

"How about thirty minutes?"

"I'm sure you're tired—"

"I'm not."

"Don't underestimate standing still in the sun all day. I've seen many a model—"

"I'm fine. And I'm certainly not one of your models."

Andy looked at his watch.

"Fine," he said. "Thirty minutes."

Kate, having no idea where she was going, started to walk away.

"Where's your lunch?" Andy called after her.

Kate didn't need to eat. She would be fine. She just needed to meditate, think about something other than Jeff. And definitely about something other than Andy without his shirt on. When he'd been leaning over her on the golf course, she would have given herself to him right then if he'd only asked. And this was only the first day in a public place surrounded by middle-aged men in tweed—not normally a place she'd ever get turned on. She was so screwed. She should spend her lunch hour thinking about her future career instead.

For the past five years, Kate had been working at a non-profit foundation. Unfortunately, because of the downward-spiraling economy, the charity was losing donations, and they'd been forced to let many of their employees go, including Kate. Before that, Kate had planned on launching a professional singing career. She joined a band, and she and Jeff were working out the details of how they were going to handle it if Kate had to be on the road all the time. After Jeff was killed, Kate couldn't sing a note.

It was a little late to be launching a singing career now, wasn't it? Although she didn't have to be a star, she could try and make a nice living singing and playing without being a household name. But five years was a long time for a singer to go without using their voice. And she was going to have to make money in the meantime.

Before she knew it, the half hour was over. She knew nothing more about what she was going to do with her life, she was still thinking of Andy's body on top of hers, and she was freaking starving.

There were five lighthouses on the Vineyard, and Andy intended to visit every one. It would've been more convenient to stay at the Gay Head Lighthouse directly after shooting on the cliff, but they had to get the golf course in before the members began to arrive. So after lunch it was back to the Gay Head Lighthouse, where Andy told her they would take just a few more shots and be done for the day. It wasn't easy, given the number of tourists frolicking about. Luckily, people were pretty considerate on the island, and for the most part they were respectful of the process. Which, to Kate's horror, didn't mean they left them completely alone; instead, they simply watched her at a polite distance, as if she were a dangerous animal in the zoo.

"Who is she?" she heard a little boy ask his mom.

"She looks just like a regular person," the mom answered. Kate couldn't help but giggle. Andy immediately put the camera down and gave her a look. Kate stopped smiling; he had already asked her to think of something "wistful." That wasn't easy. She wasn't even sure exactly what "wistful" entailed, so instead she looked puzzled. Andy put the camera down again.

"Now you look as if you've lost something," he said.

I have, Kate thought. *My mind.*

"I said wistful," Andy complained. The parents and children gawking were totally distracting her. Again, she thought she heard a woman mutter "regular person."

"I *am* a regular person," Kate called to the mom.

"Kate," Andy said. "I am not paying you to talk. So shut up." The words hit their mark. Kate noticed the children wanted to stay to see what the mean man was going to say next, but the mothers started pulling them away. "Now," Andy said when they were alone again. "I want you to think about something you regret. Something you'd take back—"

He didn't have to keep talking. Her face immediately changed. He snapped as fast as he could, all the while hating himself for making her conjure up whatever memory was causing the haunted look on her face. But it was exactly what he needed for the shoot. He finished with Kate leaning against the lighthouse, looking out at the ocean as if it held the answer to all of life's conundrums. Topped off with her look of regret, it was exactly the haunted feel Andy wanted to evoke.

But he wasn't a total insensitive jerk. He planned on ending the day on a lighter note, and as they moved to the inside stairs, he asked her to think of playful memories, something that would make her laugh. Kate stood at the top of the landing and simply stared at him. He had to admit to snapping that expression as well, for she looked like a small child lost in a big crowd.

"Come on," Andy said. "When is the last time you really laughed?"

Kate shifted on the steps and looked around as if the answer were written on the lighthouse walls.

"Without alcohol?" she asked. Andy laughed, which made Kate smile. But it never reached her eyes.

"Go back to childhood if you have to," Andy said. "It's too bad you weren't in the yard to see Amanda looking at us through the window—"

To Andy's surprise, Kate gave a genuine laugh. He snapped the picture. "Put your hands on the rail," he said. Kate did. "And I would've like to have been there when you met Mark," Andy said. "Cockroaches. He can't eat just one." Kate laughed again, a little harder this time. Andy noted her laugh filled him with a sense of satisfaction he usually only got from snapping pictures. It was addictive, making her laugh, and he continued long after he had enough footage for the project.

"Okay," he said. "Race you to the top."

They finished their shoot where they started, on top of the cliffs, this time as the sun was starting to set. The air was starting to cool, and Kate had to admit she was getting tired. Andy removed a sweatshirt from his bag. "Here," he said, handing it to her.

"What's this?" Kate asked.

"You want a sarcastic answer? Just put it on."

"Why? I thought you wanted—"

"It's not all about that. It doesn't have to be every shot."

"I thought that was the point."

"I have plenty—just let me get a few like this, okay? I'm the artist here, missy. You're just the gorgeous model."

Kate huffed, but put on the sweatshirt and tried to ignore the smell of his cologne against her skin. Before she knew it, the day was over. She couldn't believe how fast it had flown by. She stood up, stretched her arms, and was slammed by a wall of dizziness. The next thing she knew, she was headed face-first for the ground.

* * *

When she awoke, she was in Andy's arms, being carried somewhere. She groaned and tried to squirm out of his grip. He held her tighter.

"Brought your lunch, did ya?" he said. "Looks like the 'Sticky Note Diet' isn't quite working for you."

"Oh God," Kate said. "Put me down."

"No."

She could see his Jeep just a few feet ahead.

"I can walk from here, thank you very much," she said.

"I don't care."

"Stop treating me like a child."

"Stop acting like one."

Kate shut up and laid her head on his shoulder. It must have startled him, for he stopped and looked at her for a second.

"That's it?" he said. "No more fight in ya?"

"That's it," she said. Andy laughed. It was a nice, deep, sound.

When they reached the Jeep, he gently put her down by the passenger side. He opened the door and waited until she got in. "Don't go anywhere," he said. "I have to get the equipment."

Kate nodded, too exhausted to talk. She had a new respect for models. She didn't relish going home to the lovebirds, either; in fact, she had decided to take Andy up on his offer to get her a room at the inn. She couldn't take any more ups and downs with the couple, and frankly she didn't care anymore if they made up or not. So when Andy got back in and announced he was taking her to dinner and there wasn't a thing she could do about it, she didn't even pretend to argue.

She liked him again. That was the only reason she could come up with for doing what she did in the Jeep. It had been five years, and that's too long for anyone. She couldn't remember the last time she'd been so physically attracted to someone. Whether it was the intensity of his look, or his deep voice, or his slightly crooked smile—or pheromones—who knew? The only thing she knew is that if she didn't make an immediate move, she was going to lose her nerve. Andy put the key in the ignition, and Kate simply placed her hand over his. He didn't look at her right away, he just stared at her hand on top of his, as if contemplating his next move.

"Kate," he said, turning to her.

She leaned in and kissed him. Softly, he returned the kiss, then tried to pull away. She pressed harder and possessively wrapped her hands around the back of his neck to keep him close. He made a low noise into her mouth, and she knew she wasn't letting him turn back now. If only the stick shift wasn't in the way. It was dark now. Kate wanted to find someplace on the beach, near the cliffs. She only hated breaking off the kiss to talk. Talk was dangerous. Action was all that was called for now.

"Do you know of any private section of beach?" she asked, pulling away only long enough to ask the question and then kissing him again before he could answer. This time she rubbed her hand along his thigh, and she couldn't believe it, but she was getting turned on by the strangest things, like the feel of his jeans underneath her fingers, the stubble on his jawline, and the way his hair slightly curled under at the ends.

"Kate," he said, barely breaking the kiss. "I'm taking you to dinner, remember?" Kate took his hand and put it back on her waist. He rubbed the area, and then trailed his fingers up her curves, until he reached her breasts. Then, with both hands, he softly outlined each breast with his fingers before exploring them fully with both hands. His touch was soft but strong, and Kate knew she was a goner.

"Dinner can wait," Kate said. "I don't think this will take long."

Andy pulled back. "Just what do you mean by that?" he asked.

Kate laughed and put her free hand on his other thigh and leaned into his neck, where she gave it a little kiss.

"I'm not talking about you," Kate said. "I'm talking about me."

They didn't even make it to the lighthouse or a secluded place on the beach. Andy took condoms out of his glove box, and that was all Kate needed to see. As soon as they were out of the Jeep, she pulled him down to a soft patch of grass and pulled him on top of her. "Here?" he asked. "Are you sure?"

"Here," she said, reaching for him. "I'm sure."

They barely took any clothes off, driven by a sense of urgency that seemed bigger than both of them. Kate lost herself in the moment. It all felt so right, how he tasted, touched, smelled—how perfect their bodies fit together. It was just as intense and passionate as she had imagined. And she'd been right about one thing: it certainly didn't last long for either of them.

"Oh God," Andy said. "You must think I'm—"

"Starving," Kate said, kissing him. "I am, too. Let's go."

They scrambled to pull up what had been pulled down, and pull down what had been pulled up, and by the time they were back in the Jeep less than ten minutes had passed. Ten minutes that could change everything between them. Kate couldn't believe she'd only been on the job a day and she'd already slept with the boss. Jumped him was more like it. But instead of feeling guilty or ashamed, she felt amazing and renewed, and she couldn't stop smiling. Neither, she noticed, could Andy.

"Next time is going to be slow," Andy said, starting up the Jeep and reaching for her hand without taking his eyes off the road. "Very, very slow."

"I'm not usually like that," Kate said. "I don't want you to think—"

"Please," Andy said, holding up his hand. "That was amazing. Maybe the best night of my life. I know we haven't known each other very long yet, but believe me, from what I do know about you, you have my full respect."

Something in Andy's tone tripped off an alarm in Kate. *What I do know about you*—it was the exact tone people had used around her the first year after the accident. Full of sadness and pity. But she'd never said anything to Andy about Jeff. She assumed he didn't know that's how she got the scar, otherwise . . .

Otherwise, wanting to expose it for his photographs . . .

"What do you know about me?" Kate asked. Andy must have picked up on the slight alarm in her voice, for he took his time answering.

"I know you're spirited, and beautiful, and intelligent—"

"Do you or do you not know what happened to me?"

Andy pulled the Jeep over to the side of the road and put it in park. Kate couldn't believe the instant ache in her heart.

"Oh my God," Kate said. "You do."

She opened the door to the Jeep and got out. Andy was right behind her.

"Kate."

She didn't reply. She stood staring down the dark expanse of the road, as if she were waiting for another ride.

"I think you're beautiful," Andy said. "I think your scar is beautiful—"

Kate whirled around.

"Do you think lying underneath a smashed-up car on a dark highway is beautiful? Do you think not being able to move any part of your body while the man you love is losing his life a few feet away from you is beautiful? Do you think living the rest of your life knowing that *it should have been you* is beautiful?"

Kate was well aware her anger wasn't really directed at Andy but at herself. Nobody knew about those last few moments in the car, moments she could never take back. The accident was all her fault. That's why she'd been hiding her scar.

It was a daily reminder that she was responsible for the death of the only man she had ever loved. She had been foolish to think she could ever move on.

"Kate," Andy said. "It shouldn't have been you. Please don't ever say that—"

"You don't know that," Kate said. "You don't know me."

"Please," Andy said.

Kate turned back to the Jeep.

"Just take me home," she said. "Just take me home."

Chapter Fourteen

"I'm telling you, it's because he has money," Amanda said as she strolled along Main Street with Kate and Pete. They were supposed to be spending a leisurely afternoon window-shopping, but Kate soon started complaining about Andy, and now Amanda was weighing in.

"Amanda," Pete said.

"I mean it," Amanda said. "He wouldn't be treating Kate like this if he were poor."

Kate didn't respond. Instead, she lost herself in the windows of the boutiques.

"You don't know that," Pete said. "Not every rich person is an asshole."

"I disagree. I told you my theory when we first met."

"I remember all too well," Pete said.

"People with that kind of privilege—"

"Andy is one of the most down-to-earth people I know," Pete interrupted. Kate had never heard him so animated. He was almost . . . standing up to Amanda. "And if he's so bad, why'd you take him up on the offer to stay at the cottage, huh? Does an asshole loan out his home for an entire month?" Instead of answering Pete, Amanda threw Kate a look. Kate caught it all right—*Help me out here*—but she wasn't going to get involved. Amanda had always had a chip on her shoulder about people with money, mostly, Kate suspected, because she'd never been one of them.

"I didn't say Andy was an asshole," Kate said. "I just said he was cruel."

"Who wants ice cream?" Pete asked.

"Well, at least he got you to stop hiding," Amanda mumbled.

"Excuse me?"

"Come on, Kate. You've been covering your arms up for five years. He freed you from that."

"He freed me?" Kate said.

"There's a great little ice-cream place right up the road!" Pete said.

"You know what I mean," Amanda said.

"So now he's my savior?" Kate said.

"Do you have to take everything so literally?" Amanda said.

"Me!" Kate said. "You're the one getting in the way of your own happiness!"

"Just what the hell do you mean by that?"

"Or frozen yogurt," Pete said. "I'm sure they have frozen yogurt."

"Oh, come on, Amanda. It's always drama, drama, drama. And I've kept my mouth shut because you're my friend and I love you. But I've just been humiliated here, and you're siding with Andy Beck!"

"I just called him a rich asshole, didn't I? Which is kind of an oxymoron, but nevertheless—"

"All rich people aren't assholes!" Pete exploded. "Kate's right. You are a drama queen."

Kate wanted the floor to open up and swallow her whole. She could yell at her best friend, but she'd never meant to create a ganging-up-on scenario. This was not going to end well.

"You're not always dramatic," Kate said. "I didn't mean to imply—"

"Oh, don't stop now, Katie," Amanda said, stopping in the middle of the street and facing Kate. "Let her rip!"

"Amanda," Kate said softly.

"No," Amanda said. "I want to hear this. What am I so dramatic about?"

"I'm not doing this—"

"Yes, you are. I told you what I think. You've been hiding for five years, and rich asshole or not, I'm glad Andy Beck helped put an end to it. There, I said my piece and the world didn't end. So you say yours."

"I think you're immature. I think you canceled your own wedding for no good reason. Was it a dumb thing to say? Yes. But news flash—men often say dumb things. And I don't think it was Pete you were worried about as much as yourself. You're the one who's afraid to commit, and you were going to use any little excuse to get out of it!"

Pete backed up a couple of steps.

"I can't believe you just said that," Amanda said.

"See?" Kate exploded. "This is what I mean. You just forced me to tell you what I thought. Now you're punishing me for it!"

"Just because you had a perfect relationship—" Amanda started to say. Kate put her hands over her ears and screamed. Amanda stopped in her tracks and threw Pete a worried look. Kate stopped screaming, but within seconds she was quietly sobbing.

"Katie?" Amanda said.

"We were having a fight," Kate said. "It's my fault. The accident was all my fault."

"What do you mean?" Amanda asked.

"I'd just told him I wanted to break up," Kate sobbed. "That's why he was distracted."

"In the car?" Amanda said. "You ambushed him with that in the car? During a snowstorm?"

"Amanda," Pete said softly. He put his hand on her shoulder. Amanda shook it off.

"Why?" Amanda demanded. "Why did you do that?"

"I didn't mean it. We'd been fighting a lot that week."

"I never knew that."

"Over stupid things—I didn't even mean it. Of course I didn't want to break up with him—"

"Then you shouldn't have said it! Not while he's driving!"

"You think I don't know that?"

"You killed him!"

"Amanda," a new voice broke in. They all turned. Andy was standing behind Kate.

"You," Amanda said. "You rich asshole. You have no right listening to this conversation."

"The hell I don't," Andy said. "Kate is a victim here, too, Amanda. Can't you see she's been eating herself alive with guilt? Torturing herself all these years?"

"And why shouldn't she?" Amanda cried. "She killed my brother!"

Kate winced as if she'd been physically struck.

"No," Andy said. "She didn't. She had an argument with her lover. She's not responsible for what happened." Andy turned to Kate. "Do you hear me? It is not your fault. It was an accident. You did not kill Jeff." Kate couldn't answer. She was sobbing. Andy took her into his arms and held her. After a moment, she lifted her head and looked at Amanda.

"I'll never forgive you," Amanda said.

"If you have something to say, just say it," Amanda growled. Pete watched her stomp through the kitchen, yanking pots and pans out of the cupboards and dumping them on the countertop.

"You don't really think Kate killed Jeff," Pete said. Amanda threw down the last pan and then, exhausted, leaned against the sink. "You and I fight all the time," Pete continued. "What if something had happened to me after one of them?"

"Like what?"

"I don't know, but would it make one of us a murderer?"

"The roads were icy!" Amanda yelled. "And she distracted him."

"It was dark. The roads were covered in black ice, and Jeff lost control of the car, Panda. You know how many accidents were reported that evening. On the news they were practically begging people not to go out. Jeff could have been distracted over something that made him *happy* and still lost control of the car."

"I hate it," Amanda said. "I hate knowing the last thing he heard before he died was Kate telling him she wanted to break up with him."

"I know. So do I. But think of how she feels. You know she didn't mean it. You've said that to me lots of times."

"Lots of times? Have I really said it lots of times?"

"The point is, I don't just listen to the words."

"Gee, thanks."

"I mean I try to listen to what's behind the words. I can tell the difference between you being hurt and you seriously wanting to end things with me."

"You can?"

"Of course. And if anyone else was sensitive enough to pick up on stuff like that, it was Jeff. Andy was right. Kate's been torturing herself for the past five years. Do you really think Jeff would have wanted that? What if it had been Kate that died after fighting with Jeff? Would you seriously have blamed Jeff for the rest of his life? Would you want him torturing himself?"

"No."

"So don't do it to Katie. If any good is to come out of this miserable summer, let it be her happiness again. Don't do it for me. Do it for Jeff." Amanda's eyes filled with tears as she nodded her agreement. She wiped them away and then looked at the man she loved, the man she should have married.

"Do you think Kate was right?" Amanda asked. "Do you think I chickened out of our wedding on purpose?"

"I don't know. Only you can answer that. But I'm glad things happened the way they did."

"You are?" Amanda asked. "Why? Because you don't want to marry me?"

"No," Pete said, taking her hands. "Because if you agree to marry me again—I want to do it the right way. Without any secrets between us."

Amanda went in for a hug and then stopped.

"What do you mean? Pete? What secrets?"

Pete gestured for Amanda to sit down. When she didn't, he cleared some of the pots and pans out of the way, picked her up, and set her on the countertop. She crossed her arms against her chest and waited.

"Andy's not a rich asshole," Pete said. "He doesn't own this cottage or the yacht. He doesn't live on a trust fund."

"That's your big secret? So what?"

"Remember how when we first met, you went on and on about how you hated rich people?"

"Yes, and you told me he was filthy rich—oh, I see. You said that so I wouldn't go out with him."

"Yes," Pete said.

"Wait a minute. If Andy doesn't live in this cottage—"

"He does," Pete said. "He's been renting it. For a very good price, I might add."

"And the yacht?"

"He's just the . . . interim captain, I guess you might say."

"Well, if he doesn't own this house and the yacht, then who does?"

"You're looking at him," Pete said. "I'm the real rich asshole."

Chapter Fifteen

"Trust me. Just walk and look at things. Really look. When you see something that strikes your imagination—just click." Andy and Kate were back on Main Street, and Kate was wielding Andy's camera. Instead of shooting pictures of her today, he wanted her to play the role of photographer. She knew he was trying to get her mind off her argument with Amanda. He'd only had to see her face for a split second this morning to call off the day's shoot. At first Kate had been hesitant to accept his "therapy," but soon she was completely into it.

She liked the Welcome sign on Annie's Island Flowers. She snapped the picture. She liked the ceramic duck in the window of a boutique. A child's shoe sat atop a mailbox. A shiny penny dropped on the ground. A starling resting on a low branch. A golden retriever outside an ice-cream shop, tied to a pole, drool dripping from its lips as it gazed longingly into the window of the shop where its thirteen-year-old master was imbibing on mint chocolate chip. Kate was disappointed she couldn't get both the kid and the dog in one shot, but Andy's only rule had been "nothing staged." Before Kate knew it, two hours had flown by and they had barely walked a block. When Kate finally put the camera down, a peacefulness settled around her, and her face was relaxed and open.

"Lunch," Andy said. "We'll start with the shoot after that."

"Thank you," Kate said. "That was amazing."

"You have an artist's eye," Andy said. "You'd be good at this yourself."

"It's the little things in life that make it miraculous, don't you think?" Kate asked as they strolled down the street, no real destination in mind.

"Yes. It can also be the little things that make life cruel," Andy said.

"Like an icy road at night," Kate said.

"Yes," Andy agreed. "Like that." He stopped then, took both her hands and gently turned her toward him. "It wasn't your fault," he said. "Tell me you know that."

"I shouldn't have picked a fight while he was driving in bad weather," Kate said.

"It wasn't the fight," Andy said. "It was the condition of the roads. You could have been silent. You could have been joking about something. It doesn't matter—"

"I don't know if this is going to work," Kate said.

"What?"

"Those are the last words Jeff heard me say," Kate said. "I said, 'I don't know if this is going to work.'"

"I'm sorry. But don't you think you've punished yourself enough? And if our soul does go someplace after this, don't you think he knows how much you really loved him?"

"Yes," Kate said. "Jeff would have been the first to forgive me." Tears filled her eyes as she said this. Andy rubbed her back gently, and gave her space to cry.

"Then let him," he said after a minute. "Just let him."

That afternoon Andy followed Kate's lead, and instead of shooting at the ocean, or the golf course, or the lighthouses, he shot her in everyday places. Leaning against a pickup truck. Sitting cross-legged and barefoot on the sidewalk in front of the ice-cream shop, eating a butterscotch cone. Stopping to smell a hydrangea bush. Watching a mother as she stooped to tie her child's shoe. Standing in front of the movie theater pulling a ten-dollar bill out of her pocket. It was the most fun she'd had modeling for his pictures, and her good mood lasted the entire day. On a break she checked her cell phone to see if Amanda had called. She didn't even reprimand Andy when she heard the click of his camera as he watched her take in the fact that there were no messages from Amanda.

She understood Andy's point about capturing the moment without staging it. His original photo book with Michelle had been staged. All the fancy outfits and makeup artists and posing. That was a book done by someone doing a job, going through the motions. This book was one created by an artist, driven by passion. Kate was proud to be part of it. If only the relationship were strictly professional. If only she didn't want to touch him every second. She found herself longing for shots in which he would have to come and "arrange" her. She looked for any excuse to have his body near hers. Neither of them had mentioned the other night, ignoring both their passion and the argument that followed. They were overly polite, and shy, but the sexual tension was as palpable as the warm Vineyard air. Kate was determined to get through this without incident. After all, they were from two different worlds. Andy lived on this island. He owned a yacht. Kate loved visiting, but she wasn't comfortable in the land of the rich; she was destined for a down-to-earth lifestyle. If she could scrape enough money together, maybe she'd travel. Do some hands-on work instead of sitting behind a desk. It wasn't a lifestyle Mr. Moneybags would want. She'd had her rebound sex; going back for seconds could only spell disaster.

Kate tried to hide her disappointment when Andy called it a day.

"Are you hungry?" he asked.

"No."

"Me neither. Well, not exactly."

"What do you mean, not exactly?"

"I guess I'm just going to say it."

"Just say it."

"You know I have a room at the inn."

"Yes."

"Well. There's room at the inn," Andy said. They held eye contact for a long time.

"Lead the way," Kate said.

Of the island's numerous inns, the Black Sheep wasn't fancy, but it was quaint, cozy, and private. It had four petite guest rooms, and Kate was happy to note Andy had the one on the top floor. It was early evening, and the only other inhabitant was an elderly man at the front desk. Kate and Andy hurried up the stairs as if trying to outrun any lingering doubts. When Andy tried to open the door, he fumbled and dropped the key. Kate was relieved to see he was as nervous as she was. When he finally flung it open, Kate saw that the most prominent thing in the tiny room was the big bed. It was exactly where they were headed.

This time, they took their time. They touched, explored, kissed, and laughed. Nothing felt as good to Kate as Andy's arms around her, the scent of him on her skin, his voice reverberating in her chest. She hated that she was jumping ahead in her mind, but in the moment she could no longer imagine spending another night alone. Not that she verbalized this, of course. She wasn't that crazy. But nothing could stop her imagination from spinning a future that included endless nights of lovemaking like this one. As they lost themselves in each other's body, snapshots of the island ran through Kate's mind and transported her to those places with Andy.

The squeaky cheap bed of the inn was replaced with vivid images of the ocean, the Gay Head Cliffs, the stairs of the lighthouse. She thought of their first hurried encounter on the grass by his Jeep, the coffee cup with the sticky note just for her, even their heated argument by the side of the road. And it was all okay. She let herself go, and in that moment she completely opened up.

"I'm starving," Andy said a few hours later. The sheets were sweaty and tangled, running through and underneath their entwined limbs. Kate giggled. Andy pinched her.

"I'm talking about food this time," he said, kissing her on the nose.

"Me, too," Kate said. "But I never want to leave this bed."

"Think we can get Ed to deliver?"

"Who's Ed?"

"The old guy at the front desk. He has a bike with a basket. I've seen it."

Kate laughed.

"You have a gorgeous laugh," Andy said. "Among other things," he added, running his hand down the length of her body and kissing her softly.

"If you don't stop that," Kate said, leaning in to his kiss, "I'm going to lose my appetite."

The rest of the month flew by, and it wasn't long before Kate was staying with Andy at the inn. Amanda had yet to make any effort to contact her, and Kate didn't want to blow her money from the shoot on a room of her own. Besides, Andy and Kate were dying to spend every second together, counting the minutes until the shoot was over and they could be wrapped in each other's skin. And gradually, they took their relationship out of the bedroom. They took long walks on the beach, saw movies, tried all the seafood joints on the island, and went sailing with Tony. Andy had a surprise for Tony, too. Even though the official book wouldn't be out for at least a year, Andy announced he wanted to throw a party at the bookstore and preview his photographs to the public.

It would be a wrap-up celebration, an early promotional opportunity, and Andy would pay for the entire thing. It was the least he could do. Tony was thrilled and readily agreed. Kate was nervous at the thought of a roomful of people looking at images of her, but she kept it to herself. Being exposed, being out there, was something she might never be comfortable with, but this time she knew she could face it. This was Andy's project, and she wasn't going to do anything to ruin it. She couldn't help but feel sad that Jeff wouldn't be there to see the pictures. She knew two things. He would be proud of her, and he would forgive her. She only wished she could say the same thing for Amanda.

It was this thought that brought her back to Andy's honeymoon house. She noticed the porch was put back together. The swing was hanging and slightly swaying in the breeze. The flowerpots lined the steps. The heart-shaped lights were strung. Two pairs of white flip-flops, HIS and HERS, sat next to the bride-and-groom welcome mat. Kate slipped the invite under the door and walked away.

Chapter Sixteen

Grapevine Books looked fabulous. Kate loved books; just being surrounded by them made her feel at home. Andy had chosen ten photos to enlarge and display. They were hung on a black-felt backdrop, five on each side of the store. They were covered at the moment; the "reveal" would happen as soon as Tony gave the word. Kate was nervous, but not for the obvious reasons. She was praying Amanda would walk through the door. Since she would be leaving the Vineyard in a few days, it was their last chance to kiss and make up. She knew if she left the island without the two of them straightening things out, they would probably never speak again. The things Amanda had said to her had deeply wounded Kate, but she understood where Amanda had been coming from. Grief often welled up and spilled on anyone unfortunate enough to be in its path. She and Amanda had been friends long enough to weather this—as long as they had the chance. She missed Amanda, too, even with her constant complaining, and wondered how Amanda was getting along with Pete. If nothing else, their fight had probably brought Amanda and Pete closer together. Kate knew Amanda; she'd have a hard time alienating the two most important people in her life at the same time. Since Kate was "out," Pete was probably still "in."

Maybe she should just let them be, sacrifice their friendship so Amanda could stay happy with Pete. But that wasn't a long-term solution—Amanda was still Amanda, and until she learned to ease up on her expectations of others, she would never be happy. Kate tried to put Amanda out of her mind as she eyed the tables of appetizers and headed to the open bar set up at the check-out counter. She was going to have a celebratory drink and just relax. She wasn't surprised to see so many people—on such a small island, an event like this brought the vacationers out in droves.

She found Andy right away, surrounded by people, looking sexy all in black. He caught her staring at him, and the smile he gave her was a better buzz than all the champagne in the room. Tony was dressed in a spiffy tan suit with a red shirt, working the crowd like a Carnival cruise director. Kate was happy Tony was going to have his book after all, and thrilled she was a part of it. Everyone seemed to be having a good time, with the exception of Mark.

He was leaning against the counter, lording over a plate of cheese, looking disgusted. He wasn't going to find a good wife among these drinkers and artists tonight. He caught Kate's eye and waved her over. Kate reluctantly made her way toward him, already coming up with exit lines and assuring herself she wouldn't talk to him any longer than ten minutes.

"Hello, Mark," she said.

"Kate." The two stood like unwilling participants in a junior high dance. Kate was just about to try out one of her exit lines when he spoke.

"You know why he did this, don't you?" Mark said, gesturing to the photographs. For a moment Kate wasn't sure what Mark was talking about, and frankly, she didn't care.

"If you'll excuse me," she said, starting to walk away.

"Michelle was a real model," Mark said.

Kate stopped.

"Yes," she said. "I know that."

"So why do you think he picked you for round two?"

"Why do you care?" Kate asked.

Mark shrugged. "I don't really. But you should."

"I thought this is what you wanted, Mark," Kate said. "Look how happy your father is." The two stopped to look at Tony, who had a scotch in one hand and an appetizer in the other. He was surrounded by the little old ladies from the book club, and his head was thrown back in laughter.

"Oh, I'm sure he'll find a way to screw it up," Mark said, pointing at Andy. At that moment, Andy looked up. His expression clearly showed his dislike of Mark.

"Did you see that?" Mark asked. "Did you see the look on his face? He's worried I'm going to tell."

"Tell what?" Kate asked. When she looked over again, Andy was making his way toward them.

"Here he comes," Mark said. "Does he have bionic hearing or is he just paranoid?"

"Mark," Kate said. "What are you talking about?"

"Hello, Mark," Andy said, putting his hand around Kate's waist and slightly tugging her away. "You don't mind if I steal her for a second, do you?"

Mark looked at Kate and smiled. It was a smug, self-serving smile. It was the smile of someone who knew something you wish you did.

"Just a minute," Kate said. "Mark was about to explain himself."

Mark looked at Andy and the smile grew.

"Kate," Andy said. "There's someone I'd like you to meet. Perhaps this can wait—"

"Oh, you'd like it to wait, wouldn't you, Andy? You'd like it to wait forever." Mark's voice was growing in volume, enough to distract a portion of the evening's lighthearted chatter and laughter. People were starting to stare and gather, like gawkers around a bar fight. Tony descended on them and grabbed Mark by the arm.

"We're going to unveil the art," he said. "Let's not occupy them any longer."

"I want to hear what he has to say," Kate said.

"Kate," Andy said.

"He's trying to ruin your evening," Kate said. "Well, I'm going to show him he can't."

"Ladies and gentlemen," Tony interrupted, "if my assistants are ready, I'd like them to stand by their designated poster." Local kids from the island, also dressed in black, hurried to each of the photograph displays, waiting for the go-ahead to whip off the cover and reveal the picture. It was a bit showy, but it had been Tony's idea, and Kate knew Andy was going along with it to make amends with Tony.

"Ever play Texas hold 'em, Kate?" Mark asked.

"Mark," Andy said. "That's enough."

"The card game?" Kate asked. "What about it?"

"It's a betting game," Mark said. "Did you know that?"

"Kate," Andy said.

"Just spit it out, Mark!" Kate said.

"There was a bet about who could get you to take those long-sleeved shirts off, and Andy Beck here was the highest bidder!"

"You're lying," Kate said.

"Why else do you think he asked you to do the book, Kate?"

"Shut up, Mark!" Andy said.

"Because of all your modeling experience?" Mark continued. Kate looked at Andy. She didn't know what kind of a player he was, but he wasn't wearing his poker face today. He looked like a defendant who had just been proved guilty.

"Kate. It's not what you think," Andy said.

"Did you or did you not participate in a bet about my scar?" Kate asked.

"Technically," Andy said. "I did. But—" Kate held up her hand, she'd heard enough.

She felt as if she'd been physically struck. She hadn't fully realized the weight she'd been carrying around the past five years until it was back, squarely on her shoulders, heavier than she ever remembered. She felt numb, and wondered how on earth she was going to find a place to put her glass of champagne down and calmly walk out of the room. Before he could say or do anything, Tony grabbed Andy and dragged him to the front of the room. Kate slowly walked toward the exit.

"Kate," Andy shouted.

"Help me count," Tony yelled to the crowd. Kate didn't turn around.

"Kate!" Andy yelled again. "Wait!" The crowd reached the number one and burst into applause as the photographs were revealed. Kate burned, knowing that the real reason everyone was now staring at her lightning-bolt scar was because Andy had won a bet. It was probably how the jerk made all his money—betting on other people's traumas. How could she have been so naïve? How could she have slept with him? A wave of pain rolled over her as she realized she'd never touch or be touched by him again. She wished she didn't know. She wanted to go back to their little love nest at the inn, crawl under the covers, and never emerge. At least the door was close; in a few minutes she would be out of here, and with a little luck she'd be able to make her escape before the tears started.

Just as she was reaching for the handle, the door swung, revealing Amanda and Pete.

"Kate," Amanda said, immediately reading trouble on her best friend's face. "What's the matter?"

"What do you care?" Kate asked, trying to push past her. She was in no mood to kiss and make up with anyone now. Amanda reached out and took Kate by the arms.

"I'm so sorry for what I said." There were definite tears in Amanda's eyes. "You didn't kill Jeff," she said softly. "And he would have been ashamed of me for ever saying so." A bit of the weight that had crippled Kate moments ago was lifted. She threw herself into Amanda's arms.

"I loved him," she said.

"I know," Amanda said.

"I didn't mean it," Kate said. "I didn't want to break up with him."

"Shh," Amanda said, rubbing her back. "He knows that."

Kate pulled away and looked in Amanda's eyes. "Do you really think so?"

"Oh, sweetie. I know so. Don't you?" Kate nodded, afraid her voice would betray her. Amanda looked over Kate again, and tugged on her wrap.

"Why are you wearing that?" Amanda demanded.

"It was symbolic," Kate said. "I was going to take it off when they revealed the photographs."

"They're revealed," Amanda said, taking Kate by the arm and pulling her toward them.

"No," Kate said. "It's all ruined now. You were right. Andy's a con artist. He makes all his money gambling and—"

Amanda's laughter ripped through Kate's revelation.

"Andy doesn't have any money," she said. "He definitely fits the profile for starving artist. Although from the look of these photographs, he may not stay that way for long."

"What do you mean starving?" Kate said, refusing to look at the images that were fascinating everyone around her, including Amanda and Pete. Kate couldn't help but be curious and a little bit proud as she took in the expressions of those around her. It was obvious they were captivated by the images.

"What about the house?" Kate said. "The yacht?"

"They belong to another rich asshole," Amanda said, throwing a look toward Pete, who meekly put up his right hand and waved. "Why aren't you looking at these?" Amanda asked, leaving Kate's side to move closer to a photograph. Andy was suddenly behind her; he put his hands around Kate's waist and turned her toward him.

"It's not what you think," he said.

"You weren't the highest bidder?" Kate asked bitterly.

"I was," Andy said. "But only to stop drunken jerks from trying to take advantage of you because of a bet."

"Oh, but it's all right to take advantage of me because of art? Is that what you're saying?" Andy swiveled Kate around to the nearest photograph.

"Look," he said. "Just look." Kate was about to protest, but the photograph looming in front of her stopped her. It was the one on the golf course. She ran her eyes over the arresting image—her hands thrown up above her head, her hair around her face. The photograph was so beautiful, Kate almost forgot she was looking at herself. It was another woman up there, one who looked as if she'd thrown away all the cares of the world, one who looked almost unearthly in her serenity. Kate looked for her scar or a lightning bolt, but the picture was shot at such an angle that you didn't even see her scar, and there certainly wasn't any lightning bolt. Silently, Kate moved from picture to picture. They were all absolutely stunning, Kate lying on the cliff on her side, Kate leaning against the lighthouse, Kate cross-legged with the ice-cream cone. No scar, no lightning bolt.

"I'm sorry I didn't tell you," Andy said. "I thought I wanted the lightning bolt. I thought I wanted the scar. But then, when I went in for that first shot, it hit me. I just wanted you. And I was about to tell you, except there you were, exposed to the world, but instead of looking frightened— something in you had totally opened up. I couldn't risk losing that expression," Andy admitted. "That's why I didn't tell you. I guess that is exploiting you for my art. I guess—"

Kate planted her lips over Andy's and interrupted him with a kiss worthy enough to draw the evening's second round of applause.

"Do you forgive me?" Andy asked when she finally pulled away.

"There's nothing to forgive," Kate said as the last of her emotional burdens slipped off her shoulders like the wraps that used to hide them. "There's nothing to forgive."

Chapter Seventeen

Martha's Vineyard. One year later.

The wedding was picture-perfect. Everyone commented on how happy the bride and groom looked, how sweet they were to each other, how madly in love they seemed. Amanda's smile was more radiant than her dress, which she insisted was wrinkled. The attendance at the wedding was double that of the previous year. Since Amanda and Pete had moved into the Honeymoon House, they'd gotten to know all of the locals and even a handful of terminal tourists, and they wanted all of them to witness their day. Amanda didn't shed a tear until Kate sung "It Had To Be You." Andy was the wedding photographer, no small favor considering his book was about to be released and was already up for awards. Amanda couldn't be happier for the two of them, living the life in Manhattan where Andy was making inroads with the artists' community and Kate was working administratively for Doctors Without Borders during the day and singing at night. Amanda and Pete had already discussed it: when the two of them got married, they were going to let them have the Honeymoon House for a month.

"May I dance with my beautiful bride?" Pete asked, sweeping Amanda into his arms.

"You may," Amanda said.

"Can you believe," Pete said, "people are already asking when we're going to have kids?"

"The nerve," Amanda said, kissing Pete's neck.

"I couldn't imagine—"

"I can't wait—"

Pete and Amanda stopped dancing.

"You don't want kids?" Amanda asked.

"I don't know," Pete said. "I mean—not right away, you know?"

"Right, right. But how long is 'not right away'?"

"Is this a trap?" Pete asked. "Because it feels like a trap."

"I just don't understand," Amanda said. "I thought you liked kids."

"I like other people's kids," Pete said. "I just don't think I'd like *ours*." Pete stopped dancing and dropped his arms. "Oh God," he said. "That sounded bad, didn't it?" Amanda, prepared to unleash, caught the stricken look on Pete's face and just laughed. She pulled him into her arms again.

"Maybe," she said. "We can adopt."

"Like Mia Farrow and Woody Allen," Pete said.

"We," Amanda said, resuming the dance with her husband, "are never, ever, adopting."

"It's good to be back, isn't it?" Kate and Andy sat on top of the Gay Head Cliffs, watching the sun sink below the horizon. The sky was almost purple. It matched Kate's hideous plum bridesmaid dress, which, as Amanda predicted last year, Kate had been able to wear again.

"I can't believe we've only been together a year," Kate said, snuggling into Andy. "It feels like a lifetime." Kate felt Andy's breath on her ear. He kissed her cheek.

"I know what you mean," Andy said. "Because it feels like I've loved you forever."

Kate looked up and out as Andy pulled her in. The ocean lapped against the shore. A boat horn sounded in the distance. A hawk circled silently above. But none of it matched the music Kate felt within. And in that moment, nobody knew better than Kate Williams did how a few moments of "forever" could last a girl a lifetime.

The Marrying Kind

Debbie Macomber

Chapter One

Could it actually be Katie Kern? Katie, here in a San Francisco bar of all places? It didn't seem possible. Not after all these years.

Her hips swayed with understated grace and elegance as the sleek, sophisticated woman casually walked toward Jason Ingram's table. They'd been high school sweethearts in Spokane, Washington, ten years earlier. More than a lifetime ago.

Sweet, gentle Katie. That was what Jason had assumed until that fateful night so long ago. He'd say one thing for her, she'd certainly had him fooled. Then, without warning, without so much as a clue as to who and what she really was, Katie had brutally ripped his heart out and then trampled all over it.

He caught a whiff of her perfume and closed his eyes, trying to identify the scent. Jasmine. Warm and sensual. Seductive. Captivating, like the woman herself. Like Katie.

But it couldn't be Katie. It just wasn't possible. Jason sincerely hoped life wouldn't play such a cruel joke on him. Not now when he was two days away from marrying Elaine Hopkins. Not when it had taken him the better half of these last ten years to forget Katie. It would take much longer to forgive her.

Her back was to him now as she walked past him, making it impossible to identify her for certain.

Jason downed another swallow of beer. His fiancée's two older brothers sat with him, joking, teasing, doing their best to entertain him and welcome him to the family.

"Don't feel obligated to attend this potluck Mom's throwing tonight," Rich Hopkins said, breaking into Jason's thoughts.

It demanded every ounce of strength Jason possessed to stop staring at the woman. He wasn't the only one interested. Every man in the St. Regis cocktail lounge was staring at her, including Rich and Bob. She was stunning, beautiful without knowing it, the same way Katie had once been. She always had been able to take his breath away. But this wasn't Katie. It couldn't be. Not now. Please, not now.

"I'd get out of the dinner if I could," Bob added, reaching for his beer. He was Elaine's youngest brother and closest to her in age.

Jason watched as the woman approached a table on the other side of the room. The old geezer who occupied it promptly stood and kissed her cheek. Jason frowned.

"It's entirely up to you," Rich added. "You'll meet everyone later at the wedding anyway."

Wedding. The word cut through his mind like a laser light, slicing into his conscience. He was marrying Elaine, he reminded himself. He loved Elaine. Enough to ask her to spend the rest of his life with him.

Funny, he'd never told his fiancée about Katie. In retrospect he wondered why. Certainly Elaine had a right to know he'd been married once before. Even if it was the briefest marriage on record. By his best estimate, he'd been a married man all of one hour. If it wasn't so tragic he might have been amused. The wedding ceremony had lasted longer than his marriage.

"You must be exhausted."

Jason's attention returned to the two men who'd soon be his brothers-in-law. "The flight wasn't bad."

"How long does it take to fly in from the East Coast these days?"

"Five, six hours." Jason answered absently. He tried not to be obvious about his interest in the woman sitting with the old fart. It wasn't until she sat down that Jason got a decent look at her.

Dear, sweet heaven, it was Katie.

His heart pounded so hard it felt as if he were in danger of cracking his ribs.

In a matter of seconds, ten long years were wiped away and he was a callow youth all over again. The love he felt for her bubbled up inside him like a Yellowstone geyser. Just as quickly, he was consumed with an anger that threatened to consume him.

There had been a time when he'd loved Katie Kern more than life itself. He'd sacrificed everything for her. He assumed, incorrectly, that she loved him, too. Time had proved otherwise. The minute she faced opposition from her family, she'd turned her back and walked away without a qualm, leaving him to deal with the heartache of not knowing what had happened to her. To them.

"I believe I'll skip out on the dinner plans," Jason said, tightening his hand around the frosty beer mug. He deliberately pulled his gaze away from Katie and concentrated on Elaine's brothers.

"I can't say that I blame you."

"Make an early night of it," Bob suggested, finishing off the last of his beer. "It's already ten o'clock, your time."

"Right." The last thing Jason felt was fatigued. True, he'd spent almost the entire day en route, but he traveled routinely, and time changes generally didn't bother him.

Rich glanced at his watch and stood. "Bob and I'll connect with you sometime tomorrow, then."

"That sounds great," Jason answered. "My brother's set to arrive early afternoon." He could barely wait to tell Steve that he'd seen Katie. His brother was sure to appreciate the irony of the situation. Two days before Jason was to marry, he ran into Katie. God certainly had a sense of humor.

Rich slapped him across the back affectionately. "We'll see you tomorrow, then."

"You've got less than thirty-six hours to celebrate being a bachelor. Don't waste any time." Bob chuckled and glanced toward Katie suggestively. He stood and reached for his wallet.

Jason stopped him. "The beer's on me."

Both brothers thanked him. "I'll see you at the rehearsal."

"Tomorrow," he echoed, grateful when the two left.

If the woman was indeed Katie, and the possibility looked strong, he had to figure out what he intended to do about it. Nothing, he suspected.

Their marriage, if one could call it that, had been a long time ago. He wasn't sure she'd even want to see him again. For that matter, he wasn't sure he wanted to see Katie, either. She was a reminder of a painful time that he'd prefer to forget.

The cocktail waitress delivered Katie and her date's order. While still in high school, Katie had refused to drink alcoholic beverages. Her aversion apparently hadn't followed her into adulthood.

"Can I get you anything else?" the cocktail waitress asked as she approached his table.

"Nothing, thanks."

She handed him the tab and he signed his name and room number, leaving her a generous tip.

He toyed briefly with the idea of casually walking over and renewing his acquaintance with Katie. That would be the civilized thing to do. But Jason doubted that he could have pulled it off. He was angry, damn it, and he had every right to be. She'd been his wife and she'd deserted him, abandoned him and all their dreams.

Her family had openly disapproved of him when they'd first started dating at the end of their junior year. He'd never completely understood why. He suspected it wasn't him personally that they objected to, but any involvement Katie might have with someone of the opposite sex. Someone not handpicked by them.

The man she was currently with was exactly the type her parents preferred. Older, rich as sin, and pompous as hell. Quite possibly they were married. It wouldn't surprise him in the least.

Ten years ago Jason hadn't been nearly good enough for the Kerns' only child. Her family had had no qualms about voicing their disapproval and so Katie and Jason had been forced to meet on the sly. Dear, sweet heaven, how he'd loved her.

As their senior year progressed, it became increasingly apparent that her parents intended to send her away to school. Then Katie had learned she was headed for a private girls' college on the East Coast and they knew they had to do something.

The thought of being apart was more than either one could bear. They'd been determined to find a solution and eventually had. Marriage.

The night they graduated from high school, instead of attending the senior party the way everyone expected, Jason and Katie eloped across the Idaho border.

It had been romantic and fun. They'd been giddy on love, and each other, certain they'd outsmarted their families and friends.

During the wedding ceremony, when Katie read the vows they'd written themselves, her eyes had filled with tears as she'd gazed up at him with heartfelt devotion. He never would have guessed that her love would be so untrustworthy.

Jason's stomach clenched as he recalled their wedding night. He nearly snickered aloud. There'd been no such animal. If they hadn't taken time for a wedding dinner, they might have had a real honeymoon. Jason had no one to blame but himself for that. He'd been the one who insisted on treating Katie to a fancy dinner. She'd been cheated out of the big wedding she deserved and he wanted to make everything as perfect for her as possible.

He'd been nervous about making love and he knew Katie

was, too. She'd been a virgin and his experience had been limited to one brief encounter with his best friend's older cousin when he was sixteen.

After he'd paid for the hotel room, they'd sat on the edge of the bed, holding each other, kissing the way they always did. In all the years since, he hadn't met a woman who gave sweeter kisses than Katie. Not even Elaine.

Just when their love for each other overtook their nervousness, the door had burst open and they were confronted by Katie's irate parents and the local police. The horrible scene that followed was forever burned in his memory.

Katie's mother wept hysterically while her father shouted accusations at them both. The police officer had slammed Jason against the wall and he'd been accused of everything from kidnapping to rape. The next thing he knew, Katie was gone, and he was alone.

He'd never seen her again. Never heard from her, either.

Correction. She'd signed the annulment papers in short order. No letter. No phone call. Nothing. Not even a good-bye.

Until tonight. Thirty-odd hours before he was scheduled to marry another woman. Then, lo and behold, who should he see but Katie Kern. If it was still Kern, which he doubted. Her parents had probably married her off to Daddy Warbucks a long time ago.

In the beginning he'd waited and hoped, certain she'd find a way of contacting him. He'd believed in her. Believed in their love. Believed until there was nothing left. Eventually he'd been forced to accept the truth. She'd sold him and their love out. She wanted nothing more to do with him.

Briefly he wondered if she remembered him at all. He'd wager she'd obediently followed her father's blueprint for her life.

That was the way it was meant to be.

Jason stood and strolled out of the lounge as if he hadn't a care in the world. He didn't so much as glance over his shoulder. It gave him only minor satisfaction to turn his back on Katie and walk away from her. He'd go up to his room, take a long, hot shower, and watch a little television before turning out the lights. The next couple of days were sure to be busy. He didn't need the memory of another woman clouding his mind before he married Elaine.

He got as far as the lobby. If he could have named what stopped him, he would have cursed it aloud.

Katie, after all these years. In San Francisco.

He looked back just in time to see her leaving the lounge. Alone.

What the hell, he decided. He'd say hello, just for old times' sake. Ask about her life, perhaps bury some of his bitterness. Even wish her well. It would do them both a world of good to clear the air.

He waited by the pay phones.

Although the lighting was dim, it didn't take him but a moment to realize he'd been right. It really was Katie. More beautiful than he remembered, mature and sophisticated, suave in ways that had been foreign to them both ten years earlier. The business suit looked as if it had been designed with her in mind. The pin-striped skirt reached midcalf and hugged her hips. The lines of the fitted jacket highlighted everything that was feminine about her. Her reddish-brown hair was shorter these days, straight and thick with the ends curving under naturally, brushing against the top of her shoulder.

Jason pretended to be using the phone. He waited until she'd strolled past him before he replaced the receiver. He spoke her name in a manner that suggested he'd recognized her just that moment.

"Katie? Katie Kern?" he said, sounding a bit breathless, surprised.

She turned and her eyes met his. Her lips parted softly and her eyes rounded as if she couldn't believe what she saw.

"Jase? Jase Ingram?"

Chapter Two

"Jase? Is it really you?" Katie raised her hand as if to touch his face, but stopped several inches short of his cheek. "How are you? What are you doing here in San Francisco?"

Jason buried his hands in his pants pockets and struck a nonchalant, relaxed pose, wanting her to assume he happened upon her just that moment and had spoken before censuring his actions.

"You look wonderful," she said, sounding oddly breathless.

"You, too." Which had to be the understatement of the century. He almost wished she'd gone to seed. She was more beautiful than ever.

"What are you doing here?" she asked again, not giving him time to answer one question before she asked another.

"I'm in town for a wedding. My own."

"Congratulations." She didn't so much as bat an eyelash.

His gaze fell on her left hand, which remained bare.

"I've never . . . I'm still single."

He wasn't sure congratulations would be in order. He was tempted to blurt out something spiteful about making sure she knew what she wanted the next time around, but restrained himself.

"It'd be fun to get together and talk about old times," he said.

But before he could claim that, unfortunately, he simply didn't have the time, she nodded enthusiastically.

"Jase, let's do. It'd be great to sit down and talk." She reached out and wrapped her fingers around his forearm. Regret slipped into her eyes and she bit down into her lower lip and glanced toward the cocktail lounge. "I . . . I don't know that I can just now—I'm with someone."

"I saw," he murmured darkly. So much for playing it cool. She was sure to realize he'd spied her earlier now.

"You saw Roger?"

"Yeah." No use trying to hide it. "I was in the lounge earlier and thought that might have been you."

"How about dinner?" she suggested eagerly, her excitement bubbling over. He hadn't counted on her enthusiasm. "I haven't eaten and—"

"Some other time," he interrupted stiffly. He certainly didn't intend to join her and Daddy Warbucks for the night. He had never enjoyed being odd man out, and it wasn't a role he intended to play with Katie.

"But . . ."

"I just wanted to say hello and tell you you're looking good."

Her eager excitement died as she stiffened and moved one step back as though anticipating something painful. "There's so much I have to tell you, so much I want to know . . ."

Yeah, well, he had plenty of his own questions.

"Please, Jase. I'll make some excuse, tell Roger I've got a headache and meet you back here in an hour. I deserve that much, don't I?"

"All right." He may have sounded reluctant, but he wasn't. He had plenty he wanted to say to Katie himself, plenty of questions that demanded answers. Perhaps he should feel guilty—after all, he was marrying another woman in a couple of days—but God help him, he didn't. Maybe, just maybe, he could put this entire matter to rest once and for all.

"I'll meet you in the dining room," he said.

"I'll be there. Thanks, Jase," she murmured before turning and hurrying back to the cocktail lounge.

Jason headed up to his room and phoned for dinner reservations. It wasn't until he stood under the pulsating spray of the shower that his hands knotted into tight fists with a rare surge of anger. Katie had betrayed him, abandoned him, rejected his love. He'd waited ten long years to vent his frustration, and he wouldn't be denied the opportunity now. Once again he experienced a mild twinge of conscience, dining with another woman without Elaine knowing. His excuse, if he needed one, was that getting rid of all this excess emotional baggage was sure to make him a better husband.

At least that was what Jason told himself as he prepared to face the demons of his past.

Katie couldn't quell the fluttery feeling in the pit of her stomach. The last time she'd felt this anxious about seeing Jase had been the night they'd eloped. Her cheeks flushed with hot color at the memory of what happened, or, more appropriately, didn't happen. Her heart ached for them both, and for all the might-have-beens that never were.

With her heart pounding and her head held high, she walked into the hotel lobby, half expecting Jase to be waiting for her there. He wasn't, and so she headed directly for the restaurant.

Although he'd approached her, he hadn't seemed any too happy to see her. She understood his dilemma. By his own admission, he was hours away from marrying another woman. Katie should be pleased for him, glad he'd found a woman with whom to share his life. What an ironic twist of fate for them to run into each other now.

He was almost married and she was practically engaged. Roger had been after her to marry him for months and his pleas were just beginning to hit their mark. The last time he'd asked, she'd been tempted to give in. He was kind and gentle.

Affectionate. But what she felt for Roger didn't compare with the hot urgency she'd experienced with Jase all those years ago. That had been hormones, she told herself. Good grief, she'd been little more than an eighteen-year-old kid.

Jase was already seated when she joined him. The hostess escorted her to his table. He'd changed clothes, and damn it all, looked terrific. Just seeing him again stirred awake a lot of emotions she'd thought were long dead, long buried. But then, she'd always loved Jase.

"So we meet again," he greeted with a telltale hint of sarcasm. One would think he'd already experienced second thoughts.

Perhaps it hadn't been such a good idea to meet after all, Katie mused, but damn it all, he owed her an explanation, and for that matter a hell of a lot more. She'd pined for weeks for Jase, waited, believed in him and their love. She'd literally been ripped from his arms and never heard from him again.

Katie made a pretense of reading over the menu, something Jase appeared to find fascinating. She made her selection quickly and set it aside.

"Tell me, what've you been doing these last ten years?" she asked, wanting to ease into the conversation. There'd been a time when they could discuss anything, share everything, but those days were long past. Jase was little more than a stranger now. A stranger she would always love.

Slowly, he raised his head until his gaze was level with hers. She'd forgotten how blue and intense his eyes could be. What surprised her was how unfriendly they seemed, almost angry. She'd always been able to read his moods, and he hers. At one time they were so close it felt as if they shared each other's thoughts. Just when it seemed he was about to speak, the waiter approached with a bottle of Chardonnay.

Katie rarely indulged in alcohol, but if there was ever a time she needed something to bolster her nerve, it was now.

The first sip, on an empty stomach, seemed to go straight to her head.

"Let's see," he said after their server left, sounding almost friendly. Almost, but not completely. "After I signed the annulment papers you sent me, I joined the Marine Corps."

He mentioned the annulment documents as if they meant nothing to him, as if it were nothing but a legal formality, one they'd discussed and agreed upon before the wedding. Surely he realized what it had cost her to pen her name to those papers. How she'd agonized over it, how she'd wept and pleaded and tried so hard to find a way for them to be together. It would have been easier to cut out her heart than nullify her marriage. Her fingers closed around the crystal goblet as the memories stirred her mind to an age and innocence that had long since died.

"When my enlistment ended with the Marines, I went back to school and graduated. I work for one of the major shipping companies now."

"West Coast?"

"East. I'm only in San Francisco for the wedding."

She noticed that he didn't tell her anything about the woman he was about to marry, not even her name.

"What about you?" he asked.

"Let me see," she said, drawing in a deep breath. "I attended school, majored in business, graduated cum laude, and accepted a position with one of the financial institutions here in San Francisco." She downplayed her role with the bank, although she was said to be one of the rising young executives.

"Just the way daddy wanted," he muttered.

Katie bristled. "If you recall, my parents wanted me to go into law."

"Law," Jase returned, "that's right, I'd forgotten."

That wasn't likely, but she let the comment slide. They'd both carried around their hurts for a long time.

The waiter came for their order and replenished their wine.

Perhaps it was the Chardonnay that caused her to risk so much. Before she could stop herself, she blurted out, "Didn't you even try to find me?"

"Try?" he repeated loudly, attracting the attention of other diners. "I nearly went mad looking for you. Where the hell did they take you?"

"London . . . to live with my aunt."

"London. They don't have phones in England? Do you realize how long I waited to hear from you?"

Katie bowed her head, remembering how miserably unhappy she'd been. How she'd prayed night and day that he'd come for her. "She wouldn't let me," she whispered.

"And that stopped you?"

She swallowed against the tightness gathering in her throat, combating it with her anger. "You might have tried to find me."

"Of course I tried, but it was impossible. I was just a kid. How was I supposed to know where they'd sent you?"

"I told you about my father's sister before, don't you remember? We'd talked about her and how my parents wanted me to spend the summer with her before I went away to college. She's a law professor and . . ." She hesitated when the waiter returned with their salads.

Inhaling a calming breath, she reached for her fork. The lettuce was tasteless and she washed it down with another sip of wine. That, at least, calmed her nerves.

"Your aunt—sure, I remembered her, but I didn't have a name or an address. Someplace on the East Coast, I thought. A lot of good that did me." He tossed his hands into the air. "I don't possess magical powers, Katie. Just exactly how was I supposed to figure out where you were?"

"You should have known."

His mouth thinned and he stabbed his fork into the lettuce. "Perhaps it'd be best if we let sleeping dogs lie."

"No," she cried emphatically.

He arched his brows at her raised voice. She wasn't the timid young woman she'd once been, shy and easily intimidated.

"I want to know what happened. Every detail. I deserve that much," she insisted.

The waiter, sensing trouble, removed their salad plates and brought out the main course. Katie doubted that she had the stomach for a single bite. She lifted her fork, but knew any pretense of eating would be impossible.

Jase ignored his steak. "I did everything I knew how to do to locate you. I pleaded with your father, asked him to give me the chance to prove myself. When I couldn't break him, I tried talking to your mother. The next thing I knew they slapped a restraining order on me. It wasn't easy for me, you know. Everyone in town knew we'd eloped, then all at once I was home and you were gone."

"I'd never been more miserable in my life," she whispered. He seemed to think being shipped off to a heartless, uncaring aunt was a picnic. "I loved you so much . . ."

"The hell you did. How long did it take you to sign the annulment papers? Two weeks? Three?"

"Five," she cried, nearly shouting.

"The hell it did," he returned, just as loud.

The entire restaurant stopped and stared. Jase glanced around, then slammed his napkin on top of his untouched dinner.

"We can't talk this out reasonably, at least not here," she muttered, ditching her own napkin.

"Fine, we'll finish this once and for all in my room."

Jase signed for their dinners and led the way across the lobby to the elevator. They stood next to each other, tense and angry on the long ride up to the twentieth floor. She paused, wondering at the wisdom of this, as he unlocked the room. She relaxed once she realized he had a mini-suite. They wouldn't be discussing their almost-marriage with a bed in the middle of the room, reminding them they'd been cheated out of the wedding night.

"All right," she said, bracing her hands against her hips. "You want to know about the annulment papers."

"Which you signed in short order."

She gasped and clenched her fists. "I signed those papers while in the hospital, Jason Ingram. I ended up so sick I could barely think, in so much pain and mental agony I was half out of my mind."

The color washed out of his face. "What happened?"

"I . . . went on a hunger strike. My aunt constantly stuck those papers under my nose, demanding that I sign them, telling me how grateful everyone was that they found me before I'd ruined my life."

Jase turned and stood with his back to her, looking out over the picturesque San Francisco skyline.

"Day after day, I refused to sign them. I insisted my name was Katie Ingram. I wouldn't eat . . ."

"You could have phoned me."

"You make it sound so easy. I wasn't allowed any contact with the outside world. I was little more than a prisoner. What was I supposed to do? Tell me!"

Her question was met with stark silence.

"I tried, Jase, I honestly tried."

"You ended up in the hospital?"

The years rolled away and it felt as though she were a naïve eighteen-year-old all over again. The tears welled in her throat, making it difficult to speak "In the beginning I thought the stomach pains were from hunger. I'd lost fifteen pounds the first two weeks and . . ."

"Fifteen pounds?" he whirled around, his eyes wide with horror.

"It was my appendix. It burst and . . . I nearly died."

"Dear God." He closed his eyes.

"My mother was there when I came out of surgery. She

looked terrible, pale and shaken. She pleaded with me to sign the annulment papers and be done with all this nonsense. She claimed it was what you wanted. . . . I was too weak to fight them any longer. You're right, I should have been stronger, should have held out longer, but I was alone and afraid and so terribly sick. I remember wishing that I could have died—it would have been easier than living without you."

Jase rubbed his hand along the back side of his neck. "I thought . . . assumed you wanted out of the marriage."

"No. I tried to hold out, really I did. More than anything I wanted to prove that our love wasn't going to fade, that what we felt for one another was meant to last a lifetime."

"Then I signed the papers," he whispered, "and joined the Marines."

"When I came back, you were gone."

The distance between them evaporated and he brought her into the warm circle of his arms. "I'm sorry, Katie, for doubting you."

"I'm sorry for failing you."

"We failed each other."

"I loved you so much," she whispered and her voice cracked with the depth of emotion.

"Not a day passed for five years that I didn't think about you."

His kiss was soft and sweet, reminiscent of those they'd once shared. An absolution, forgiveness for being young. For not trusting, for allowing doubts to separate them as effectively as her parents had once done. For giving in to their fears.

"If only I'd known," he whispered. His lips grazed her cheek, seeking her mouth a second time, and Katie tried not to think about this other woman Jase was about to marry. But when he kissed her again, any guilt she might have experienced died. She turned her head in an effort to meet his lips, expecting him to kiss her with the hunger she felt, the hunger he'd fired to life with the first kiss. Instead, his mouth simply slid over hers in moist forays, back and forth, teasing, coaxing, enticing.

Excitement began to build, fires licking awake the tenderness of what they'd once so freely shared.

After what seemed like an eternity, his mouth settled completely over hers and he kissed her in earnest. Jase groaned and wrapped his arms around her, lifting her from the floor, grabbing hold of the fabric of her suit, kissing her with a hunger that was so hot she felt the heat emanating from him like the warmth coming from a roaring fire.

"All these years, I believed . . ."

"So did I." She wept and laughed at the same moment.

"I loved you so damn much."

"I've always loved you . . . always."

He kissed her in a frenzy of hunger and breathless passion. When his tongue broached her lips, she was ready. Her lips parted, welcoming the invasion, greeting him with her own.

He groaned again.

His hands unfastened her suit jacket, slipped it from her shoulders, and let it fall to the floor.

She twined her arms around his neck, panting, breathless with wonder and shock. "Jase, oh, Jase, what are we doing?"

Chapter Three

"We're finishing what we started ten years ago." Jason repeated Katie's question without really hearing the words. He slanted his mouth over hers and devoured her lips with a hunger and need that had been buried deep inside him all these years. He sank his hands deep into her hair, loving the feel, the taste, the sense of her.

"Jase, oh, Jase."

She was the only person in the world who'd ever called him Jase, and the sound of it on her lips was more than he could stand. He took possession of her mouth before he could question the right or wrong of what was happening.

Her hands struggled with the buttons of his shirt while he fumbled with the openings to her blouse. They were a frenzy of arms, tangling, bumping against each other in their eagerness to undress. The raw, physical desire for her all but seared his skin. He sighed when he was finally able to peel the silky material from her shoulders and capture her breasts with both hands, fondling them while kissing her lips.

Their kisses became desperate as their hands caressed each other. Jason was never sure how they made it into the bedroom. He didn't stop to turn on the light or shove back the covers. He'd waited ten years for this moment and he wasn't about to be cheated a second time.

Their clothes were gone, disappeared, evaporated like the early morning fog over the bay. All that existed in that moment was their overwhelming love and need for one another.

He gently placed Katie on the mattress, then joined her, kneeling above her. She wrapped her bare, sleek legs around his thighs and raised her hips in unspoken invitation.

Through the haze of his passion, he saw her stretch her arms toward him, silently pleading with him to make love to her. In the dim light of the full moon, he watched as the tears rolled from the corners of her eyes and onto the bedspread. Her tears were an absolution for them both, for the hurts committed against them, for the long, lonely years that had separated them.

"Love me," she whispered.

"I do. God help me, I do."

His entire body throbbed with need as Jason eased forward, penetrating her body with one swift upward thrust. Katie buckled beneath him, sobbing with an intense pleasure as she buried her nails in his back. Her heels dug into his thighs as she rocked against him, meeting each pulsating stroke, riding him, pumping him.

He cried out hoarsely at the explosion of his climax, rearing his head back, blinded by the pure, unadulterated pleasure, breathless with the wonder and the shock.

He loved Katie. He'd never stopped. If anything the years had enhanced the emotion. He didn't speak as he gathered her in his arms. He was grateful when she didn't feel the need to discuss what they'd shared. If they stopped to analyze what had happened, they might find room for regrets and Jason experienced none of those now.

He eased next to Katie, keeping her wrapped protectively in his embrace. Her head was on his shoulder, her legs entwined with his. He stroked the silky smooth skin of her back, needing the feel of her to admit this was real. She was in his arms the way she should have been all those years ago. He dared not think beyond this moment, or look into the future for fear of what he'd see. Eventually he felt his mind drifting toward the mindless escape of sleep.

Katie woke when Jase stirred at her side. She rolled her head and read the illuminated dial of the alarm clock on the nightstand. It was three minutes after two.

"Are you cold?" he whispered, kissing her neck.

"A little." She assumed he meant for them to pull back the covers and started to climb off the bed.

His hand stopped her. "No."

"No?"

"I'll warm you."

He'd already done an excellent job of that, and seemed intent on doing so again, this time without the urgency or haste of the first.

"Jase," she whispered, unsure if they should continue. Her head, her judgment, had been clouded earlier, but she was awake now, prepared to put aside whatever emotion had driven them earlier. "We should talk first . . . we need . . ."

"Later. We'll discuss everything later." He captured her nipple between his nimble lips and sucked gently.

Katie sighed and curled her fingers into his hair as the sensation sizzled through her. It didn't seem possible that he could evoke such an intensity of feeling from her so soon after the first lovemaking.

He loved her with a slow hand and an easy touch, whispering erotic promises as his lips explored the sensitive area behind her knees, then moved up the small of her back, eventually making his way to the nape of her neck. Shy and a little embarrassed, Katie couldn't keep from sighing. Again and again he coaxed a response from her, insisting she participate fully in their loveplay. She hesitated, reluctant, fearing recriminations in the morning on both their parts, but she held back nothing, including her head and her heart. She was his and had been from the time she was seventeen. His in the past, the present, always.

"I've dreamed of us like this," he whispered between deep, bone-melting kisses. "Some nights I'd wake and feel an emptiness in the pit of my stomach and realize I'd been dreaming about you."

Katie ran her fingers through his hair. "I can't believe you're here."

"Believe it, Katie, believe it with all your heart."

He entered her then and the sweetness, the rightness of their love was almost more than she could bear. Locking her arms around his neck, she clung to him on the most pleasurable ride of her life.

Eventually they did fall asleep, but it was from sheer exhaustion. Jase shoved back the sheets and they lay, a tangle of arms and legs unwilling to separate for even a moment. She'd never known happiness like this. She should have realized, should have expected it to be fragile. She just didn't know how breakable it truly was until the phone jarred her awake.

The piercing shrill sliced rudely through their lazy contentment.

Apparently jolted out of a deep sleep, Jase jerked upright and looked around as if a fire alarm had sounded.

"It's the phone," she murmured, only slightly more awake than he.

Blindly, he reached for the telephone, nearly throwing it off the nightstand. It rang a third time, the loudness causing Jase to wince.

Katie looked at the clock and groaned aloud. It was nearly nine and she was due to meet with the vice president of Grand National Bank, Roger, and two other bank executives at ten. She couldn't be late.

"Elaine." Jase shouted the other woman's name and glanced guiltily toward Katie. "Sweetheart. What time is it?"

Sweetheart? He spent the night making love with her and he had the gall to refer to Elaine as *Sweetheart?*

"It's nine, already? Meet your Aunt Betty and Uncle Jerome for lunch? Sure. Sure. Of course . . . all right, all right, I'll say it. I love you, too." He rubbed a hand down his face and ignored Katie.

Katie didn't know if she could listen to much more of this without getting sick to her stomach. Tossing aside the sheet, she climbed out of bed and headed for the bathroom.

Slapping cold water on her face, she stared at herself in the mirror and didn't like what she saw. Her reflection revealed a woman who'd been well loved. Well used. She wasn't the woman in Jase's life any longer. Elaine was. Jase was engaged to marry the other woman.

A sick sensation assaulted her. She'd always been a fool for Jase, and the years hadn't changed that. But she wasn't about to become embroiled in an affair with a married man, or a near-married man.

"Katie."

Feeling naked and shy, she looked around for something to cover herself and grabbed a towel. Securing it around her torso, she walked back into the bedroom with her chin tilted at a regal angle.

"Mornin'," he murmured, yawning loudly. He sat on the edge of the mattress, a sheet wrapped around his waist, studying her. The appreciative look in his eyes said he wouldn't be opposed to starting the morning over on a completely different note.

How dare he act as if nothing had happened. "That was your fiancée?"

His face sobered and he nodded. At least he had the good grace to lower his gaze. "I'm sorry about that . . ."

"Not to worry—it's well past time I left." Doing her best to conceal her nakedness, she reached for her blouse, jamming her arms into it without bothering to put on her bra.

"What are you doing?" he demanded, as if it wasn't evident.

"Dressing." She glanced at her wristwatch and groaned. "I have to be in a meeting by ten. If I hurry I can get home, change clothes, and make it into the office before then."

He looked stunned. "Don't you think we should talk first?"

"I don't have time." She found her skirt and stepped into it, hastily tugging it over her hips and sucking in her stomach to fasten the button.

"Like hell. Make time."

"I can't. Not this morning." Then, realizing he probably had a point and that they did need to talk, she sighed expressively and suggested, "Meet me this afternoon."

"I can't."

"Why not?"

"My brother and his wife are arriving. Later I've got the wedding rehearsal and a dinner."

An unexpected pain momentarily tightened her throat. "That says it all, doesn't it?"

"Don't do this to me, Katie. We made love. You can't just walk out of here. Not now, especially not now."

"You're marrying Elaine." She made it a statement, unsure of what she wanted. They were different people now, not teenagers. He had his own life, and she hers. By clouding their heads with the physical they'd stepped into a hornet's nest.

"Elaine," he repeated and plowed all ten fingers through his hair, holding his hands against the crown of his head as if that would help him sort matters through. "Hell, I don't know what to do."

"Let me make the decision easy for you. *Elaine. Sweetheart. Of course I love you.*"

His face tightened. "I'm in San Francisco for my wedding. I told you that."

"I know." She sounded like a jealous shrew, but she

couldn't help herself. Although it was painful to say the words, one of them needed to. It hurt, but it was necessary. "It's too late for us, Jase," she whispered, unable to disguise her misery. "Far too late."

"I suppose you're going to marry Roger," he accused, tossing aside the sheet and reaching for his pants. He jerked them on, stood, and yanked up the zipper. "He's perfect for you. Did your father handpick him?"

It was so close to the truth that Katie gasped. "Roger is generous and kind and caring and—"

"A pompous ass."

"I've never met Elaine but I know exactly the type of woman you'd marry," she cried. "She must be a simpering, mindless soul without a thought of her own."

Jase's eyes narrowed into thin slits.

"Let's just end this here and now," she shouted, throwing the words out at him like steel blades. Stuffing her bra, pantyhose, and shoes into her arms, she headed for the door.

"You're not walking out on me. Not again."

"Again?" she challenged. "That's the most ludicrous thing you've ever said to me." Turning her back on him, she took a great deal of pleasure in hurrying out of the suite and slamming the door.

"Katie! Don't you dare leave. Not like this."

As far as she could see, she didn't have a choice. Jase was marrying Elaine. He loved the other woman—she'd heard him say so only moments earlier. It was too late for them. Spending the night with him was quite possibly the worst mistake of her life. What a deplorable mess they'd created. She hadn't meant what she'd said about Elaine. She didn't even know the woman, but his fiancée certainly didn't deserve this. Katie was so furious with Jase and herself that she wanted to weep.

Despite the fact that her underwear was crunched up in her arms, she hurried down the hallway toward the elevator.

"Katie. For the love of heaven, stop."

Katie groaned aloud when she realized Jase had followed her. Barefooted, and with no shirt, he caught up with her at the same time the elevator arrived.

"Jase, please, just leave it."

The doors glided open and a middle-aged man wearing a pin-striped suit and carrying a garment bag stared openly at them. A blue-haired lady in a pillbox hat, who held a small dog under her arm, inhaled sharply.

Her dignity lay in a pool at her feet. Nevertheless, Katie stepped into the elevator and silently pleaded with Jase to let her go. He returned her glare and joined her.

"We've got to talk," he whispered heatedly, standing next to her as if nothing were amiss.

"It's too late for that."

"Like hell."

The two other occupants of the elevator moved as far away from them as possible. Fully aware of her state of undress, Katie wanted to crawl into the nearest hole and die.

"Jase, it's over."

"Not by a long shot. We'll discuss what happened now or later, the choice is yours."

"You're getting married later, remember?"

The elderly woman huffed disapprovingly.

Jase turned and glared at her. "Do you have a problem?"

The dog barked.

Never had it taken an elevator longer to descend to the ground floor. Katie was convinced she'd die of mortification before the doors opened to the opulent hotel lobby. The two other occupants left as if escaping a time bomb.

"We need to sort this out," Jase insisted in low tones.

She offered him a sad smile, and with as much dignity as she could muster, which at this point was shockingly little, she stepped out of the elevator.

"You're walking out on me again," Jase shouted, calling

attention to them both. "That's what you've always done, isn't it, Katie?"

"Me?" She whirled around and confronted him, her voice tight and raised. "You're the one who abandoned me. You're the one who left me to deal with everything." Then, swallowing a sob, she turned and ran out of the hotel.

Chapter Four

Jason resisted the urge to slam his fist against the polished marble column when Katie literally ran out of the lobby. It was obvious nothing he said was going to convince her to stay and sort through their predicament.

Defeated and depressed, he walked back into the elevator and punched the button for the twentieth floor. Luckily he had his room key in his pants pocket or he'd be locked out of the suite, which at this point would have been poetic justice.

Once inside his room, he slumped onto the sofa and leaned forward, placing his elbows against his knees. It felt as if the weight of the world rested squarely on his shoulders. The last thing he expected Katie to do was run out on him. To prove how completely unreasonable she was, her parting shot was that *he* was abandoning *her*. That made no sense whatsoever. He didn't know how she could even think such a thing.

Fine, he decided, if that was the way she wanted it. Good riddance. He was better off without her. But he didn't feel that way. He felt the same empty sensation he had the night they'd eloped and her parents had literally ripped her out of his arms.

Although he comforted himself with reassurances, Jason didn't believe them. He'd loved Katie as an eighteen-year-old kid and God help them both, he loved her now. Nothing had changed. Except for one small, minute detail.

He was scheduled to marry Elaine on Saturday.

Elaine. Dear God, how would he ever explain how he'd spent the night with another woman? He didn't even want to think about it. Until now, Jason had always thought of himself as an honorable, decent man. He'd have to tell Elaine—there was no way around it.

Dread settled over him like a concrete weight. He expelled his breath in a long, slow exercise while he sorted through his options—which, at the moment, seemed shockingly few.

He couldn't possibly marry Elaine now, not when he still loved Katie. Love! What the hell did he know of love anyway? Sixteen or so hours ago when he first arrived in San Francisco, he'd assumed he was in love with Elaine. He must love her, Jason reasoned, otherwise he'd never have asked her to be his wife. A man didn't make that kind of offer unless he was ready, willing, and able to commit the rest of his life to a woman.

Whether he loved or didn't love Elaine wasn't the most pressing point, however. He needed to decide what to do about the wedding. Really, there was only one choice. He couldn't go through with it now. But canceling it at the last minute like this was unthinkable. Humiliating Elaine in front of her family and friends would be unforgivable.

Elaine didn't deserve this. She was a wonderful woman, and he genuinely cared for her. The wedding had been no small expense, either. Her father had a good twenty grand wrapped up in the dinner and reception. Jason had invested another five thousand of his own savings.

He leaned against the sofa and tilted his head back to stare at the ceiling. It would be the height of stupidity to allow a few thousand dollars to direct the course of his life.

By all that was right he should put an end to the wedding plans now and face the music with Elaine and her family before it was too late, no matter how unpleasant the task.

Again, the thought of confronting his fiancée and her family, plus the dozens of relatives who'd traveled from all across the country, boggled his mind.

Something was fundamentally wrong with him, Jason decided. He was actually considering going ahead and marrying Elaine because he felt guilty about embarrassing her and inconveniencing their families. First he needed a priest, then a psychiatrist, and that was only the tip of the iceberg.

No clear course of action presented itself and so Jason took the easy way out. As painful and difficult as it was, he'd confess to her what had happened with Katie and then together, Elaine and he could decide what they should do.

He showered, dressed, and still felt like he should be arrested. Actually, jail sounded preferable to facing his fiancée and her family. He'd deal with Elaine first and then find Katie. If his high school sweetheart, his teenage wife, thought she'd escaped him, she was wrong. As far as he was concerned it wasn't even close to being over between them.

With an hour to kill before meeting Elaine and her aunt and uncle, he drove the rental car around the streets of San Francisco, allowing his eyes to take in the beauty of the sights while his mind wrestled with the problems confronting him.

He arrived outside Elaine's family home at noon.

Elaine stood on the porch and smiled when he parked the car. She was petite, slender, attractive, and as unlike Katie as any woman he'd ever met. His heart ached at the thought of hurting her.

Jason remembered the day they'd met a year earlier. Elaine worked as a secretary in the office across the hall from him, efficient, hardworking, ambitious. She'd asked him out for their first date, a novelty as far as Jason was concerned, but then he appreciated a woman who knew what she wanted. It didn't take her long to convince him they were good together.

As time passed, he discovered that they shared the same goals. Her career was important to her and she'd advanced from being the secretary to the vice president to lower level management and was quickly making a name for herself. She'd surprised him when, two months before their June wedding, she'd decided to change jobs and had accepted a position with a rival shipping company. It seemed a lateral move to him, but her career was her business and Jason was content to let her make her own decisions.

"Did you sleep well?" she asked, wrapping her arms around his neck and bouncing her lips over his.

It was all Jason could do to keep from blurting everything out right then and there. He might have done exactly that if Elaine's mother hadn't stepped onto the porch just then. Helen Hopkins was an older version of Elaine, cultured and reserved.

"It looks like the weather is going to be lovely for the wedding," Helen announced, sounding pleased and excited. "It's always a risk this time of year, and I want everything to be perfect."

Guilt squeezed its ugly fingers tightly around his throat. Elaine was the only daughter, and her parents had pulled out the stops when it came to her wedding. He wondered if it were possible for the Hopkinses to get a refund at this late date, and was fairly confident that would be impossible. It was too late for just about anything but biting the bullet.

Elaine's Aunt Betty and Uncle Jerome were both in their early eighties and spry, energetic souls. They greeted Jason like family . . . which he was about to become, or would have if he hadn't run into Katie.

"I'm pleased to make your acquaintance," Jason said formally. He glanced toward Elaine, hoping to attract her attention. The sooner he explained matters to her, the better he'd feel. Or the worse, he wasn't sure yet. It might just be easier to leap off a bridge and be done with it.

"I thought we'd have lunch out on the patio," Helen said, gesturing toward the French doors off the formal dining room.

"What a lovely idea, Helen," Betty said, leading the way

outside. Her husband shuffled along behind her. A soft breeze rustled in the trees as Jason followed along. He could hear birds chirping joyously in the distance, but instead of finding their chatter amusing or entertaining, he wanted to shout at them to shut up. As soon as the thought flashed through his mind, he realized his nerves were about shot. He had to talk to Elaine, and soon, for both their sakes.

"I need to talk to you," he whispered urgently in Elaine's ear. "Alone."

"Darling, whatever it is can wait, can't it? At least until after lunch."

"No." If she had any idea how difficult this was, she'd run screaming into the night. He was two steps away from doing so himself. The need to confess burned inside him.

"In a minute, all right?" She flew past him and into the kitchen, leaving Jason to exchange chitchat with her vivacious aunt and uncle until she returned with a pitcher of iced tea.

"What time did you say your brother was arriving?" Helen directed the question to Jason as she sat down at the round glass and wrought-iron table. A large multicolored umbrella shaded the area, although the sky had turned gray and overcast. Jason's mood matched the gathering clouds. He felt as if he were standing under a huge cumulus, waiting for lightning to strike.

"Steve and Lisa should be here sometime around two," he answered when he realized everyone was waiting for his response.

"He had to be here to organize the bachelor party," Elaine explained.

"Naturally, Rich and Bob will help out. You met them last night, didn't you?" Helen passed the hard rolls to Jason and he nodded. He wasn't likely to forget Elaine's brothers. He'd been with Rich and Bob when he'd first seen Katie.

"They got him so drunk, Jason decided to make an early night of it, remember?" The salad bowl went from mother to daughter.

Jason was about to explain that the lone beer wasn't responsible for his "early night," then thought better of it.

"Don't pick on your fiancé," Betty advised Elaine, winking at Jason.

"At least not before the ceremony," Jerome added, chuckling.

Helen spread the linen napkin across her lap. "You can't imagine what our morning's been like, Jason. Elaine and I were up at the crack of dawn, running from one end of town to another. It's been a madhouse around here."

"I can't believe you slept half the morning away. That's not like you." Elaine dug into her shrimp-filled Caesar salad with a hearty appetite.

"I . . . I had trouble falling asleep," he muttered, certain her entire family knew exactly what he'd been doing.

Elaine gifted him with a soft, trusting smile. Not once since they'd decided to marry had she expressed doubts or voiced second thoughts. If she was experiencing any such notion now, it didn't show.

"Just think," Betty said, glancing fondly at her niece. "At three o'clock this time tomorrow, you'll be a married woman."

Married. Jason broke out in a cold sweat.

Elaine reached across the table and squeezed his hand. "I'm the luckiest woman in the world to be marrying Jason."

He actually thought he was going to be sick.

"Isn't love grand?" Betty murmured, and dabbed at the corner of her eye with her napkin.

By the sheer force of his will, Jason managed to make it through the rest of the meal without anyone noticing something was amiss, although he considered it nothing short of a miracle. He never had been much good at subterfuge.

He managed to answer Jerome's questions about the shipping business and make polite small talk with the women. Elaine glanced at him curiously a couple of times, but said nothing that led him to believe she'd guessed his true feelings.

"I want to steal Elaine away for a few minutes," he insisted when they'd finished with their salads. He stood and held his hand out to her.

"I keep telling him he'll have me for a lifetime after tomorrow, but he refuses to listen," Elaine joked.

Helen glanced at her watch and Jason knew what she was thinking. Steve and Lisa's flight was due to land in little more than an hour and he was a good forty minutes away from the airport.

"Ten minutes is all I'll need," he assured Elaine's mother.

"Take him out into the garden," Helen suggested indulgently.

Jason wanted to kiss his future mother-in-law. The more private the area the better. Elaine was known to have a hot temper at times and he was sure she'd explode. Not that he blamed her. Heaven almighty, what a mess he'd made of this.

The garden was little more than two rows of flowering rosebushes in the back side of the property. A huge weeping willow dominated the backyard. Elaine swung her arms like a carefree child as they strolled toward the cover of the sprawling limbs of the willow.

"I know you, Jason Ingram. You want me alone so you can have your way with me." Before he could stop her, she wound her arms around his neck and planted a wide, open-mouthed kiss across his lips.

"Elaine, please," he said, having trouble freeing himself from her embrace. She was making this impossible. The woman was like an octopus, wrapping her tentacles around him, refusing to let him go.

"Loosen up, sweetheart."

"There's something I need to tell you."

"Then for the love of heaven, say it," she replied impatiently. She leaned against the tree trunk and waited.

Jason's heart ached. He found it difficult to meet her gaze so he stared at the ground, praying for wisdom. "Before we go ahead with the wedding, there's something you should know about me."

"This sounds serious."

She hadn't a clue how serious.

This wasn't easy, and he suspected the best place to start was in the beginning. "You know that I was born and raised in Spokane."

"Of course."

"At the end of my junior year of high school . . ."

"Are you about to tell me you had a skirmish with the law and I'm marrying a convicted felon?"

"No," he snapped, thinking that might be preferable to what he actually was about to tell her. "Just listen, Elaine, please."

"Sorry." She placed her finger across her lips, promising silence.

"I started dating a girl named Katie, and we were deeply in love."

"You got that sweet young girl pregnant, didn't you? Jason Ingram, you're nothing but a little devil."

"Elaine," he snapped, growing impatient. "Katie and I never. We didn't . . . No."

"Sorry." She squared her shoulders and gave him her full attention.

"As I said, Katie and I were deeply in love." He could tell that Elaine was tempted to say something more, but he silenced her with a look. "For whatever reasons, her family didn't approve of me. Nor did they think we were old enough to be so serious." He glanced her way and found he had her full attention. "Her parents had plans for Katie and they didn't include a husband."

"I should hope not," Elaine said stiffly.

"But Katie and I vowed that we wouldn't let anything or anyone keep us apart." He experienced the same intensity of emotion now as he had all those years ago. "When we learned that her family intended to separate us, we did the only thing we could think of that would keep us together." He sucked in a deep breath and watched Elaine's eyes as he said the words. "We married."

"Married." She spit out the word as if it were a hair in her food. "That's a fine thing to tell me at this late date."

"I know . . . I know." Jason couldn't blame her for being angry.

"Jason Ingram, if you tell me that you've got a wife you never bothered to divorce, I swear I'll shoot you." Her eyes flashed fire, singeing him.

"We didn't need to bother with a divorce," he told her quietly, sadly. "The marriage was annulled."

"Oh, thank heaven," Elaine murmured, planting her hand over her heart, her relief evident.

This was where it got difficult. Really difficult. Now was the time to mention how, through no one's fault, he'd run into Katie right here in San Francisco. Now was the time to explain how, when they saw each other again for the first time in ten years, they realized how much they still loved each other. Now was the time to explain how one thing led to another and before either of them was fully aware of what they were doing they ended up in bed together.

Now was the time to shut up before he ruined his entire life.

"Is there a reason you never mentioned this other woman before?" Elaine asked, sounding suspiciously calm. "You asked me to marry you, Jason, and conveniently forgot to mention you'd been married before."

"It was a long time ago." Canceling the wedding was as painful as anything in his life, including his own father's death.

"You should have told me."

He agreed completely. "I know."

"Well," she said, doing that sighing thing once more, as if to suggest she'd been burdened but not overly. She could deal with this. "We all make mistakes. It's understandable . . . I appreciate you letting me know now, but I must tell you I'm hurt that you kept this from me, Jason. I'm about to become your wife, but then," she whispered, "we all have our secrets, don't we?"

It was now or never. Jason held his breath tight inside his chest. "I loved her. Really, truly loved her."

"Of course you did, but that was then and this is now." She frowned, but seemed willing to forgive him.

Now. He opened his mouth to tell her everything, but the words refused to come. His heart felt like it was about to burst straight through his chest.

"Elaine." Her mother called, and Elaine looked toward the house, seemingly eager to escape.

"I'm not finished," Jason said hurriedly, before she left and it was too late.

"I'll be right back." She kissed his cheek and hurried toward her mother's voice.

Jason clenched both fists and squeezed his eyes closed as he sought a greater source for the courage to continue. Swearing under his breath, he started pacing, testing the words on his tongue. Elaine had a right to know what had happened. It was his duty to tell her.

She returned breathless and agitated a couple of moments later. "Darling, it's a problem with the caterer. We specifically ordered pickled asparagus tips for the canapés, and now they're telling us the order came in without them."

"You're worried about asparagus spears?" Jason couldn't believe what he was hearing.

"It's important, darling. Mother's on the phone with them now. Is there anything else, because this is important. I really need to deal with this. Mother thinks we may have to run down and confront these people right here and now."

"Anything else?" Jason knew he was beginning to sound suspiciously like an echo. "No," he said hurriedly, hating himself for the coward that he was.

"Good." She smiled broadly and then raced back to the house.

Jason stayed outside several minutes, condemning himself. Thanks to the years he served as a Marine, his swearing vocabulary was extensive. He called himself every dirty name he could think of, then slumped down onto a bench.

"Jason," Helen shouted from the back door. "Don't forget your brother."

"Right." He made his way back to the house. "Where's Elaine?"

"She's dealing with the problem with the caterer. It's nothing for you to worry about." She escorted him to the door. "We'll see you at five, right?"

"Five."

"The rehearsal at the church."

"Oh, right, the rehearsal." Jason didn't know how he would get through that, but he hadn't given himself any option. As far as Elaine and her family were concerned, the wedding was still on.

Chapter Five

A headache pounded at Katie's temple like a giant sledge-hammer. Keeping her mind on track during this all-important meeting was almost impossible. She wanted to blame the wine, but she knew her discomfort had very little to do with the small amount of alcohol she'd consumed. Jase Ingram was the one responsible for her pain, in more ways than one.

Katie lowered her head to read over the proposal on the table, but her thoughts were muddled and confused, refusing to focus on the matter at hand. Her mind and her heart were across town with Jase.

"Katherine?"

She heard her name twice before she realized she was being addressed.

"I'm sorry," she murmured, "what was the question?"

"We were thinking of tabling the proposal until next week," Roger supplied, frowning slightly.

Katie didn't blame him for being irritated. She'd been use-less as a negotiator this morning. Her thoughts were a million miles away with the girl she'd once been. At eighteen life had seemed so uncomplicated. She loved Jase and he loved her and their being together was all that was important.

"Tabling the proposal sounds like an excellent idea. Forgive me if I've been inattentive," she said in her most businesslike voice, "but I seem to be troubled with a headache this morning."

"No problem, Katherine," Lloyd Johnson, the first vice president of Grand National, said kindly. "Your headache may well have given us a few more days' time, which is something we could all use just now."

Katie smiled her appreciation. "Thanks, Lloyd."

The men shifted papers back inside their briefcases. Soon the meeting room was empty save for Roger and Katie.

She knew she owed him an explanation, but she could barely find the courage to face him after her lie from the night before. She'd said she wasn't feeling well then and had him drive her home so she could sneak back to the hotel and rendezvous with Jase. It was an ugly, despicable thing to do to a man who genuinely cared for her.

"You're still not feeling well, are you?" Roger asked gently.

"I'm doing slightly better this morning." Another lie. She was worse, much worse.

"Tonight's our dinner engagement with the Andersons," he reminded Katie, eyeing her hopefully.

Katie groaned inwardly. She'd forgotten all about the dinner date which had been set weeks earlier. Had she arrived at her usual time this morning, she would have seen it on her appointment calendar. Instead she'd rushed into the office, barely in time to make the meeting.

The Andersons were longtime friends of Roger's. The couple was in town to celebrate their wedding anniversary and had invited Roger and Katie along for what promised to be a fun-filled evening on the town. They were going back to the Italian restaurant where they'd met fifteen years earlier. Fresh from graduate school, Roger had been with Larry that night as well.

Katie suspected Roger wanted to show her that he wasn't as much of a stuffed shirt as it seemed. With his friends he could let down his hair, as if that was what it took to convince her to marry him.

"You'll feel better later, won't you?" His eyes were almost boyish in his eagerness.

She couldn't refuse him, not after the callous way she'd dumped him the night before. The irony of the situation didn't escape her. She hadn't been eager to join him for drinks at the St. Regis. Roger knew she didn't indulge often, but he'd insisted they had reason to celebrate. They'd worked hard on this deal with Grand National Bank and would be meeting with the first vice president. It was a small coup and so Katie had given in.

She'd never thought of herself as a weak person. After her marriage was annulled she'd promised herself that she wouldn't allow anyone to control her life ever again. Yet here she was, trapped in a relationship with a man her father considered perfect for her. A man who constantly pestered her to marry him.

Marry.

By this time tomorrow Jase would be married. In her mind's eye she pictured him standing in a crowded church exchanging vows with a beautiful, sophisticated woman.

"You seem a million miles away." Roger waved his hand in front of her face, dragging her back into the present, which, unfortunately, was as painful as her dreams.

"I'm sorry."

"About tonight?"

She owed Roger this even if she did feel like staying at home, burying her face in a bowl of chocolate ice cream. But she couldn't do that to Roger, and it would do her no good to sit home and cry in her soup. Or in her case, ice cream. What was done was done. Jase would marry his "sweetheart" and they'd both get on with their lives.

With time and effort they'd put the one small slip in their integrity behind them. Pretend it didn't happen. That was the solution, she realized. Denial. For the first time since she raced out of the St. Regis, Katie felt comforted. Everything was going to work out. She'd forget about him and he'd forget about her.

They'd gotten along perfectly well without one another this long. The rest of their lives wouldn't matter.

Now if she could only make herself believe that.

Standing outside the jetway at San Francisco International, Jason waited for his older brother and his wife, Lisa, to step from the plane and into the terminal. If ever there was a time Jason needed his brother's counsel it was now.

The minute he spied Steve and Lisa, his heart lightened. He stepped forward, hugged his sister-in-law, and impulsively did the same with his brother, squeezing tightly.

"That's quite a welcome," Steve said, slapping him across the back. "You ready for the big day, little brother?"

"Nope."

Steve laughed, not understanding this was no laughing matter. Jason felt about as far from being ready as a man could.

"I need to talk to you as soon as you're settled in at the hotel." His eyes held his brother's, hoping to convey the extent of his distress.

"Sure."

Jason led the way toward the baggage claim area.

Lisa eyed him skeptically. "Is everything all right?"

He longed to blurt out the whole story right then and there, but he couldn't.

"Jason?" Steve pressed. "What's wrong?"

He exhaled sharply. "I'll fill you in later. Come up to my room as soon as you're settled, all right?"

Steve nodded. "Something tells me you've gotten yourself into another fine mess."

Jason couldn't wait to see his brother's expression when Steve learned this "fine mess" involved Katie Kern. Three years his elder, Steve had played a significant role in advising Jason when he'd lost Katie the first time. The two had talked long and hard in the days and weeks following his and Katie's elopement. Frankly, Jason didn't know what would have happened if it hadn't been for his brother.

It seemed to take an eternity for Steve and Lisa to get checked in at the hotel. Jason returned to his own suite, but he couldn't sit still. He paced and snacked on a jar of peanuts out of the goodie bar that cost more than anybody had a right to charge. And waited, impatiently, for his brother.

By the time Steve arrived, Jason had worn a pattern into the plush carpet.

"All right, tell me what's got you so worked up," Steve said and helped himself to a handful of peanuts.

"Where's Lisa?" Jason half expected his sister-in-law to show. A woman's perspective on this might help.

"Shopping. It's only three hours until the rehearsal and she didn't know if she'd have time to hunt down those all-important souvenirs after the wedding. Mom's visiting Uncle Philip and he's driving her to the wedding tomorrow," he added unnecessarily.

Jason sat down across from his brother and rammed his hand though his hair. "I saw Katie Kern."

"Who? Katie?" Jason recognized the instant his brother made the connection. Steve's face tightened. "When? Where?"

"Last night. Here. The crazy part was she was sitting in the cocktail lounge downstairs having a drink with some old fart."

Steve watched him closely. "Did you talk to her?"

"You might say that," he muttered, rubbing the back side of his neck. "The fact is we did a whole lot more than talk."

"How much more?" Steve asked cautiously.

"We . . . ah, spent the night together."

Steve vaulted to his feet. "Oh, God."

"My sentiments exactly," Jason muttered. "I couldn't help it, Steve. Damn it all, I love her. I always have."

"But you're marrying Elaine."

"Maybe not." This wasn't exactly news to Jason. He'd wrestled with his conscience all day. The guilt was eating giant holes straight through his middle. He regretted cheating on Elaine, but not loving Katie.

"All right," Steve said, sounding calm and rational, "let's reason this out."

"Good luck," Jason said under his breath. He'd been trying to do exactly that all day and was more confused than ever.

"Where's Katie now?"

"I don't know. She ran out of here first thing this morning." He didn't confuse the issue by explaining Elaine's untimely phone call and how it had set everything off between them. "Get this. Katie ran out of here, claiming I was doing the same thing I'd done before by abandoning her."

"You? She betrayed you."

"She didn't," Jason returned heatedly. "Her parents shipped her off to her aunt's place in England. She had no way of contacting me." He didn't mention the hunger strike or that she'd nearly died when her appendix ruptured.

"You believe her?"

He nodded. Perhaps because he so desperately wanted it to be the truth.

"You were little more than kids."

"I loved her then and God help me, I love her now."

Steve sat back down. "What about Elaine?"

If Jason knew the answer to that he wouldn't be in such a state of turmoil. "I decided this morning that the only fair thing to do was tell her . . ."

Steve stopped him by raising his hand. "That would be a big mistake."

"I slept with another woman, Steve. I can't just stuff that under the carpet."

His brother jerked his hands back and forth in a stopping motion. "You might think confession is good for the soul, but in this case I don't think so."

"I tried to tell her."

"What does she know about Katie?"

Steve assumed that he'd confessed his teenage marriage early on in their relationship, but he hadn't. "Only what I was able to relay this afternoon. I intended to tell her everything, but chickened out at the last minute."

"Thank God. The worst thing you could have done is tell her about what happened last night. Even the advice columnists think it's a bad idea. You read 'Dear Abby,' don't you?"

Jason stood and jammed his hands into his pants pockets. "Okay, so I don't say a word to Elaine about Katie. Don't mention a thing about last night. That doesn't change the way I feel."

"What do you mean?"

Jason took in a deep breath. "I . . . don't know that I want to go through with the wedding."

"What? You're joking. Tell me you're joking!" Steve was back on his feet. His brother had turned into a human pogo stick. He fastened his hand against his forehead and slowly shook his head.

"How can I marry Elaine now?"

Steve glared at him. For a minute, he seemed to be at a complete loss for words. "You're right, you're right," he said finally. "This is one of the most important decisions of your life and marriage isn't something to be taken lightly."

Jason felt part of the burden lifted from his shoulders. Steve understood. If no one else, his brother would stand at his side, support his decision, help him through this mess. Together they'd muddle through the same way they had as boys.

"But, Jason, have you considered the ramifications of canceling a wedding at the last minute like this?"

He'd thought of little else all day.

"Elaine's family has invested a lot of money in this." Why his brother felt it was necessary to remind him of that Jason didn't know. It was something he preferred not to consider at the moment.

"I know."

"Lisa mentioned that the wedding gown came from the Young Lovers. She said there wasn't a gown in the entire store under five grand."

Jason knew that, too.

"You're sure you want to cancel the wedding?"

"They're having pickled asparagus tips," Jason muttered, knowing it was a completely illogical statement.

"Pickled asparagus tips?" Steve repeated.

Jason shook his head to clear his thoughts. "Never mind." It seemed a damn shame to marry a woman he wasn't sure he loved because she planned to top the canapés with asparagus. He didn't even like asparagus. He'd never liked asparagus, and generally he enjoyed vegetables.

"I have to tell her, Steve," he murmured. "Even if it means ignoring Dear Abby's advice. Then Elaine and I can make an intelligent decision together." Surely his fiancée would realize that if he fell into bed with another woman only two days away from their wedding, something wasn't right. True, there were mitigating circumstances, but that didn't excuse or absolve him.

"I hate to see you let Katie do this to you a second time," Steve said, sitting back down and reaching for the peanuts. "There are people in this world who are just bad for us."

Jason had never thought of Katie in those terms but he didn't want to get into a verbal debate with his only brother.

"What's she like these days?" Steve inquired.

"The same." The outward trappings were more sophisticated, but it was the same wonderful, generous Katie.

"Daddy's puppet?"

Jason knew what Steve was doing and he didn't like it. "Leave her alone."

"Alone. I don't intend to contact her if that's what's worrying you. She ran out on you, remember? It isn't the first time, either, is it?"

"I said stop it," he shouted.

"All right, all right." Steve raised both hands. "I apologize— it's just that I don't want you to make the biggest mistake of your life."

"Trust me, Steve, I don't want to, either."

Chapter Six

The church was filled with people Jason didn't know. The priest directed traffic while the organist practiced the traditional wedding march. The musical score echoed through the sanctuary, bouncing off the ceiling and walls, swelling and filling the large church.

Everyone talked at once and soon Jason could barely hear himself think. Rich and Bob and their wives and children sat impatiently in the front pew. Bob's wife bounced a squirming toddler on her knee. A handful of kids raced up and down the aisles, refusing to listen to Elaine's mother, who chased after them.

Jason's stomach was so tight he didn't know how he'd make it through this rehearsal without being sick. He had to talk to Elaine, explain what happened with Katie, despite his brother's advice. He felt he owed her the truth.

Once he confessed the error of his ways, they could reason everything out like two mature adults and decide what they should do. The only clear answer, as far as he could see, was to cancel the wedding.

Steve elbowed him in the side. "Father Ecker says you're supposed to step toward the altar as soon as Elaine starts down the aisle with her father."

At the mention of his fiancée's name, Jason turned toward the back of the church, hoping to find her. He hadn't seen her since lunch. Quite possibly she was still involved with the asparagus tip disaster.

When he finally did see her, his heart sank with dread. She stood just inside the vestibule with her bridesmaids gathered around her like a gaggle of geese. She wore a mock veil and carried a frilly bouquet made up of a hundred or more ribbons in a variety of colors and sizes. They came from her five wedding showers, if he remembered correctly. Oh, no. All those gifts would need to be returned.

"I have to talk to Elaine," he announced tightly.

"Now?" Steve asked incredulously.

"Yes." He wasn't putting this off any longer. He walked over to where Father Ecker stood. "I need a few minutes alone with Elaine." He didn't ask if the moment was convenient. He didn't care if he did hold up the entire rehearsal. This was by far more important.

Marching down the center aisle, he sought her out. "Elaine."

Giggling with her friends, she didn't notice him at first.

"Elaine." He tried again.

She glanced away from her maid of honor. "Jason, you're supposed to be in the front of the church," she teased.

"We need to talk," he announced starkly.

"Now?" Her eyes grew round and large.

"Right now."

Elaine cast a speculative glance toward her women friends before following him into the back of the church in the dim light of the vestibule. "What's going on? You haven't been yourself all day."

"I have something to tell you." The best way he could think to do this was to simply say it without offering her any excuses or explanations. He had no justifications to offer for sleeping with Katie.

"You need to talk to me again? Really, Jason, you're carrying this thing a bit far."

"What thing?" Maybe she knew more than she was telling.

"Nerves. Darling, everyone has them."

She didn't appear to be affected. "It's a lot more than nerves."

"You sound so serious." She laughed, making light of his distress.

"I *am* serious." He held her gaze for a long moment before he spoke again. "This afternoon I told you about Katie and me."

"Yes," she said, sounding bored. "We've already been through all that, Jason. Really, you don't have anything to worry about—I understand."

"I saw her last night."

"Katie? Here in San Francisco? I thought you said you met her in high school."

He nodded. "I did. I haven't seen her in ten years . . . the last time I did she was my wife."

Elaine's mouth thinned slightly. "But she isn't now, right?"

"No," he agreed readily enough. He paused because what he had to say next was so damned difficult.

She glared at him with agitation. "Jason, really, can't you see we're holding up the entire rehearsal? I'm beginning to lose patience with you and this woman from your past. So you saw your high school sweetheart after ten years. Big deal."

"That isn't all." His voice sank so low he wondered if she heard him.

Elaine crossed her arms and tapped her foot. "You mean to tell me there's more?"

He nodded, and swallowed hard. Lots more. "Katie and I had dinner together."

She laughed nervously. "So you had dinner with an old girlfriend. You should know by now that I'm not the jealous type. Frankly, Jason, you're making much more of this than necessary. I trust you, darling."

She might as well have kicked him in the balls. It was what he deserved.

"Katie came up to my room afterward." It demanded every ounce of fortitude he possessed to face her, but he owed her that much.

"You don't need to tell me anything more," Elaine insisted tightly. "I already said I trust you."

She glared at him as if to will him to keep from telling her what she'd already guessed.

"Your trust isn't as well placed as you think." He ran a hand down his face and found he was shaking with nerves and regret.

"Jason," she insisted in a voice wrapped in steel. "Would you kindly listen to me? This isn't necessary."

"It is," he insisted. This was by far the most difficult thing he'd had to do in his entire life. "Elaine," he said, holding her with his eyes. "I wouldn't hurt you for anything in the world."

"Fine, then let's get back to the rehearsal. Everyone's waiting."

He didn't know why she was making this nearly impossible. "I need to tell you what happened between Katie and me."

"Must you really? Jason, please, this has gone far enough."

"Katie spent the . . ."

"Jason, stop," she snapped. "I don't want to hear it."

". . . night with me."

It felt as if all the oxygen had been sucked from the room. The silence between them throbbed like a living, breathing animal. Jason waited for her to respond. To shout, to scream, to slap him. Something. Anything.

"I can't tell you how sorry I am," he murmured, his voice so hoarse with regret that he barely recognized it.

"Well," Elaine murmured tightly, "do you feel better now that you've bared your soul?"

"Yes . . ."

Her face tightened with a mild look of displeasure. "Do you have any other confessions you care to make?"

"Ah . . . no."

Her shoulders swelled and sank with a sigh. "Well, that's one thing to be grateful for." She started back toward the sanctuary.

"Elaine, where are you going?"

She tossed him a look over her shoulder that suggested he should know the answer to that. "The rehearsal, where else?"

"But doesn't this change things? I mean . . ." He hesitated and lowered his voice. "I made love to another woman."

"Okay, so you had a momentary lapse. Your timing was incredibly bad, but other than that I'm willing to look past this indiscretion. Just don't let it happen again."

Look past this indiscretion. She made it sound as if his night with Katie meant nothing, as if he'd used the wrong fork at a formal dinner. A minor faux pas.

She turned back to face him. "You aren't thinking of doing something really stupid, are you?"

"I thought . . . I assumed . . ."

"You thought I'd want to cancel the wedding?" She made the very idea sound ludicrous.

"Yes." That was exactly what he'd assumed would happen. He wouldn't blame her if she did decide she wanted out of the marriage. Forgiving him was one thing, but the ramifications of what he'd done went far beyond the obvious. He'd betrayed her faith in him, destroyed her ability to trust him ever again. Surely she understood that. His sleeping with Katie should have told them both something important. He wasn't ready for marriage.

"We're not calling off this wedding just because you couldn't keep your zipper closed."

"But . . ."

"Don't think I'm pleased about this, because I'm not. I'm furious and I have every right to be."

"I know . . ."

"What you did was despicable."

"I couldn't agree with you more."

"And it won't happen again."

"I still think we should . . ."

"Then I don't see what the big deal is," she said, cutting him off. "I'm willing to overlook this one incident. I have to say I'm disappointed; I never thought I'd have this sort of problem with you."

He gave her credit—she handled the news far better than if the tables had been turned. "Then you want to go ahead with the wedding?"

"Of course." She laughed, the sound grating and unnatural. "Of course, we'll still be married. After all the trouble and expense? You're joking, aren't you? I wouldn't dream of calling it off."

"Elaine . . ."

"But I want it understood that I won't tolerate this kind of behavior again."

"I wouldn't think . . ."

"Good. Now let's get back to the others before someone thinks there's something wrong." Without another word, she marched back into the sanctuary.

Rarely had Katie spent a more miserable evening. She enjoyed Wanda and Larry. Liked them. Envied them. Their love for each other was evident, even after fifteen years of togetherness, three children, a mortgage, and all the rest. Being with the couple, listening to them laugh with one another, made it all the more difficult to return to her own home, alone.

That was the crux of it, Katie realized. She was alone when she so desperately wanted the deeply committed relationship the Andersons shared. She longed for a husband, a family. It shouldn't be so much to ask. Nor should it be so difficult. Every man she'd met in the last ten years had fallen short of what she wanted in a husband. After seeing Jase again she understood why. She'd never stopped loving him. He was her heart. Her soul.

Mentally saying his name was like peeling back a fresh scab. The pain rippled down her spine. Within a matter of hours he would be forever lost to her.

"You're still not feeling well, are you?" Roger whispered. He'd been attentive all evening, and she knew why. When it came time to drop her off, he was going to bring out a dazzling diamond ring and ask her to marry him.

As tempting as the offer was, she couldn't. Roger was her friend. He'd never hurt her, never desert her or leave her emotionally bankrupt the way Jase had. Roger was kind and generous. But to marry him would be cheating this wonderful man out of the kind of wife he deserved.

Katie didn't love him. She was fond of him, cared about him, but she didn't love him. Not the way a wife should love her husband.

"I'm feeling much better," she assured him.

"More champagne?" He replenished her glass without waiting for her answer. He seemed to think a couple of drinks would fix whatever troubled her.

"You know that we met in this very restaurant, don't you?" Larry's gaze slid away from his wife's long enough to glance in Katie's direction.

"That's what Roger said."

Larry waved a breadstick in Roger's direction. "He was here, too."

"So I heard. In fact," Katie said, smiling, "he accepts full credit for getting the two of you together."

"No way." Larry chuckled.

"As I recall," Roger muttered, setting aside the goblet, "I had first dibs on Wanda."

"You make me sound like a piece of meat." Wanda pretended to be outraged, but she didn't fool anyone.

"You were such a cute little thing," Larry teased, and added pointedly, "then."

The other woman glared at her husband and then laughed. "You try keeping your hourglass figure after three children, fellow."

Larry stood and undulated his hips a couple of times. "I managed just fine, thank you."

Katie couldn't keep from laughing. Roger's gaze captured hers and he reached for her hand, squeezing it gently. He was a handsome man, not the old fart Jase claimed. At forty-three Roger's hair was just beginning to show streaks of silver, giving him a distinguished air. While he did tend to maintain a businesslike attitude, she wouldn't call him pompous.

"Here's to another fifteen equally happy years," Roger said, toasting his friends.

"Hear, hear," Larry agreed.

Their dinners arrived and soon after they'd eaten, Roger made their excuses, surprising Katie.

After hugs and congratulations, Roger and Katie left the restaurant. She'd worked all day to keep the memories of Jase and the woman who would soon be his bride at bay. Her efforts had worked fairly well until that evening with Larry and Wanda.

For ten long years, Jase had been lost to her. Then life had played a cruel joke and sent him back for one all-too-brief interlude just so she'd know what she'd missed. One night of memories was all she would have to hold on to through the years.

"Thank you for a wonderful evening," she said as she looped her arm in Roger's. He led the way outside and paid the valet, who delivered his BMW.

"I was hoping you'd invite me up for coffee," he said as they neared her condominium.

"Not tonight."

Although she knew he was disappointed, he didn't let it show. He pulled into the crescent-shaped driveway outside her building and kissed her on the forehead. A touching, sweet gesture of affection. "Sleep well, my love."

"Thanks for everything," she whispered and slid out of the car. She waved when he pulled away and then greeted the friendly doorman as she entered the lobby.

By the time Katie stepped into the elevator, unexpected tears had filled her eyes. Silly, unexplainable tears. She wasn't sure whom she wept for. Jase. Roger. Or herself.

Wiping the moisture from her cheek, she decided she was a mature woman, long past the days of crying over might-have-beens.

She'd fallen in love with Jase far too early in her life, and found him again far too late. Her parents had taught her years ago that life was rarely fair.

She let herself inside her condo and walked over to the large picture window that revealed the bright lights of the city. Her gaze wandered to the twentieth-floor tower of the St. Regis Hotel.

Hugging one arm around her stomach, she pressed her fingertips to her lips. Fresh tears filled her eyes as she stood and looked at the bright, glittering lights of the city. Once more her gaze returned to the St. Regis and Jase. Closing her eyes, she smiled and blew him a kiss, sending him her love.

Chapter Seven

"You're going to go through with the wedding then?" Steve asked Jason in the hallway outside his suite. It was well past midnight and he was scheduled to pick up his tuxedo first thing in the morning.

Elaine's brothers seemed disappointed that he'd cut his bachelor party short, but he wasn't in the mood to celebrate. He'd let the others have their fun, but hadn't participated much himself.

"That's what Elaine wants," Jason said, and slipped the plastic key into the hotel door.

"I can't believe you told her. You're a braver man than I am."

"I didn't have any choice."

"Sure you did. There are some things in life that are best left unsaid."

After the shock of Elaine's reaction, he was almost willing to agree. Frankly, he was sick of the entire matter. "I'll see you in the morning."

"You want me to pick you up?"

"Sure." He didn't show much enthusiasm for a man who was about to be married.

"'Night," Steve said, hesitated, then added, "Jason, don't do anything stupid, okay?"

"Like what?" He resented the question.

"Contact Katie."

"No way," he said emphatically. "She was the one who ran out on me, remember?" As far as he was concerned, she'd done that one too many times. She had some gall, racing across the hotel lobby accusing him of abandoning her. No, he was finished with Katie Kern. He'd learned his lesson. Besides, she'd let him know the entire episode was a mistake and that she wanted him out of her life.

Elaine was right. They'd both put this unfortunate episode behind them and build a meaningful marriage the way they'd planned all these months. Katie had her life and he had his. It was too late for them, far too late.

Walking over to the picture window, Jason stared out over the lights of the city. He jerked his tie back and forth to loosen the knot. By this time tomorrow, he'd be on his honeymoon.

Sitting down in the large, comfortable chair, his feet on the ottoman, he reached for the television remote. No sooner had he found a sports station than the phone rang. He glanced at his wrist and saw that it was almost one. Not the time most folks would make a phone call.

"Hello."

Nothing. A wrong number or a crank call, he wasn't sure which.

"Hello," he said again impatiently. He was in no mood to deal with a jokester.

Then he knew. He wasn't sure how or why he recognized that it was Katie, but he knew beyond a doubt that the person on the other end of the line was his one-time wife.

His hand tightened around the receiver. "Katie?" He breathed her name into the mouthpiece. If he were smart he'd sever the connection now, but he couldn't make himself do it. His heart beat with happy excitement. He'd wanted to talk to her all day, needed her to help him make sense of everything— and she'd walked away.

"I shouldn't have phoned." Her voice was as fragile as mist

on a moor. He heard the regret, the pain, the worry, knew her voice was an echo, a reflection of his own.

Jason clicked off the television, closed his eyes, and leaned back in the chair. "I'm glad you did."

Neither spoke. Jason suspected it was because they were afraid of what the other would say. Or wouldn't say.

Try as he might he couldn't push the memory of their night together from his mind. It had haunted him all day. Would stay with him the rest of his life.

"I . . . I wanted you to know how sorry I am," she whispered.

"Yeah, well, that makes two of us."

"I don't know how I could have let that happen." Her voice was so low, Jason had to strain to hear her.

"I'm not in the habit of that sort of behavior myself." He felt obliged to reassure her of that.

"Nor me."

That much he knew. "Why'd you run away from me this morning?" His day had been hell from the moment she'd raced out of the hotel.

He could hear her soft intake of breath against the mouthpiece.

"What made you say I'd abandoned you?" Jason asked. Her parting shot had burned against his mind all day.

She ignored the questions. "Does she know?"

He hesitated, then murmured, "Yeah, I told her."

"Oh, Jase, she must be so hurt. Hurting Elaine is what I regret the most. My heart aches for her. How . . . how'd she take it?"

He wasn't sure how to answer. Elaine had acted as if infidelity were no big deal. Certainly it wasn't a problem as far as their wedding was concerned. She knew what had happened between him and Katie, but she didn't want him to tell her.

Because he had no answer to give Katie, he asked a question of his own. "Did you tell Daddy Warbucks?"

"No." A bit of defiance echoed in her husky voice. "I'm not sleeping with Roger if that's what you're asking."

It wasn't. Then maybe it was.

"I should go." She was eager to end the conversation.

"No." There were matters that needed settling first. He wouldn't let her break the connection when so many questions remained unanswered.

"The only reason I called was to tell you how very sorry I was. And . . ."

"And?" he coaxed.

"To wish you and . . ."

"Elaine."

"To wish you and Elaine every happiness."

Happiness was the last thing Jason felt. He was bone tired, weary to the very bottom of his soul. "Thanks."

He waited for her to disconnect the line. She didn't. He couldn't make himself do it. The telephone was the only contact he had with her. Would probably ever have.

"Katie?"

She didn't answer right away. "I'm here."

He already knew that. Knew she wanted to maintain the contact with him as long as she could, the same way he wanted to keep hold of her.

"She's all right?"

"She?"

"Elaine." Katie said the name quickly as though voicing it caused her pain. "If I learned you'd slept with another woman two days before our wedding, it would have killed me."

"She's fine." She'd been more upset with the caterers over the asparagus tips than she had been with what he'd done.

"Good . . . I worried about it all day."

So had he, but for naught. Elaine simply hadn't given a damn.

"Why'd you run out on me?" He wasn't going to let her off the hook so easily. His day had been hell and it had all started when she left him in a huff.

"I . . . don't know that I can tell you."

"Try." He rubbed his hand down his face. "I need to know."

She took her own sweet time answering. "You called her *Sweetheart*." He heard the hesitation and the pain. "You'd spent the night making love to me and . . . and then you called Elaine your sweetheart."

"I was taken off guard by her phone call. You have to admit, the situation was a bit awkward."

"I know all that. Really, Jase, it doesn't make any difference now, does it? I suppose I was jealous, which is ridiculous in light of the circumstances." She tried to laugh and failed, her voice trembling as she continued. "All at once I was eighteen all over again and I felt," she said as she struggled to regain control of her emotions, "I felt so alone, facing an impossible situation, loving you, wanting you. Only this time it wasn't my family that stood between us, it was life."

"You ran away from me ten years ago, too."

"I didn't," she cried. "I explained what happened."

"This morning," he said, "I was that eighteen-year-old kid again, the same as you. I needed you to help make sense of what happened. Instead you walked out on me."

"All we seem to do is hurt each other."

He didn't disagree with her.

"Good-bye, Jase."

"Good-bye." He was ready to end it now. He'd gotten the answer to his question.

In the morning he'd be marrying Elaine.

Katie slept fitfully all night and was up midmorning. Saturdays she generally did her shopping for the week and took care of any errands. This day would be no different, she decided. It wasn't the end of the world just because Jase was marrying Elaine. No matter how much it felt like it.

She dressed in jeans and a sleeveless blouse and headed for the local grocer's, but soon found herself wandering aimlessly down the aisles, her cart empty. Her mind refused to focus on the matters at hand. Instead it seemed focused on her short conversation with Jase the night before.

There'd been so much she'd wanted to tell him. Even now she didn't know where she'd found the courage to actually contact him. She'd gone to sleep, awakened, her heart heavy and sad. As she lay in bed, she knew she couldn't let it end abruptly with Jase like that. With her running out of the hotel never to see him again. And so she'd phoned, calling herself every kind of fool when he actually answered. She'd expected to wake him from a sound sleep. To her surprise he'd answered on the first ring as if he, too, were having trouble sleeping.

Instead of helping her bring some sort of closure to their relationship, their conversation created longing and wonder. To have found each other after all these years and still have it be too late.

She walked down the aisle and paused in front of the baby-food section and was immediately assaulted with a sudden, unexpected flash of pain. Drawing in a deep breath, she forced herself to look straight ahead.

It wasn't until she was at the checkout stand that she realized her entire week's menu consisted of frozen entrees.

Back at the apartment, she noted the flashing light on her answering machine. It was probably Roger and she wasn't in the mood to talk to him. Not today. She was going to be completely indulgent, cater to her own whims and nurture herself. A long walk in Golden Gate Park sounded perfect.

The afternoon was cool and overcast as was often the case in San Francisco in June. Katie wore a light sweater and her tennis shoes as she briskly followed the footpath close to the water. Runners jogged past, daredevils on Rollerblades, kids on skates. The breeze off the bay carried with it the scent of the ocean, pungent and invigorating.

When she'd completed her two-mile trek, she felt better. Her heart was less heavy. She checked her watch and noted that Jase and Elaine had been married all of two hours.

Because she was a glutton for pain, she went out of her way to stroll past the church where Jase had mentioned he and Elaine would be married. The guests would have left long ago. Katie wasn't entirely sure why she was doing this. It wasn't wise, she knew, but she was indulging herself and she wanted to see the church where Jase had married his "sweetheart."

The church was situated on a steep hill overlooking the bay. By the time Katie had walked up the hill, she was breathing hard. She paused, leaned forward, and braced her hands on her knees.

Her gaze studied the sidewalk where she saw bits of birdseed left over from the wedding. A few small seeds had fallen between the cracks. The analogy between her life and those lost seeds didn't escape her. She felt as though her own life had fallen between the cracks. Mentally she gave herself a hard shake. She refused to give in to self-pity.

Slipping inside the darkened church, Katie's gaze went immediately to the huge stained-glass window above the pulpit. A couple of older women were busy in the front, setting huge bouquets of arranged flowers around the altar.

Katie recognized that they were probably the very ones used for Jase and Elaine's wedding.

Walking up the side aisle, she heard the murmur of voices as the two women chatted, unaware she was there.

"Never in all my years as an organist have I witnessed what I did this day," the first woman said in hushed tones.

"From what I heard the bride threw a temper tantrum."

Katie's head perked up in order to better listen in on the conversation.

"While the mother dealt with the daughter, the father dealt with the groom. I don't mind telling you I felt sorry for that young man. Not that I blame him. Good grief, if he was going to change his mind, he might have done it a bit sooner than when he was standing in front of the altar."

"Excuse me," Katie said, making her way toward the two.

"I couldn't help overhearing. You wouldn't by chance happen to be talking about the Ingram wedding, would you?"

The two women glanced at each other. "No," answered the first.

"Just a minute, Dorothy, I thought that might have been the name."

Dorothy shook her head. "Nope. It was Hopkins. I'm positive it was Hopkins. I played for the Ingram wedding earlier. Don't know when I've seen a more beautiful bride, either. Those two were so in love, why, it did my heart good just being here. Now that's a marriage that'll last."

"Thank you," Katie whispered as she turned away. For a moment she'd dared to hope for a miracle.

Katie speed-walked back to her condominium and took a long, hot shower. She hadn't eaten lunch and wasn't in the mood to cook so she slapped a frozen entree into her microwave. She wasn't sure when she got into the habit of eating her meals in front of the television, but it was well ingrained now. A voice, a friend, someone to share her dinner with so she wouldn't be alone.

Her favorite show was the evening news. The newscaster stood in front of a homeless shelter, a congenial soul who gave the weekend reports. "This evening the men and women dining at Mission House are enjoying Beef Wellington and succulent baked salmon fit for a king, or, more appropriate, a groom."

Groom. Great, she was going to be assaulted once again. Everywhere she turned people were talking about weddings.

"This groom experienced a sudden change of heart. Unfortunately, it was too late to warn the caterers. Rather than discard the dinner, the groom opted to serve the meal to San Francisco's homeless."

The scene changed to a group of ragged-looking men and women enjoying their elegant dinner. The camera zeroed in on a table of hors d'oeuvres, and petite canapés topped with asparagus spears.

"When asked about the wedding, groom Jason Ingram . . ."

"Jase." A flash of sheer joy raced through Katie as she roared to her feet.

Jase had called off the wedding.

Chapter Eight

Jason sat in the cocktail lounge at the St. Regis Hotel, wishing he was the type who found solace in a bottle of good whiskey. He never had been one to drown his sorrows in liquor, but if ever there was a time a man should drink, it would be after a day like this one.

He'd stood before the priest, Elaine at his side and the organ music surrounding them, and realized he couldn't do it. That very morning, he'd had every intention of going ahead with the wedding. Frankly, he couldn't see any other option. It was what Elaine wanted. What his brother, his own flesh and blood, advised. Everyone he knew seemed to think Elaine was perfect for him.

Everyone except him.

Then when he stood before Father Ecker and looked at Elaine, he knew otherwise. He remembered Katie's words on the phone from the night before. She'd claimed that if she'd learned that he'd cheated on her two nights before their wedding, she would have died. The pain of his betrayal would have killed her.

Elaine had barely been troubled by what she referred to as his indiscretion. Not that he'd ever wanted to hurt her. He would have given anything to spare her this embarrassment, save his soul. But that was what marriage would have demanded. In that moment, he realized that no matter how painful this was to them both, he couldn't go through with it.

All this came down on him as the music swirled around them at the foot of the altar. Before the priest could start the wedding, Jason leaned over to Elaine and suggested they speak privately before the ceremony proceeded any further.

Elaine pretended not to hear him.

Fortunately, the priest did hear and paused. Jason tried to tell Elaine how sorry he was, but he couldn't marry her. Then her father had gotten into the act and her mother. Soon the entire wedding party had gathered around them. Everyone seemed to have an opinion, but could reach no consensus.

When Elaine realized that he'd actually called off the wedding, she'd thrown down her bouquet, stomped all over the flowers, and then gone at him with both fists. It'd taken the priest and two ushers to pull her off him.

Jason worked his jaw back and forth to test the discomfort. He'd say one thing for his former fiancée—she packed quite a punch. But the beating Elaine had given him didn't compare with what her father had in store. Jason would almost have preferred a pounding to the financial burden facing him. Elaine's father had left Jason to foot the bill for the dinner and reception. As best as he could figure, Jason would work for the next ten years to pay for the wedding that never was.

He took another swallow of beer and looked up to find his brother and sister-in-law. They looked pleased with themselves, as well they should. Jase had gifted them with his honeymoon. The two were scheduled to fly to Hawaii first thing in the morning. The honeymoon suite awaited them on Waikiki.

"We're checked out of the hotel," Steve said, pulling out the chair across from Jase and plopping himself down.

"I feel a little guilty having Steve and me go on your honeymoon," Lisa told him, sitting next to her husband.

"You're turning down two weeks in Hawaii, all expenses paid?" Jason joked. His brother was no fool.

"No way," Lisa laughed.

"I had vacation time due me anyway. It's a little short notice, is all." Steve gave him a worried look, as if he wasn't square with this even now.

"But you swung it."

"We swung it."

"Enjoy yourselves," Jason said, meaning it. "I sure as hell won't be needing it." He wasn't sure what the future held for him.

"What about you and Katie?"

Jason mowed five fingers through his hair. "I don't know. We're different people now. I'd like to believe that we could make it, but she lives here and I work on the East Coast."

"You can move, can't you? Or she can," Lisa advised. "Don't sweat the small stuff."

"Have you talked to her yet?"

"No." He'd tried phoning her twice, and each time reached her answering machine.

"What are you waiting for, little brother?"

It'd be nice for the swelling to go down on his eye, but he didn't say so. He raised his hand and tentatively tested the tenderness and winced at the pain.

Steve's gaze drifted toward the door. "Time to go, Lisa," he announced unexpectedly. "Jason's got company."

"Who?" He tossed a look over his shoulder and found Katie standing in the doorway. Her eyes lit up with warm excitement when she found him.

"Good luck," Lisa said, kissing him on the cheek as she followed Steve.

Jason had the feeling his luck was about to change. He'd found his pot of gold in his high school sweetheart.

"Jase?" Katie took one look at his face and bit into her lower lip. "What happened?" She gently cupped one side of his jaw and the pain he'd experienced moments earlier vanished.

"You don't want to know," he muttered.

"Elaine's father?"

"Nope," he said with a half-laugh. "Elaine."

"You look . . ."

"Terrible," he finished for her. He'd seen his reflection and knew that his face resembled a punching bag. He had a bruise alongside his chin and one eye was swollen completely shut.

"Not terrible, but so incredibly handsome I can't believe you called off the wedding," she said all in one breath as she slid in the chair recently vacated by his sister-in-law.

"So you finally listened to your messages?"

"My messages. That was you? I thought . . . no, I didn't play them back. I heard about it on the six o'clock news."

There seemed to be no end to his humiliation. First Elaine punching him and now this. "They reported that I'd called off the wedding on the San Francisco news?"

"No, that you had the caterer serve the dinner at the homeless shelter."

"Oh." That salved his ego only a little. "I couldn't see any reason for all that expensive food to go to waste."

"It was a generous, thoughtful thing for you to do."

He smiled, despite the pain it caused. "I never did much care for asparagus canapés."

"Me, either." Now that Katie was here, Jason wasn't sure what to say or where to start.

"I can't believe I'm here with you. You actually stopped the wedding."

He shrugged, making light of it when it was the most difficult thing he'd ever done. "I had to," he said, taking Katie's hand in both of his. "I was in love with another woman. The same woman I've loved since I was a teenager. I've always loved you, Katie."

Her beautiful eyes welled with tears. "Oh, Jase."

"I don't know how many times I told myself it was too late for us, but I couldn't make myself believe it. We live on different coasts . . ."

"I'll move."

"I'm in debt up to my eyebrows for a wedding that never took place."

"I'm really good at managing money. In fact, I know a great place to get a loan. I've got an 'in' with the manager." She knocked down every objection he offered.

"Your 'in' doesn't happen to be Roger, does it?" he asked with a frown. He didn't want any help from Daddy Warbucks.

"No, me."

"You?" He knew she'd done well, just not that well. He felt a fierce pride for her accomplishment and at the same time was a bit intimidated. "You mean to say you'd be willing to give all that up for me?"

"Is this a formal marriage proposal, Jason Ingram?"

The question gave him pause—not that he had any qualms about marrying Katie. He'd already married her once, but his head continued to ring from his last go-around at the altar. The least he should do before considering it a second time was look at his options.

It took him all of two seconds. He was crazy about Katie and had been for more years than he cared to remember.

"Yes," he admitted, "that's exactly what I'm asking."

Her smile was probably one of the most beautiful sights known to man. Her eyes were bright with unshed tears and a happiness that infected him with a joy so profound it was all he could do not to haul her into his arms right then and there.

"I love you so damned much, Jase Ingram."

Her words were a balm to all that had befallen him that day. "I hope you're not interested in long engagements."

"How about three hours?"

"Three hours?"

"We can drive to Reno in that time."

Are you suggesting we elope, Katie Kern? Again?" It didn't take him long to realize it was a fitting end to their adventure.

"I can be ready in say . . . five minutes."

He chuckled, loving her so much it felt as if his heart couldn't hold it all inside. "Are we going to have a honeymoon this time?"

"You can bet the house on that, Jase Ingram. My guess is it'll last fifty years or longer."

"I only hope that's long enough."

Jason paid for his beer and with their arms wrapped around each other, he brought her up to his room to collect his suitcase.

Eight hours later, they exchanged their vows. The very ones they'd promised each other ten years earlier.

Only this time it was forever.